STREETWISE

ROBERTA KRAY

sphere

SPHERE

First published in Great Britain in 2013 by Sphere
This paperback edition published in 2014 by Sphere

Copyright © Roberta Kray 2013

The moral right of the author has been asserted.

*All characters and events in this publication, other than those
clearly in the public domain, are fictitious and any resemblance
to real persons, living or dead, is purely coincidental.*

A CIP catalogue record for this book
is available from the British Library.

ISBN 978-0-7515-4986-7

Typeset in Garamond by M Rules
Printed and bound in Great Britain by
Clays Ltd, St Ives plc

Papers used by Sphere are from well-managed forests
and other responsible sources.

MIX
Paper from
responsible sources
FSC® C104740
www.fsc.org

Sphere
An imprint of
Little, Brown Book Group
100 Victoria Embankment
London EC4Y 0DY

An Hachette UK Company
www.hachette.co.uk

www.littlebrown.co.uk

Roberta Kray was born in Southport. In early 1996 she met Reggie Kray and they married the following year; they were together until his death in 2000. Through her marriage to Reggie, Roberta has a unique insight into the world of London's gangland.

For Janelle Posey
A much-loved and much-missed friend.

1

As Ava Gold walked along the streets of Shoreditch she began to have second thoughts. Was this really such a good idea? Probably not, she decided, but when it came to options hers were rapidly shrinking. Three weeks searching for work had yielded nothing even remotely tempting and now her money was starting to run out. Beggars couldn't be choosers, she told herself. Of course she could always go back on the minicabs, but the memory of all those drunks cursing or crying or chucking up in the back of the car was enough to make her think again. Anything had to be better than that.

She paused to check her reflection in the window of a butcher's shop, running her fingers through her cropped dark hair while she wondered, yet again, if she'd worn the right clothes. She had been aiming for that fine line between not too prim and not too slutty, but wasn't convinced that she'd successfully pulled it off. Was her navy dress too short or not short enough? Were her heels too high or too low? Was she wearing too much make-up or not enough?

Ava pulled a face, her gaze drifting down to the meat, to the rows of chops, beef joints, sausages, liver and kidney. She glanced over her shoulder towards the club. She gave a sigh, knowing that she had no other choice. Like a lamb to the slaughter, she thought.

Before she could find a good reason to change her mind, she crossed the road and walked up the path to Belles. It was eleven o'clock in the morning and the lap-dancing club, owned by the infamous Street family, wasn't due to open for another hour. A man with a van was busy ferrying boxes into the lobby, watched over by a massive black guy with bulging muscles and a mean expression.

Ava skirted around the van and went inside, trying to look as though she knew where she was going. The reception area, smelling of air freshener, had lots of shiny chrome and potted palms. The dark red walls were covered with photographs of semi-naked girls with large jutting breasts and pouting mouths. She let her gaze slide over them, doubt creeping into her mind again. But this wasn't the time for a moral debate. She had rent to pay, bills to sort out.

Immediately ahead of her was the main part of the club, the tables ready and waiting, the lights already dim. There was the chink of bottles as preparations were made for the lunchtime session. There was a counter to her right but no one was behind it. Her heels clattered on the marble floor as she strode purposefully towards the door marked *Staff Only*.

At any moment she was expecting to be stopped, for someone to ask who she was or where she was going, but nobody questioned her presence. She pushed open the door and found herself in a long empty corridor. Above her, set into the ceiling, a series of small lights blinked red. Was she being watched? The thought made her feel as nervy as a burglar.

She carried on walking almost to the end where she came across another door with a plaque saying MANAGER. She paused only for a second, took a deep breath and knocked.

'Yeah?'

Ava turned the handle and stepped inside. Chris Street, dressed in a smart dark grey suit, white shirt and silver tie, was sitting behind a wide curved desk with a pile of papers in front of him. She smiled, recognising him instantly. He was older of course – it was getting on for seventeen years since she'd last seen him – but he hadn't changed that much: dark hair, dark eyes, razor-sharp cheekbones in a well-defined face. A good-looking man, although probably not one to be trusted. She waited a moment thinking he might recognise her too, but there wasn't even a flicker.

'Yeah?' he said again, this time with a touch of impatience.

'Ava,' she said. 'Ava Gold.' The name clearly didn't mean anything to him either. She had, it appeared, been a less than memorable ten-year-old. 'I'm here about the job.'

Chris Street shook his head. 'And what job would that be?' He blatantly looked her up and down as if checking out her vital statistics. He didn't seem overly impressed. She thought there was a faint sneer on his lips as he focused on her modest breasts, but she could have been imagining it.

Closing the door firmly behind her, Ava advanced into the room. The office was almost disgustingly opulent with royal blue walls, gold paintwork and a cream carpet that was soft enough to sleep on. Two crystal chandeliers hung from the ceiling. On the walls, carrying on the theme from the lobby, were three framed paintings displaying the finer points of the female form.

'You don't remember me,' she said.

Chris Street's face took on a wary, defensive look as if they might once have shared an intimate moment that had long since slipped his mind. 'I'm sorry?'

'That's okay,' she said, quickly putting him straight. 'There's no reason why you should. It was ages ago. I'm Ted Gold's niece. You used to come to the car showroom in Kellston when I was a kid.'

'Ah,' he said, obviously relieved. 'And how is Ted these days?'

'Pretty good, I think. He retired to Spain, you know. I haven't seen him in a while.'

Chris gestured towards the chair that she was standing next to, his demeanour more cordial now that he knew who she was – and that he was off the hook. 'Sit down, please. Grab a seat.'

Ava lowered herself on to the swing chair, her short dress riding up as she did so. She quickly tugged at the hem, aware as she lifted her eyes that he was staring at her legs.

'So, you're after a job,' he said, his eyebrows lifting slightly.

She glanced towards one of the pictures on the wall, looked back at him and grinned. 'Not *that* sort of a job. I heard you were looking for a driver.'

'And who told you that?'

'Are you saying it's not true?'

Chris Street leaned back, folded his arms across his chest

and studied her carefully. A smile twitched at the corner of his mouth. 'To be honest, we usually employ men in that position.'

'Yeah?' she said. 'And how's that been working out? I hear you've had three drivers in as many months.' As he didn't deny it, she continued with her pitch. 'I've been around cars all my life. I'm reliable, trustworthy and very discreet. Anyway, it's sex discrimination saying that you only employ men. What's wrong with a woman?'

'I employ lots of women.'

Ava gave a snort. 'So the men drive and the women strip? Is that how it goes?'

Chris Street laughed, opening his mouth to reveal a row of white even teeth. 'The women don't strip, they *dance*. And they earn more cash than the men. I don't hear them complaining.'

She pulled a face, shrugging off his response. 'Look, why don't you give me a trial? I can start any time – straight away if you want. I won't let you down. Early mornings, late nights, whatever you need. Give Uncle Ted a bell, he'll tell you how good I am.'

'In Spain?' he said.

'They do have phones in Spain.'

Chris Street seemed amused by the exchange if not exactly convinced of her suitability for the job. She had the feeling he was humouring her, but she pushed on regardless. 'I worked for Alec Harmer for five years. He runs an executive car service based in Mayfair.'

He gave a nod. 'Yeah, I've heard of Harmer's.'

'I've got references if you'd like to see them.' She took an envelope out of her bag and laid it on the desk. 'All my details are in here as well.'

'I'm sure your references are excellent. You wouldn't be giving them to me otherwise. But perhaps you could tell me why you left?'

Ava gave a wry smile. 'I made the mistake of marrying the boss. And he made the mistake of not being able to keep it in his pants. I'll spare you the details. But after we split up, I couldn't carry on working there.'

'Kind of awkward, huh?'

'Kind of awkward,' she agreed. 'But I'm over it now.' This wasn't exactly true, but she didn't want to give an impression of weakness. No one wanted a driver prone to excessive bouts of weeping. 'The divorce came through six months ago. I'm just trying to get on with my life.'

Chris Street nodded. 'Well, I know that feeling.'

'You too?' Hoping that this shared experience might tip things in her favour, she made a final plea. 'So how about it, then? I need a job and you need a driver. Why don't you give me a chance? If you don't, I'll be forced to go back on the minicabs, and believe me you don't want that on your conscience.'

Chris Street smiled. He thought about it for a while, scratching his chin. 'And how would you feel about being hassled by Old Bill?'

'Am I likely to be?'

'How do you think I lost my licence?' he sighed. 'Everywhere I turn these days, there's some bloody copper lurking in the shadows.'

'I can handle it,' she said. 'I'm no stranger to the law. My dad was in and out of nick for most of his life.'

Chris Street continued to gaze at her, mulling it over.

'Please,' she begged. 'Give me a chance. You won't regret it.'

'Okay,' he said finally. 'I'll give you a trial. A week, yeah? And if it doesn't work out—'

Ava reached over the table to grasp and shake his hand. 'It will. I won't let you down, I swear I won't. Thanks. Thanks very much.'

'Here's the address,' he said when he eventually managed to retrieve his fingers. 'And my phone number.' He scribbled the details down on a slip of paper and passed them over to her. 'Do you know Kellston?'

'I live in Kellston.'

'No excuse for being late, then. Ten o'clock sharp. I'll see you tomorrow.'

Ava put the address in her bag and then leapt up before he could consider changing his mind. 'I'll be there.'

She left the office with a smile on her face and in the happy knowledge that she'd be able to pay the rent at the end of the month. Things were finally on the up. Chris Street might be a villain but there were worse men to work for. She knew that for sure. Hadn't she wasted five stupid years on Alec Harmer? Still, that was all in the past now. She walked through the lobby with her head held high. Her gaze raked the images that lined the walls, but her smile didn't falter. She might not have a 34DD cup or a backside that looked like a peach, but she didn't give a damn. She had a job and that was all that mattered.

2

Chris Street drummed his fingers against the top of the desk, wondering how the hell he'd just managed to employ a woman driver. Ava wouldn't exactly be handy in a scrap. Still, she was easy on the eye and she smelled a damn sight better than her predecessors. Plus, she'd had the guts to come here and plead with him for the job. It wasn't as if decent drivers were queuing round the block. Out of the last three, two had spent more time in the pub than the motor and the third had managed to reverse the Mercedes into the gates of the house. Perhaps, all things considered, he'd made the right decision. Yeah, the girl wasn't ideal but she'd do until he found someone better.

He frowned as he thought about the morons he'd had to fire. What the hell was the matter with people these days? Lazy fuckers, that's what most of them were. Once upon a time he'd have no bother at all in finding someone suitable: anyone who wanted to be someone would have beaten a path to the door of the Street family. Now, however, there was little interest and sod all respect. It came to something when—

Chris pulled himself up, realising that he was sounding – even if it was only in his own head – exactly like his old man. Jesus, if he wasn't careful he'd turn into Terry Street, forever complaining, forever harking back to the good old days. And although there was no doubting that his father had been a major player in his time, the empire that he'd built up had been in steady decline for the past ten years. The Streets no longer ruled the East End and had little influence in the West End either. Other more powerful firms had moved in, gradually squeezing them out. The glory days were over and there wasn't much chance of them returning. Kellston was the only place where Terry had any influence and he was clinging on to that by the skin of his teeth.

Chris knew that once his dad was gone – and with the amount he drank that could be sooner rather than later – what power they retained would quickly crumble. That was why he was trying hard to ring-fence the more legitimate sides of the business, the clubs and the pubs, so that when that day came there would be something to fall back on.

The mail was piled up in front of him and he flicked through the envelopes, putting the bills and a small parcel to one side. He opened the letter from the agents that contained the details on the Fox. The best pub in Kellston had recently come on the market and he was lobbying hard for the family to buy it. His pleas, however, were falling on deaf ears. The investment was sound, the profits excellent, but still his father refused to listen.

'Forget it. I've already owned that place once. It's more bloody trouble than it's worth.'

Quite what the 'trouble' was, Chris hadn't been able to discover. Terry had bought the pub about forty years ago after its then owner, Joe Quinn, had been murdered. Why he'd sold it again was a mystery. With its real ale and excellent food, the Fox was the focal point of Kellston: the rich, the poor, the criminal and the strictly legit all mingled together there. Along with the Blind Beggar – where Ron Kray had shot dead George Cornell – it was one of the most famous pubs in the East End.

Chris heaved a sigh, frustrated by his father's refusal to even discuss the matter further. And Danny, his younger brother, wasn't much help either. Danny's interest in the business extended only to what gave him pleasure – the girls, the cash, the drugs, the violence. His viciousness and unpredictability were useful when it came to dealing with the scumbags who stepped out of line, but he contributed little to the day-to-day running of the firm. There was only one person who put any effort into keeping the business afloat and that was the mug who was sitting in the office all alone at half eleven on a Tuesday morning.

Chris knew that if he dwelled on it too much his mood would only worsen. He reached out for the parcel, saw that it was addressed to his father but ripped off the brown paper anyway. If it was anything personal it would have gone to the house. Inside was a rectangular cardboard box and he flipped this open in an absent-minded fashion, his thoughts still pre-occupied by other things.

As his gaze focused, it took a second for the contents to

register with his brain – and then, startled, he rocked back in his chair. 'What the fuck . . .'

It was the shock of it more than anything else. He jumped up, feeling the acceleration of his heartbeat, the sudden dryness of his mouth. The dead brown rat was lying on its side, its glazed eyes still open, its sharp yellowy teeth bared in the final torment of death. He stared at it, disgust sweeping through his body. Shit, he hated rats, even those that weren't breathing any more.

As if it might suddenly spring back to life, Chris kept his distance. The stench of death drifted into his nostrils and made him grimace. A dead rat in a box. A message from someone his father had pissed off. But who? Well, that could be a long list. And there was no knowing whether it was a historical grudge or the result of something more recent.

Eventually, cautiously, he leaned forward and took hold of the brown paper, studying the writing on the front and the postage label. He learned little from either of them. The address had been printed in block capitals, and the label had been stamped *London* along with yesterday's date. He folded it up and slipped it into the top drawer of his desk.

Then, steeling himself, he peered down into the box again. There was no note so far as he could see, but then one wasn't really needed. The message came with the corpse. Just some nutter, he told himself but as he gazed at the rat he felt the hairs stand up on the back of his neck. A cold sensation swept over him like an icy premonition. Quickly, he shook the feeling off. That damn rodent was just playing with his head!

Before his revulsion could get the better of him, Chris sat down, shut the lid and dropped the box into the waste-paper basket. But still the smell lingered. Shit, he'd have to take it outside and dump it in the garbage. Anyway, he shouldn't leave it lying around in the office. It would be just his luck if Health & Safety turned up, decided that the club was a hazard and closed them down.

Just as he was tentatively reaching back down, the door to the office opened and Danny walked in. Chris sat up straight again, glancing at his watch.

'Nice of you to put in an appearance.'

Danny gave a shrug. 'What's the problem? I'm here, ain't I?'

Danny, however, hadn't come alone. His latest squeeze, Silver Delaney, came waltzing in behind him wearing a tiny pink dress and bringing with her the heavy musky smell of perfume. She was the nineteen-year-old daughter of retired London gangster, Vic Delaney, and was trouble with a capital T. With her long fair hair and wide blue eyes, she looked like an angel but nothing could be further from the truth.

'Hey, babe,' she said, coming to perch on the edge of his desk and crossing her long legs provocatively. 'How are you today?'

'Busy,' Chris said, making a determined effort not to stare at her pale thighs or the ample display of cleavage that was on view.

'Ah, sorry, darlin',' she said without appearing at all sorry. 'Are we bothering you?'

Everything about Silver Delaney bothered Chris, not least her father. There were rumours that one of Silver's previous boyfriends had ended up with a bullet through his head.

Danny was playing with fire, but then he already knew

that. Danny didn't do safe and he didn't do smart. Silver was one of those girls who oozed sexuality, but there was something sly and cruel about her too. 'Just trying to keep the business ticking over.'

'Oh, hon,' she said, leaning forward to squeeze his shoulder, 'you're all tense. Would you like me to give you a neck massage?'

'No, ta,' Chris said, shifting away from her.

'He's all tense, Dan.' She glanced over at him. 'Why's your brother all tense?'

Danny grinned back at her. 'Because he hasn't had a decent shag since Jenna dumped him.'

'Do you mind?' Chris said sharply. He was annoyed, partly because it was true but mainly because he didn't like being mocked. He preferred to keep his private life private. It wasn't as if he didn't have the opportunity – he was surrounded by fit birds every day – but somehow, other than a few unsatisfactory one-night stands, he hadn't seen much action in the last couple of years.

'What you need is a girlfriend, hon,' Silver said. 'We can fix you up with someone.' She glanced over at Danny again. 'We can fix him up, can't we, Dan? We can find him a nice girl to share his lonely evenings with.' She leaned down towards Chris again, her breasts almost touching his face. 'What do you prefer, babe – blondes or brunettes?'

'Thanks, but no thanks,' Chris said. 'I don't need fixing up.'

'Come on, bro,' Danny chipped in. 'Admit it. You need help. Even the old man gets more than you do and that's saying something.'

Chris shook his head. He wasn't in the mood for this. 'Drop it, huh?'

But Danny, once he'd touched a nerve, always liked to press home the advantage. 'Hey, it's not my fault if you can't find a bird. Everything okay downstairs, is it?' He grinned at Silver, enjoying himself. 'There's stuff you can get, you know. You should check out the internet.'

'As it happens,' Chris said sharply, 'I'm already seeing someone, so just get off my back, right?'

'Oh yeah?'

'Yeah.'

'So how come we've never met this mystery bird of yours. Something wrong with her, is there?' Danny folded his arms across his chest and smirked. 'What's her name then?'

'None of your damn business.'

'You're making it up. What d'ya reckon, Silver?'

Silver put her thumb in her mouth and giggled.

Chris glanced from one to the other before plucking the first name he could think of out of the air. 'Ava, okay? She's called Ava.' As soon as he'd said it, he wished he hadn't but there was no going back now. 'Matter of fact, she'll be driving me around for a while 'til I get a proper driver.'

'You gonna let a tart drive the Merc?'

'She can handle it.'

Danny gave a snort. 'Shit, it must be love.'

It was at that very moment that Chris felt a movement by his feet. At first he thought it was Silver, but then he heard a snuffling noise and looked down to see Danny's bull terrier, Trojan, poking his nose into the waste paper bin.

Chris tried to pull the bin away, but the dog snarled and

14

snapped at his fingers. 'For God's sake, Danny, I've told you about bringing that *thing* into work.' He couldn't stand the dog. It had the same nasty character traits as its owner and its cold cruel eyes gave him the creeps. 'If he pisses all over the carpet again, you can clear it up.'

But lifting his leg was the last thing on the dog's mind. He'd smelled something good in the bin and wasn't going to stop until he'd got it. Seconds later, Trojan had forced his way into the cardboard box and grabbed hold of the rat in his teeth. He shook it violently back and forth, growling softly.

Chris wasn't stupid enough to try and take it off him. He only had two hands and didn't fancy losing one of them.

'What's he got?' Danny asked, leaning over the desk.

'A rat, a dead rat.'

'What?'

'It came in the post this morning, a gift for the old man.'

'And you put it in the bin?'

'What did you expect me to do with it?'

Trojan took his prey and dashed to the far corner of the office. He stopped, dropped it, picked it up again and proceeded to rip its belly open. Rat guts spilled out over the carpet. And then, as if this wasn't enough, he began to gnaw at the head, grinding the skull until the bone splintered between his teeth.

'Jesus,' Chris said, grimacing. 'Do something, can't you?'

Danny grinned like an over-indulgent parent watching his child behaving badly. 'Like what? He's only doing what comes natural.'

Chris looked at Silver. She was staring at Trojan with a small, strange smile on her face. She seemed unperturbed, even pleased, by the savagery she was witnessing. He felt that odd, cold feeling roll over his body again. Quickly, he got to his feet and made for the door.

'Where are you going?' Danny asked.

'You sort it out. I've had enough.'

Out in the corridor, Chris strode towards the bar. He needed a drink and he needed a strong one. He felt tired and angry and frustrated. When he'd got up that morning, everything had seemed normal – well, at least as normal as it ever was. But in the space of a few hours he had somehow acquired a female driver, an imaginary girlfriend and a carpet that would stink for weeks. What the hell was going on?

3

On Wednesday morning, Ava was up early, showered, dressed and in the kitchen by seven-thirty. Whatever happened during the day, she was determined to make a good first impression and arrive exactly on time at the Street residence. She couldn't afford to blow this opportunity. With her dwindling bank balance, she needed to make some cash and fast. There were times – usually when she opened her bank statements – that she regretted letting Alec off the hook. He was the one who'd been unfaithful and she could have made him pay for it, but she had wanted the divorce over and done with as quickly as possible. A nice clean split with no haggling over money.

Her flatmate Tash was already seated at the kitchen table, sipping a mug of coffee.

'Oh, very smart,' she said, looking up and flicking back her long brown hair.

'You don't think it's too much?' Ava glanced down at her clothes. Indecisive about what to wear, she had started with a black suit and white shirt but then decided that she looked like a waitress. She had changed from the white shirt into a pink one, decided that was too girly and finally settled on a pale blue one.

'No, you look great. Anyway, I'm sure he doesn't care what you're wearing so long as you don't smash his beloved Merc into the nearest lamppost.'

Ava grinned. 'No pressure then.' She made herself a coffee and sat down on the other side of the table. 'And thanks again for the tip-off. If it hadn't been for you, I wouldn't even have known about it.'

'That's okay. You get to hear about everything working at the Fox.'

Ava gave a nod. 'The rumour capital of Kellston. Any news on a buyer yet?'

'No, but I wish Maggie wasn't selling. It won't be the same without her – that's if I even get to keep the job.' She lowered her chin on to her hands and sighed. 'Whoever buys it may want to bring in their own staff and then what will I do?'

'You'll be okay,' Ava said. 'Who wouldn't want to keep you on? Anyway, you won't even need the job when the business takes off.' Tash was actually trained as a milliner. She made beautiful hats and although she sold some of them to the fancy West End designer outlets, she was still waiting for her big break. In the meantime she supplemented her income by renting out the spare room to Ava and working shifts at the pub. 'It's only a matter of time. Your hats are amazing. Everyone who's anyone is going to want one.'

'Ah, thanks, hon,' Tash said, leaning across to squeeze her hand. 'You always make me feel better.'

It was at that very moment, naturally, that Tash's girlfriend, Hannah, chose to walk into the kitchen. She frowned as she saw her partner's hand lying on top of Ava's. 'Sorry,' she said icily, 'am I disturbing something?'

Ava mentally raised her eyes to the ceiling. 'No, you're not disturbing anything.' Hannah was a smart attractive woman in her early thirties, but despite all her accomplishments – she worked as an accountant for a firm of top City lawyers, earned a six-figure sum and owned a fancy apartment in Hampstead – she still viewed any other female of a certain age as a possible threat to her relationship. Even the fact that Ava was straight didn't deter her. 'I was just saying that Tash is going to be a big success one day.'

'Well, of course she will.' Hannah bent to give Tash a proprietary kiss on the lips, her eyes darting sideways towards Ava. 'She's not going to work in a pub for the rest of her life.'

Ava was tempted to ask what was wrong with working in a pub, but knew she would only be adding fuel to the fire. It was best to keep her mouth shut. Whatever she said would be taken the wrong way and so she simply smiled instead. How Tash coped with Hannah's insecurity, with her intense jealousy, was beyond her – she wouldn't have been able to bear it herself. Still, it took all sorts and when it came to relationships she was hardly an expert. One six-month marriage to the world's greatest philanderer hardly qualified her to pass judgement on others.

'Ava starts her new job today,' Tash said.

'For the Streets, right?' Hannah said, somehow managing to imbue the short question with a distinct undertone of disapproval.

19

'For Chris Street,' Ava said.

Hannah gave a light shrug as if a Street was a Street and it didn't matter what their Christian name was. 'Do you think that's wise?'

'Wise?' Ava echoed, feeling her hackles rise and trying hard to keep them in place. The job might not be the greatest in the world but she didn't need career advice from the likes of Hannah Canning.

'Aren't they ... you know ... a bit on the iffy side?'

'Chris is okay,' Tash said, joining in the exchange. 'It's that Danny you have to watch. He's the weird one. You wouldn't believe the things I've heard about him. He's a real crackhead and loony tunes with it. God, that guy could start a fight with his own shadow. And don't get me started on how he treats women ...'

'Oh, thanks for that,' Ava said.

Tash sat back and laughed. 'Sorry, babe. I didn't mean to put you off on your first day.'

Hannah visibly winced at the *babe*, her brows jumping together in a scowl. She threw Ava a dirty look as she placed her hands on Tash's shoulders. 'You coming over to my place tonight, love?'

'I'm not sure what I'm doing yet,' Tash said. 'I'll give you a bell, yeah?'

'Why? What are you doing?'

'I'm not sure yet.'

'What do you mean, you're not sure?'

'Just what I said, hon. I'm not sure.'

Hannah's eyes instantly darkened with suspicion. She lifted her hands from Tash's shoulders, flounced over to the kettle, flicked on the switch and slammed a mug down on the counter. 'Well, you've either got plans or you haven't.'

Sensing the onset of a row, or at the very least a cross-interrogation, Ava decided to leave them to it. She'd barely started her coffee, but it was worth the sacrifice. It was too early yet to arrive at the Street house, but she thought she'd take a drive down there and suss out exactly where it was. Although she'd grown up in Kellston, the south side had changed a lot since she'd been a kid. 'Okay, folks,' she said. 'I'll see you later.'

'Bye,' Tash said. 'And good luck. Hope it all goes well.'

'Thanks.'

Hannah didn't say a word. She had her back turned and was angrily shovelling coffee into the mug.

Outside, the November air was sharp and cold. An icy wind was sweeping along the street, making the striped awnings of the stalls flap and snap. Living in Market Square had its disadvantages – the early, noisy start of the stallholders being one of them – but Ava was still happier here than she'd ever been in Alec's luxury Barbican apartment. She liked the hustle and bustle, the colour, the smells and scents, the sheer life of it all.

For her, Kellston would always be home despite her mum's decision to move away from London all those years ago. Ava had been ten then and less than overjoyed at having to leave her mates behind. But it was her mates that her mum had been worried about. Ava had started hanging around with a gang of girls from the Mansfield Estate, girls who smoked and swore, drank and thieved. With trouble never far away, and with Dad doing yet another stretch in the Scrubs, Sharon Gold had decided to up sticks and join her sister in Norwich.

Ava walked to the high street, crossed the road to Connolly's and ordered a round of toast and a coffee to take away. While she waited she looked around at the people in the café, working men mostly who were drinking their strong morning brews while they flicked through the paper. Although she'd been born in Kellston and had spent her childhood here, now that she was back she wasn't sure if she completely fitted in. Her time away had altered her, made her different, so that she wasn't quite a local, but not quite a stranger either.

Ava paid the guy behind the counter, thanked him, picked up the brown carrier bag and left the café. She strolled along to Violet Road where she always left the car. It was hard to find a space around Market Square even when the market wasn't in full swing. The small, pale yellow Kia Picanto was where she'd left it, parked alongside a row of neat two-up, two-down terraced houses. The secondhand car was scratched and dented but the engine still ran smoothly. She climbed inside, placed the bag on the passenger seat and set off for the Streets'.

On her way, Ava passed the car lot that her uncle had once owned. She frowned as she thought about him. It still made her sad that her parents had split and she held Ted partly responsible. She knew that her dad had free will and that he'd never *had* to do anything that his brother requested, but Ted was older and extremely persuasive. Although not an out-and-out villain, Ted Gold had always been involved in one dodgy deal or another, but somehow, when things had gone wrong, it was always her dad who'd been nabbed and ended up doing time. He should have learned his lesson but he never had and in the end her mum, sick of being a prison widow, had lost patience and decided to call it a day.

Despite the heavy commuter traffic, it didn't take long to get to the south side of Kellston. Gradually the long rows of terraces gave way to larger, detached and more expensive houses. This was where the moneyed residents of the East End gathered, their homes vigorously protected by high walls and banks of security cameras. It was ironic, she thought, that this exclusive enclave, designed specifically to keep out the local lowlifes, was home to one of the most powerful criminal families of the district.

Ava cruised along the pleasant tree-lined streets until she came to Walpole Close. Slowing as she arrived at number eight, she peered through the tall wrought-iron gates at the house beyond. She gave a low whistle as she took in its splendour. Whoever said crime didn't pay hadn't seen this place. It was a grand white Colonial-style building, three storeys high with pretty shuttered windows. The central front door was sheltered by a portico and there was a long drive with a front garden laid to lawn. She passed on by and then drove to the corner where she pulled up and parked.

As she ate her toast and drank her coffee, Ava wondered if her mother might have been more forgiving of her father had he been less of a failure in his criminal exploits. While Uncle Ted's business had grown and prospered, her dad's prospects had steadily declined. He'd drifted into petty crime and more often than not ended up in the slammer.

Ava had decided long ago that she would never be beholden to any man. She had watched her mum struggle to feed and clothe her, to pay the rent and the bills while her father had been banged up. She knew it was important to be self-sufficient, to be able to make your own money and not rely on anyone else. Which brought her smartly back to what she was doing here today.

Ava glanced at her watch and saw that it was ten to ten. She wiped the crumbs from her lap, finished her coffee and put the debris on the back seat. She checked her face in the rear-view mirror, tidied her hair and reapplied her lipstick. Then, when she was as prepared as she'd ever be, she took a deep breath, started the engine and headed back to the Street residence.

She wasn't nervous about working for Chris Street – she'd grown up surrounded by villains of one sort or another – but she was anxious to make a good impression. Any mistakes today and she would end up back on the minicabs. She knew she only had one chance and she had to make the most of it.

4

Ava pulled up the car in front of the locked electric gates and sat there with the engine idling. She waited for a while, peering through the windscreen at the two security cameras, unsure as to whether anyone knew she was there or not. Perhaps she needed to go and press the intercom. She slipped off her seat belt and opened the door, but just as she got one foot on the ground the gates slid smoothly apart. Quickly, she pulled her foot back, closed the door and headed up the driveway.

Ava swung the car into a space to the left of the house at the same time as Chris Street came out of the front door. He was smartly dressed, suited and booted and wearing a dark overcoat, but his face fell as his gaze roamed over the outside of the Kia.

'I'm not late, am I?' she said as she got out.

'No,' he said shortly, staring hard at the rear of the car with all its dents and scratches.

'Oh, that wasn't down to me,' she said, following his gaze. 'It was like that when I got it.'

Chris's eyes held an expression of ill-disguised scepticism. His fingers tightened around the keys to the Mercedes.

'Really,' she insisted, holding out her hand. 'You don't need to worry.'

He hesitated, but only for a second. 'Okay,' he said, passing them over. 'But just be careful, huh?'

Ava gave a nod. 'I'm always careful.' Before he could change his mind, she walked across to the other side of the drive where the sleek midnight blue Mercedes was parked. As she climbed inside, she drank in the smell of the expensive leather seats. Much as she loved her little Kia – it was great for zipping around town – she'd missed driving the luxury cars for which Harmer's was renowned.

Chris got in beside her. He was in the process of pulling his seat belt across when the front door to the house opened again.

'Let's go,' Chris said.

Ava could see Danny Street walking towards them. 'I think your brother wants you.'

'My brother always wants something.' His voice grew sharper. 'Come on, let's get out of here.'

Ava started the engine and prepared to move off, but Danny wasn't having any of it. He strolled straight in front of the car, placed his hands on the bonnet and smirked at them.

Chris gave a hiss. 'For fuck's sake.'

Ava looked at Danny. He had the same dark hair, the same prominent cheekbones as his older brother, but none of his charm or geniality. As a kid she'd been scared of Danny. She'd sensed something off, something weird about him, and she had the same shivery feeling now.

Chris opened the window. 'Get out of the way. Shift it! What are you playing at?'

Danny went around to the passenger side of the car, still grinning. He leaned down and looked across his brother. 'So,' he said softly. 'You must be Ava.'

She smiled, trying not to show her discomfort. 'Ava Gold. Hi.'

'What do you want?' Chris asked. 'I'm in a hurry, yeah, so make it snappy.'

But Danny didn't seem to be in a snappy frame of mind. 'What's the problem, bruv? I'm just being friendly.'

'Well go and be friendly someplace else. I've got work to do.'

Danny winked at Ava. 'He's been keeping you under wraps, hon. Ain't said a word until we forced it out of him yesterday. Can't figure out what the big secret is. You from round here then?'

'Originally,' she said.

'So how long have you two been—'

'We're going,' said Chris, quickly interrupting. He closed the window, turned to Ava and said brusquely, 'Can we just get the hell out of here?'

She didn't need asking twice. 'Sure.'

Danny stood back, his hands on his hips. As Ava carefully swung the car round, an ethereal-looking girl, dressed in a flimsy white dress, appeared in the doorway of the house. She was young, late teens, with long fair hair flowing down her back. Although undoubtedly pretty, she had a wasted quality

27

about her. Her face was a little too gaunt and there were purplish shadows under her eyes. More heroin chic, Ava thought, than fallen angel.

'Jesus,' Chris muttered under his breath.

Ava wasn't sure if he was referring to his brother or the girl. She was curious about the latter but sensed that now was not the time to start asking questions. 'Where to?' she enquired brightly, hoping that his mood would improve once they were away from the house.

'The Hope and Anchor. Do you know where that is?'

'Yes, I know it.' The pub was about fifty yards from the Fox and was owned by the Streets. She had only been in there once, but that had been enough. It was a meeting place for the local villains, and strangers weren't made welcome.

At the end of the drive, Chris opened the gates with the remote control. Ava slid the Mercedes smoothly out on to the road. As she drove back towards the centre of Kellston she was overly aware of her passenger's scrutiny and of the way he visibly flinched every time she changed gear or put on the brakes. She could feel how tense he was, but wasn't sure how much of that was down to her driving and how much to the exchange that had just taken place with his brother.

Ava was still thinking about Danny as they hit the high street and came to a halt at the queue waiting at the traffic lights by the station. The guy had a reputation and it wasn't a nice one. Hopefully, she'd be able to keep out of his way. Chris, on the other hand, didn't bother her. He might be a villain, but he wasn't a psycho. Despite his silence – he hadn't said a word since they'd left Walpole Close – she still felt comfortable sitting beside him.

It was only as the lights changed and they shifted forward that he finally spoke again. 'Do you have any brothers or sisters?'

'Just the one. A brother. Well, a half-brother.'

'And do you get on?'

'Yes,' she said, 'pretty much. But he's a lot younger than me. He's called Jason. He's only thirteen.' She paused before adding, 'And I don't have to live with him.'

Chris's mouth slid into a smile. 'Yeah, well that makes a difference.'

'He'd probably drive me crazy if I did.' She turned right at the lights, went past the Fox and travelled on up Station Road until she came to the Hope and Anchor. She pulled in to the kerb and switched off the engine. 'You ever thought about moving out?'

Chris made a noise in the back of his throat. 'Only a couple of hundred times a day. But someone has to keep the peace. Danny and my dad don't exactly . . . Well, let's just say that they know how to wind each other up.' He opened the car door, got out and leaned down. 'I'll be fifteen minutes. Will you be okay?'

Ava lifted her eyebrows. 'Would you ask that if I was a man?'

He grinned, shut the door and walked over to the pub. It was closed but his knock was quickly answered by a middle-aged man with thinning salt-and-pepper hair and a heavy paunch. She watched as Chris went inside and then she settled back to wait. Driving jobs often involved a lot of hanging about but she was used to it.

Ava took her iPod out of her bag, stuck in the earphones

and started listening to Florence and the Machine. She gazed through the windscreen, the glass splattered by rain, and looked at the people going by. She knew why Chris had asked if she would be okay: they were parked only twenty yards from Albert Road, the traditional haunt of the local toms. The dealers always gathered there too, along with the pimps and the junkies. It was, however, way too early for the girls to be out and there wasn't much other activity either.

Five minutes after Chris had gone inside, a smart black Bentley drew up behind the Mercedes. The driver, wearing a traditional chauffeur's uniform, got out of the car and walked round to the rear door. He opened an umbrella and held it over the man as he climbed out. The man, in his early fifties, was tall and impeccably groomed with short grey cropped hair. Ava studied him in her rear-view mirror. She reckoned, from his features, that he might be Russian or East European.

The chauffeur delivered the guy to the pub and even knocked on the door for him. Once the man had disappeared inside, the driver strolled back to the Bentley. As he passed the Mercedes, he threw Ava a disdainful glance, but didn't acknowledge her further. They might both be drivers but he clearly considered himself a class above – Mr Chauffeur, she figured, thought of himself as more Knightsbridge than Kellston.

Ava looked across towards the pub again. It didn't take a genius to work out that a deal was going down. And if the Streets were involved, it was bound to be dodgy. Still, that was none of her business. See no evil, hear no evil. It was, she knew, a slightly skewed moral perspective but she couldn't afford too many principles at the moment.

5

It was closer to half an hour before Chris Street emerged again. He was with the older guy and the two of them walked over to the Bentley where they shook hands and separated. Chris got back into the Mercedes with a pleased expression on his face. Ava knew better than to ask how it had gone; anything he volunteered to tell her was fine but it didn't do to probe.

'Where to now, boss?' she asked.

'That shop on the high street, the one with all the stuffed animals.'

'Beast?' she said, surprised by the request.

'Yeah, that's the one.'

Ava pulled the car into the traffic. Chris seemed more relaxed about her driving now or maybe his mind was on other things. She knew the place he was talking about. When she was a kid, it had been the local undertaker's, a family business established for generations. But some bad stuff had happened there, a gruesome murder that had finished off the business for good. A few years ago the premises had been taken over by a taxidermist. Personally, she couldn't see the attraction but apparently it was back in fashion and all the rage. 'You like that kind of thing?'

'It's not for me. It's a present for a friend.'

Ava gave him a sidelong glance. 'Not a girlfriend, I hope. I think they usually prefer perfume and flowers.'

'No, not a girlfriend. A business associate.'

She wondered if it was for the man she'd just seen him with. 'Good,' she said, smiling. 'You could kill a relationship with a gift like that.'

It only took them a couple of minutes to get there and fortunately there was a parking space not too far away. The sky had darkened and the rain was coming down hard, bouncing off the pavement and swirling into the gutters. As Chris opened the passenger door, he turned to her and said, 'Would you mind coming with me? A second opinion would be handy.'

'I don't know anything about stuffed animals.'

'Join the club,' he said.

Ava gave a shrug. 'Okay.' She had never been inside before and, despite a faint distaste, was curious to see what it was like.

They ran from the car to the gallery, sloshing through the puddles. Chris opened the door and then stood aside to let her enter. Almost as soon as she'd crossed the threshold, Ava was struck by the surreal quality of the place. Animals of all varieties – stoats and weasels, foxes, mice, rats, reptiles, bats, birds and fish – were displayed in various poses around the room.

For a while they drifted from cabinet to cabinet, examining the contents. There was a hushed, almost reverential air about Beast. Although they weren't alone – there were at least half a dozen other customers in there – everyone spoke in whispers. Ava felt as though she'd stumbled upon a bizarre animal cemetery – except all the bodies were above ground. Eyes followed her wherever she went. She knew that they were glass and yet they still felt uncomfortably real.

'Have you got any ideas?' she asked, looking up at a large brown bear that was standing in the corner. The bear, she thought, had a slightly mortified expression. 'Do you know what he likes?'

Chris pulled a face. 'Not a clue. Someone told me about it, said his house was full of the stuff.'

'Weird,' she said. 'Would you put any of this in your home?'

'Only if it was called Trojan.'

'Trojan?'

'My brother's dog,' he explained. 'The bull terrier from hell. Now there's one animal I wouldn't mind seeing stuffed and shoved in a cabinet.'

They carried on browsing, moving from case to case. After a while a tall, stooped man with very pale skin and a shock of white hair approached them. It was hard to tell how old he was. He could have been anything from fifty to seventy.

'Morton Carlisle,' he said with a small bow of his head. 'I'm the proprietor of Beast. Would you like some assistance?'

'Yeah,' Chris said. 'I'm looking for something, for a colleague. He's interested in ... you know ...' He made a general sweeping gesture with his hand. 'Stuffed animals.'

33

Ava noticed Carlisle wince at the word *stuffed* although he was quick to cover it up.

'Well, as you can see we have a wide selection of mounted animals. Is there anything in particular you'd care to take a closer look at?'

'I'm not sure. To be honest, I don't really know what he's into.'

'Your colleague,' Carlisle said patiently. 'Is he a collector? If so, we may have already met. The world of taxidermy is a small one.'

Chris hesitated as if pondering on the wisdom of divulging his business contacts to a complete stranger. His eyes raked the room before coming back to rest on Carlisle. He weighed up his options for a few seconds more, but then, unwilling to make the wrong choice, decided to throw caution to the wind. 'Borovski,' he said. 'Anatoly Borovski.'

'Ah, Mr Borovski,' Carlisle said, bringing his long slender hands together as if in prayer. He briefly touched his chin with his fingertips. 'Indeed. I may have just what you're looking for. Come this way.'

Carlisle turned and swept off towards the rear of the store. As they followed him, Ava recalled again how this had once been a funeral parlour. It was here that the bodies had been cleaned and embalmed and laid out in the chapel of rest. Strange, she thought, how the business had changed but that the premises continued to be inhabited by the dead. There was something inescapably macabre about the place.

Carlisle led them into a room where he lifted his arms in a wide dramatic gesture as if welcoming them to previously unknown delights. 'Here we are!' he exclaimed. 'The birds!'

'The birds,' Chris repeated glumly, glancing not altogether tactfully at his watch. 'And Mr Borovski likes these?'

'Oh, indeed. He has a very keen interest.'

'And are there any in particular that—'

'Over here, over here,' Carlisle said, ushering him towards the larger cabinets at the back.

Ava followed in their wake, peering at the collection as she trudged behind. There was a vast array of birds both of the native and more exotic variety. There were birds small enough to fit into the palm of her hand and ones with the kind of wingspan that would strike terror into their prey. There were pheasants, owls, buzzards and eagles. There were parakeets and parrots and toucans. She stopped to peer into a dome containing two pretty European bee-eaters with jade-green breasts.

'Ava?' Chris called out.

She hurried over to join the two men. Chris was scrutinising the contents of a large glass case. Inside, perched on a rock, was a gyrfalcon with brown-flecked plumage and black eyes ringed with yellow.

'What do you think?' he asked. 'It's either this one or the sparrowhawk.' He turned to look at the case behind him, indecision etched on to his face.

Ava studied both mounted birds. Although she could appreciate the skill involved, she couldn't see the beauty. For her the loveliness, especially of birds of prey, was in the flying, in the swooping and soaring, in the graceful way that they travelled through the sky. These poor creatures had been grounded forever. Sensing, however, that a choice had to be made – and that Chris wasn't likely to make it in a hurry – she pointed confidently towards the falcon. 'That one,' she said. 'Yes, definitely that one.'

Morton Carlisle nodded sagely. 'Yes, an excellent choice. Quite excellent.'

Ava gave him a thin smile, suspecting that the response would have been exactly the same if she'd chosen the hawk.

'Okay,' Chris said. 'I'll take it.'

Carlisle bowed his head again. 'I'm sure Mr Borovski will be very pleased.'

They went back into the other room where the sale was rung up on the till. Ava drew in her breath as she saw the amount – sixteen hundred quid. Jesus, you could buy a second-hand car with that. Or an awful lot of shoes. Whatever was cooking with Borovski must be one hell of a deal.

Chris put his credit card into the machine and punched in his number. 'You deliver?' he asked.

'Of course.'

He took a business card for Belles out of his wallet and gave it to Carlisle. 'Any time after eleven in the morning. Call me if there's a problem.'

Carlisle held the card between his finger and thumb, quickly reading off the details before dropping it beside the till. Ava saw a flash of what might have been disgust fly across his face. She figured that he wasn't a fan of lap-dancing clubs although he was, apparently, perfectly happy to do business with their owners.

Chris waited for the receipt and put it in his pocket. 'Thank you.'

'A pleasure,' Carlisle said.

Chris turned to Ava. 'Okay. Job done. Let's get out of here.'

They were halfway across the room when the door to the shop opened and a fair-haired man in his mid-thirties walked in. Ava was simultaneously aware of two strong physical reactions. One was her own – the man had the kind of good looks that would make any girl's heart miss a beat – and the other came from Chris. She felt his whole body stiffen as a hissing breath escaped from between his lips.

Ava looked quickly from one to the other before her gaze settled on the stranger again. He had a beautifully sculpted face with a strong chin and piercing blue eyes. But it wasn't just his handsome features that had captured her attention; the guy had an extraordinary air about him, a kind of magnetism, something that could only be described as charisma.

Chris, however, wasn't feeling the love. He glared at the man with pure hate in his eyes. Ava could feel the rise in testosterone levels. Like two male dogs meeting on neutral territory, they stood their ground, each trying to stare the other out. Neither of them spoke. It was an animalistic exchange, cold and nasty.

The impasse was broken only by the arrival of Morton Carlisle. Sensing that an 'incident' was brewing – and not relishing the collateral damage that was likely to result from two grown men scrapping in his gallery – he inserted himself smartly between them. 'Ah, Mr Wilder. How nice to see you again. Please, do come with me.'

As Wilder allowed himself to be gently propelled away, he glanced over his shoulder and said in a soft mocking tone, 'I hear they can stuff anything in here – even rats.'

Chris made as if to lunge for him, but then thought better of it. 'You'll pay for that, you bastard!'

'Is that a threat?'

Chris Street's cheeks were tinged with red, his hands clenched into two tight fists. 'No, mate, it's a fuckin' promise!' And with those angry words, he turned his back and stormed out of the gallery.

Ava, startled by the exchange, hurried after him. 'Who on earth was that?' she asked as they got into the Merc.

Chris didn't answer. He pulled out a pack of cigarettes, lit one, opened the window and glared at the door to Beast. He smoked furiously, staring at the gallery as if he was in two minds whether to go back in or not.

Ava didn't ask again. She could see that he was steaming and didn't want to aggravate him further. The best thing to do, she thought, was to try and put some distance between him and Mr Wilder. Quickly, she started the engine, placed her hands on the wheel and said, 'Where to?'

'What?'

'Where would you like to go now?'

He threw the butt of the fag on to the pavement and closed the window 'Belles. Take me to Belles and then you can drop the car off at the house. I won't be needing you again today.'

'Already? But it's only—' She stopped, seeing the look on his face. 'Belles it is,' she said. 'Will there be someone at the house to let me in?'

Chris took the remote control for the gates out of his pocket and threw it on the dash. 'You can hang on to that.'

'Okay. Thanks.'

Ava waited for a gap in the traffic, pulled out and started

heading for Shoreditch. The atmosphere in the car was tight and strained. She knew that the smart thing to do was to keep her mouth shut and hope that he would calm down soon. She was feeling none too happy herself. It wasn't even eleven o'clock and already she'd been dismissed for the day. They hadn't discussed her salary yet – and now certainly wasn't the time to be raising the subject – but if he was paying her by the hour she wasn't going to be earning much.

'You know what that bastard did?' said Chris, his voice still full of rage.

Ava gave him a sidelong glance. 'What did he do?'

'The fuckin' bastard sent a dead rat through the post!'

'What?' She jumped, shocked by the revelation. 'What . . . why . . . why the hell did he do that?'

'Because that's the kind of guy he is. He's sick and he's twisted.'

Ava frowned, trying to reconcile the vileness of the act with Mr Wilder's remarkable features. She knew it was wrong to judge by appearances, but it was often hard not to equate beauty with goodness. 'No other reason?' she asked. And then, worried that it might sound like an accusation, she rapidly added, 'I mean, you're right, it's sick, it's really disgusting, but why would he do that?'

'He doesn't need a reason.'

'You two have history, huh?'

Chris gave a nod. 'Oh yeah, we've got history all right.'

Ava waited, but he didn't elaborate. In fact, he didn't say anything else at all until they got to Belles and she pulled up by the door. 'Are you sure you don't want me to pick you up later? I can come back. It's no trouble.'

'No, I'll get a lift home with the old man.'

'Well, call me if you change your mind.'

'I won't,' he said, undoing his seat belt. 'Look, sometimes it's like this, yeah? Other times we'll be on the go all day, maybe until late at night. Short hours, long hours. It balances out in the end.'

'Okay.'

Chris got out of the car and leaned down to speak to her like he had when they'd stopped outside the Hope and Anchor. 'Oh, and one other thing,' he said. 'About your driving . . .'

Ava braced herself for some unwelcome macho criticism. 'Yes?'

He nodded. 'I've seen worse,' he said before slamming the door.

Ava raised her eyebrows. And that, she thought, was about as close to a compliment as Chris Street would ever get.

6

Noah Clark picked up the pitcher, poured out two Mojitos and added a wedge of lime and a mint leaf. He placed the glasses on a tray and passed it over to the cocktail waitress. Throughout the process, he'd had one eye on the drinks and the other on the end of the bar. It was there that Guy was standing with a group of customers. He was, as always, the focal point of the room. People were drawn like moths to a flame. They gathered round, their social wings fluttering, jostling for his undivided attention.

Noah understood Guy's appeal. He'd known and adored him for over twenty years. They were friends, business partners and lovers. Tonight, however, he was worried. He knew who the tall, slender blonde was and he knew that Guy was going to sleep with her. His eyes raked over the woman. She was nothing special, he thought, just one of a breed – an Essex girl with peroxide hair, cosmetically enhanced breasts and very white teeth. She was wearing a short red dress and sporting enough bling to pay for a deposit on a house.

Noah felt a tightening in his chest, but it wasn't jealousy at the root of his anxiety. He had long ago become resigned to the fact that Guy Wilder was incapable of monogamy. No, he could cope with that – he knew that Guy would always come back to him – but this was something else entirely. There was trouble brewing and the result could be explosive. The girl in question was called Jenna and she was Chris Street's ex-wife.

Noah looked at Guy, caught his eye and beckoned him over.

Guy excused himself from the group and joined him at the other end of the bar. 'Problem?'

Noah leaned forward, put his elbows on the counter and lowered his voice. 'There will be when Chris Street finds out that you're messing with her.'

'And that should bother me because . . . ?'

Noah gave a shake of his head. 'Are you crazy, man? He's going to go ballistic.'

'Let him. It's not my fault if he can't hold on to his wife.'

'You're just trying to wind him up.'

The corners of Guy's mouth twitched. 'That isn't difficult. Did I tell you I saw him today? He was in Beast. God knows what he was doing there. Maybe he was making arrangements to have the old man stuffed.'

Noah glanced at Jenna, pulled a face and looked back at Guy. 'Just be careful, huh? I don't want to be scraping you off the pavement.'

Guy laughed. 'He wouldn't dare. Anyway, we're all set for next week.'

'Next week?'

'Morton Carlisle's show. We're doing the cocktails, remember? Thursday, three 'til five at the gallery.'

Noah gave a shudder. 'That place is weird. And don't change the subject. What's the point in making Street mad? He'll come after you. You know he will.'

'It's none of his business any more. She's a free agent. She can do as she likes.'

Noah knew that there was no point in arguing. When it came to the Streets, Guy was never rational. He gazed over at Jenna and said, 'She's not worth it. She's just using you to get back at him.'

Guy gave a light shrug. 'Well, there you go. That's something the two of us have in common.'

'It's not funny, man.'

'Who's laughing?'

The waitress came back with a new batch of orders and passed the slips of paper over to Noah. It brought the conversation between the two men to a halt.

'Catch you later, then,' Guy said. 'And send over another bottle of champagne when you've got a minute, yeah?'

'Just think on,' Noah said, but he knew his warning would fall on deaf ears. He watched as Guy walked back to the group, observing the way the men and women responded, their body language changing as he joined them again: shoulders becoming straighter, faces lighting up, smiles instantly appearing. Noah understood the effect he had on people; for him a room was always empty if Guy wasn't in it.

Noah got to work on the drinks: two Cosmopolitans, two Cuba Libres and a Bloody Mary. It was only early evening, but already it was getting busy. They had launched the business over seven years ago, starting off as a wine bar but gradually becoming more renowned for their cocktails. It was a calm, laid-back lounge where folk came to chill. There was flattering lighting, wide comfortable sofas, and black-and-white photographs of the old Hollywood stars on the walls – Gable, Monroe, Hepburn, Bogart and Bacall. The music was soft jazz and blues.

Noah knew that without Guy the bar would never have become as popular as it had. He was its centre, its very heart. Wilder's wasn't in the most fashionable part of town, but the most fashionable people came to drink here. Despite its relaxed nature, there was still a buzz about the place, a unique atmosphere that existed nowhere else.

Glancing over again towards the small group at the end of the bar, Noah saw that Guy's hand was now resting lightly on the base of Jenna's spine. He felt a shiver run through him. This could only end badly, but there was nothing he could do to stop it. Guy's obsession with the Streets was escalating, his need for retribution growing stronger by the day. Sending a dead rat through the mail was one thing, but screwing Chris Street's ex was quite another. It was a declaration of war.

7

Faced with an unexpectedly empty afternoon, Ava had used the time to do her washing and clean up the flat. There was no sign of Tash other than the debris lying on the table in the living room, scraps of felt and cotton and ribbon that she used when she was making her hats. Tash wasn't the tidiest person in the world, but Ava didn't mind. She liked sharing with her. It was easy, uncomplicated. She enjoyed the chat and the laughs and the companionship. It felt like an oasis after the gruelling battleground of her relationship with Alec.

In the bedroom, Ava changed into a clean pair of jeans and a white jumper. She ran a comb through her hair and gazed at her reflection in the mirror. There had been a time when she'd hated her dark hair and olive skin – an inheritance from her Italian grandmother – but now, finally, she was coming to terms with her appearance. She would never be a leggy blue-eyed blonde and that was just the way it was.

She tilted her chin, reviewing her current situation: twenty-seven, divorced, childless and working for a local gangster. Not exactly what she'd envisaged for her future, but despite past disappointments she still felt optimistic. Life was certainly better than it had been. She'd gone down as far as she could and now the only way was up.

Checking her watch, Ava saw that it was almost six-thirty. She grabbed her jacket and bag and headed for the door. She was due to meet her dad in the Fox and didn't want to be late. Outside, it was dark and a sleety rain was falling. The temperature had dropped a few degrees and she could feel the cold biting at her fingers. She pulled up her hood, put up her umbrella, bent her head and set off for the pub.

Ava thought about the morning's events as she tramped along the high street. Things had gone well enough on one front – at least nothing disastrous had happened to the Merc – but she wasn't so sure about the rest. She had the feeling that Chris Street wasn't entirely comfortable with a female driver. As there was nothing she could do about her sex, she would have to find another way of convincing him to keep her on.

Ava walked past Beast, closed now with a latticed iron grille pulled down over the shop front. From between the slats, she could see a light shining in the back. She had a sudden image of Morton Carlisle bent over a table, his fingers peeling back the fur on some poor dead creature. She hunched her shoulders, a shudder running through her.

Seeing the gallery reminded her of the antagonistic meeting between Chris and the fair-haired man called Wilder. Why did they hate each other so much? And what would she have done if it had all kicked off? She hoped that there wouldn't be too many altercations like the one she had witnessed today.

A hundred yards on, she turned left into Station Road, continued until she was opposite the Fox and then waited for a gap in the traffic. She was standing on the edge of the pavement when a white van careered past, sending up a wave of water from the gutter. She jumped back, but it was already too late. The spray rolled over the bottom part of her legs, drenching her jeans and shoes.

'Pig!' she muttered, glaring after the van. But the driver was well gone, probably with a big fat smile on his face.

With her feet squelching, Ava jogged across the road, gave her umbrella a shake and opened the door to the pub. Inside, it was wonderfully warm with a real log fire burning in the grate. The place was busy, but not too crowded, and she immediately saw her father standing by the bar. He was holding a twenty in his hand and waiting to be served.

'Hey, Dad,' she said, going over to stand beside him.

He turned and put an arm around her. 'Sweetheart,' he said, smiling as he gave her a peck on the cheek. 'How are you doing?'

'I'm good.' Ava noticed that his face was flushed, his eyes a little brighter than usual. She could smell the beer on his breath and knew that he was already tipsy. How long had he been here for? She nodded towards the score he was holding. Usually, he didn't have two pennies to rub together. 'You in the money, then?'

'Oh, just a lucky flutter on the gee-gees.'

Ava narrowed her eyes. Her father was a lovely guy,

even-tempered and kind, but he was a dreadful liar. He wasn't even capable of fibbing to the law, which probably accounted for the number of times he'd been sent down. 'The gee-gees, eh?'

'So what do you want to drink, love?' he said, making a feeble attempt to change the subject.

'Dad?'

'What?'

'You know what.' She glanced around, lowering her voice. 'What have you been up to?'

'Nothing, I swear.' He gave a shrug. 'Just a bit of business, nothing to worry about.'

But Ava couldn't help worrying. She still had a clear recollection of all that prison visiting she'd done as a kid – the chipped magnolia walls, the Formica-topped tables, the hard uncomfortable plastic chairs – but most of all the weary disappointment on her mother's face. 'It's not worth it, Dad. You know it's not. What if—'

But Jimmy Gold was saved from Ava's remonstrations by the arrival of the barman.

'Yes, guv'nor, what can I get you?'

Jimmy pushed his empty glass across the counter. 'Ta, yeah. You can put another pint in there.'

'And I'll have a Coke, please,' Ava said. 'Ice and a slice.'

While they were waiting, she resisted the temptation to probe him further. It was a waste of time and it would only spoil the evening. She didn't want to see him banged up again, but there was no point in nagging.

After they'd got their drinks, they took them over to an empty table near the fire. Ava put her dripping brolly on the floor. She shrugged off her jacket and placed it over the back of her chair.

'God, you're soaked,' Jimmy said.

Ava glanced down at her wet jeans. 'Some sod of a van driver deciding to have a laugh at my expense. I'll soon dry out. Anyway, I haven't told you my news. I started a new job today.'

'Oh, well done, sweetheart. Good on you. You back on the cabs?'

'No,' she said. 'I'm working for Chris Street, driving him around. But it's only a trial. I think he wanted a bloke really, but I persuaded him to take me on.'

'Chris Street, huh?' he said. 'You're not his getaway driver, are you?'

'Ha ha. Very funny.'

'And there you were having a go at me for—'

'Yeah, well,' she interrupted, 'I'm not planning on doing anything illegal.' She took a sip of her Coke and grinned. 'But he seems okay. I remembered him from when he used to come to Uncle Ted's car lot.'

Jimmy gave a nod. 'Yeah, he's sound enough. Chris won't give you any bother. What does your mum think about it?'

Ava glanced away before looking back at him. 'Well, I haven't exactly told her yet. You know what she's like. She'll only start fretting.'

'Ava Gold,' he said with mock sternness, 'I hope you've not been lying to your mother.'

'Not *lying*,' she insisted, 'just not sharing all the details. She won't approve. You know she won't. She'll think I'm on the first step to a life of crime. And I might not get to keep the job so what's the point of worrying her?'

He played with his glass for a moment, swirling the beer around. 'Well, I suppose what she doesn't know won't cause her any sleepless nights.'

'Exactly!' Ava said. She smiled and he smiled back. She had the feeling that he was inwardly pleased that the two of them shared a secret. He'd missed out on so much when she was growing up that now even the smallest of confidences meant a lot to him.

'So how is your mum? She doing all right?'

They'd been divorced for fifteen years, but Ava suspected that he still held a torch for her. 'She's good. She's fine.' Before he could start to dwell on what had been lost and could never be recovered – something he tended to do after a few bevvies – she leaned forward, lowered her voice and said, 'Actually, there was something I wanted to ask you about Chris Street. We came face to face with a bloke called Wilder today – a blond guy, good-looking – and the two of them weren't exactly friendly. I just wondered if you knew anything about him.'

Jimmy Gold laughed. 'Shit,' he said. 'Face to face? Which one of them is dead?'

'Neither as it happens. Although it was a near thing. So what's the deal between those two? It was like some kind of hatefest.'

'Yeah, they're not what you'd call close.'

'But why?' If Ava was going to go on working for Chris, she reckoned it would help to find out as much about him as she could. 'What's the history?'

'They're family, sweetheart – that's the history.'

'You're kidding me? Those two are related?'

'Brothers,' Jimmy said. 'Well, stepbrothers. Do you remember Lizzie Street, Terry's wife?'

Ava nodded. Lizzie was entirely memorable, a ballsy blonde who'd clawed her way out of poverty to become one of the most powerful women in the East End. She was the one who'd run Terry's businesses while he was banged up – and made a damn good job of it too. 'He's her son?'

'Got it in one. Guy Wilder. He owns the cocktail joint on the high street, just round the corner.'

'Ah,' Ava said. 'Wilder's.' She must have driven past it a hundred times but hadn't made the connection with the man she'd seen today. 'So what's with the aggravation?'

Jimmy took a pull on his pint and licked his lips. He always enjoyed telling a good story. 'It's a can of worms, this one. It all goes back to when Guy Wilder was a kid. Six or seven he must have been. Lizzie hooked up with Terry – he was a widower then, bringing up the boys on his own – and Guy was sent to live with his grandmother.'

'Why's that? Why didn't he live with the rest of them?'

'Depends whose story you believe. From what I've heard, and it's all gossip, mind, Terry and the kid didn't get on. Wilder claims that Terry knocked him about, that he didn't want to bring up another man's child and that he made his mother choose between the two of them.'

'Ouch,' Ava said, frowning. 'That must have hurt. Nothing like being rejected by your own mum.'

'But Lizzie's take on it was always different. *She* reckoned that she'd only been protecting Guy, that she didn't want him growing up in that world. She had big ambitions for the lad, a fancy school and all that, and didn't want him turning into a villain. Marrying Terry gave her the money she needed to give him a better start in life.'

Ava stretched her legs out towards the fire, feeling the warmth spread up her shins. 'And who do you think is telling the truth?'

'God knows. Lizzie Street could twist anything to suit her own purpose, and her son's got a massive chip on his shoulder. All I do know is that you don't want to get involved. Keep out of it, love. That kind of family stuff, it's always messy.'

'I intend to. But I still don't understand the deal between Chris and Guy Wilder. I mean, I can see why there's bad blood, but the two of them looked like they wanted to kill each other.'

Jimmy took another drink and put the glass down on the table. 'Ah, that's because you haven't heard the end of the story yet.'

Ava waited while her father paused for effect. 'Go on, then,' she urged.

'You know about Lizzie being murdered a few years back?'

'Yeah, I heard about it.'

Jimmy glanced to either side to make sure no one was listening. He leaned forward, keeping his voice low. 'Well, rumour has it that Terry was the one who had her bumped off. He was just coming to the end of a ten-stretch and wanted her out of the way before he got out. The marriage wasn't exactly a happy one – neither of them were the faithful sort – and she'd grown pretty powerful while he'd been inside. They say that Terry wanted his empire back and didn't want a row about it.'

'Jesus,' Ava murmured.

'And Guy Wilder has always believed that Chris and Danny were involved, that Terry wouldn't have trusted anyone else. And Wilder might have hated his mother's guts – he didn't ever forgive her for abandoning him – but he didn't want to see her dead.' He scratched his chin where a day's growth of beard gave the skin a bluish hue. 'But like I said, it's only a rumour. The cops never found any evidence and no one was ever charged. Could just be a pile of bollocks.'

Ava tried to imagine Chris Street lifting a gun and shooting his stepmother through the heart. Was he capable of such a thing? She didn't really want to think about it. There were enough horrors in the world without creating imaginary ones too.

Jimmy finished his beer and raised his empty glass. 'You got time for another?'

'Of course. Let me get these.' She reached for her bag, but her father was already on his feet.

'Keep your cash,' he said, flapping a hand. 'These are on me.'

As Ava watched him standing at the bar, she wished that he could find someone to settle down with. The girlfriends came and went – usually arriving when her dad was in the money and leaving as soon as it ran out. And okay, maybe he wasn't the greatest catch in the world, but he still had his own hair and teeth, was kind and loyal and never bore grudges. There were far worse guys out there.

She saw him pay for the drinks and that nagging worry came back to haunt her again. Where had he got the dosh from – and how long before the law came knocking on his door? Her father never could say no to a 'sure thing'. Hope always triumphed over experience. Raising her eyes to the ceiling, she silently prayed to the heavens above: *Please God, just for once, let him get away with it.*

8

Terry Street was sitting at his usual table in Belles, near the back and off to the side where he could see everything that was going on. He was staring at the girls, but he wasn't really seeing them. After a while, one half-naked body looked much the same as another. Tits and bums, tits and bums. He felt no lust for them, no desire. The only thing that brought him any pleasure these days was the booze.

He reached for his glass and drank some of the whisky. When he put the glass down, he frowned. He'd been mulling over something, but now he couldn't remember what it was. It had been happening to him a lot recently, this weird disconnection halfway through a train of thought. And he kept putting things down and forgetting where he'd put them. Age creeping up, he supposed, although he was only in his sixties.

Terry picked up his glass again. He glanced across at the bar and saw Chris standing there, chatting to a group of banker types. Once Terry would have been the one to do the schmoozing, but lately he couldn't be bothered. It was too much of an effort and basically he didn't give a toss about the customers. So long as they paid their money, drank the champagne and kept away from him, he was happy.

Terry knew that he was becoming anti-social. The truth was that most people bored him these days. The younger generation didn't know the meaning of a proper conversation; it was mobile phones and texting, Facebook and all the rest of that crap. Even the villains were bland. Back in his time, there had been real characters, men with personalities. Now you were lucky to find someone who could string more than a couple of sentences together.

He looked hard at Chris. Both of his boys, in different ways, had been a disappointment to him. Neither of them had what it took to be a real success. Chris was smart enough but he lacked the killer instinct. If he could avoid trouble, he would – and everybody knew it. He had some charm but not enough to make up for his deficiencies. Danny, on the other hand, had a fuckin' screw loose. It was a tough thing to admit about your own son, but there it was. Danny was a bleeding liability and that was never going to change.

Only Liam, his eldest son, his long-dead son, had had the potential to really go places. Liam could have stepped into his shoes if he'd been given the opportunity. Instead, he'd got half his head blown off when he was only seventeen. Terry felt a sudden searing pain in his heart, the symptom of a grief that never diminished no matter how many years passed by.

He knocked back the whisky and caught the eye of one of the waitresses. He didn't say anything. He didn't need to. She came and took his glass and went over to the bar. A minute later, Chris came back with the drink.

'Here,' he said, placing the glass on the table. 'I need a word.'

Terry gestured ungraciously towards the chair in front of him. He would have preferred to be alone with his whisky and his thoughts. 'Just tell me this ain't about the Fox again.'

'We need to talk about it.'

'We've already done that.'

Chris frowned. 'Have we? The way I remember it is that I suggested buying it and you said forget it. Not what I'd call a conversation. You want to tell me why we shouldn't?'

Terry glared at him. There was a time when Chris wouldn't have questioned a decision he had made, a time when his word would have been law. But there was no respect any more. A father couldn't even expect it from his son. 'Okay,' he said. 'I'll tell you why not.' He counted out the reasons on his fingers. 'For one, Maggie McConnell ain't going to sell it to us. For two, even if she did we'd never get a fuckin' licence. For three, we ain't got that kind of spare cash lying around. And for four, I don't *want* to own the fuckin' place again.'

'We could find the money,' Chris said. 'That place is a goldmine. We'd soon be raking it in. And we've already got a licence for the Hope so why should getting one for the Fox be a problem?'

'It ain't the same.'

'No, it ain't the same. The Fox is a damn sight more profitable.'

Terry shrugged his shoulders. Although all the reasons he had given were perfectly valid, there was one that he hadn't mentioned and wasn't about to. Years ago, when he'd been a young man, he'd murdered Joe Quinn outside the cellar door to the Fox. Bludgeoned him to death with a baseball bat – and got away with it too. Quinn had owned the pub back then, had owned half the East End in fact, and Terry had wanted it all.

'At least give it some thought.'

'Sure,' Terry said, eager to be rid of him. 'Now piss off and leave me in peace.'

Chris got to his feet and then leaned back down and said, 'And we need to sort out Wilder too.'

'Who?'

'Wilder,' Chris repeated.

For a moment, Terry couldn't place the name. Who the fuck was Wilder? As he struggled to find a path through the fog in his brain, he was aware of his son waiting impatiently. 'What about him?' he asked, playing for time.

Chris gazed at his father and gave a light despairing shake of his head. 'Well, if that's how you feel, you can open your own bleedin' post from now on. I'm not handling any more dead rats that were meant for you.'

It was then that the name finally slotted into place. Wilder. Christ, Guy Wilder. Lizzie's boy. How could he have forgotten that? Quickly, Terry tried to cover his confusion. 'He ain't worth the bother. You really gonna let that scrote get to you?'

Chris threw him a dirty look. 'For God's sake, he sent you a filthy rotting rodent. Since when did you let that bastard walk all over you?'

Terry gave a shrug. 'The only person he's walking over is you. That's if you let him. He's a worthless piece of shite. Just forget about it, huh?'

'Right, so forget about the rat, forget about the Fox. Anything else you want me to forget about?' Chris turned on his heel and strode back towards the bar.

'Fuckin' kids,' Terry muttered under his breath. He wasn't going to buy the bloody pub and that was that. All this recent talk of the Fox had stirred up old memories. He could be walking down the road, sitting in the office or lying in bed trying to get some shut-eye, when suddenly an image of Joe Quinn would rise up in his mind. He would see him sitting in Connolly's, expertly rolling his skinny cigarettes. He would see him holding court at the Fox, supping on his pint and snarling out orders. He would see him climbing into the rusty old van at the start of the last journey he would ever make.

Terry took a large gulp of whisky. On the whole, he didn't hold much truck with the concept of karma, with the idea that what goes around comes around, but these constant reminders of Joe had begun to unnerve him. Why couldn't the bastard leave him alone? What was done was done and nothing could change it. And okay, it was true that he'd let Joe's two sons go down for a murder they hadn't committed, but innocence was relative – completely relative in this instance – and he didn't regret what he'd done. Dog eat dog, the survival of the fittest – those were the rules of the criminal world. There was no room for finer feelings.

Terry felt a prickling sensation on the back of his neck. He turned his head but no one was paying him any attention. All eyes were firmly fixed on the glistening bodies of the tarts on stage. But still the feeling continued as if somewhere, in the shadows, he was being watched. Although it was the last thing he wanted, he suddenly found himself thinking about

Lizzie. The bitch might be six foot under, but she still continued to haunt him.

He scowled as he buried his face in his glass. Lizzie was the only person he had ever told about the murder of Joe Quinn. He had done it in that first flush of passion when they had shared everything. He had thought then that Lizzie was the love of his life, but as the years passed by she had become his greatest enemy. Had she told anyone else? He didn't think so, but there was no knowing for sure.

Terry was still dwelling on this when he felt a tap on the shoulder.

'Boss?'

He turned to look up at the tall black man called Solomon Vale. 'Yeah? What is it? What do you want?'

Vale bent his head and said softly, 'Vic Delaney's out front. Says he wants to talk to you. I told him I wasn't sure if you were here or not, said I'd check. You want me to let him in? You want to see him?'

Terry didn't want to see him, but he couldn't put it off forever. He'd been expecting a visit for the past few weeks. Now that he was here, might as well get it over and done with. 'Yeah, show him in.'

'Will do, boss.'

Terry watched as Vale strode back towards the door. Solomon, although tough and reliable, was a man of few words. He'd been with the firm for years, but Terry still didn't know him that well. He was always polite, always respectful, but he was Chris's right-hand man and it was with Chris, ultimately, that his loyalty lay. Terry wasn't sure who he could trust any more. There was no one left of the old firm, the men he'd inherited from Quinn. They were all dead now. And although Terry hadn't had any problems in recruiting new members, he had always been wary of them. Just as he'd betrayed Joe Quinn, he knew that one of them might do the same to him.

Now, of course, the firm was a quarter of the size it had once been. Nothing was the same. The East End wasn't the same. He missed the old days when people had looked up to him, when he'd wielded the kind of power that other villains could only dream about. Those had been the glory days and nothing could compare to them.

Terry was still absorbed in the past when Vale returned with Vic Delaney in tow. Delaney was a fat man, almost as wide as he was tall. He had an ugly pug face, multiple chins, and a pair of piggy eyes peering out from between creamy folds of flesh. It didn't do, however, to underestimate him. Delaney was one tough guy and those who crossed him usually lived to regret it.

Terry got to his feet and held out his hand. 'Vic. Good to see you again.'

'Terry,' the other man said, unsmilingly.

'You'll have a Scotch?'

'Yeah.'

Terry looked at Vale. 'Get one of the girls to bring it over.'

Solomon Vale gave a nod and walked off.

Terry and Vic Delaney sat down. Terry watched as Delaney's gaze flew briefly to the dancers on the stage before returning again.

'You know what this is about,' Delaney said.

'Sure,' Terry said. 'Although I don't know what you expect me to do about it.'

Delaney leaned forward a little, placing his thick arms on

61

the table. He was younger than Terry, although not by that much. They came from the same era and had mixed in the same circles for years. Delaney's manor was up Chigwell way and he'd made his money from property and drugs. 'I want you to keep your son away from my girl.'

'And how am I supposed to do that?'

'I don't care how,' Delaney said sharply. 'Just sort it, huh?'

'He's a grown man. I can't tell him who he can or can't see.'

'Yeah, and Silver's just nineteen. You think it's right for him to be hanging around with a girl half his age?'

Terry could have retorted that he'd seen Delaney with plenty of girls young enough to be his daughter, but decided not to go there. Raising the subject of double standards was only going to inflame the situation. Instead, he made a calming gesture with his hands. 'Look, I can see where you're coming from. For what it's worth, I agree with you. I'd rather they weren't together. He is too old for her. But you know what, the minute we start telling them what to do, they'll only go and do the bloody opposite.'

The drink arrived, carried by a topless waitress with long pink hair. Delaney stared blatantly at her tits, his damp lips parting slightly.

'Ta,' Terry said to her.

As she waltzed off in her high heels, Delaney took the opportunity to scrutinise her backside too. He might have come to discuss the moral welfare of his daughter, but that wasn't going to stop him grabbing an eyeful while he was here. When he'd finished leering, he turned his head back towards Terry. 'So what are you saying?'

'That we just leave them to it. Odds are it'll all fizzle out in a couple of weeks. But if we start interfering . . . well, there's every chance they'll stay together just for the hell of it.'

Delaney lifted his glass and then put it down again. 'So do nothin', huh? That's your plan?'

Terry gave a shrug. 'Sometimes nothin' is the best thing to do.' A part of him felt sorry for Delaney. He knew what it meant to have a crazy kid, and Silver was both disturbed and disturbing. You didn't need to be a psychiatrist to work that one out. The girl had been out of control for years, running wild. He'd heard all sorts of rumours about her, none of which he'd have willingly repeated to her father.

Delaney wasn't won over by the suggestion. 'It ain't right,' he muttered. 'I don't like it.'

Terry could have said that Danny didn't do girlfriends. His son shagged the local toms and picked up the occasional bit of skirt, but never got involved in actual relationships. However, as he couldn't see this as being an entirely reassuring piece of information, he kept it to himself.

'We gonna fall out over this, Terry?'

Terry held Delaney's gaze, a hardness coming into his eyes. 'I ain't got a problem, Vic. *You're* the one with the problem.'

'Your bloody son's my problem!'

'So take it up with him. I'm not his bleedin' keeper.'

Delaney glared at him, his lips curling away from his teeth. 'Then you'd better tell your boy to watch his back.'

'I'll do that,' Terry said. 'Thanks for dropping by.'

Delaney scraped back his chair and hauled up his bulk. He loomed over Terry for a moment, his huge gut stretching at the fabric of his shirt. 'This ain't over,' he said. 'It ain't over by a long chalk.'

Terry gave a nod. 'I'll take your word for it.'

Delaney growled, turned around and marched off. Terry followed his progress until he disappeared into the crowd. He mulled over the exchange, knowing that Vic Delaney wouldn't let it lie. Well, he'd tip Danny the wink, but it'd make sod all difference. Danny always did exactly as he wanted.

Beside him, at a table to his right, a group of young men suddenly burst out laughing. Terry instantly got the idea that he was the subject of their amusement. An indignant rage blossomed in his chest. Did they know who he was? Did they have any idea who they were mocking? But as he glowered over at the table, he realised that none of them were looking back. And then he thought he heard another laugh, a lighter one, a female one, a familiar one. He would know that laugh anywhere. It was *hers*. It was Lizzie's. He was sure of it.

Terry's eyes wildly searched the room, behind, in front, to the sides, his gaze probing the crowd. His heart started to beat faster. He jumped up, knowing she was there somewhere. As he continued to look, to frantically scan the club, his hands curled in frustration. A red flush of anger rose to his cheeks. Where was the bitch? Where the fuck was she?

'Lizzie!' he yelled out.

Gradually, he became aware that he actually was the centre of attention now. Heads were turning to stare, the focus on him rather than the dancing girls. A sea of faces, frowning, curious, amused, swam in front of him. His legs suddenly buckled and he slumped down into the chair. In front of him was Delaney's Scotch, still untouched. He poured the whisky into his own glass and knocked the whole lot back in one.

9

The black Mazda MX-5 was parked round the corner from Beast and away from any direct light from the streetlamps. Danny Street laid out the coke across the hand-sized mirror, using a credit card to shift the powder into neat straight lines.

'Keep an eye out, babe,' he said.

Silver gave a cursory look over her shoulder. 'No one's gonna see. It's pissing down.'

'Just do as you're told, huh? You think the filth cares about a bit of rain? Those bastards are out to get me. They've been hanging round the club for weeks, and around the house. Everywhere I go, I've got a bleedin' shadow.'

'The street's empty. There's no one here but us.'

Danny leaned over, snorted a couple of lines and waited for them to take effect. He screwed up his eyes and gazed out through the windscreen. 'Just 'cause you can't see 'em, don't mean they ain't there.'

Silver took the tray off him and picked up the straw. 'They

won't ever get you, hon. You're too smart for the filth.' She inhaled the coke and laughed out loud. 'Hey, Danny,' she said, 'you ever killed anyone? Bet you have, bet you've killed loads. What does it feel like? Does it feel good?' She leaned her head back against the seat and sighed. 'Yeah, I bet it feels good.'

Danny smiled, but said nothing.

Silver turned to him, her eyes gleaming. 'Tell me how many? How did you do it?'

But Danny wouldn't be drawn. He was high as a kite, but still knew that no woman could be trusted. One minute they'd be sucking your cock, the next they'd be stabbing you in the back with a kitchen knife. 'Your old man must have topped a few in his time.'

'My old man's a fuckin' dickhead.'

'Well, your fuckin' dickhead of a father wants to see me six foot under.'

'Sleeping with the fishes,' she said. 'Or propping up the nearest motorway. He hates any bastard who screws his daughter.'

'That's 'cause he wants you for himself.'

Silver gave a childlike giggle. 'Everybody wants me, baby. I'm the best. I'm the fuckin' best in the whole wide world.'

'Yeah, well I know one old geezer who's gagging for it. You ready?' Danny took the empty tray off her and shoved it in the glove compartment. 'Come on, he'll be waiting for us.'

The two of them walked around the corner to the gallery. It was dark, after nine, and the place was locked up, but they could see a light in the back. Danny pressed the bell beside the door and then pressed his face against the glass. Silver wrapped her arms around her chest and hopped from one foot to the other.

'Is he there, babe?'

'Course he's there,' Danny said. 'Where the fuck else would he be?'

It was only a few seconds more before the tall shadowy figure of Morton Carlisle glided through the shop and slid back the bolts. 'You're late,' he hissed softly as he ushered them inside. 'The back. Go through to the back. And mind the cabinets!'

'Well, if you'd put the bleedin' light on . . .'

But Carlisle was the cautious sort. You never knew who might be walking past and he didn't want Danny Street to be recognised. He glanced quickly along the street, left and right, before shutting the door and locking it behind them. 'The back,' he urged again. 'Go straight through.'

As Danny reached the door to the basement, he felt his pulse quicken. He stopped and glanced over his shoulder at Silver. 'You know what they used to do down there, babe?'

'What?'

'It's where they embalmed the bodies when this place was an undertaker's.'

'How do you know that?'

Danny looked at Carlisle. 'It's true, ain't it, Morton? This place used to be a funeral joint.'

'I believe so.'

'See,' Danny said. His mouth slid into a smile. 'I saw it done once. I saw a body being embalmed.'

Silver stared back at him, her expression sceptical. 'Oh yeah?'

'Yeah, straight up. It was a girl, a blonde, a bit older than you. Fact, she looked a bit like you too. I watched her blood being drained, and the fluid being sucked from her organs.' He felt a stirring in his groin and his smile widened. 'It was very educational.'

'The office,' said Carlisle, his voice sounding strained as he tried to edge them forward. 'Over there, to the right.'

Danny gave one last lingering look at the door before walking towards the room where the light was coming from. The office was small and cluttered with a desk, a couple of filing cabinets, two chairs and a heap of cardboard boxes. Danny sat in one of the chairs while Silver hovered behind him.

Morton Carlisle walked around the desk and sat down too. He looked at Danny. 'So, have you got it?'

'Of course.' Danny put a hand in his inside jacket pocket, pulled out a wad of notes and threw them on to the top of the desk. 'Two k,' he said. 'As we agreed.'

Carlisle snatched up the notes, opened a drawer and dropped the money inside. 'Good.'

'Ain't you gonna count it?' Silver asked.

Carlisle gave her a weary smile. 'Mutual trust, my dear. It's the only way to do business.' He transferred his gaze to Danny. 'No problems, then?'

'None at all. The tosser paid up without a murmur. We could probably go back for seconds.'

'No seconds,' Carlisle said sharply. 'We agreed, right? One hit and that's it. Any more and they'll start to panic, think that it's never going to end. And that's when they'll throw caution to the wind and end up going to the law.' He put his elbows on the desk and steepled his fingers. 'We don't need the police sniffing round, do we? It would hardly be advantageous for either of us.'

'Whatever,' Danny said. 'Don't bother me either way. So, you got someone else lined up?'

Morton Carlisle pulled a large blue ledger towards him, flicked the book open and ran a finger down the page. 'There are several possibilities, but ... Yes, I think this could be our man.' He glanced up at Danny. 'Squires. Jeremy Squires. He's forty-six, a businessman – something tedious to do with computers – but he's also a local councillor with ambitions to stand for Parliament. As such, any scandal would be decidedly unwelcome.'

'Married?' Danny asked.

'Naturally. Although rumour has it that he has a penchant for the *younger* ladies.' His gaze slid towards Silver where it settled for a few seconds. 'He also has two teenage daughters.'

'Nice,' Danny said, gently rubbing his hands together. 'Sounds like he's our man. Loaded, I take it?'

'Apparently so.'

'Best give us the details then.'

Morton Carlisle gave a nod of his head before writing out the name and address on a notepad. He ripped the sheet off and passed it to Danny. 'Let me know when it's done. How were you thinking of—'

'You let me worry about that,' Danny said, rising to his feet. 'Let's just stick to what we're good at, eh? I'll be in touch.' He took hold of Silver's elbow. 'Come on, babe. Time to go.'

'Hold on.' Carlisle sat back, frowning. 'Aren't you forgetting something?' His eyes darted towards Silver. 'We have a deal, remember?'

'Oh, *that*,' Danny said, smirking. He gave Silver a small push. 'Go on, hon. Go and be nice to Mr Carlisle.'

Silver obediently walked around the desk until she was standing right beside his chair. She stood for a moment gazing down at him, before slowly undoing first the belt and then the buttons on her raincoat. She took her time, occasionally pausing to sweep back her long fair hair. An enigmatic smile played around her mouth, but her eyes were cold and empty.

Carlisle's tongue darted out like a snake, briefly wetting his lips before disappearing back inside. His breathing grew audible and his hands slid down into his lap.

Silver let the coat slip from her shoulders on to the floor. It made a light swishing sound like an indoor breeze. Underneath, she was naked, her skin as smooth and pale as porcelain. All she was wearing now was a pair of red stilettos. She put her left hand on her hip and stood very still as if she was posing for a magazine picture.

Carlisle stared hard at her full breasts and tiny waist before his gaze gradually descended to her pussy, her thighs, her ankles and feet. Then his eyes quickly swept up again to focus on the small brown nipples of her breasts. Almost immediately, he reached out a hand, but Silver stepped smartly out of reach.

She laughed, leaning forward to wag a finger in his face. 'Uh-huh, you know the rules, babe. You can look – you can look as much as you like – but you can never ever touch . . . '

10

From her bed, Ava gazed across at the thin grey light sliding through the gap in the curtains. Morning or afternoon? At this time of year it was impossible to tell. She reached out, scrabbling for her watch on the table, but couldn't find it. Now she was awake she knew that she would have to get up, but still she lingered for a few moments, enjoying the warmth and snugness of the duvet.

While she delayed the inevitable, she thought back over the previous day. In the afternoon, Chris had informed her that he had to go to Manchester and they'd set off within the hour. She'd enjoyed the drive up the motorway, getting some speed out of the Mercedes for once instead of being stuck in a perpetual traffic jam. He had spent most of the journey on the phone, making calls, sending texts or checking out the Facebook page for Belles.

Once in Manchester, she'd dropped him off in the city centre at a pub called the Crown and then found somewhere to park before going to get a burger. There had been some nice-looking restaurants around the area, but she hadn't fancied eating in them on her own. The burger place was busy and anonymous, easy to blend into. Surrounded by northern accents, she'd felt like a stranger, but not an unwelcome one. Natural curiosity had made her wonder what Chris's business was up there, but she hadn't asked and he hadn't said. It was probably for the best. What she didn't know, she couldn't tell.

It had been the early hours of the morning before they'd got back to London. He'd been chattier on the return journey and the time had passed quickly. She guessed that the meeting, whatever it had been about, had gone well. She'd also had the feeling that Chris had wanted to say something to her, but hadn't quite been able to find the words. He'd begin, glance at her, and then change his mind.

Ava stretched out her arms and yawned. It was over a week now since she'd started the job and she had managed to get through it without incurring any damage, major or minor, to the precious Merc. The hours, as predicted, varied widely, but this didn't bother her. It wasn't as if she had a rich social life to fit in around her work. She hadn't had a date since splitting up with Alec – not that she'd wanted one – and the recent highlight of her social calendar had been a drink with her dad in the Fox.

Eventually, with reluctance, Ava pulled back the covers and slipped into her dressing gown. As she went through to the living room, she rubbed at her eyes with the heels of her hands. She peered at the clock on the wall: twenty past eleven. Tash, who was sitting at the table, attaching pink feathers to one of her latest creations, looked up and grinned.

'So, you dirty stop-out, where did you get to last night? It must have been one hell of a party.'

'Manchester,' Ava said.

'Wow. That's different. Was it good?'

'Not exactly. I had to drive Chris Street up there.' Ava walked on through to the kitchen where she switched the kettle on. She felt tired and sluggish, in need of a caffeine boost to wake her up properly. Grabbing a mug from the draining board, she shovelled in two teaspoons of coffee. 'You want one?' she called back over her shoulder.

Tash joined her in the kitchen, leaning against the door jamb. 'Yeah, go on then. So what's so important you had to go all the way to Manchester?'

'I didn't ask.'

'Mm, probably wise. So how's it going? You think he's going to keep you on?'

Ava poured hot water into the mugs and got the milk out of the fridge. 'God, I hope so. I can't afford to lose this job. I've done the trial week and he hasn't said anything one way or the other. I don't want to ask in case ... well, if it is bad news I'd rather not hear it.'

'It won't be,' Tash said, forever the optimist. She paused and then added, 'Are you doing anything this afternoon?'

'No, nothing planned, although the sofa's looking pretty attractive right now. I'll probably just crash, have a lazy day.'

'Do you fancy coming to an exhibition with me? It's at that Beast place so it's not far to go. It's from three to five and there are cocktails too.'

Ava pulled a face, remembering her last experience at the

gallery. 'Not really. Since when did you have an interest in stuffed animals?'

'I don't, but I've always reckoned it's a sin to turn down the offer of free drinks. Besides, there'll be a lot of rich, fashionable people there. I might be able to make some contacts, do a bit of social networking. Lydia gave me a ticket. It's a plus one but I don't have anyone to go with. Hannah's at work and I don't really want to go on my own.'

'Who's Lydia?'

'She works there, at Beast. Just sales and that. She comes into the Fox sometimes. That's how I got to know her.'

'Well, you won't be on your own then.'

'But she'll be working, won't she? She won't have time to talk to me.' Tash flashed one of her brightest smiles. 'Oh, come on,' she wheedled. '*Please.* It's only for a couple of hours and you never know, it might even be fun.'

'You reckon?'

Tash gave a sigh. 'Ava Gold,' she said. 'You're in danger of becoming seriously boring.'

'Good. I like boring. I *love* boring. Is there anything wrong with wanting a nice quiet life?'

'And how old are you exactly?'

Ava blew on the top of her coffee and took a couple of quick sips. 'Old enough to know that there are better ways of spending an afternoon than staring at a stuffed weasel.'

But Tash wasn't giving up without a fight. 'You're coming with me,' she said. 'Even if I have to drag you there.'

11

Ava's first surprise, as she walked through the door into Beast, was the number of people who were there. Who'd have thought that an exhibition of stuffed animals would have drawn such a crowd? Her second surprise came as her eyes alighted on the good-looking blond man standing by a makeshift bar.

'Oh, God,' she murmured, nudging Tash with her elbow.

'What?'

'It's him. It's Guy Wilder.'

Tash followed her line of sight. 'So?'

Ava gazed at Wilder as he handed out brightly coloured cocktails. He was surrounded by a group of women, all stylishly dressed and all vying for his attention. 'So it's embarrassing, isn't it? Last time we met, I was with Chris Street – and the two of them were just about ready to kill each other.'

Tash gave a shrug. 'I shouldn't worry. He won't remember you.'

'Really? Well, thanks for that. It's good to know I'm so instantly forgettable.'

Tash tilted her head and grinned. She was wearing one of her cuter hats, a bright red pill box with a short net veil. 'Hey, I didn't mean it like that. You know I didn't. All I'm saying is that he was probably preoccupied. And anyway, what does it matter? It's not as though he's got anything against you.'

'I suppose.' But Ava still felt awkward about coming face to face with him again. 'Look, why don't you go and get the drinks and I'll wait here.'

'Okay, what do you want?'

'It doesn't matter. Anything. Surprise me.' While Tash headed for the bar, Ava began to wander along the cabinets, reading the names of the various exhibits. She wasn't really interested in the contents, but she took the opportunity to do some people-watching and to eavesdrop on their conversations. Morton Carlisle, sporting a tweed jacket and a green bow tie, appeared a few feet away from her and began talking to a middle-aged expensively dressed couple. She could hear him holding forth on the merits of a mounted red fox, on the *exquisite* artistry and *sophisticated* technique.

Ava peered between the couple until she spotted the animal in question. The red fox was standing alert with its ears pricked and its head turned a little to one side. For a second it seemed to be looking straight back at her, its wily eyes staring directly into hers. She felt an odd jolt followed by a pang of sympathy for the remains of the creature trapped forever inside its glass cage. She wondered how it had died, if it had been fast or slow, and if it had even understood the concept of mortality.

The view of the fox was obscured as the middle-aged woman shifted position. Ava looked across the gallery towards the bar, wondering where Tash had got to with the drinks. There was no sign of her. Guy Wilder was now chatting with a slender, elegant black man and an older grey-haired guy in a suit. His female entourage lurked to one side, waiting – or so she surmised – for an opportunity to join him again.

As Ava watched, the older guy moved and turned his head slightly. It was then that she thought that she recognised him. But she couldn't quite place the face. It niggled away at her, her frustration growing by the second. Who was he? Not wanting to be caught staring, she walked along a row of cabinets, pretending to be absorbed in a display of freshwater fish. It was only as she surreptitiously lifted her gaze again, that she suddenly realised. Yes, she'd got it – he was the bloke she'd seen outside the Hope. It was! It was the Russian man, Borovski, the man Chris had bought the falcon for.

Ava frowned. There was, she knew, no reason why the Russian *shouldn't* be here – he obviously had an interest in taxidermy – but something smelled wrong. He seemed very pally with Wilder. Their body language, their easiness with one another, made her certain that they'd known each other for some time. But so what? Just because Wilder and Chris were at loggerheads didn't mean that Borovski couldn't have an amiable relationship with them both. And yet . . .

Ava drifted along with one eye on the cabinets, the other on the Russian. *Don't get involved*, she told herself. Chris Street was old enough and smart enough to take care of himself – he didn't need her watching out for him. She was paid to be his driver, nothing else. But still her gaze kept flicking towards the two men. They were laughing now, slapping each other on the back, enjoying a private joke. Could she really say nothing to Chris? Was it better or worse to keep her mouth shut about what she was witnessing?

A waitress walked by with a tray full of cocktails. As Tash still hadn't come back, Ava grabbed a glass containing something as red as her friend's hat, thanked the girl and took a few quick sips. Cranberry and some kind of liqueur, she thought. Well, whatever it was, it slipped down nicely. What to do next? Ava was in two minds as to whether to continue her spying activities or to move to another room when she turned to find herself standing right in front of Morton Carlisle.

'Ah,' he said. 'Miss ... er ... '

'It's Ava, Ava Gold.'

'Indeed,' he said, as if he had once known her name and it had only temporarily slipped his mind. 'How nice to see you again. Thank you for coming today.' His eyes slid away from her and made a quick nervous survey of the surrounding area. 'And is, er ... is Mr Street with you?'

'No, I'm here with a friend.' She found herself glancing around for Tash, but she was nowhere to be seen.

'Ah,' he said, relief spreading over his face. 'And you're enjoying the exhibition?'

'Yes, it's very ... ' Ava scrabbled for a suitable response. 'Very inspirational.'

'Indeed,' he said again, clasping his hands together. 'I'm so glad.'

'Absolutely,' Ava said, trying to edge away from him. 'And

there's so much more to see. I'd better get on. I don't want to miss anything.'

Morton gave a small bow, releasing her from his attention.

Ava moved off with a sense of relief. She didn't care for Morton Carlisle, although she couldn't say exactly why. It was a gut reaction, something that came from deep within her. He was like a shudder under her skin. He reminded her of darkness, of nightmares, of creepy things that went bump in the night.

Slowly skirting around the main room, Ava made her way closer to the bar. The Russian was still talking to Wilder although others had joined them now. Had she been wrong about what she'd seen? She loitered by a cabinet of snakes, pretending to make a study of the leathery-looking reptiles. The last thing she wanted to do was to stir up trouble. But if she kept silent and Borovski *was* closer to Wilder than Chris realised . . .

'Ah, here you are!'

Ava, lost in her thoughts, whirled around to find Tash and another girl standing behind her.

'We've been looking all over for you,' said Tash, as if Ava was the one who'd done a disappearing act rather than herself. There was no sign of the drinks she had gone to get; either she had never reached the bar or the cocktails had been drunk along the way. 'This is Lydia. She's been a real sweetheart, introducing me to everyone. You wouldn't believe the people who are here today. God, if I could get a few commissions for my hats it would really make a difference.' She paused and then quickly added, 'Oh, Lydia, this is Ava.'

'Hi,' Ava said.

'Sorry,' Lydia said. 'I didn't realise Tash was with anyone or I wouldn't have kept her so long. Have you been okay?'

'Fine, thanks. I've just been checking out the exhibits.'

'Seen anything you liked?'

'Oh,' Ava said, not wanting to offend. 'This and that.'

Lydia smiled at her. She was a slight, pretty girl with silky blonde hair and wide blue eyes. 'It's okay, you don't need to be polite. I know it's not to everyone's taste.'

Tash spotted someone she knew and waved to them across the room. 'Oh, there's Amanda,' she said. 'I'm just going to nip over and say hello.'

As Ava watched her disappear again, she found herself thinking of that nice comfy sofa that she'd sacrificed – and all the delights of trashy afternoon TV. So much for Tash needing company; she could have easily come on her own! Her gaze flicked over to settle on Wilder again. If she hadn't let Tash persuade her into coming, she'd have never seen the exchange between him and Borovski, and wouldn't have had to decide what, if anything, to do about it.

Lydia saw her looking and said, 'That's Guy Wilder. Would you like me to introduce you?'

'What? Oh, no. No thanks.'

'Gosh,' Lydia said. 'I think you're the first woman who's ever turned that offer down!'

Ava gave a thin smile. 'Yes, he does seem kind of popular, but we've already met . . . sort of.' She glanced over at Wilder again, remembering what her dad had told her. It was hard to imagine how a man so outwardly handsome could harbour such inner resentment. 'And he is very good-looking. It's just that . . . to be honest, he's not really my type.'

'I suppose you're immune to his charms.'

Ava frowned, not understanding. 'Immune?'

'Well, you know, with you and Tash being . . .'

It took Ava a moment to realise what she was saying, and then she laughed. 'Oh, we're not . . . we're not a couple, just flatmates, nothing else.'

Lydia's cheeks flushed pink. 'Oh, God, I'm sorry . . . I didn't mean . . . I thought . . . Jesus, I'm always putting my foot in it.'

Ava laughed. 'You haven't. Don't worry about it.'

Lydia looked down at the floor and then up again. She pulled a face. 'Now I feel like a complete idiot.'

'Don't. It doesn't matter, honestly.' Ava had intended to make her excuses and leave – Tash clearly wasn't in need of her support – but she didn't want Lydia to think that she'd taken offence. As such, she felt an obligation to stay on for a little small talk before heading for the door. 'So, have you worked here for long?'

Lydia shook her head. 'Only a few months. I moved here in July. It's interesting, though. I like it.' She leaned in and lowered her voice. 'Well, most of the time. To be honest, Morton's a bit odd, but I think he's harmless enough.'

Ava grinned at her. 'Are you sure about that?'

Lydia bared her teeth in a half-grimace. 'I hope so. Hey, have you seen the Rogues' Gallery yet? Why don't you come and take a look.'

Ava, who was now yearning more than ever for that sofa, suddenly found herself being led towards the rear of the room. So much for making a quick escape. Still, Lydia seemed nice enough, if a little nervous, and she had the cocktail to finish. She drank the last inch as they squeezed through the crowd and then she placed the empty glass in a handy space between two cabinets.

The Rogues' Gallery was in a completely separate room to the rest of the exhibition and Ava's eyes widened as she went inside. The cabinets in this area did not contain real animals at all, but ones that had been created using the body parts of several different species. Some were mythical like dragons, griffins or unicorns; others were works purely of the artist's imagination.

'A lot of taxidermists don't approve of this,' Lydia said. 'They don't consider it *real* taxidermy. But it's kind of interesting, don't you think?'

Ava wasn't sure what she thought. It was like stepping inside another universe, where creation had taken a completely different path. There was a rabbit with wings, a two-headed lamb, a fish wrapped in squirrel fur. Some of the exhibits were just plain strange, others faintly frightening, like the rat with three tails pulling the bloody entrails from its own stomach. 'It's certainly weird,' she murmured.

Lydia tilted her head and gazed through the glass. 'Yes, they are a bit bizarre. They remind me of a book I used to have when I was a kid, all about fantastical creatures, mermaids and the like.'

The room was busy, but above the buzz of conversation Ava was convinced she heard Guy Wilder's voice. She swung around, her eyes scanning the crowd, but he wasn't there. Had she just imagined it? As she slowly turned back towards the cabinets, her gaze came to rest on the rat again. She wrinkled her nose, not wanting to look and yet feeling oddly compelled to do so. And then, from somewhere deep inside her, she was assailed by a sudden sense of dislocation, a notion that nothing and no one were what they appeared to be. She wrapped her arms around her chest, but it was too late. A coldness was already seeping into her bones.

12

Vic Delaney stood by the side of the swimming pool, pushed his hands into his pockets and scowled down at the water. An empty cheese-and-onion crisp packet was floating on the surface, bobbing around, shifting from one place to another as the wind caught its edges. He thought about getting the net from the pool house and fishing it out – but why should he? It wasn't his job. That was what he employed the bloody staff for. Not that any of them earned their wages; a pile of lazy, good-for-nothing skivers the whole fuckin' lot of them.

Vic wasn't in a good frame of mind. He'd woken up in a temper that morning and, like a festering sore, it had been growing worse ever since. Now he was just about ready to blow his top. Walking over to the small metal table, he picked up the glass of brandy, knocked it back in one and refilled the glass.

It was starting to sleet again and still he didn't go inside.

The cold evening air made him shiver and the booze wasn't good for his blood pressure – he'd been told to lay off the alcohol by his doctor – but he wanted to stay angry. Anger was his fuel for getting things done and something had to be done about Danny Street. In his mind, he went over the meeting with Terry, his hackles instantly rising. Who the hell did he think he was, giving him advice on what to do? *Just leave them to it.* Jesus, what kind of a response was that? Danny Street was a nutter, a druggie, a fuckin' weirdo, and he didn't want him anywhere near his daughter.

Vic lit a cigar – another vice that had been banned by his doctor – and began pacing impatiently round the pool. He kept his eyes fixed on the crisp packet as if it represented everything that was wrong with the world. He thought about Silver and slapped a hand against his thigh. She wasn't a bad kid. She was just easily led. And not having a mother hadn't helped either. What kind of a woman just took off like that, leaving her child behind? A bitch, he decided, a selfish shitty bitch. And okay, so the marriage hadn't exactly been perfect, but blood was blood and nothing should get in the way of it.

'Boss?'

Vic turned and glared at the man who had just stepped out from the open French doors that led into the living room. 'What time do you call this?' he snarled. 'I said six. Ain't you got a fuckin' watch?'

'It is six, boss,' he said.

Vic lifted his wrist, screwing up his eyes as he peered at the dial of his own watch under the dim pool lights. It was true, it was six o'clock exactly, but that only annoyed him all the more. Even the fuckin' time was conspiring against him.

'What you got for me, then?' he snapped. 'What's going down?'

Raynard, who was used to his employer's irascible moods, didn't bat an eyelid. 'No change,' he said. 'She's still hanging out with Street. Only one odd thing; last night the two of them went to a shop on Kellston High Street, place called Beast.'

'Beast?'

'Yeah, they sell stuffed animals. And the shop was closed. It was after nine. They had to ring the bell to get in. They stayed for about twenty minutes.'

'Who'd they meet there?'

'Can't say for sure, boss. I reckon it was the owner who let them in – a bloke called Morton Carlisle – but there's no knowing who else was inside. No one came out before them though, so I reckon it might just have been those three.'

Vic puffed hard on his cigar, coughing as the smoke invaded his lungs. 'What do we know about this Carlisle geezer?'

'Not much at the moment. I've put a few feelers out, but it's early days yet. He's in his sixties, been in the trade a long time. He opened the shop in Kellston a couple of years back. That stuff's becoming popular again, all the rage apparently. There's money in it now.'

Vic frowned, trying to figure out what the angle was. What the hell was Danny Street up to? He glared at Raynard again, but only because he had no one else to take his frustration out on. In truth, Raynard was the only person he trusted these days. Vic had inherited him from an old pal, a Clacton villain called Badger Campbell. Badger had managed to get himself garrotted by a rival gang, and Raynard – not wanting to end up on a cold slab beside him – had decided to hotfoot it to London and take his chances elsewhere. That had been three years ago and Vic had never regretted hiring him.

'You want me to have a word with Carlisle?' Raynard asked.

Vic thought about it, but then shook his head. 'Nah, not yet.' Raynard, despite his slim build, was very persuasive when it came to 'talking'. What he lacked in muscle, he made up for in sheer sadism. He liked to hurt people and to do it slowly. 'Let's try and find out what the fuck's going on first.'

'Okay, boss.' Raynard gave a nod. 'And Terry Street? What about him?'

Vic snarled, his upper lip curling to reveal a row of brown stained teeth. He was still seething about the conversation that had taken place at Belles. Disrespectful, that's what Terry had been – and no one disrespected Vic Delaney and got away with it. 'Let's go inside before we freeze our bollocks off. We'll talk about it there.'

13

It was ten to eleven and Ava was about to take a shower and go to bed when the phone started ringing. She stared at it for a moment, tempted to ignore it and let it go to the answering service. She was tired and wasn't in the mood for talking. It was probably for Tash anyway. No one she knew would ring her at this time of night. But then she had one of those uneasy thoughts that something bad might have happened to her mum or dad, an emergency, an accident, a sudden illness . . .

Ava jumped off the sofa, crossed the living room and snatched up the receiver. 'Yes?'

'It's only me,' Tash said.

'Oh, hi. You okay?' She felt a small wave of relief flow over her.

'Yeah, yeah, I'm fine but . . . Look, I'm at the Fox. Terry Street's here. He's been here for a few hours now. We've just called last orders, but Terry says he's not leaving until Joe Quinn gets here.'

Ava frowned. 'Joe Quinn? But he's been dead for years.'

'Exactly. And Maggie's in a spin. I wondered if . . . well, I wondered if you could get in touch with Chris, maybe get him to come down and pick up his dad. I wouldn't ask, but we don't really know what else to do. He seems kind of confused.'

'All right, I'll try and call him.'

'Thanks, love. You're an angel. I'll see you later.'

Ava put the phone down, picked up her bag and dug out her mobile. If Chris was at Belles it would take him a while to get back to Kellston, especially if he had to call a cab. She found his number and pressed the button. It was answered after a couple of rings.

'Chris Street.'

'Hi, it's Ava.'

'Yeah?' he asked shortly.

She hesitated, wishing now that she'd taken a minute to work out what she was going to say and how to phrase it in a suitably diplomatic fashion.

'Oh, don't tell me,' he said drily. 'You can't make it in the morning, right? Doctor's appointment, dentist, imminent hangover? I was wondering how long it would take.'

Ava scowled down the phone, offended and annoyed by the presumption. 'As it happens, none of the above. I just got a call from a friend who works at the Fox. Your father's there. I think . . . er, I think you might want to go and pick him up.'

'Had a skinful, has he?' Chris gave a snort. 'Well, he hasn't got far to walk. I'm sure he'll make it home on his own.'

'It's not that.' Ava paused again. 'Apparently, he's a bit . . . a bit confused.'

'Pissed, you mean.'

'I don't know,' she said, 'but I don't think so. He's saying that he won't leave until he's seen Joe Quinn.'

Chris drew in his breath, a sharp sound that travelled down the line. 'But Joe Quinn's—'

'Yes,' she said. 'That's why I'm calling you.'

'He's probably just pissed,' Chris said again, but his voice lacked its earlier certainty. 'Okay, I'll get over there and sort it out.'

'Are you at Belles?'

'No, I'm at home. The duty manager's dealing with the club.'

Ava, still riled by his earlier response, felt an unwelcome rush of sympathy for him. She knew what it meant to have to worry about a parent. Before she'd had time to think about it properly, she blurted out the offer. 'Do you want me to come over? It's no trouble. I'm only down the road. I can be there in five minutes.'

'No, it's . . .' He stopped. 'I dunno . . . maybe that would be better. Could you?'

'I'll see you soon.'

'I'll start walking,' he said. 'You can pick me up along the way.'

Ava put the phone down, wondering what had possessed her to volunteer her services at this time of night. She might be his driver, but this was over and above the call of duty, especially after the long haul to Manchester. Still, if she wanted to keep the job, it was worth going the extra mile. And that was the only reason she was doing it. Wasn't it? Before she could examine her own motives too closely, she grabbed the car keys from the coffee table, pulled on her jacket and rushed out of the flat.

Outside, the cold air hit her like a slap in the face. She half walked, half jogged to Violet Road where the Kia was parked. Shivering, she jumped in, switched on the engine and the heat and headed for the south side of Kellston. It was a good thing she'd only had one cocktail this afternoon, else she wouldn't have been fit to drive. She had, she thought, shown considerable restraint. Being surrounded by dead stuffed creatures, real or otherwise, was enough to drive anyone to drink.

The traffic was light and Ava kept her eyes peeled as she approached the area where Chris Street lived. It was only a few minutes before she saw him, his shoulders bent, his head down against the freezing wind. She gave a quick beep of the horn and drew up by the kerb.

Chris gave her a nod as he got into the car. 'Ta,' he said softly.

'No need for thanks,' she said. 'I'm your driver, aren't I? It's what I'm here for.'

He gave her a quick glance. 'You pissed off about what I said before?'

Ava did a U-turn in the road and headed back towards the Fox. She kept her eyes straight ahead, her voice low and steady. 'Why should I be pissed off just because you thought I was the kind of person who would ring in with some lousy excuse as to why I couldn't come to work tomorrow?'

'You *are* pissed off.'

'Only a bit,' she said. 'But don't worry, I'll get over it.'

'I could have got a cab.'

'Yeah, and waited half an hour.'

There was a short silence during which Ava wondered if she'd overstepped the mark. But, much as she wanted to keep the job, she knew it would only work if there was at least a modicum of mutual respect. She'd been walked over too many times by her ex and didn't intend to throw herself under any other man's boots.

'Well, if it helps,' he said, 'I appreciate you coming out tonight.'

Ava gave a light shrug of her shoulders. 'Yeah, it helps.'

'Good,' he said. 'And I'm sorry if I suggested that you were anything less than the perfect employee. I've got used to people taking the piss. The minute I take anyone on, they're already looking for ways to skive off.'

'Maybe that's because you employ the wrong people.'

'I employed you,' he said.

'I don't count. I'm only on trial, remember?'

Chris Street turned his head and smiled at her. 'Are you saying you don't want the job?'

'Are you saying that you're offering it to me?'

Ava never got the chance to hear his answer. The traffic lights at the junction were on green and as she sailed through them, indicating right and then right again before turning the Kia into the almost empty car park of the Fox, the headlamps illuminated the figure of a man loitering by the cellar door at the side of the pub. Chris didn't need to say anything for her to know that it was Terry Street. As soon as she stopped the car, he leapt out and rushed across to him.

Ava stayed where she was, not sure what to do, but not wanting to intrude. She thought about going into the pub and seeing Tasha but decided against it. Instead, she kept the engine running and peered through the windscreen as the two men talked. A few flurries of snow drifted down from the sky, gathering briefly on the glass before melting away. She remembered Terry from when she was a kid but hadn't seen him since she'd come back to Kellston. He was older now, of course, a lot older. What she remembered most were the brutal scars on his throat from where he'd been shot and the hoarse, slightly strangulated sound of his voice.

It was another five minutes before Chris led his father to the car. He opened the back door and gently propelled him inside. 'Come on,' he said. 'Time to go.'

Terry settled himself into the back, waited until Chris had climbed into the passenger seat and then sat forward. 'I thought you wanted to buy the bloody place.'

'I do.'

'So how are you going to do that without talking to Joe?'

Chris snapped his seat belt across his chest before glancing over his shoulder. 'There's no rush,' he said. 'He ain't going anywhere. We can talk to him tomorrow.'

Ava looked at Chris. 'Home?'

'Yeah,' he said. 'Quick as you can.'

Ava turned the car around and set off for Walpole Close. As she drove, she was aware of Terry lurking by her left shoulder. He was leaning so far forward, he was almost breathing down her neck. He wasn't drunk, or at least she didn't think so. There was a faint whiff of whisky, but nothing overwhelming. And he had walked quite steadily across the car park.

'So which one are you, then?' he said.

Ava glanced at him. 'I'm sorry?'

'You're one of Tommy Quinn's girls, ain't you? Debs, is it, or are you Karen? You two always looked so alike, I never could tell the difference.'

Chris twisted around to stare at him. 'This is Ava,' he said. 'She ain't one of Tommy's daughters. How could she be? That was years ago. They must be ... shit, they must be in their fifties by now.'

'It's okay,' Ava said.

'Ava Gold,' Chris said. 'She's Ted Gold's niece. You remember Ted, don't you?'

There was silence from the back seat.

'He used to run the car lot down by the station.'

'Where are we going?' Terry asked.

'We're going home, Dad. We're going to Walpole Close.'

Terry gave a sigh, sat back and stared out of the window.

Ava could feel the frustration leaking from Chris Street. He sat beside her, tense and agitated. She noticed him reach into his pocket for his cigarettes and then withdraw his hand, realising that he wasn't in his own car. 'You can smoke if you want,' she said.

Chris shook his head. 'It doesn't matter.'

Ava wanted to say something reassuring, but nothing came to mind. It wouldn't get any better; she knew that from personal experience. Her granddad on her mother's side had been the same, deteriorating week by week, month by month, a gradual drifting away from the core of himself until the person he had been had completely disappeared. 'Are you okay?' she asked softly.

Chris's mouth twisted a little. 'He's fine. He's just had a skinful. He'll be all right in the morning.'

Ava stopped in front of the wrought-iron gates, opened the window and pressed the remote. Did he believe what he was saying or did he just *want* to believe it? As the gates swung smoothly back, she drove the Kia carefully up the drive and pulled up outside the front door.

'Thanks,' Chris asked. 'You want to come in, grab a coffee?'

Ava couldn't tell from his tone whether he was being polite or whether he actually wanted the company. 'Best not,' she said. 'It's getting late. I'll see you in the morning.'

'Ta, love,' Terry said as he got out of the car. 'Give my best to your mum.'

'Will do,' Ava said. She gave a wry smile as she turned the car around and retreated back down the drive. She could imagine her mother's horror if she passed on Terry Street's best wishes – but, of course, she wouldn't. His regards hadn't been meant for her, but another woman entirely.

14

After she'd turned back into the close, Ava stopped again and got out her phone. She gave Tash a call at the Fox, told her that Terry Street was safely home and offered her a lift. 'I'm only down the road. I'll be passing in five minutes.'

The night sky was a deep purplish-grey and the snow was starting to fall faster. It clung to the rooftops and the pavements and the bonnets of parked cars. By the morning, if this continued, conditions would be icy and the traffic would be dire. She hoped that Chris wasn't planning on making any long-distance journeys. The Mercedes would handle the conditions just fine; it was other cars – and other drivers – that posed the greater danger. She still wasn't sure if she'd actually secured the job or not and didn't want to scupper her chances through some minor accident.

Ava released a long low sigh. She knew it was selfish to be thinking about herself, especially after what she'd witnessed tonight, but she couldn't help being worried about her own future too. All she wanted was a bit of stability, a steady job and the means to get back on her own two feet. That wasn't too much to ask, was it? The trouble was that she'd lost her confidence somewhere along the road; it had, she suspected, been neatly filed away with the divorce papers.

Thinking about Alec was a big mistake. Quickly, she pushed him out of her mind. That was history. It was over and done with, finished. But was it ever that easy? She thought about Terry Street, thrust back into a past that no longer existed and from where there was no escape. Surrounded by ghosts, he would gradually lose touch with the present, with his own children, and finally with his very essence. She had watched her granddad go through the same slow painful process.

Ava felt a dull depression settling over her. If she wasn't careful it would gather, like the snow, numbing all her senses. She tried to think of other things, good things, like her mum and dad, Jason and Tash. She drummed her fingertips impatiently on the steering wheel, eager now to get to the Fox and have the distraction of another person's voice.

The pub was closed by the time she got there, the last customers gone and the lights turned off. Tash was waiting by the main entrance, huddled under an umbrella.

'God, you're a life saver,' she said as she hurried over and climbed into the passenger seat. 'I didn't fancy walking home in this.' She dropped the wet umbrella by her feet and pulled on her seat belt. 'Oh, and Maggie says thank you too. She didn't want to chuck him out, not when he was in that state.'

'He was in the car park when we got here,' Ava said, pulling away from the kerb again.

'Yeah, he kept going in and out all evening, hanging round the cellar door.'

'Was he drinking? I mean, was he drinking a lot?'

Tash shook her head. 'No, he bought a few whiskies, three or four, but that's not much for Terry. Mind, I don't know how much he'd had before he turned up. He didn't seem drunk, though.'

'No, I didn't think so either.'

Tash gave a shudder. 'It's spooky, though, the way he kept going back to the cellar.'

'Spooky?' With the traffic lights on green, Ava passed straight through and on to the high street. 'Why spooky?'

'Well, you know, after what happened there.'

Ava glanced at her. 'No, I don't know. I don't have a clue.'

Tash shifted in her seat, eager to tell the story. When it came to rumour and gossip, she was up there with Jimmy Gold. 'Well, that's where Joe Quinn was murdered, wasn't it? Battered to death with a baseball bat. By his own son too. Right there by that cellar door.'

Ava's eyebrows shifted up a notch. 'Really?' Although she was aware that the gangster had been killed at the Fox, she'd had no idea of the exact location. In fact, her knowledge of the Quinn family was decidedly slight. She knew that they had once been a major force in the East End, almost as powerful as the Krays, but that was about as far as it went. She would probably have learned more if her mother hadn't taken her away from Kellston at such an early age.

'Joe was a right nasty bastard by all accounts,' Tash continued. 'He used to own the Fox and Terry worked for him. Not in the pub, he wasn't a barman or anything . . . more on the other side of things, collecting extortion money, putting the screws on, that kind of stuff. Course, Terry was only young then – we're talking forty-odd years ago – but everyone could see that he was going places.'

'How do you know all this?' Ava asked.

'Maggie told me.'

'Ah.' Maggie McConnell, the current landlady of the Fox, was a small, slim lady, a widow in her late fifties. Despite her size, she was a real tough cookie. Everyone was welcome in her pub – including the cops, the villains and the local toms – so long as they abided by her rules. Anyone caught soliciting, thieving, fighting or dealing would be out on their ear with no second chances. 'So was Tommy Quinn the son?' Ava asked, remembering Terry's earlier mistake when he'd thought she was one of Tommy's daughters.

Tash gave a nod. 'One of them, but not the one who killed him. That was the older brother, Connor. Tommy still got sent down though, for helping to dispose of the body.'

Ava turned the car into Violet Road and slowed down until she found a parking slot. The Kia, fortunately, was of a size to fit into spaces other cars couldn't manage. She switched off the engine and looked at Tash. 'Well, I suppose that's why Terry was there then. If Joe was his old boss and that's where he died—'

'Except that's not the whole story,' Tash interrupted. She lowered her voice as though someone might be trying to eavesdrop from the back seat. 'Connor and Tommy always swore that they were innocent, and some people reckon they were set up. In the end it was Terry who profited most from Joe's death – he got to take over the firm, control the money and buy the pub at a knockdown price. If you're asking who had most to gain, Terry comes right at the top of the list.'

Ava slipped off her seat belt. 'Yeah, but the East End's full of rumours – rumours and conspiracy theories. Doesn't mean any of its true.'

'Doesn't mean it isn't, either. Maybe Terry's got a guilty conscience.'

From what Ava knew about Terry Street, she didn't think he had much of a conscience at all. You couldn't afford finer feelings if you were going to be a gangland boss. But then again, the past could come back to haunt anybody. She gazed out through the windscreen for a few seconds, watching the snow come tumbling down. She recalled what her dad had said about the murder of Lizzie Street. If a man could have his own wife murdered, he was probably capable of anything. 'Does Maggie think he did it?'

Tash gave a dismissive flap of her hand. 'Oh, you know Maggie. She likes a good gossip but she's always careful not to say *too* much.'

Ava thought about the landlady of the Fox as they got out of the car. Maggie McConnell, even though she was a few years older than her father, would make the perfect partner for him. She was an attractive woman of strong character and independent means, the kind of lady who might be able to whip him into shape. It was supposed to be parents who worried about their kids, but in Ava's case – well, with her dad at least – it was usually the other way round.

Tash put up her brolly and the two of them tried to shelter under it as they hurried towards home, crossing over the main street to an empty Market Road and then into the square.

They were both quiet for a while. A thin layer of snow scrunched beneath their feet, the only noise other than the muffled sound of an occasional car travelling along the high street. Ava's thoughts had returned to Terry Street, but Tash's had taken a completely different direction.

'So what did you think of Lydia?'

It took Ava a second to place the name. With everything that had happened this evening, she had almost forgotten the events of the afternoon. But of course, Lydia was the girl who worked at Beast, the pretty one who had showed her the Rogues' Gallery. 'Yeah, she seems nice enough.'

'She is, isn't she? I thought I might invite her round one night.'

They were almost at the flat and Ava took her hands out of her pockets, feeling the cold bite into her fingers as she scrabbled in her bag for the door key. 'And are you going to tell Hannah?'

'Tell her what?'

They jogged up the steps and Ava unlocked the door and flicked on the hall light. 'You know what. She won't be best pleased if she finds out you've been entertaining attractive women behind her back.'

Tash closed the door behind them. 'It's not like *that*,' she protested. 'Lydia hasn't lived here for long. She doesn't know many people. I'm just being friendly.'

Ava grinned at her. Tash was the biggest flirt she'd ever come across, man or woman. 'Ah, friendly. Right, I get it.'

Tash grinned back at her. 'Anyway, what Hannah doesn't know, Hannah won't grieve over. I mean, it's not as though you're about to tell her, is it?'

'Ugh, don't involve me in this. I've seen Hannah when she's angry and she scares me half to death.'

'You just need to know how to handle her, babe.'

As they climbed up the flight of stairs, Ava glanced over her shoulder. 'Anyway, is Lydia even ... you know, that way *inclined*.' Her female gaydar was rubbish; unless a woman was wearing Doc Martens and dungarees with a gay rights badge pinned to her chest, she had no idea whether she was lesbian or not.

Tash laughed. 'Who knows – inclinations come and go – but it could be fun finding out.'

'Ah, fun,' Ava said. 'I can remember the days when I used to have fun.'

'Men aren't worth the trouble, hon.' Tash gave her a mischievous nudge. 'Maybe you should try something new.'

Ava unlocked the door and the two of them walked in. 'If you're trying to convert me, you haven't got a hope. I'm sworn off relationships, any kind of relationships, for the foreseeable future.'

'That's what you say now, but things change. You don't know how you're going to feel tomorrow.'

But tomorrow wasn't a day that Ava was looking forward to. She still had to decide whether to tell Chris Street about Wilder and Borovski. And she was sure, especially after the events of this evening, that the very last thing he needed was more bad news.

15

Usually Noah loved this time of day, the quiet hours after the cleaners had been in and before the bar opened for business, but this morning he couldn't settle. He started the stocktaking and abandoned it halfway through. He polished some glasses, put them down on the counter and forgot about them. He wandered aimlessly between the two connecting rooms, checking for dust and spills although the place was immaculate with every surface gleaming.

He knew what was bugging him, but he couldn't do anything about it. Chris Street's ex, Jenna, had turned up at the bar last night and Guy had been all over her. The two of them had spent the entire evening together, making it clear to everyone that they were a couple. They couldn't have made it more obvious if they'd put a neon sign above their heads. How long before Chris Street heard the news? The East End was like one giant rumour machine, pulling in the gossip and churning it out. And news travelled fast with phones and texts and Facebook. It was only a matter of time before it all kicked off.

Noah had long ago ceased to torment himself as regards Guy's sexual adventures – he could live with the pain of short-term infidelities – but by screwing Jenna, Guy was deliberately taunting Chris Street, provoking him to the point where it was bound to end in violence. Street wasn't the type to turn the other cheek – he would see the relationship as a personal insult – and Guy wouldn't back down either.

Noah returned to the bar, picked up a cloth and ran it along the shiny surface. If he could find a way to delete Guy's past he would, but it wasn't possible to turn back the clock. The hate and anger was ingrained and could never be wiped clean. At some point, and it might not be long, all hell was going to break loose.

He slapped the cloth down on the counter, wishing there was something he could do, but he could no more control the future than he could the weather. For a while, he gazed out of the window, watching the snow fall on the street. And then, because idleness didn't suit him, he started polishing the counter again. Time passed slowly when you were waiting for bad things to happen.

It was almost nine o'clock before Noah heard the door to the upstairs flat open, followed by the clickety-click of high heels on the wooden steps. A few seconds later Jenna appeared in the bar, wearing the same dress from last night and with a fur coat draped around her shoulders.

'Hi, babe,' she said, walking over to the counter and perching on a bar stool. She crossed her long brown legs. 'And how are you today?'

'Good,' he said, forcing a smile. He thought she had a slightly smug expression but it could have been his own prejudice coming into play. 'Where's Guy?'

'He'll be down in a minute. He's just making a call.'

Noah stared at the coat. He reckoned it was real, not artificial, which gave him another reason to dislike her. Suddenly, he remembered an expression he'd once heard Guy's mother use: *All fur coat and no knickers.* Despite the damage she'd done, Noah had always had a soft spot for Lizzie Street; when he'd been a teenager, she had been one of the few people who had judged him on himself and not on the colour of his skin or his sexuality.

Jenna swept back her long blonde hair and looked at him. 'What is it?'

'Huh?'

'You're frowning.'

'Am I?' Noah shook his head, glancing off towards the window. 'I was just thinking about something . . . someone.' Whenever he thought fondly about Lizzie Street, he always felt disloyal. The abysmal mother–son relationship had tainted Guy's whole life, leaving him incapable of moving on, of being unable to attach himself properly to anyone else. Guy was good-looking, full of charm, but it was all on the surface; deep down, where it really mattered, was a heart that was fractured. Noah knew that Guy cared about him, even needed him, but that wasn't the same as love.

Jenna put her elbow on the bar, tilted up her chin and batted her long, false lashes. 'Someone nice?'

Noah's thoughts skipped back to Lizzie Street. 'I'm not sure if nice is the word exactly.' No, no one could ever have accused Lizzie of niceness. She'd been single-minded, greedy and reckless. But there had been another side to her too. She had, on occasion, been capable of great acts of kindness and generosity. It was impossible to know whether her marriage to Terry Street had altered her character or simply brought out the worst in what was already there.

'Oh, right,' Jenna said. And then, because she wasn't the sort of girl who could deal with silence, she quickly added, 'I suppose you've known Guy for ages.'

'Quite a while. Since we were in school, in fact.'

'Really?' she said. 'What was he like back then?'

'Much the same.' Noah saw the hunger in her eyes, the need to find out more, and understood it. It was an irony that Guy inspired great love, great passion and devotion and yet was incapable of returning it. He had wondered if Jenna was using Guy in the way that he was using her – simply to get under the skin of Chris Street – but could see now that it was more than that. She'd already fallen for him. She was trapped in the web and she didn't even know it.

'I bet all the girls were crazy for him.'

'Actually, it was an all-boys school.'

Her red slash of a mouth widened into a sly smile. 'All the lads, then.'

Noah gave a shrug. He wasn't going to tell her the truth about the two awkward eleven-year-olds who hadn't fitted in, who had always been outsiders in a school that catered mainly for the privileged. Back then, Guy had not yet smoothed out his vowels or developed that sleek layer of charm that served him so well now. His working-class accent and Noah's black skin had marked them out as different. They had come together for protection and companionship, stayed together out of . . .

Noah was still searching for the right word when Guy came down the stairs with his pale grey overcoat hanging over his arm.

'Are my ears burning?'

Jenna turned to him, her eyes lighting up. 'I was just asking Noah about when you were at school.'

'Oh, that was a long time ago,' Guy said dismissively. 'Ancient history. The bad old days, eh, Noah? Best forgotten.'

Noah smiled, but said nothing. For him those days still meant something, still mattered. They might not always have been happy, but at least they had been spent with the person he loved.

Guy shrugged on his overcoat. 'Ready to go, sweetheart?'

Jenna stood up, went over to him and slipped her arm through his. 'Are you sure? I'm only parked down the road.'

'It's no bother.' Guy glanced over at Noah. 'I'm just going to walk Jenna to her car.'

'Bye, Noah,' she said, giving him a wave. 'Have a good day.'

'You too.'

Noah watched as they walked out of the door, past the window and along the street. He felt his guts turn over and placed a hand against his stomach. Jenna wouldn't last. She was merely a means to an end – but it could prove to be a disastrous one.

16

Ava picked up Chris Street from outside the Eagle, waited for him to put his seat belt on and then pulled away from the kerb. She drove carefully through the streets of Soho, trying to concentrate as she manoeuvred the Mercedes through the tangle of traffic. It was still snowing and everything static was covered in a blanket of white. The people hurried by on the pavement, umbrellas up and heads down. The ice, churned up by the wheels of passing cars, had formed a nasty grey slush in the gutters. She kept an eye on the vehicle in front and on the one behind, hoping that her reflexes would be fast enough if anything untoward happened.

The bad weather, however, wasn't the only thing that was bugging her. She had slept badly and her eyes felt dry and scratchy. She had dozed and woken, dozed and woken, and now her head was full of the remnants of bad dreams – dreams about treacherous Russians, about villains with caved-in skulls, about dead rats with their entrails hanging out.

Ava gripped the wheel, trying to shake off the nightmarish images. Chris Street sat silently beside her. Since they'd met up this morning, he hadn't said a word about the previous evening and she hadn't mentioned it either. That was okay with her. If he didn't want to talk about it, she wasn't going to force the issue. But what about that other sticky problem? She still hadn't decided whether to tell him about Guy Wilder and Borovski. Despite having weighed up the pros and cons – the pros being that the knowledge could save him from making a costly mistake and would show that she was loyal to him, the cons consisting mainly of not sticking her beak into things that didn't concern her – she was still wavering.

'Where to?' she asked. 'To Belles?'

Chris nodded. 'Yeah, back to Belles.'

It was half an hour before they made it to Shoreditch, the traffic creeping along at a snail's pace. As they passed a row of shops, Ava noticed that Christmas was already in evidence, the storefronts filled with big red Santas and galloping reindeer, the windows framed by twinkling multi-coloured lights. The sight of it made her heart sink. The trouble with the festive season was that it stirred up so many memories, most of them Alec-related ones that she wanted to forget. 'Lord, is it that time of year already?'

Chris looked up from his phone. 'Huh?'

'Christmas,' she said.

'It's still November.'

'Only just. So do you do anything Christmassy at Belles?'

'Like what?'

'I don't know,' she said. 'Put up a tree? Drape a bit of tinsel round the girls? Buy one lap dance, get one free?'

He grinned. 'Why, are you after a spot of overtime? The tips are good, excellent in fact.'

'It's probably best to know your own limitations. I think I'll stick to the driving, if that's okay with you.' Ava waited, hoping that he'd get the hint and that he might actually confirm she had a full-time job. But the seconds ticked by and he still didn't bite. Unable to bear the uncertainty, and realising that subtlety wasn't going to work, she decided to address the problem head on. 'I do *have* a job, don't I?'

Chris gave a shrug. 'You're still here, aren't you?'

Ava pondered on his apparent inability to give a straight answer to a straight question, and came to the conclusion that this was as good as it was going to get. It wasn't the most formal offer she'd ever received, but at least she appeared to be gainfully employed. Should she thank him? By the time she'd thought about it, the moment had passed.

A couple of minutes later, they arrived at Belles. As Ava swung the Mercedes on to the forecourt and into the reserved parking space, Chris undid his seat belt. His phone started ringing and he glanced at the screen, checking the ID of the caller before picking up. 'Lee, mate. Long time, no see. How are you doing?' But then, after listening to what Lee had to say, his tone suddenly changed. 'What? With Wilder? No way! Tell me you're fuckin' joking!'

Ava switched off the engine, feeling that awkwardness that comes with being trapped in a confined space with someone who is receiving bad news. What to do? Where to look? His body had stiffened and she could see his face growing redder. The call had to be about Borovski. Maybe someone else had been at Beast yesterday and had seen the two men together.

Seeing his reaction, she was relieved that she wasn't the one passing on the information.

'When? Who else was there?' There was a pause. Chris raked his fingers through his hair as if he'd like to tear it from its roots. 'Are you sure, are you absolutely sure?' Another longer pause. 'Jesus! The bastard, the fuckin' filthy fuckin' bastard!'

Ava inwardly winced, wondering if she should get out of the car to allow him some privacy. But that would mean standing out in the snow and getting wet, or heading over to the foyer of Belles where the massive black guy – who she now knew was called Solomon Vale – was waving in the punters for the midday session. She shifted uncomfortably in her seat, not especially enamoured of either of the options. As the call appeared to be coming to an end, she decided to stay put.

'Yeah. Yeah, I will. Ta, mate. I'll call you. I'll call you later.' Chris jabbed at the button to disconnect the line. 'Fuck it!' he stormed, slamming his fist down on the side of the seat. He banged the back of his head three times against the head rest, and then slumped forward again, still cursing. 'The bastard, the fucker, the filthy pathetic pile of shit!'

If there had been a brick wall handy, Ava was sure he would have thumped it. Unsure of what to say – *Bad news?* seemed something of an understatement – she decided to keep her trap closed and not risk antagonising him even more.

Chris glared hard at the phone as if that small metal oblong, rather than the information received through it, was responsible for his outburst of temper. A long low hiss escaped from his lips. Then, as if suddenly becoming aware of her presence again, he turned and looked at her. 'Sorry,' he said. 'You didn't need to hear that.'

'That's okay,' Ava replied, trying to be blasé about it. 'I've heard worse.'

Chris sat back, marginally calmer now, but clearly still seething. He dropped the phone on to his lap. He was breathing loudly, the sound coming from deep within his chest. His hands clenched and unclenched, his knuckles white with rage. 'Can you believe that? Can you fuckin' believe it?'

As some kind of enquiry was obviously required at this point, Ava duly made it. 'What is it?' She had a sudden worrying thought that whoever had been at Beast might have seen her there too, but thought on balance that the chances were low. She hadn't been working for Chris for long and doubted if any of his associates would recognise her. 'What's happened?'

He reached into his pocket for his cigarettes, lighting one and inhaling deeply before he replied. 'That bloody bitch!'

Ava frowned, confused at this sudden turn of events. 'Bitch?' she echoed faintly. She couldn't see where a woman fitted into the scheme of things.

'Jenna,' he said, virtually spitting out the name. 'My bloody ex. Turns out she's shagging that bastard Wilder.'

Ava didn't need to feign her surprise. 'You're kidding me?'

'I wish,' he said, tugging on the cigarette again before flicking the ash carelessly on to the floor. 'I mean, why the fuck would she do that? She's already bled me dry. Isn't that enough for her? No, of course it fuckin' well ain't. That ball-crushing cow has to go and screw that lousy lowlife too.'

'Are you sure it's true? All kinds of rumours go around and—'

'Yeah, it's true all right. My mate knows someone who was at the bar last night, said the two of them were all over each other like a rash. And she didn't leave when the place closed. She stayed there. He's got a flat upstairs. I bet the two of them were at it like—'

He didn't finish the sentence and didn't need to. Ava could see that there was more than anger in his face; there was hurt and betrayal too. The divorce, she suspected, had not been down to him, and some lingering feelings for Jenna remained. It was a cruel thing, she thought, for any woman to do – sleeping with your ex's enemy was about the lowest blow you could inflict.

Chris turned his attention back to the phone. 'Well, let's see what the bitch has to say for herself.'

Ava stared at him, aghast. 'God, you're not going to call her, are you?'

He started scrolling through the menu. 'Why not? Why shouldn't I?'

'Because if she is doing this to annoy you, to get some kind of a reaction, then you're about to make all her dreams come true.'

He considered this for a moment, his finger still on the button. 'So I just let her get away with it?'

'Get away with what? She's not cheating on you. You're not together anymore, are you?'

But as soon as she'd said it, she knew she'd made a mistake. It wasn't just his heart that had been damaged but his pride too. 'I mean, think about it at least. Maybe she's doing this to wind you up, maybe she isn't, but either way the one thing that's going to annoy her the most is if you don't react. There's nothing worse than being ignored.'

He wound down the window and chucked the half-smoked cigarette on to the forecourt. 'Do nothing? She's taking the piss. She's making me a fuckin' laughing stock.'

'Well, it's your decision,' Ava said. 'But personally I wouldn't give her the satisfaction.'

Chris cursed softly under his breath. Then he put the phone away, quickly opened the car door, got out, leaned down and said, 'Five minutes. Wait for me.'

Ava watched him stride across to the entrance to Belles. He stopped to say something to Solomon Vale and then disappeared inside the club. She sat forward, hunched over the wheel, her shoulders tense. Trouble was brewing, a great rumbling volcano that was about to explode. And she still hadn't told him about Wilder and Borovski.

17

Ava waited, wondering what was going to happen next. She watched as the punters rolled up for the midday session. Most of them arrived in black cabs in groups of five or six, young City lads, suited and booted, and sporting flash gold watches on their wrists. They laughed as they tumbled out of the cabs. So much for an economic recession. These boys were clearly making enough to not think twice about squandering their dosh on lunchtime bottles of champagne, naked flesh and sexual thrills.

Solomon Vale guarded the entrance to the club, having a quiet word with the rowdier clients, waving in the regulars. Nobody argued with Solomon. The size of him was enough to deter even the boldest of men. He must have felt her looking because he glanced over, gave her a half smile and raised his hand. It was the first time since she'd started the job that he had actually acknowledged her. Did this mean she was now officially on the firm? She smiled back and gave him a wave.

Five minutes passed by, and then ten. There was still no sign of Chris. She watched as a girl in her early twenties, wearing a lot of slap, tottered towards the club in a pair of high heels. Ava's thoughts turned to what was going on inside. When it came to lap dancing, she was on the fence. She had heard all the arguments, for and against, but her own feelings on the subject remained ambiguous. Were the women the ones in charge, exploiting the men's sexual desires and making good money simply for stripping off their clothes? Or did the whole process objectify women, reducing them to sexual commodities where they were lusted after, leched over, but never genuinely cared about? It was all about sex: sex and money. There was, perhaps, a soul-destroying emptiness to the whole exchange.

Ava was mulling this over when Chris strode out of the club again. She could see from the thunderous look on his face that the time he'd spent inside hadn't done anything to moderate his temper. He got into the Merc and slammed the door.

'Wilder's,' he said.

She could smell the whisky fumes coming off him, strong and pungent. 'What?'

'The cocktail bar,' he said impatiently. 'Wilder's. On the high street.'

'I know where it is.'

'So why are we still sitting here? I've had enough of that bastard. He ain't going to get away with it. Not this time, not this bloody time.'

Ava hesitated. 'Er . . . do you think that's a good idea?'

Chris Street glared at her. 'Are you my goddamn driver or not?'

'Yes, but I was just thinking that—'

'I don't care, okay? I don't care what you were thinking. Just get this fuckin' thing started and take me where I want to go.'

Ava scowled back at him, resenting his attitude and his tone. She didn't know what to do for the best. It was, of course, her job to drive him wherever he wanted, but he'd been drinking and was clearly itching for a fight. If he attacked Guy Wilder – and that, she presumed, was his intention – then he was likely to end up in the slammer on a GBH charge. Or maybe something even worse. And while there was probably nothing she could do to prevent it, she was reluctant to actually help him in the enterprise.

'Ah, for God's sake,' he spluttered, getting out of the car again. He marched around to her door and pulled it open. 'Get out. I'll drive.'

'You can't,' she said. 'You haven't got a licence.'

'What are you gonna do, arrest me?'

'Not me,' she replied, 'but you said yourself that the law have been hanging around. How long do you reckon it will take for them to pick you up?'

'I'll take my chances. Come on, get out.'

But Ava didn't move. 'And you've been drinking. You want to lose your licence for good?'

Chris slapped his hand down on the roof of the car. He wasn't used to people disobeying him. He made the rules and others followed them. 'Out! Now!'

Ava shook her head. She had the feeling that he would have physically tried to drag her out had they not been in a public place.

Solomon Vale, seeing the disturbance, jogged over to join them. 'Everything okay, boss?'

'No, it's not fuckin' okay. My so-called driver has decided that she's going to pick and bloody well choose where I can go and where I can't.'

'I didn't say that,' Ava objected. She looked at Solomon, willing him to help. 'I only suggested that now might not be the best time to be paying Guy Wilder a visit.'

Solomon's eyebrows shifted up a notch. 'Wilder, huh?'

If Ava had been expecting some support, she was quickly disillusioned.

Solomon frowned at her and then looked at Chris. 'You want me to get cover for the door? Give me five minutes and I can drive you there.'

Ava stared at the big man. Now it was getting even worse. If the two of them were to turn up at the bar, egging each other on, it would probably end in carnage. God, what was the matter with these guys? Why couldn't they use their brains instead of their fists? There had to be a smarter way of getting back at Guy Wilder than beating him to a pulp. Well, there was only one thing for it. She made a decision, shifted forward and switched on the ignition.

'What are you doing?' Chris asked. He grabbed hold of the car door as if she was about to drive away.

'You want to go to Wilder's,' she said. 'I'll take you to Wilder's.'

Chris hesitated for a second as if it might be some kind of trick, but then he walked around the Mercedes and got in beside her. 'About bloody time,' he grumbled.

Ava reached out and closed her own door. It was better,

she'd decided, that she took him to the bar rather than Solomon. At least she'd have a chance to try and talk him down along the way. Failing that, she could always attempt to stop things from getting out of hand once they got there. How exactly she could achieve this she hadn't quite figured out yet. She'd just have to play it by ear.

She manoeuvred the car out of the parking space, paused to let a black cab go past, and then went on through the gateway. In her rear-view mirror she could see Solomon Vale standing with his hands on his hips. He had the disappointed look of a man who had just let the opportunity of a good scrap slip through his fingers.

Chris lit up another cigarette and wound down the window. The cold air rushed in. As he smoked, he threw her a series of small irritated glances, but didn't say anything.

'You going to fire me for this?' she asked.

'Want to give me a good reason why I shouldn't?'

Ava was quick to reply. 'Well, I'd consider myself fortunate to have a driver who cared about whether I ended up in the slammer or not. I mean, is he really worth it? Is she?'

'Is that any of your business?'

'Yes, I think so. If you're banged up, I don't have a job.'

'Maybe you don't have one anyway.'

Ava gave a shrug. 'You won't find anyone better.'

'You reckon so?'

'I know so.'

He let out a brittle laugh. 'You've got a high opinion of yourself.'

'Someone has to,' she said, hoping to lighten the

atmosphere with a bit of easy banter. 'My popularity is at an all-time low.'

But Chris Street just shook his head, refusing to relinquish his ever-darkening mood. As they drove through Shoreditch, he smoked fast and furiously, lifting the cigarette to his lips and exhaling the smoke in long angry streams. He glanced at the speedometer. 'Any chance of putting your foot down? At this rate it'll be midnight before we get there.'

'It's icy,' she said. 'You want us to have an accident?'

'If you're such a good driver, that ain't going to happen.'

Ava didn't rise to the bait, and didn't increase her speed. She had no desire to get to Wilder's any sooner than she had to. 'So what's the plan?'

'Plan?'

'For when you get there. What are you going to do?'

'Jesus,' he hissed. 'What is it with you? I pay you to drive, not to ask bloody stupid questions.'

'Okay,' she said. 'I get it. Just shut my mouth and get on with it, huh?'

'If you think you can manage it.'

Ava frowned, her hands tightening a little on the wheel. So much for calming him down; she appeared to be doing the very opposite. It was best, she decided, to leave well alone. With no other bright ideas springing to mind, she might have to rely on a miraculous intervention from above. God moved in mysterious ways, apparently, although he probably had better things to do than interfere in Chris Street's macho arguments.

It was another quarter of an hour, fifteen minutes spent in total silence, before they drew up outside the bar. Chris opened the door and shot out before she'd even stopped the car properly. She wasn't supposed to park here – there were double yellow lines – but she only had two choices: either she moved the Merc around the corner or she risked a ticket. She looked quickly up and down the street, couldn't spot a traffic warden and so decided to take a chance. Anything could happen in the time it took her to find a legal parking space.

Ava ran around the car and followed him inside. What was she intending to do? She hadn't got a clue. As the door closed behind her, she scanned the room and saw that it was busy. The place was doing a brisk lunchtime trade. Chris was already at the far end. He was checking out the tables, moving stealthily between the customers like a hunter stalking his prey. The black guy, the one she had seen with Wilder at Beast, was watching him from behind the bar.

Eventually, when it became obvious that Guy Wilder wasn't there, Chris went over to the counter. 'Where is he? Where is the bastard?'

'Not here,' said the black man, who obviously didn't have to think twice to know who he was talking about.

'I can see he's not fuckin' here, Noah,' said Chris, raising his voice. 'Where the fuck is he?'

'No idea.'

'And I don't suppose you've any idea when he's coming back either?'

Noah gave a shrug. 'Sorry.'

By now most of the customers had their heads turned in the direction of the bar. There was a thin mutter of disapproval – the atmosphere had abruptly changed – but no one was prepared to risk Chris Street's wrath by making any objections clear enough to be heard.

Ava kept her distance. She watched as Chris's fingers curled into fists, his hands bouncing off his thighs. He displayed all the frustration of a man who, having whipped himself into a fury, now found himself with no one to vent it on. She felt a wave of relief flow over her. Perhaps God hadn't been too busy after all.

Chris looked to his left, towards an oak door that had a sign saying PRIVATE. 'Is he up there? Is that where the scumbag's hiding?'

'No one's hiding nowhere, man. He's out, right?' Noah waved a hand in the direction of the window. 'You see his motor?'

Chris glanced towards the row of cars parked on the opposite side of the street to the Mercedes. 'Don't mean he ain't here.'

Noah gave a weary shake of his head. 'Don't mean he is either.'

Ava saw Chris look towards the pine door again. He went over and rattled the handle, but the door was locked. His eyes narrowed, and for one awful moment she thought he was going to try and break it down, but then he stepped back. 'You tell him,' he said, glaring at Noah and pointing a finger, 'this ain't over. Tell him I'll be back.'

I'll be back? thought Ava. Not the most original line she'd ever heard, but what did that matter so long as it meant he was about to leave. As he turned away from Noah, she retreated into the street and got into the car.

Chris joined her shortly after, his face still full of rage.

'Home,' he ordered. 'If it's not too much trouble.' Even while he was fastening his seat belt, he was glowering over at the bar.

She didn't need telling twice. Before Guy Wilder could put in an ill-timed appearance, she set off for Walpole Close. She was expecting Chris to ask why she'd followed him inside, but he didn't. Perhaps he was saving the lecture for later. Or perhaps it was no more than he'd expected. Either way, it was one more nail in the coffin of her job.

She passed quickly through the lights at a junction, eager now to put as much distance as possible between Chris and the cocktail bar. The confrontation might have been postponed, but it hadn't been cancelled. At some point he was going to have it out with Wilder. She had only travelled fifty yards when she noticed the flashing blue light in the rear-view mirror.

'What now?' she murmured.

Chris whirled around. 'Shit! Don't stop!'

'What?'

'Don't stop. Put your foot down! Get the fuck out of here!'

'What?' she repeated, stunned by the order. The patrol car was right on her tail now, the driver making it clear that he wanted her to pull over. 'I haven't done anything wrong.' Ava looked across at Chris. Had he gone stark staring mad? His face had turned pale and there were beads of sweat on his forehead. 'What's going on?'

'This is what's going on.' He opened his overcoat a fraction to reveal the butt of a gun sticking out of his inside pocket.

Ava pulled in her breath. 'Christ! What the . . . why the . . .' But there wasn't time for an interrogation. Had he actually been planning on *killing* Guy Wilder? She realised now what the stop-off at Belles had been for; he'd been after more than a few stiff drinks. What should she do? If she took off, the Merc could easily outrun the patrol car, but only if the roads were clear. And she'd be landing herself in a heap of trouble with the law. How was she going to explain why she hadn't stopped? All these thoughts ran through her head in one mad rush as she gradually slowed the car.

'What the fuck are you doing?' he snarled.

'If we take off and they catch us, they'll know you have something to hide. Did anyone see the gun at the bar? Did Noah see it?'

Chris shook his head. 'Nah, nobody. They couldn't.'

She hoped he was right. It was possible that Noah or one of the customers had called 999, but it seemed unlikely that the cops would have responded so quickly. Perhaps this was about something else entirely. If they took Chris down Cowan Road police station, he'd be searched and the gun would be found. There was only one thing to do. 'Give it to me,' she said. 'Put it in my lap.'

Chris stared at her. 'Are you crazy?'

'Jesus,' she said. 'Do you want to be caught carrying? Come on, quick! Don't hang about.'

He hesitated, but eventually reached into his pocket and did as she asked. She found a safe place to pull in, switched off the engine, leaned over to the back seat, grabbed her handbag and dropped the gun into the bottom of it. The cops were already walking towards the Merc as she got out and smiled at them.

'Officers,' she said politely. 'Is there a problem?'

The older of the two men, a grizzled grey-haired man, frowned at her. 'Took you a while to stop, didn't it?'

Ava, who had the bag slung over her shoulder, could feel the weight of the gun. She could also feel her heart hammering in her chest. What on earth was she doing? It had been an impulsive decision, an insane one, and she might spend a long time regretting it. 'Sorry. I didn't realise it was me you wanted.'

'You know you jumped a red light back there?'

'I don't think so,' said Ava. She was sure the car had been clear of the line even as the lights had changed to amber. Her lips felt dry, but she resisted the temptation to run her tongue along them. 'I'm sure I didn't.'

'Red. It was definitely red.'

Ava knew he was lying, but in some way this gave her hope. Perhaps she was panicking unnecessarily. This could just be part of the general harassment that Chris had complained about the day she had turned up at Belles begging him to give her a job. She could have argued the point, but now wasn't the time to be kicking up a fuss. 'I'm so sorry. I honestly thought . . . I must have made a mistake.'

'Can I see your licence, please?'

'Of course.' As Ava unzipped the side pocket of her bag, she was aware of the other cop walking slowly around the Mercedes, examining the tyres and the lights. Chris had got out and was leaning with one elbow on the roof of the car. She wasn't sure if the position was designed to look deliberately casual or if he was having trouble standing up. Perhaps the whisky had finally caught up with him.

She handed her licence over, and the PC peered at it carefully. 'Ava Gold,' he said, glancing up at her.

'That's me.'

He looked at the Merc. 'And is this your car?'

She stared at him, knowing that *he* knew exactly who the car was registered to. 'No,' she said. 'It belongs to Mr Street.'

'Ah, of course.' He gave a smirk. 'Mr Street. Well, I'll be issuing you with a ticket.'

Ava knew that that meant a sixty quid fine and three points on her licence. 'Are you sure it was on red?' She would have argued her innocence more vehemently if it hadn't been for the presence of the gun in her bag. As it was, all she wanted to do was to get away as soon as possible.

'Saw it with my own eyes,' the copper said. 'Clear as day.'

Ava could have retorted that the day was far from clear. The snow was still falling, coming down in fast swirling flurries. Instead, forgoing the temptation to make any further protestations, she simply gave a sigh. 'Sorry,' she murmured again.

While the older cop did the paperwork, the younger one continued to prowl around the car.

She watched the latter out of the corner of her eye. He had a sour expression on his face. What was he up to? It took only a few seconds for her to find out. Stopping by the rear of the car, he looked at her and said, 'Would you mind opening the boot, miss?'

'What for?' Chris said sharply. 'You stopped her for jumping a light, nothing else.'

The two cops exchanged a look, their mouths simultaneously curling up at the corners.

Ava felt her heart sink. Oh God, what was in the boot? Maybe there was a whole arsenal of weapons in there. Or drugs. Jesus, please don't let there be drugs! Fear coiled like a knot in her guts. Her fingers tightened around the keys.

'You got a problem with that?' the young cop asked.

Chris curled his lip. 'Yeah, I've got a problem. I'm sick to death of you lot hassling me. Ain't you got nothing better to do?'

Ava stared at him, dumbfounded. What the hell was he doing? Why was he provoking them? Was he too drunk to realise the enormity of what was happening? Adrenalin was pumping through her blood, prompting that fight-or-flight impulse. She had a sudden mad urge to sprint off down the street. It took a real effort of will for her to stay where she was.

'This is out of order,' Chris said. 'You're taking liberties.'

'Miss?' the younger cop asked again. There was impatience in his voice now.

She hesitated. The keys, grasped tightly in her right hand, were starting to dig into the soft flesh of her palms. What could she do? Her gaze darted towards Chris, but all he did was scowl back at her. A fat lot of help. If she refused, they'd both end up nicked, but if she went ahead there was no saying what might be revealed. She was buggered whatever choice she made. She was caught between a rock and a hard place.

When she could no longer delay the inevitable, Ava stepped forward and slid the small key into the lock. She held her breath, preparing herself for the worst as the boot swung slowly open. She could hardly bear to look. And then, as her gaze settled on the contents, she couldn't believe what she was seeing. There was nothing there but the spare tyre, a jack and a can of motor oil.

She looked up and caught Chris's eye. He winked back at

her. She gave him a withering stare in return. Although relieved, she felt a spurt of anger too. *The bastard.* He'd let her go through that for nothing. All he'd been doing was winding up the cops.

The young PC, unable to disguise his disappointment, slammed shut the boot and strode back to the patrol car. The older cop grinned. He'd been around long enough to know that some you win, some you lose. He passed Ava the ticket and said, 'Try and be more careful in future, huh?'

'Yes, officer,' she said.

'You'll be hearing from my solicitors,' Chris said.

The cop ignored him and went off to join his partner.

Ava only had to walk a few steps to reach the door and get inside the Mercedes, but that short distance felt like a mile. Her legs were lead and her knees were knocking together. At any second she expected the officer to turn around, to call out for her to stop, to hurry back with some excuse to search her bag. When she finally climbed into the driver's seat, it was with such a sense of relief that she had to sit back and close her eyes for a moment.

When she opened them again, Chris was sitting beside her. 'Thanks for that,' she said. 'Were you trying to give me a heart attack?'

'Sorry, love, but it's what they expect. You have to play the game. If I hadn't had a go, they'd have been suspicious.'

He had some front, she thought, but he was a fool too. What kind of an idiot carried a gun around? She waited for the patrol car to move off, before taking the gun carefully out of her bag and handing it over to him. 'What the hell were you thinking?'

'It's not loaded,' he said. 'I wasn't going to . . .'

'What? Shoot him?'

'No, I wasn't going to shoot him.'

'Well, three cheers for that,' she said caustically. 'No harm done, then, apart from almost getting yourself arrested.'

Chris slipped the gun in his pocket. 'I owe you one.'

'You owe me sixty quid,' she snapped. 'And that's just for starters.'

18

Ava dropped Chris off at Walpole Close, hoping that he'd sober up and stay away from Wilder. She changed cars and made her way towards the Mansfield Estate. She needed someone to talk to and her dad seemed like the best bet. She was starting to wonder if she'd made a big mistake about the job. Was it really worth the hassle? She knew that Chris hadn't forced or even asked her to take the gun – it had been her suggestion entirely – but if she'd been caught with it, she would have been in a whole lot of bother.

Although the snow was still falling, she decided to leave the car in Violet Road. No motor was safe on the Mansfield, not even her little Kia. The feral kids that roamed the estate weren't fussy about what they went joyriding in. She began to walk, shivering in the cold and wishing that she'd worn a warmer coat.

She turned on to Lincoln Road and from there cut up on to the Mansfield. The three tall, concrete towers were familiar to her from her childhood. Although the family had never lived on the estate – they'd had a little two-up, two-down terrace off the high street – she'd spent plenty of time there with her friends. She remembered the dark threatening passageways, the rusting balconies and graffiti-covered walls. Nothing much had changed. There had always been an edge of menace to the place, and an air of downtrodden resignation too.

As she walked along the main path, she kept her eyes peeled. Muggings were rife on the Mansfield and she had no desire to be relieved of the small amount of cash she was carrying. Usually the estate was awash with dealers, but the bad weather had driven all but the most hardy, or most desperate, of them inside. Only a few hooded figures lurked ominously in the shadows.

Ava opened the door to Haslow House and stepped inside the dimly lit foyer. It was cold and empty and smelled of dope. Her dad had a one-bedroom flat on the third floor. She was glad he wasn't higher up; it saved her the trauma of having to ride in a lift that stank of pee. Ignoring the elevators, she jogged up the stone steps, brushing the snow off her shoulders as she went. By the time she'd climbed three flights, she was out of breath and could feel the pull of the muscles in the back of her legs.

After turning the corner on to the walkway, she stopped for a while to look out across the estate. Even the Mansfield had a certain charm when it was covered with snow. Then, when her breathing had returned to normal, she carried on by the row of doors until she came to number thirty-one.

She rang the bell and it was answered straight away. Her father quickly ushered her in, rubbing his hands together as if he was the one who'd been out in the cold.

'Come on in, love, before you freeze to death. What a day, eh?'

After the events of the last few hours, she was glad to see a friendly face. The flat, although small, was warm and cosy. They went through to the kitchen where he took her wet coat and put it over the radiator. They made small talk while he got out the tea bags and organised a brew. When the two mugs were on the table, he sat down opposite to her.

'So what's the problem, sweetheart?'

Ava wasn't sure how grown-up it made her, running to her dad at the first hint of trouble, but she had no one else to turn to. She could share most things with Tash – her flatmate would never deliberately break a confidence – but with this she needed to be extra careful.

'You mustn't tell anyone. Will you promise me?'

His eyebrows lifted. 'Cross my heart,' he said. 'Now come clean before your old man dies of curiosity.'

Ava took a welcome sip of tea before beginning her story. She started with the phone call to Chris and the news about his ex. 'He went ballistic,' she said. 'You wouldn't believe they were actually divorced. He was acting like she was cheating on him.'

'But with Guy Wilder,' he said, shaking his head. 'That must have rubbed him up the wrong way.'

'You don't know the half of it.' She went on to tell him about the stop-off at Belles, about Solomon Vale and her reluctance to drive Chris to Wilder's. 'But he was going there no matter what I said and so I reckoned it was better to take him there myself.'

'You're not wrong there.'

She gave him a quick summary of the events at the bar before moving on to the more important bit. 'And then, just when I was heading for Walpole Close, thinking that the worst was over, there's a flashing blue light behind me.'

'Old Bill.'

'Yeah, the cops. The sods claimed I went through a red light, but I swear I didn't. They were just looking for an excuse.'

'They give you a ticket?'

'You bet, but that's not the worst of it. Chris didn't even want me to stop. He told me to put my foot down, for God's sake. He wanted me to try and shake them off.' She paused before revealing why, briefly lowering her eyes to the table before raising them again. 'He had a gun, Dad. He was carrying. He went to try and find Guy Wilder with a gun in his pocket.'

Jimmy Gold took a breath. 'Christ. You don't think he was going to—'

'He said he wasn't, said it wasn't even loaded, but . . . I don't know. What if he was lying? What if he had shot him? I could have ended up an accessory to murder!'

'But the cops didn't find it?' His eyes widened with alarm. 'Shit, they didn't, did they?'

'No, of course not.' She'd been intending to tell him about how she'd hidden it in her bag, but for some reason decided not to. The stupidity of what she'd done was slowly dawning on her. He would ask her why and she wouldn't she able to tell him. How could she? She didn't know herself. It had been a mad, impulsive thing to do. 'I just . . . I'm not sure. Maybe I'm not cut out for this job. Do you think I should chuck it in?'

Her father reached across the table and laid his hand over hers. 'That's up to you, love. Although ... no, I don't know ... I'm just glad you're okay. What do you think?'

Ava didn't know what she thought. A part of her wanted him to tell her to walk away, to make the decision for her. 'Maybe I should call it a day.'

'It might be for the best.'

'Should I?'

The two of them looked at each other across the table. Her father scratched his forehead. 'He shouldn't have done that. He shouldn't have put you in that position. I don't want you getting into trouble, love.'

'Except it wasn't his fault that the cops stopped us.' She picked up the mug, drank some tea and put it down again. 'Am I overreacting? No, I'm not, am I? If he had been caught with that gun, I could have been for the high jump too.'

'Perhaps you should quit.'

'Should I? Yes, you're right. Should I?'

'Or you could sleep on it. See how you feel in the morning.'

She gave a sigh. 'I don't even know why I'm thinking about it. He'll probably fire me anyway. End of. Problem solved.'

'And if he doesn't?'

She sat back, putting her hands behind her head. 'Then I'll resign.'

'And go back on the cabs?'

'I'd rather stick hot needles in my eyes.' But what was she going to do? Driving positions weren't that easy to find. She'd had to beg for this one. And Christmas was rapidly approaching. On top of all her bills, she needed money for presents.

She couldn't afford too many scruples. And the truth was that she liked Chris – except when he was pissed and behaving like a dick – and didn't want to throw the job away.

'You'll get something else,' he said. 'I know you will.'

Ava sat forward again. There was a copy of the *Kellston Gazette* on the table. She flicked to the back where the classified section was. 'Look at this. There's hardly anything: deliveries, deliveries, deliveries . . . cabs. And they're all paying peanuts.'

Her father reached into his pocket and took out his wallet. 'Here,' he said, pulling out three twenties. 'Have this to tide you over. It'll pay that fine, at least.'

She waved the money away. 'Thanks, but I'm okay at the moment, Dad. And I'm not paying the fine, Chris is.' She closed the paper and nodded towards the notes. 'I see you're still flush, then.'

'I'm being careful with it.'

'Must have been a good win.'

'Everyone deserves a bit of luck now and then.'

Ava gave him an enquiring look, but he wasn't coming clean. Her gaze dropped down to the paper again. She scanned the headlines and then turned over the page where the first thing she noticed was a report about a break-in at a local warehouse. Finian's, a retail supplier of electronic goods, had been relieved of their stock by a gang of robbers. She wouldn't have thought much else about it if her father hadn't chosen that moment to make a clumsy attempt at trying to distract her.

'So what else have you been up to, love? Been anywhere nice?'

She looked up at him. 'Tell me you didn't have anything to do with it.'

'What's that?'

'This,' she said, prodding the article with her finger. She turned the paper around and pushed it across the table. 'Finian's. That's in the business park on Lincoln Road, isn't it?'

'Is it?'

'You know it is.'

He gave a shrug, but his eyes wouldn't meet hers. There was a short silence filled only by the ticking of the kitchen clock and the occasional click of the radiators.

'Dad?'

He screwed up his face, not wanting to lie to her, but not wanting to tell the truth either. 'It was a last-minute thing,' he eventually admitted. 'They needed a driver and ... well, things have been a bit tight lately. I know I said I wouldn't, but it was just too good to pass over. I checked out the plans. It was all sweet, neatly planned. We were in and out in fifteen minutes.'

Ava's heart sank and she shook her head despairingly. 'You'll end up back inside.'

'Only if they catch me,' he said.

'You haven't got any of the stuff, have you? I mean, here, in the flat?' Among other things, Finian's sold computers, TVs, iPads and phones. She looked quickly around the kitchen. 'You didn't bring anything back with you?'

'No,' he said. 'Cash. It was strictly cash.'

'You swear?'

'Yeah, yeah. I swear, sweetheart. There's nothing here.'

She hoped he was telling the truth. Some people learned

from experience, but Jimmy Gold wasn't one of them. 'That's something, I suppose.' There was no point in having a go. What was done was done and couldn't be changed. And anyway, who was she to pass judgement when she was working for one of the biggest villains in the district? 'And no cops sniffing around? They haven't given you a tug?'

'Why would they? They've got no reason, love. The job went off fine, sweet as a nut, and I've been clean for years. Well, nothing heavy.'

She wanted to feel reassured, but she didn't. When it came to her dad, things rarely ran smoothly. The last thing she wanted was to see him behind bars again.

19

Danny Street glanced at his watch. It was half past five exactly. He kept an eye on the building while Silver carefully examined her face in the mirror. She spent a lot of time gazing at her own reflection. It was her third favourite pastime after shagging and snorting coke. This evening, she seemed preoccupied by her pale pink mouth. She pouted and smiled and pouted again.

'What the fuck are you doing?'

She frowned as if he'd interrupted her midway through an especially arduous task. 'I'm getting into character, babe. It's what all the best actresses do. I've read about it. You have to *think* yourself into the part. You have to imagine what they'd be feeling, how they'd behave, all that sort of stuff.'

'Oh yeah?'

'Yeah.' She pushed a strand of fair hair away from her face. 'I'm thinking myself into Ava's head. What would she say? What would she do?'

'Ava?'

'Well, I need a name, hon. I can't give him my real one.'

'I thought we'd decided on Emma.'

Silver pouted again. 'I don't like Emma. I want to be Ava.'

'You want to be the girl who's shagging my brother?'

She turned her head and smiled at him 'Why not? What's wrong with that?' She laid a hand on his thigh, squeezed and then ran her fingers closer to his balls. 'Are you jealous, babe? Are you angry?'

Danny grinned back at her. 'You're a whore,' he said. 'You're a fuckin' tart, a tom. What's there to be jealous about?'

Silver tilted back her head and laughed. 'I'm Ava,' she said. 'I'm your brother's filthy little whore.'

'And you're about to cheat on him.'

'I am, aren't I?'

Danny pushed her hand away. His cock had hardened, he even felt in the mood, but he wasn't going to go there. He had more important things on his mind. 'So you keep concentrating on that while I watch out for Mr Squires.'

'Mr Squires,' she repeated, giggling. 'Mr Squires, Mr Squires.'

Danny would usually take his time checking out the mark, establishing what their movements were, when they came and went, but on this occasion he'd decided to go with the flow. He already knew the basics – the guy lived in Highgate and usually caught the train home – and that was probably enough. With the weather on their side he figured it was smart to take advantage of it. A girl could easily slip in conditions like these, especially if she was wearing high heels, and any half-decent bloke would feel obliged to go to her rescue.

Jeremy Squires had an office on the second floor of an ugly steel-and-glass construction at the top of the high street. The land had once been occupied by a cinema, but that had been pulled down years ago. Danny could still remember it, though, a plush Odeon with a grand foyer smelling of popcorn, and an auditorium with red velvety seats. He had liked going there as a kid and felt resentful about its demise.

He kept his eyes on the building. For the past half-hour, people had been coming out, walking towards the station or the bus stop. He kept looking at the photo on the dashboard, waiting for Squires to appear. He didn't know for sure that he was there – he might not have even gone to work today – but was working on the laws of probability. He felt lucky, on a high, on a roll. It might have been the gear – it always made him optimistic – but he didn't see how anything could go wrong.

It was another ten minutes before Danny finally clocked the man he'd been waiting for. 'Here we go,' he said triumphantly. He gave Silver's shoulder a push. 'There he is. Quick, shift it! Get out, get over there!'

Silver opened the door. 'Wish me luck.'

'You don't need luck, babe. Just go screw him.'

Danny peered through the windscreen as Squires walked across the forecourt and out on to the high street. He was a smartly dressed middle-aged man, carrying a briefcase in one hand and an umbrella in the other. The snow was coming down in thick fast flurries. Silver weaved her way across the road, her white coat blending in with the snow, her red stilettos bright as blood.

'Come on,' he muttered as she advanced towards the mark. 'Take it easy, take it easy . . .' For a moment, he thought she was going to blow it. She was almost level with him and still hadn't made her move. But then she did it – and did it with style. Appearing to slip, she gave a small yelp, skidded and fell at his feet. As Squires crouched down to help, Danny knew that the deal had been sealed.

He watched, grinning with satisfaction, as Silver winced and rubbed her ankle. She was gazing up, giving Squires that little-girl-lost look. He couldn't hear what they were saying, but he already knew the script. It wouldn't be long before Squires offered to help her home . . . and that's where the fun would begin.

Danny got out of the car, put the hood up on his jacket and walked quickly towards Silverstone Heights. It was a gated community not far from the station, an estate protected by high walls and iron gates. He knew a guy, a broker in the City, who had a place there. The two of them had a nice little deal going: Danny kept him well supplied with coke, and in return he had use of the flat whenever he needed it.

He slowed down as he approached the gates, knowing that he was already well ahead. Silver would limp her way back to the Heights, clinging on to Squires's arm, thanking him, flattering him, saying he was a gentleman. She would ask him in for coffee and he would accept. Of course he would accept. He would make the discreet call to the wife, the excuse for being late – an emergency or a meeting or a client who had turned up out of the blue – and then he would follow the call of his loins.

Danny used the electronic card to get though the gates. He

walked past a row of mews houses and made his way over to the main block of flats. The large redbrick building had once been a Victorian asylum, although he doubted if any of its former inmates, had they been brought back from the dead, would recognise it now. It had been converted into luxury apartments, each one with its own balcony.

The foyer was warm – no scrimping on the heating here – and full of plants. The tiled floor was immaculately clean, or at least it had been until he'd stamped the snow off his shoes. He took the lift up to the third floor. The lift was spotless too, the metal panels polished and gleaming.

He unlocked the door to the flat and stepped inside. The spacious living room was decorated in neutral shades, the carpet beige, the curtains a pale mushroom brown. There was a brown leather sofa and two matching easy chairs, a table, some lamps and a widescreen plasma TV.

In order to disguise the obvious masculinity of the room, he and Silver had come over earlier and done their usual makeover. Now there were pink and cream cushions scattered on the sofa, a vase with pink roses, and copies of *Cosmopolitan*, *Vogue* and *Heat* magazine piled up on the coffee table. They had even emptied the bathroom cabinet of all the male toiletries and replaced them with female ones. It didn't do to be careless, to make stupid mistakes. It would be all too easy for the mark to get spooked, to figure something was wrong and do a runner.

Danny did a mental check. Yes, everything was in order. There was wine in the fridge, a few lines of coke in the kitchen drawer. You could never tell what these blokes were into. He went into the master bedroom and looked up at the camera that was attached to the ceiling and disguised as a smoke alarm. All set and ready to go.

He left and walked into the second, smaller bedroom, picked up the laptop and sat down on the bed. It wouldn't be long now. He listened out for the sound of the key in the lock. Whatever the guy was into, 'Ava' would oblige. Jeremy Squires was about to have all his dreams come true ... and then he would pay for it.

20

By the time Ava got back to Market Square, it was knocking on for seven. She had stayed at her father's for something to eat and then he had walked her off the estate and along to the corner of the high street. She'd told him she'd be fine, but he'd insisted on accompanying her.

'It's dark, love. There are all sorts hanging around.'

She hadn't raised any further objections. In truth, she was glad of the escort. The estate was a dubious place in daylight, but at night it was positively sinister. The lighting was bad and there were too many shadowy places for people to hide. She had linked her arm through his and together they had trudged through the snow. After the day she'd had, it had been nice to feel safe and secure, to know that – for the next five minutes at least – nothing bad was going to happen.

Ava didn't feel so confident, however, about the future. Now that she'd found out about the robbery, and her dad's part in it, she was scared that the law would catch up with him. The job might have gone off without a hitch, but that didn't mean anything. People had loose tongues. If another member of the gang got nabbed, they probably wouldn't think twice about grassing him up in exchange for a lighter sentence. The old rules of keeping shtum no matter what had long since gone out of the window and now it was every man for himself.

She slowed as she crossed the square. It might be Friday night, but she had nothing special to rush home for. 'Ava Gold,' she murmured, 'you have to get yourself a life.' She passed the cinema where there was a short queue waiting outside. It was ages since she'd last been to see a film. The couples huddled together against the cold, their intimacy reminding her of her own solitary status. Would she ever start dating again? The thought of trusting her heart to someone new filled her with fear and anxiety. Perhaps she would get a cat instead.

As she entered the flat, she could hear voices and music coming from the living room. She pushed open the door and three faces turned to look at her.

'Ah, there you are,' Tash said. 'Where have you been? We've been waiting ages.'

Ava, who hadn't been aware of any arrangements, frowned back at her. 'At my dad's. I didn't know—'

'Lydia's here,' said Tash brightly, gesturing with her hand in case Ava had failed to notice.

'Hi, Lydia.'

'Hi.'

Hannah crossed her legs and stared at her through suspicious eyes. 'What happened? Did you forget?'

Before Ava could reveal that there hadn't been anything to

forget, Tash jumped in again. 'It doesn't matter now. We've got wine. Why don't you grab yourself a glass?'

It only took Ava a few seconds to figure out what was going on. She smiled at Lydia and said, 'Sorry, have you been here long?'

'Only half an hour or so.'

'Good, that's good. I'll just go and get a glass, then.'

Tash followed her into the kitchen under the pretext of getting more snacks. 'Sorry,' she said in hushed, hurried tones. 'Hannah turned up out of the blue. I had to tell her that you'd invited Lydia over or ...'

'Or she'd have thought you were up to no good.'

'Something like that.'

'So now Lydia's my new best friend?'

Tash reached into the cupboard and took out a large pack of dry roasted peanuts. 'Not your *best* friend,' she said. 'That would be me. Just *a* friend, and Lydia's nice. I thought you liked her.'

'I do, although obviously not as much as you.'

Tash grinned. 'She's cute, don't you think?'

Ava took off her wet coat and draped it over the back of a chair. 'And what about Hannah?'

Tash glanced towards the living room and put a finger to her lips. 'What about her?'

'They can't hear us, not above the music. Look, if you don't want to be with her, why don't you tell her?'

'I do want to be with her. I love Hannah. It's just ... she can be so serious. And she gets so jealous. What's wrong with having a bit of fun now and then? It's not as if I'm going to cheat on her or anything.'

146

As if on cue, Hannah's voice rose over the dulcet tones of Emeli Sandé. 'What are you two doing in there?'

'Two secs,' Tash called back. She leaned over and squeezed Ava's arm. 'Thanks for this. You're a sweetheart.'

Ava shook her head, waiting a moment before joining the others. Personally, she thought Tash was playing with fire, but that was up to her. Although she wasn't happy about the deception, she knew she'd go along with it. She rummaged in her bag and took out her phone. No new messages. No missed calls. She wondered if she'd hear from Chris Street before the end of the day. As things stood, she still didn't have a clue if she was expected in on Monday or not. Hired or fired? If he made a decision, it would save her the trouble.

Ava left the phone on the table and picked up a clean glass from the side of the sink. Then she went into the living room. Tash and Hannah were sitting on the sofa, and Lydia was in the easy chair. Not wanting to squeeze in beside the happy couple, she got a cushion and sat down on the floor instead.

'Here,' said Tash, passing over the bottle of Chablis. 'Pour yourself a large one. You've got some catching up to do.'

Ava filled the glass and put the bottle down on the coffee table. She took a sip of wine, aware of Hannah's eyes boring into her. Tash's cover story, she suspected, hadn't been entirely believable. Quickly, Ava looked over at Lydia. 'So hey, thanks for coming. I'm sorry I was late. How's work going? I enjoyed the show. Did you sell much?'

Lydia sat forward and smiled. 'Oh yes, lots. It went really well. Someone even bought the rat.'

'You're kidding?' The image of the rat with its guts hanging out leapt into her head. 'My God, who'd want to own a thing like that?'

'You'd be surprised. Some of the collectors like the grotesque.'

'It's all grotesque,' said Hannah, giving an exaggerated shudder. 'Dead animals. It's sick.'

Lydia's smile faded away. She looked over at her, but didn't say anything.

'But some of the animals are quite beautiful,' Tash said.

Hannah snorted. 'Since when did you become such a fan? That's a new one. You told me you didn't like—'

'I said I didn't like a few of the exhibits. That's not the same as all of them.'

'Well, pardon me for hearing something completely different.'

Ava caught Lydia's eye and raised her eyebrows. She felt sorry for the girl, invited round for what she must have hoped would be a pleasant evening. There was an atmosphere that would make the most thick-skinned individual feel like running for the hills. 'So, are we staying in or should we go out somewhere?'

'What about Wilder's?' Lydia suggested.

Ava pulled a face, remembering the drama with Chris Street earlier that day. 'Anywhere but Wilder's.'

'What's wrong with it?' asked Hannah, itching for a fight. 'At least you can get a decent bottle of wine there.'

Ava was prepared to do pretty much anything to help out Tash, but she drew the line at returning to that bar. 'I'd rather not.'

'Oh, sorry, I forgot,' Lydia said. 'You don't like Guy Wilder, do you?'

'It's not that. I don't even know the man. It's just sort of awkward at the moment.'

'Awkward?' Hannah echoed. 'How do you mean awkward?'

Ava didn't want to go into detail, but she had to give some kind of explanation. 'Well, my boss doesn't get on with him so it makes things a bit difficult.'

Hannah stared at her. 'Right, so because Chris Street has a problem, we're not allowed to drink in Wilder's?'

Ava stared back. 'No one's saying you can't,' she replied coolly. 'You can drink wherever you like. I'd just prefer to keep my distance right now.'

'He's actually very nice,' Lydia said. 'Guy, I mean. He's very sweet. You should meet him sometime.'

'Yes,' Hannah said. 'And then you could make your own mind up instead of letting someone else make it up for you.'

Ava felt her hackles rise and made a point of mentally counting to ten. Hannah was out to provoke, but she wasn't going to rise to it. 'You're probably right,' she said, forcing a smile. 'Still, I'd rather not get involved in other people's arguments.'

'Aren't you already doing that?' Hannah said.

Ava bit her tongue. She'd had enough confrontation for one day.

'Let's go to the Fox instead,' Tash said.

Hannah shook her head. 'You work at the Fox, love. You don't want to go there on your night off.'

'Oh, I don't mind. It'll make a change being on the other side of the bar.' Tash jumped up. 'Yes, let's go the Fox.'

Ava uncurled her legs and stood up too. 'I'll get my coat.' She went into the kitchen, saw her phone on the table and checked again for any messages. The screen was still blank. As she was standing there, she heard the distant sound of a police siren and the breath caught in her throat. She thought of her father first – what if they were going to arrest him? – but quickly dismissed the idea. They wouldn't advertise the fact that they were on their way. Chris Street, however, was a different matter. Maybe he'd decided to go back to the bar and have it out with Wilder.

21

Chris stared hard at the gyrfalcon and the falcon stared back at him. It was a competition that he could never win, but he persisted in trying out of sheer perversity. He'd been drinking on and off all day, and although he wasn't slaughtered he had reached that point where his thoughts were getting frayed around the edges.

'So,' he said to the bird. 'Is this how it's going to be from now on? Me doing all the talking and you just sitting there? I mean, you could at least try and make an effort.'

The glass dome had been delivered to Belles and then sent on by taxi to Walpole Close. Chris could have picked it up from the office in the morning, but for some reason – perhaps because of the whisky he'd been pouring down his throat – he'd decided he had to have it straight away.

'You're a bloody expensive bird, considering you do fuck all,' he said.

The bird's glassy eyes gazed back at him.

'You'd better be worth it.' The deal with Borovski was still hanging in the balance. The Russian's new casino, slap on the border of Shoreditch and Kellston, was due to open in a couple of months. It was a matter of opinion as to whether this was actually in Street territory or not. Borovski, however, was reluctant to pay out protection money. A compromise deal was being negotiated, whereby the Streets would provide the security, and possibly some girls. It would be a nice little earner if it came off. But you couldn't trust the Russians. Say one thing and do another. Jesus, you couldn't trust anyone these days, not even your bloody ex-wife.

'Okay,' he said to the falcon. 'You win.' He dropped his gaze to the mobile phone, still sitting silently on the arm of the chair. Despite Ava's advice, he had been trying to ring Jenna all evening. The cow wasn't picking up. Straight to voicemail every time. So she was avoiding him. That didn't come as any great surprise. But she'd have to talk to him eventually.

His hands curled into two tight fists. He'd been fighting the urge to storm down to Wilder's for the last couple of hours. But it would be a waste of time. He knew it would. Noah would have tipped his partner off about the earlier visit, and Wilder would be keeping his head down.

He jumped up, poured himself another glass of whisky and went over to the French windows. He opened them out and stepped on to the patio. He felt the air hit his face, a blast of icy cold that partly sobered him up. The garden was covered in a thick blanket of snow. He pictured what he'd like to do to Guy Wilder and the thought was crystal clear. It would almost be worth the time he'd serve for the satisfaction of putting a bullet through the bastard's heart.

He heard a car pull up on the drive and then the sound of the engine cutting out. Two doors slamming. And then voices, laughter. Danny and Silver. A minute later, they breezed into the living room.

'For Christ's sake,' Danny said. 'Shut the bleedin' doors. It's freezing in here.'

Chris turned to look at them. 'Where's the old man? Isn't he with you?'

'Why would he be with us?'

Chris went back inside, closing the French windows behind him. 'I thought you might have been at Belles.'

'Nah, we've not been to the club.'

Silver took off her white fur coat and draped it over the back of the sofa. 'We've been somewhere else, babe.' She gave that little-girl giggle that Chris found so irritating. 'We've been keeping well busy.'

Chris watched as she sat down and flipped off her bright red shoes. Her toenails were painted the same shade of scarlet. 'I'm sure you have.'

She ran her tongue along her lips. 'Don't you want to know what we've been doing, hon?'

'No, he don't,' Danny said, throwing her a warning glance. 'He don't want to know fuck all.'

Chris reckoned they were both high. When weren't they? They were always shoving something up their noses, or smoking dope, or popping pills. The two of them were a walking, talking chemical factory. 'You're right. I couldn't give a toss. So you don't have a clue where Dad is?'

Danny gave a shrug. 'Out and about.'

But out and about was what Chris was worried about, especially if his father was back at the Fox going on about Joe Quinn again. How long before people began to talk? He'd been kidding himself for ages now that it was just the booze, that there was nothing wrong with the old man, but it was getting worse by the day. And it was more than mere forgetfulness; some of the things he was doing were completely off the wall. Take that episode at Belles, for instance, when he was shouting out for Lizzie. That wasn't right. That wasn't normal.

'No hot date tonight?' Silver asked.

Chris sat down on one of the black leather recliners. He swirled the whisky around in the glass and checked his phone again. Still nothing. Not even a text. 'Does it look like it?'

Danny poured a couple of drinks, gave one to Silver and sat down beside her on the sofa. 'Not going so well with Mercedes Girl, then?'

'Ava,' Silver said. 'Her name's Ava.' She looked over at Chris. 'Isn't it, hon?'

Chris gave a grunt, wishing that he'd never lied about Ava being his girlfriend. If the truth came out, he'd be a bloody laughing stock.

'Are you waiting for her to call? Ah, ain't that sweet.' She gave Danny's leg a nudge with her foot. 'Ain't that sweet, babe?'

'If you say so.'

'It is. It is sweet. And how is the lovely Ava, Chris? What's she doing tonight?'

She and Danny exchanged a look and they both sniggered.

154

Chris stared back at the two of them. What were they up to? There was something going on. Did they know the truth about Ava? Were they laughing at *him*? No, they couldn't know. How could they? He was being paranoid. It was just the booze messing with his head.

Danny leaned back and smirked. 'You need to keep an eye on your bird, bro. She could be up to all sorts.'

'Oh yeah?'

'Yeah, you got to keep 'em on a tight leash or they'll screw you over. It's in their nature, see. They just can't help themselves.'

Chris shook his head. 'Tell me you're not trying to give me relationship advice.' Ironically, Ava appeared to be the one person he *could* actually trust. If he'd been caught with that shooter, he'd be down the cells right now. He wondered why she'd done it. She'd taken one hell of a risk. But then what motivated women to do anything? Take Jenna, for example. Of all the men in London, she had to choose Wilder to shag. He felt the familiar fury growing in his chest again. Why? Why had she gone there? If he'd dumped *her*, he'd have understood. Revenge is sweet and all the rest of it. But she was the one who'd done the walking.

'Now you've made him angry,' Silver said. 'Look, his face has gone all red.'

Chris glared at her. 'I'm not angry.'

'Well, you look mad. You look all hot and bothered. Don't you reckon, Danny? Don't you think he looks angry?'

'Nah, he always looks like that.'

Silver inclined her head and gazed at Chris. 'No, not always. I think Ava might be breaking his heart.'

'Can we stop talking about her, please.'

'See?' Silver said. 'He doesn't want to talk about her. That's not a good sign.'

Chris buried his face in his glass. She was like Trojan; once she got her teeth into something, she wouldn't let go. He was reminded of the dead rat, of the stench of death. There was something wrong about Silver. She pretended to care, but she didn't really. She just liked to mess with other people's heads.

Danny finally noticed the falcon and screwed up his eyes as if he might be seeing things. 'What the fuck's that thing doing here?'

Chris, glad of the change of subject, tapped the top of the dome. 'It's for Borovski. What do you reckon?'

'Where did you get it?'

'Beast.'

Silver gave another of her giggles. 'Did you buy it off Morton Carlisle?'

Chris frowned. 'How do you know Carlisle?'

She leaned into Danny's shoulder and gave one of her sly smiles. 'I know everybody, hon.'

'How much you pay for it?' Danny asked.

'Too much.'

Silver got off the sofa, knelt down by the coffee table and stared into the dome. 'Is it a boy or a girl?'

'How the fuck would he know?' Danny said. 'When it comes to birds, he hasn't got a clue.'

Silver giggled again and pressed her nose against the glass. 'Look at its claws.'

'Talons,' Danny said. 'Didn't they teach you nothin' at that posh school of yours?'

'Schools,' Silver said. 'I got expelled from most of them.'

Chris was tempted to ask what she'd been expelled for, but then decided that he'd rather not know. He wondered how much money Delaney had squandered in trying to turn his daughter into something other than she was.

'We should open a casino,' Danny said. 'It's easy money. The house always wins in the end.'

Chris finished his drink and put the glass down on the coffee table. 'Yeah, next time we've got a few million in the bank, we should do that.'

'The Russian's got cash, loads of it.'

'And he didn't get rich by giving it away.' Chris picked up his phone and rose to his feet. 'Right, I'm off to bed.'

Silver gazed up at him, her eyes flicking quickly from the phone to his face. 'You going to call her? You going to call Ava?'

'Why should I do that?'

'Maybe she's missing you, hon. Maybe she *wants* you to call.'

Chris thought he heard a kind of mockery in her voice, but he couldn't be sure. You could never be sure of anything with Silver.

22

The text from Chris Street was waiting on Ava's phone when she woke up in the morning. **Meet me in Connolly's at ten.** No please or thank you. No indication of what it was about. Well, she could guess what it was about. But what did the actual summoning mean? Maybe he was going to fire her. Or maybe he just wanted to make sure that she was going to keep her mouth shut about the gun. As she still hadn't come to a firm decision about what *she* wanted to do, she decided that the best thing was to hear him out and take it from there.

She brushed her teeth, took a shower, and dressed in jeans and a warm jumper. In the kitchen, she made toast and a cup of coffee and sat down at the table to eat. Tash and Hannah, thankfully, were still in bed. She'd had enough of Hannah's sniping last night and didn't want a re-run over breakfast.

The evening at the Fox had been interesting if not entirely comfortable. Hannah, suspicious of Lydia's intentions, had subjected the girl to an interrogation of which the Gestapo would have been proud. If Lydia had been at all fazed, however, she hadn't shown it. She had answered Hannah's questions with smiling equanimity.

. Ava buttered her toast, added a thin layer of marmalade and took a bite. While she chewed she thought some more about Lydia. Although she seemed on the surface a pleasant enough sort of person, there was something a little odd about her. She couldn't exactly put her finger on it. Was she aware of Tash's attraction to her or had she accepted the invitation to come round to Market Square purely on face value? Ava still had no idea if she was straight or gay, or if Tash's interest in her was in any way reciprocated. Hannah clearly suspected the worst, but then that was Hannah's nature.

At ten to ten, Ava put on her coat and made her way out to the square. The snow had stopped falling, but there was still a thick layer on the ground. It scrunched under her boots, the cold seeping up through her soles. The market was in full swing, the traders doing brisk business despite the weather, and she breathed in the mingling smells of frying onions, curry and soup.

She stopped to browse through a display of hand-knitted scarves, almost tempted to buy one until she remembered that she might not actually have a job any more. Reluctantly, she laid the scarf back on the stall. Maybe she would come back later.

By the time she had forged a path through the crowds, it was almost ten o'clock. Dodging the cars, she crossed over the high street and pushed open the door to Connolly's. She was met by a welcome rush of warm air and a babble of voices.

The café was packed and there were no empty tables. She looked around, wondering if he was there yet, but then suddenly spotted him.

Chris Street was sitting by the window. He raised his head and gave her a nod. It was impossible to tell from his expression whether this was a friendly greeting or not.

'I wasn't sure you'd come,' he said as she pulled out the chair and sat down opposite him.

'Well, here I am.'

There was a brief awkward silence. Ava filled it by shrugging off her coat and hanging it over the back of the chair. Then she turned to face him again. He looked tired, as if he hadn't slept. He clearly hadn't shaved either. There was a bluish tinge to his cheeks and jaw that might have passed for designer stubble if his eyes hadn't been rimmed with red.

'You want a brew?' he asked.

'Coffee, please. White, no sugar.'

Chris caught the attention of a passing waitress and placed the order. He picked up his mug of tea, raised it to his lips and then put it down again without taking a drink. 'I think we need to talk.'

'Fire away,' she said.

'About yesterday.'

Ava waited, but he didn't carry on. A few seconds passed. 'About yesterday?' she prompted.

'Yeah. It was stupid, what I did.' He leaned in closer to her, lowering his voice. 'I shouldn't have ... I put you in a bad position. I just got wound up, you know, about everything. It all got out of hand.'

'Right,' Ava said.

'So I was thinking maybe we could draw a line under it, start again.'

Just like that, she thought. All swept under the carpet and forgotten about. He hadn't even apologised, not properly. It was his lack of contrition that provoked her reply. 'Maybe I don't want the job any more.'

'Don't you?'

The waitress arrived with the coffee and put the white mug down on the table.

'Thanks,' Ava said. She waited until the woman had left before answering. 'I'm not sure. I haven't decided. Not if . . . well, not if you make a habit of . . . ' She couldn't say the words out loud, not when they were surrounded by people. 'You know.'

'It was a one-off,' he said. 'It won't happen again.'

She shrugged. 'Easy to say.'

Chris Street smiled for the first time. 'Come on, you don't really want to go back on the cabs. Especially with Christmas coming up – all those drunken parties, all the abuse, all those fares throwing up in the back seat of your taxi. It'll be hell and you know it.'

'Good tips, though,' she said.

'It'll cost you more in detergent.'

'That's emotional blackmail.'

Chris lifted his hands, palms up. 'So what do you want me to say?'

'Sorry would be a start.'

'Okay, I'm sorry. I'm really sorry. I behaved like an arse.' He paused and smiled again. 'Now will you come back or do you want me to beg?'

'You can easily get another driver.'

'Not one I can trust,' he said.

Ava thought about that moment when she'd recklessly slipped the gun into her bag. 'I didn't do what I did to protect you. Don't flatter yourself. Don't even think that because it isn't true. I did it because I needed the job. I wouldn't have had the job if you were caught with . . . if you were nicked and thrown into the slammer.'

'Job's still here,' he said. 'Be a shame to waste it.'

She drank some coffee and looked at him over the rim of the mug. 'So we just start again?'

'Why not? A clean slate. What do you reckon?'

'And what happens next time you want to pay Mr Wilder a visit?'

He flinched a little at the mention of the name. 'Then I'll walk,' he said. 'Or I'll take a taxi.'

'And you won't get me involved?'

'No, I won't get you involved.'

She gave a nod. 'Fair enough.'

'So shall we say Monday, ten o'clock. Pick me up as usual?'

She hesitated. 'Erm . . . '

'What now?'

'Well, if we're talking clean slates, there's something I need to tell you. I would have mentioned it yesterday only . . . '

'What is it?'

Ava drank some more coffee while she tried to formulate the words in her head. Was she doing the right thing in telling him? He might go off at the deep end again. But she didn't want to go back to work with it still hanging over her. Finally, she put the mug down and began to explain. 'There was an exhibition at Beast Thursday afternoon. I wouldn't have gone only my flatmate dragged me along. Anyway, Wilder was there doling out the cocktails.' She paused, waiting to see how he'd react. A muscle twitched at the corner of his left eye, but nothing more drastic. She carried on. 'And there was someone else there too: the Russian bloke, the guy you bought the falcon for.'

'Borovski?'

'Yes, that's the one.' She worried on her lower lip for a moment. 'I mean, there was no reason why he *shouldn't* be there. It was a taxidermy exhibition and he's obviously into that kind of stuff, but . . .'

'But?'

'But he spent quite a while talking to Wilder and I got the impression . . . well, I got the impression they knew each other pretty well. Pally, you know. No, more than that. Comfortable, easy. Like they'd been friends for a long time.' She stopped again and gave a shrug. 'It probably doesn't mean anything, but if you're doing business with him . . .'

Chris frowned and thought about it. 'Wilder and Borovski?'

'I could have got it wrong,' she said. 'It was only an impression. I didn't hear anything they said.'

He frowned some more and then scratched his chin. 'Okay. That's interesting. Thanks for telling me.'

Ava gave a nod. Well, he'd taken that more calmly than she'd expected – or was he just too hungover to be able to think it through properly? 'So that's it,' she said. 'Everything out in the open.'

Chris gave a nod, but his eyes wouldn't meet hers. He quickly lowered his gaze to the table.

'Isn't it?' asked Ava, feeling a flicker of apprehension.

He glanced up at her again. 'If we're clearing the decks, there is *one* other thing.'

Ava sighed. What now? She braced herself for bad news, for some disturbing revelation that she might not be able to deal with. 'Go on.'

'It's to do with Danny.' He pulled a face, looking embarrassed. 'He's kind of got the idea that we're an item. You see, being the male chauvinist pig that he is, he doesn't think I'd actually hire a woman to be my driver and so he reckons something else must be going on.'

She smiled, relieved that it was nothing more serious. 'So why don't you just put him straight?'

'Ah, well, I would, only his crazy girlfriend keeps trying to fix me up with one of her mates, and so . . . '

'And so you'd prefer to have an imaginary girlfriend.'

'Something like that.'

Ava laughed. 'God, how old are you?'

Chris looked taken aback. 'What's that got to do with anything?'

'You're a grown man,' she said. 'Can't you just tell him to push off and mind his own business?'

'I could, but it wouldn't make a blind bit of difference. And I'm telling you, this girl he's seeing is completely nuts. Believe me, it's easier this way.' He picked up a teaspoon and twisted it around in his fingers. 'Unless you're uncomfortable with the idea. I mean, I'd understand if you were. It's a bit weird, I guess.'

'No,' she said. 'I sort of get it. After I split up with Alec, people were always trying to fix me up with someone else.

They just don't get that you might be happier on your own. God, the amount of dinner parties I was invited to where there was always a spare male who would be "just right" for me.'

'And are you?'

'Am I what?'

'Happier on your own?'

'Yes,' she said. 'I think so. For the most part. It can be lonelier being with someone who doesn't love you than it is being single.' She felt his eyes on her and coloured a little, realising that she'd said more than she meant to. 'But anyway, isn't there a flaw in this great plan of yours? I mean, aren't they going to wonder why I'm never round at your place, why I never stay over?'

'Oh, I'll think of something.'

'A dog, maybe,' she suggested. 'I could have a dog that I don't like to leave on its own overnight.'

'What kind of dog?'

'How should I know? You decide. Something not too big, though – and not too small either. I don't want one of those handbag dogs. And we'll have to come up with a name. You can't have a dog with no name.'

He drank some of his tea and grinned. 'This could get complicated.'

'You started it. Maybe next time you'll think twice about getting involved with an employee.'

'So does that mean you'll be coming back to work, then?'

'I suppose so. I've not had any better offers.'

'Monday, then. I'll see you at ten.'

Ava took a couple of pound coins out of her purse and put them on the table for the coffee.

Chris waved the money away. 'It's on me.'

'Thanks,' she said. 'But you still owe me sixty quid.'

'You'll get it.'

'I know I will.' She got up, put on her coat and said goodbye. As she left the café, she wondered if she'd made the right decision. Oh well, there was no going back now. She gave a small shake of her head as she trudged towards the flat. Last night, courtesy of Tash, she'd had to pretend that Lydia was her new best friend. Now she had to pretend – to his brother and his crazy girlfriend – that Chris Street was her lover. Her imaginary life had taken on a whole new dimension. Still, at least her job was real. That was something to be grateful for.

23

DI Valerie Middleton gazed through the slats of the blind into the incident room beyond. It was early Saturday afternoon and everything was quiet. It was, however, only the lull before the storm. When darkness fell, the partying would begin and then it was just a matter of time before things started to fall apart. Even before last orders had been called, parts of Kellston would erupt into booze-fuelled chaos. There'd be the usual brawling, rows and recriminations. Not to mention the human debris sprawled in the gutters. Still, unless something especially bad happened, it wouldn't be her problem. It made her glad she was no longer in uniform.

She watched as DS Laura Higgs walked across the incident room and perched on the edge of Preston's desk. Higgs leaned down and said something and Preston glanced towards the office and laughed. Were they talking about her? Even though she'd been doing the job for years – and doing it successfully enough to gain regular promotions – she was aware of not being particularly liked. Respected, hopefully, but not liked. She was the Ice Queen or Blondie or any of a number of other deprecating nicknames that came and went depending on the current mood.

All senior officers had their own style. Some were chummy, one of the lads, but she preferred to keep a professional distance. She knew it made her seem standoffish, even cold, but it was the way she coped with the responsibilities of the job. Being a woman and a blonde meant that she often had to try twice as hard in order to be taken seriously. Occasionally, she would join her team for a drink at the Fox, but she never felt entirely comfortable. It was as if her presence inhibited the natural flow of conversation, creating an atmosphere in which the others couldn't completely relax.

Laura Higgs stood up and walked towards the office, still grinning from the exchange with Preston. She was a solid, sturdy-looking woman in her early thirties with a round face and short brown hair. Under her arm, she was carrying a folder. She knocked lightly on the door.

'Come in.'

'It's about Finian's, guv,' said Higgs, flapping the folder in the air. 'We might finally have something.'

Valerie nodded. 'Good.' She gestured towards the chair on the other side of her desk, and Higgs sat down. The robbery at Finian's had been a slick professional job, the gang getting away with thousands of pounds' worth of stock. The small amount of grainy CCTV coverage – acquired before the cameras had been smashed – revealed that five men had been involved, all of them wearing masks. The plates of the dark-coloured van had been obscured. Despite pulling in the usual suspects, they hadn't yet got a result. The gang had gone to ground and there wasn't a sniff of the stolen goods.

Laura Higgs put the folder on the desk and flipped it open. 'I got a couple of names from my snouts, but one's a definite no-go. Barry Tanner?'

'He's inside, isn't he?'

'Doing a five-stretch in Pentonville. Been there since August.'

'And the other one?'

'Well, this one's more promising: Jimmy Gold. He's Ted Gold's brother.' Higgs paused, and then added somewhat disdainfully, 'Oh, Ted Gold used to run the car lot on the high street. He was a bit of a villain, but we never caught him at it. Getaway cars, stolen vehicles, that kind of thing. He retired to Spain a while back.'

Valerie smiled tightly back at her. 'I'm well aware of that.' Despite the fact that Valerie had been at Cowan Road for years, Higgs always insisted on treating her as if she'd turned up yesterday. It was one of the reasons she disliked her so much. Another was the fact that the woman was a compulsive gossip. 'Jimmy's been clean for ages, hasn't he?'

'Well, he hasn't been charged with anything,' Higgs said. 'Maybe he's just getting smarter in his old age.'

Valerie reached across the desk, retrieved the file and studied the hazy photographs that had been taken off the CCTV. 'The driver, I presume?'

'Yeah.'

Valerie continued to stare at the pictures, but there was no way of identifying any of the men. 'You can't tell a damn thing from these. You couldn't prove it one way or the other.'

Higgs leaned forward with a smug expression on her face. 'Except I just heard something interesting from Kevin Wheelan.'

'Go on.' Wheelan was a uniformed constable, an older officer who kept his ear to the ground. He'd been in Kellston longer than any of them and had an encyclopaedic knowledge of every villain that frequented the area.

'He says that he stopped Chris Street's Mercedes the other day. It jumped a red light, apparently.'

Valerie gave a short laugh. 'Oh, make my day. Please tell me that he was driving.' If she had one ambition in her life, it was to nail at least one of the Streets. They ran half the crime in the area, and took a percentage of the other half.

'Sadly not, but guess who was?'

'Don't tell me. Jimmy Gold?'

Higgs shook her head. 'Not quite.'

'So who?'

'His daughter, Ava.'

Valerie frowned. The name didn't mean anything to her. 'Has she got form?'

'Nothing. Wheelan ran a check, but she's clean. Bit of a coincidence, though, don't you think? Jimmy's in the frame for this robbery and his daughter's driving Chris Street around.'

'A warehouse robbery, though? That's not like the Streets.'

'Times are tough,' Higgs said. 'Maybe they're branching out. And the stock in that place was worth a mint. How about doing a search of Belles or the Lincoln? They could have the gear stashed there.'

Valerie shook her head. 'We'd never get a warrant, not on that kind of evidence. It's way too flimsy.'

'Depends on how you present it,' said Higgs slyly.

'Whichever way you present it.' Valerie liked to do things by the book, straight down the line and no funny business. Other officers were less fussy about how they got their convictions. She knew that if you started bending the rules it wouldn't be long before you were as corrupt as the villains you were trying to catch.

Higgs, however, wasn't giving up. 'But if we wait, guv, they could shift the gear. That's if they haven't got rid of it already. It could be halfway across the country by now.'

'It could be, but then again they might just be sitting tight and waiting for the dust to settle. If we do a search of Belles or the Lincoln and the Streets *are* involved, they're going to know we're on to them. Anyway, I don't think they'd stash the gear in either of those places. It's way too risky. It's more likely they've got a lock-up somewhere.'

Higgs wrinkled her nose. 'What about giving Jimmy Gold a tug?'

'No, we'll hold fire for now.'

Higgs pulled a face, her expression as sour as if she was sucking on a lemon.

'You got a problem, Sergeant?'

'No, guv.'

'Good.' Valerie closed the folder and pushed it back across the desk. 'Do a bit of digging into this Ava Gold and see what you can find out about her. And let's check out the security guys at the business park again. It could have been an inside job. Keep me informed, huh?'

'Yes, guv.'

Higgs picked up the folder and left the office.

Valerie watched through the slats as the sergeant crossed the incident room. She never thought she would say it, but she actually missed her usual right-hand man, Kieran Swann. He might be irritating and provocative, but at least she knew where she stood. It was typical that he'd chosen to take his annual leave just as the Street connection had emerged – although why anyone would choose to holiday in Clacton in November, one of the bleakest months of the calendar year with its short dark days and almost guaranteed bad weather, was beyond her.

She sat back and thought some more about the Streets. They'd been getting away with it for way too long. Perhaps, finally, she would get the opportunity to rid Kellston of the whole damn lot of them.

24

When Ava got back to the flat in Market Square, it was to find Hannah lounging on the sofa reading a copy of Saturday's *Guardian.*

'No Tash?' asked Ava, looking around.

'She's gone to pick up supplies, some ribbon and the like. She won't be long.'

'Oh, okay.' Reluctant to try and make small talk – Hannah was always hard work in that department – Ava headed for the kitchen and put the kettle on even though she'd only just had a coffee in Connolly's. She'd known Hannah for months, but the two of them had never clicked. Having endured her sniping the previous night, she wasn't in the mood for another round of verbal sparring.

Unfortunately, Hannah decided to follow her. She stood leaning against the door with her arms folded across her chest. 'Been anywhere nice?'

'Just some window shopping,' said Ava, not wanting to

reveal what she'd really been doing. 'But it's too cold to hang about out there.'

'Yes, I popped out for a paper earlier. It is a touch chilly.'

Ava picked up a couple of mugs from the draining board. She had no choice, now that Hannah was almost in the kitchen, but to ask the polite question. 'I was just making a drink. Would you like one?'

'Go on, then. Thanks. I'll have a tea. Lappie, please, no milk or sugar.'

Ava reached into the cupboard for the box of Lapsang Souchong tea bags that was never touched unless Hannah was here. She dropped one of the bags into a mug along with a teaspoon.

'That's a lovely sweater,' Hannah said. 'The colour really suits you.'

Ava glanced down at the dark red sweater that Hannah must have seen her in twenty times before. What was with the sudden niceness? Perhaps she was feeling bad about last night, regretting that she'd been so rude. 'Thank you. I got it from the market.'

'Really? You couldn't tell.'

Ava smiled and turned back towards the boiling kettle. Somehow, even when Hannah was trying to be nice, it didn't quite come off. She made the drinks and passed over the tea, hoping that Hannah would retreat into the living room, but no such luck. Instead she sat down at the kitchen table, making it clear that she wanted to chat.

'So how's the job going?'

'Good, thanks,' replied Ava breezily. She hadn't mentioned the episode with the gun to Tash. Pillow talk could be a dangerous thing, and she hadn't wanted to take the risk of it becoming common knowledge. 'Yours?'

'Oh, you know, same as.'

Ava didn't know. What did accountants do all day? She had a mental image of a dusty Dickensian office with rows of identically dressed men totting up figures with quill pens. But things, she presumed, had progressed quite a lot since then.

There was a short silence.

'Well,' said Ava, thinking that she might use this opportunity to escape to her bedroom.

She was still standing with her back against the sink. 'I suppose I'd better get on.'

But Hannah had other ideas. 'So how long have you and Lydia been friends?'

The question was posed with a casualness that didn't deceive Ava for a second. Ah, so that was what this was all about. 'Not long. She only moved here a few months back.'

'Where was she living before?'

'I've no idea. Why?'

Hannah gave a shrug. 'I was just curious. Don't you think she's a little . . . I don't know, evasive?'

'Is she? I can't say I've noticed.'

'Yes. It's hard to get a straight answer out of the girl.' Hannah paused as if waiting for Ava to respond, but when she didn't she carried on regardless. 'The minute I started asking her about herself, where she came from, if she had a partner or not, she completely clammed up. I could hardly get a word out of her.'

'Maybe she's just shy.'

'She doesn't give that impression.'

'Private, then. Perhaps she doesn't like talking about herself.'

Hannah gave a small dismissive shake of her head as if this explanation didn't wash. 'No, I don't think so. I reckon there's more to it.'

'Such as?'

Hannah didn't answer directly. 'And working in that place, that taxidermy shop. That's weird, don't you think? I mean, what sort of person wants to be surrounded by dead animals all day?'

'It's a job,' Ava said with a touch of impatience. Hannah, with her colossal salary and high-flying position in the City, didn't have a clue when it came to how the other half lived. 'People can't afford to be fussy when they've got bills to pay.'

'But she *likes* it. She told me she did.'

'Well, so what? We can't all like the same things.' Ava glanced at her watch as if she had things to do, people to see.

Hannah, having gained an unexpected chance to interrogate her while Tash was out of the way, now sensed that time was running out. Before Ava could make her escape, she said rather slyly, 'I suppose it must make it awkward, her being so close to Guy Wilder and all.'

'I wasn't aware that she was.'

Hannah gave a small triumphant smile. 'Oh, yes. Hadn't you heard? Those two are real buddies. Why do you think she wanted to go to the bar last night? I'm surprised you didn't know, you two being such good mates.'

Ava, aware of being wrong-footed, racked her brains for a suitable response. Why hadn't she known? And since when had Hannah become an expert on Lydia Hall? So far as she was aware, last night was the first time the two women had met. She wanted to ask, but wasn't prepared to give Hannah the satisfaction. 'What difference does it make? She can be friends with whoever she likes. I haven't got anything against Wilder.'

'But your boss has.'

'So what?'

Hannah's eyebrows shifted up a little. 'You don't think he might be concerned, knowing that you're spending so much time with someone who's that close to his greatest enemy?'

'One evening,' Ava said. 'It's hardly a huge amount of time.'

'Still,' said Hannah smugly. 'He might not like it.'

Ava knew that she was trying to drive a wedge between herself and Lydia. Realising that Tash had an interest in the younger girl, Hannah wanted her out of the way. She thought back to the day of the exhibition at Beast when Lydia had offered to introduce her to Guy Wilder. *I suppose you're immune to his charms.* Wasn't that what she'd said? 'Actually, I think Lydia's got a bit of a crush on Wilder.'

Hannah's face instantly brightened at this piece of news. 'Really?'

Ava didn't have a clue as to whether this was true or not, but if it got Hannah off her back it was worth claiming. 'Don't say anything to her, though. She'll only be embarrassed.'

'No, I won't. Of course I won't.'

Before the exchange could continue, the door to the flat opened and closed, and seconds later Tash came into the kitchen carrying a shopping bag. Her cheeks and the tip of her nose were pink from the cold, and her eyes were shining.

'Hi there,' said Tash, rubbing her hands together. 'God, it's cold out there.' She dumped the bag on the table and went to perch on the radiator.

'You'll get piles doing that,' Hannah said.

Tash laughed. 'Better that than a cold bum.' She glanced from one woman to the other. 'So what have you two been up to?'

Hannah rose to her feet. 'Oh, nothing much. Just having a natter. I need the loo. I'll be back in a minute.'

Ava waited until she heard the bathroom door close before saying softly, 'A natter? I've just been interrogated to within an inch of my life.'

'About Lydia?'

'Who else? She's suspicious, Tash. She's definitely on to you.'

Tash tilted her head and grinned. 'Actually, I've been to see the lovely Lydia. I popped into Beast on my way home.'

'Are you mad?' Ava gave her a despairing look. 'If Hannah finds out, she'll have a fit.'

'She won't find out.'

'You hope.'

'I know,' Tash said. 'Anyway, it doesn't matter because Lydia isn't interested in me. She likes you, though.'

'What makes you say that?'

'Because she kept asking questions about you.'

'She was probably just making conversation.'

Tash pushed a strand of hair behind her ear. 'No, it was more than that. She was definitely fishing. Wanting to know what you liked doing, what kind of music you were into, that kind of thing. She even asked if Chris Street was your boyfriend or just your boss.'

Ava furrowed her brow. 'Why would she want to know that?'

'Because she likes you, hon. That's what people do when they like you.'

Ava wasn't so sure. She remembered what Hannah had said earlier about Lydia being close to Guy Wilder. 'Can I ask you something?'

But Ava never got the chance to ask. There was the sound of the loo flushing, then a brief pause before the door to the bathroom opened again. Tash quickly raised a finger to her lips.

'Later,' she whispered. 'Ask me later.'

25

Noah slid out of bed and went to the bathroom for a shower. By the time he got back, Guy was awake, propped up on an elbow with the duvet pushed aside. He was gazing towards the window which, despite the layer of snow on the ground, revealed a square of sky the colour of cornflowers.

Even after all these years, Noah was still aroused by the sight of his lover's nakedness. His gaze raked over Guy's body, taking in the strong muscular arms, the smooth planes of his chest, the curve of his spine. A shaft of winter sun came through the glass, turning his fair hair to a gleaming gold.

It was Guy's expression, dark and brooding, that prompted him to ask a question he would never normally ask.

'What are you thinking?'

Guy's lips parted as if for once he might be about to share the innermost secrets of his mind, but then the familiar mask slid over his features again. He smiled and shook his head. 'Nothing worth repeating.'

Noah didn't press him. He sat down on the edge of the bed, knowing that this intimate time together would shortly be coming to an end and wanting to savour what remained of it.

Soon they'd be putting on their clothes, going downstairs and opening the bar. Guy would be absorbed into the lunch-time crowd, the centre of other people's attention instead of his own.

'Is Jenna coming over tonight?' asked Noah as casually as he could manage.

'Yes.'

'No second thoughts, then?'

Guy twisted round to lie flat on his back. He put his hands behind his head. 'Life's too short for second thoughts.'

'Yeah? Well yours is going to be even shorter when Chris Street catches up with you.'

'That man's prehistoric, a machismo-fuelled dinosaur. It's none of his business what his *ex*-wife chooses to do.'

But Noah couldn't be so blasé about it. He'd spent the last twenty-four hours in a state of anxiety, wondering when Street would walk back in and finish what he'd started. Guy wasn't so much fearless, he thought, as utterly reckless. If Jenna had actually meant something to him, then the risk might have been worth taking, but Guy was only using her. She was bait, a tethered goat, a means to an end.

'What time is it?' Guy asked.

Noah picked up his watch from the bedside cabinet. 'Twenty to eleven.' Then, in an absent-minded fashion, he opened the top drawer and closed it. It was only after he'd closed it that he became aware of something being missing. Quickly, he opened the drawer again.

'Where is it?'

'What?'

'You know what. The gun. Where's the gun?'

'Oh that,' said Guy in a languid fashion. 'I got rid of it.'

The gun, a small Beretta semi-automatic, had been in the drawer for the past five years. Noah had always hated the thing, but now that it was gone he wished that it wasn't. 'And what if Chris Street does come after you? How are you going to defend yourself?'

Guy's mouth widened into a smile. 'Well, not by saying *Excuse me while I just nip upstairs for my gun.* I mean, it's not exactly practical, is it?'

'But why now?' Noah asked.

'You've been telling me to get rid of it for ages.'

'And since when did you listen to anything I said?'

'Don't be like that,' Guy said. 'I've done what you wanted. You should be pleased.'

Noah ran his fingers over the smooth mahogany of the cabinet. 'What did you do with it?'

'I put it out with the rubbish.'

Noah stared at him, his eyes widening with alarm. 'You did what? For Christ's sake, if anyone . . . ' But then he saw Guy's face and stopped. 'Yeah, very funny. So what did you really do with it?'

'Dumped it in the river. It's gone. You don't have to worry any more.'

Noah thought of the gun leaving Guy's hand, moving

through the air and falling down towards the water. He thought of the splash it would make, and then the twisting and turning as it spun through the cold murky depths until it came to rest amidst the tangled weeds of the river bed. He gave an involuntary shudder. Sweat prickled on his forehead. He was having one of those eerie, inexplicable sensations as if someone was walking over his grave.

26

Danny flicked through the photos on his phone, trying to decide on the best picture to use. They were all good, all compromising, but he needed to find one that was thoroughly obscene. Although it was only twenty-four hours since the set-up, he wanted to strike while the iron was hot. Eventually, he chose a particularly graphic shot that left nothing to the imagination. He got it ready to send and then dialled the number that Morton Carlisle had given him.

It was picked up after a couple of rings. 'Yes?'

'Mr Squires?'

'That's right. Who is this?'

'My name's Danny, Mr Squires. I just wanted to make sure that you had your phone on you.'

'I'm sorry?'

'I'm about to send through a message. It's a little delicate, something that you might not want the wife to see. I'd appreciate it if you'd call me straight back.'

'What are you—'

Danny hung up before he had the chance to finish the sentence. Then, with a grin on his face, he sent through the photograph. It would be a few minutes, maybe even five or ten, before he got a call back. The man would panic, sweat, shit himself and think about his options. And then, when he realised that he didn't have any, he would finally make the call. That was okay. That was fine. He didn't mind waiting.

Danny lit a cigarette to help pass the time. He bent down and patted Trojan. 'It won't be long now, boy. Everyone has to pay for their sins in the end. And he ain't no different, is he?'

The dog lifted his head and wagged his tail.

'Yeah,' Danny said. 'There's no such thing as a free ride. And this one's gonna be a fuckin' expensive one.'

It was seven minutes before the phone started ringing. Danny checked the number and then let it ring a few more times before he picked up. 'Yeah?'

'What the hell do you want?' asked Squires, his voice cold and abrupt.

'Well, a little civility for starters. There's no need for that tone. I was thinking ten k would be a fair amount.'

'What?'

'Or I send the pictures to your wife.'

'That's blackmail.'

'Sure it is,' Danny said. 'You screw around, mate, you have to pay for it. Or you could come clean and tell the missus what you were doing last night.' He paused. 'No? No, I didn't think so. Women don't tend to be very understanding about these things, do they? So, I don't think it's an unreasonable sum, not when you think of the peace of mind involved.'

'And what's to stop you coming back for more?'

'I'm not greedy, Mr Squires, and I don't take any more risks than I need to. You pay me the cash, I give you the photographs, end of story. You won't ever hear from me again.'

'It's a Saturday. How am I supposed to get that kind of money on a weekend?'

'There's plenty of banks open on a Saturday. It's only ten k, Mr Squires. Peanuts to a man like you. I'm sure you won't have any trouble in raising that.'

'This is blackmail. I could go to the police.'

'Sure you could. And then you could explain to them why you had sex with a fifteen-year-old girl.'

There was a swift intake of breath from the other end of the line. 'She wasn't ... she's not fifteen.'

'Try telling that to the cops when they're reading her birth certificate.'

Squires's voice turned pleading. 'But I didn't know that. For Christ's sake, I didn't have a clue.'

'You've got a daughter about that age, ain't you? Shit, that's gonna be a bit confusing for her, her old man shagging a teenager.'

'Keep my daughter out of this.'

'That's up to you. Send me a text when you've got the money and I'll tell you where to meet me tonight.'

'It can't be tonight. I'm busy. I've got ... I've got things I have to do.'

'Then you'll have to get un-busy. Text me. And don't leave

186

it too long. I'm not the patient sort.' Danny hung up before he could respond. He sat back and grinned. It was fortunate, he thought, that so many men listened to their dicks rather than their brain. This would be the most expensive shag Squires had ever had. But then, as Silver never tired of reminding him, she was worth it.

27

Jeremy Squires turned up at Belles at exactly eight o'clock. Solomon escorted him to the corner where Danny was sitting waiting.

'Right on time,' Danny said. 'Take a pew.'

'I'd rather not,' replied Squires somewhat stiffly. 'Let's just get this over and done with, shall we?' He glanced nervously around the room. Although it was still relatively early, half the tables were already taken. There were two girls dancing on stage, their bodies glistening with oil. 'Can we go somewhere more private?'

Danny sniggered. 'What, like the Gents', you mean? Better not. People might talk.'

Squires stared down at him, his face full of anger and contempt. 'Do you want your money or not?'

'All in good time. Sit down before you draw even more attention to yourself.'

Squires hesitated, but eventually, reluctantly, lowered himself into a chair. 'So how do we do this?'

Danny could see that he was ill at ease and not just because of the circumstances that had brought him here. He was the kind of man who probably claimed, especially to his wife, that he disapproved of such establishments, and now he was worried that someone he knew might recognise him. 'Relax,' he said, enjoying his victim's discomfort. 'Where's the fire? How about a drink? Fancy a Scotch? You may as well enjoy the show while you're here.'

'I'm not here to socialise.' Squires glanced pointedly at his watch. 'I've a dinner to attend and I'm already late. Do you want the money or not?' He took an envelope out of his jacket pocket and smacked it down on the table.

Danny looked at the envelope, but didn't pick it up. For him, part of the pleasure in these transactions was in watching the men squirm. Just for a while he had complete and utter power over them; he could destroy their lives by the single simple action of pressing a button on his phone. 'I dunno. Maybe I don't fancy doing a deal after all.'

'Don't mess me about.'

'Why? What are you going to do about it?'

Squires opened his mouth and then closed it again. He swallowed hard, his Adam's apple jumping in his throat.

Danny despised hypocrites like Squires, men who were all respectability and moral high ground on the outside, but who gave in to temptation at the mere sniff of some free fanny. He stared at him, taking in the perfectly cut silver hair, the expensive shirt and jacket, the gold Omega watch, the wedding ring. Yes, they could easily have stung him for more than ten k. The pathetic piece of shit would have paid twice that.

After a while, Danny leaned down and picked up the large

brown envelope that was leaning against the leg of his chair. He placed it on the table in front of Squires. Inside, were ten A4 prints, a sordid record of the events of last night. In this digital age, the physical photographs were meaningless – the images could still exist on a computer or a phone – but Danny always liked to provide a set, just so the victims knew exactly what they were paying for. It also provided them with the dilemma of what to do with the pictures, where to hide them or how to destroy them.

Squires ran his tongue along his dry upper lip. He waited a few seconds and then his hand snaked out to grab the envelope. Once he had it, he didn't seem sure what to do next. He dithered for a moment before curling the envelope into a tube and sliding it into his jacket pocket. 'This is it,' he said, standing up. 'I won't be paying out any more.'

Danny took the other envelope. He didn't bother opening it to count the money. He knew it would all be there. 'Anybody ask you to?' He got to his feet too. 'It's been a pleasure doing business. Let me walk you out.'

'There's no need for that.'

'Oh, I insist.' He weaved between the tables until they were at the door and then out in the foyer. He knew that it wouldn't take Squires long to uncover his identity, but this didn't concern him. Why should it? If anything, it made it even more unlikely that his victim would go to the law. Once Squires discovered that he was part of the notorious Street family, he would think twice about doing anything stupid.

It was this feeling of being able to do as he liked, of being invincible, that was the real turn-on for Danny. He savoured the sensation as they walked along the red carpet towards the main entrance. Squires, eager to be rid of him, hurried forward.

Danny gave a nod to Solomon Vale as they passed through the door and stepped out into the oblong of light on the forecourt. 'Need a cab?' he asked Squires.

'No.'

Danny stopped to light a cigarette before he followed Squires to the dimly lit far corner of the car park. The spaces, clearly marked, were supposed to be for staff only, but he supposed he could overlook it on this occasion. Squires took out his keys and beeped open the doors of a racing green Land Rover Discovery.

'Nice motor,' said Danny as he ran his hands along the gleaming bodywork.

'What do you want?' Squires said. 'Why can't you leave me alone?'

Danny took a long draw on his fag and grinned back at him. 'Nothin', mate. Nothin' at all. No need to be so jumpy.'

Jeremy Squires had one hand on the door when Danny heard the noise. Three loud cracks in quick succession, like a car backfiring. And then the sudden pain in his right arm – sharp, hot, agonising. The cigarette slipped from his fingers and as he bent over, grasping his arm with his left hand, he was aware of Squires dropping like a stone.

Danny's brain, raddled with coke, took a moment to process what was happening. *Shit, shit, shit.* He'd been shot. They'd both been shot. He threw himself on the ground, down by the wheels of the Discovery. Squires was close by and he wasn't moving; he was face down with a couple of holes in his back. Was he dead? Jesus, was the fucker dead?

Danny kept his head down in case the bastard with the shooter was still hanging around. He was aware of the noise of the traffic, of the faint sound of the music coming from the club. What he couldn't hear was any sign of life from Squires. Not a moan, not a groan, not a single bloody breath.

Solomon came flying across the forecourt, his boots scrunching on the gravel. 'What the—' He crouched down by the two men, his eyes wide with alarm. He glanced over his shoulder and then back at them. 'You okay?' he asked, staring at Danny. 'What happened? What the hell happened?'

'Do I fuckin' look okay?' The blood was pouring down his arm now, covering his hand in red. He could feel a throbbing, a rhythmic painful pounding that made the breath catch in his throat.

'Stay cool. Help's on its way, man.' He took his phone out of his pocket and dialled 999. While he was talking, he leaned over and placed a couple of fingers against Squires's neck. 'Still with us, but not much of a pulse.'

While Solomon had the phone pressed to his ear, Danny gradually became aware of the increasing activity around them. People, alert to an incident, were starting to gather. He could hear the murmur of curious voices, the shuffling of feet. It wouldn't be long before half of Shoreditch had come to get an eyeful. And as this thought sank in, he had another more urgent one. *Christ, the envelope with the photographs was still in Squires's pocket!* Knowing that he had to get it back before Old Bill turned up, he waited until Solomon had got off the phone and then demanded, 'Get rid of the fuckers! Move them back. Clear some space.'

As Solomon stood up to drive back the onlookers, Danny scrambled desperately towards Squires. Could anyone see? Was anyone watching? He tried to use his own body as a shield, to pretend that he was trying to help the man. In order to get hold of the envelope he had to release his grip on his injured arm. The blood flowed down on to Squires's jacket, adding to the dark stain that was already spreading.

Panic started to flood his veins. Once the law found the photos, it wouldn't take them long to find Silver and then the game was truly up. He tried to dig his fingers under the body, but the guy was a dead weight and with only one usable arm – and that was his left – he didn't have the strength to shift him. He felt his breath coming in short fast pants. Desperate, he lay down beside Squires and shoved one leg roughly under his hip. Eventually, he managed to lever up the body and scrabble underneath until he found the envelope.

Danny now had the photos, but his relief was short-lived. What the hell was he going to do with them? He looked frantically around, knowing that the cops would go over the ground with a fine-tooth comb. He couldn't hide them and he couldn't keep them on him. There was only one other alternative. 'Sol,' he hissed. 'Come here, come here.'

Solomon Vale crouched down beside him again. 'Boss?'

'Take this,' he said, thrusting the blood-splattered envelope into his hands. And then he remembered the money. He'd better get rid of that as well. He reached into his pocket, wincing with pain and passed that envelope over too. 'Keep them safe, huh?'

Solomon didn't ask any questions. He unzipped his leather jacket, slipped the envelopes inside, and zipped it up again.

Danny struggled out of his jacket, folded it over and used it to try and stem the flow of blood from his arm. He pressed down hard and felt his brains begin to spin. He put his head between his knees, retched twice and then threw up over the shiny rear wheel of the Discovery.

28

Valerie Middleton was ploughing through what appeared to be an endless heap of paperwork when her mobile started ringing. She glanced at the phone and smiled. 'Jeff Butler,' she said, picking up. 'To what do I owe the pleasure?'

'Ah, the pleasure's all mine. How are you, Val? Haven't seen you for a while.'

'That's because they've locked me up in a small room and won't let me out until all the overtime sheets have been done.'

'Then this is your lucky night,' he said. 'I've just got you a get-out-of-jail-free card.'

'Oh, sounds good. Tell me more.'

'There's been a shooting at Belles, two casualties, and one of them is Danny Street.'

Valerie's posture instantly changed. She sat up straight, every part of her alert. 'Fatal?'

DCI Butler gave a low laugh. 'If I didn't know you better,

Inspector, I might have thought there was a hint of hope in that question. But no, not fatal, not for Mr Street at least. It's not looking so good for the other guy, though. Jeremy Squires. Do you know him?'

'Squires?' she said, surprised. 'Yes, he runs a business in Kellston. My God, he's been shot?' She paused for a second. Jeremy Squires was a respectable local businessman, a member of the Rotary Club and a generous donor to the Police Benevolent Fund. 'Was it Street? Did he do it?'

'I don't think so, but look why don't you come down and we'll go through it all when you get here. We're at the hospital, waiting to talk to him.'

Valerie was already on her feet. 'I'll do that,' she said. 'I'll be with you soon.' She thanked him for the call and hung up. Quickly, she grabbed her coat and bag and went out into the incident room. 'Laura, we've got a shout.'

Twelve minutes later they were striding along the hospital corridors. They made their way to the Accident and Emergency Unit, which was rapidly filling up. It wasn't even nine o'clock and already the doctors and nurses were run off their feet. They came across DCI Jeff Butler feeding coins into a drinks machine.

'Hey, good to see you again,' he said. 'Fancy a drink?'

'No, thank you. I've tasted that stuff and only just lived to regret it.'

'Well, I'm desperate. So long as it's hot and wet, it'll do for me.'

'Don't say I didn't warn you.'

Butler picked up his plastic cup of tea and grinned. 'Cheers.'

Valerie smiled back at him. She liked Butler. He was in his mid-forties, a placid, unflappable Yorkshireman who took things in his stride and was rarely fazed by the trials and tribulations of the job. He worked out of Shoreditch, where Belles was located, but when it came to dealing with the Streets the two stations often collaborated.

'This is DS Laura Higgs,' she said, making the introductions. 'Laura, this is DCI Butler.'

'Just call me, Jeff. Nice to meet you, Laura.'

'You too.'

Butler took a sip of the tea and pulled a face. 'Right, let's find somewhere to park ourselves and I'll get you both up to speed.'

They carried on a little way up the corridor until they came to a small row of blue plastic chairs. Butler sat down and immediately leaned forward. 'To be honest, we don't know that much yet. Only that it happened at around eight fifteen. They've taken Squires into theatre – he was shot twice – and it isn't looking good. He was conscious when they brought him in, but only just.'

'And Danny Street?' Valerie asked.

'Oh, he'll be okay. It's only a flesh wound, nothing serious. They're patching him up now. We should be able to see him soon.'

'I'm sure he'll be overjoyed at the welcome committee.'

Butler shifted up his broad shoulders. 'Even Danny Street probably takes exception to being shot.'

'Doesn't mean he'll tell us anything, though. I take it we're presuming that he was the intended victim and that Squires just got in the way?'

'Seems the most likely scenario, unless there are things about Mr Squires that we don't know.'

Valerie gave a nod. 'What on earth was he doing at Belles in the first place?'

Blunt looked at her and grinned again. 'What do most men go there for? It sure as hell isn't for the witty conversation.'

'But Squires?' she said. 'He doesn't seem the type. And it doesn't quite fit in with the image he likes to project – you know, family man, pillar of the community.'

'Maybe he had a secret life.'

'Not very secret if he was hanging around Belles. Anyone could have seen him there.'

'Did he say anything before he went into theatre?' Laura asked. 'Or in the ambulance?'

Butler shook his head. 'Not as far as I know.'

Laura Higgs stood up and gazed along the corridor. 'Right, I'll see if I can find the paramedics who brought him in. If he was conscious, he might have told them something.'

Butler watched as she strode off and then turned to look at Valerie again. 'So what happened to Swann? I thought you two were inseparable.'

'On holiday,' she said. 'In Clacton.'

'Clacton? In November?'

'Don't ask.'

Butler sipped on his tea for a while before saying, 'I've got a couple of lads down at Belles taking statements from the punters and people who were passing by. We don't know for sure that Squires was actually inside the club yet. He could have just parked his car on the forecourt, come back to pick it up and found himself in the wrong place at the wrong time.'

'What are the chances?'

'Slight,' he said. 'Of all the places to leave your motor, Belles would hardly come top of the list. Anyway, there are security cameras on the building. We'll be able to see if he went in and out. Unfortunately, they only cover the space directly in front of the entrance and not the far part of the car park.'

'And what was he doing with Danny Street? That doesn't add up. It doesn't make any sense at all.'

'Yeah, well, maybe Mr Street can enlighten us.'

'Don't hold your breath,' Valerie said. 'He's hardly known for his burning desire to help the police. And if something dodgy was going on between him and Squires, he won't want us to know about that either.'

'Maybe we'll catch him before the shock wears off. No one likes getting hit by a bullet, no matter how crooked they are.'

'What about Squires's wife? Has she been told?'

'Amanda,' he said. 'Yeah, we finally managed to track her down. She's been informed. She's on her way in.'

'I think I met her once at some charity do. God, this is going to be a nightmare for her. Not only has her husband been shot, but he's been shot outside a sleazy lap-dancing club.'

'Maybe he made a habit of it. Maybe he's not quite as squeaky clean as he'd like everyone to believe.'

Valerie gave him a look.

'Got to keep an open mind,' he said. 'She wouldn't be the first wife to decide she'd had enough.'

'And bump him off?'

'Or pay someone else to do it.' Butler placed the still half-full cup on the seat beside him. 'You were right about the tea. It's filthy stuff.'

It was another five minutes before a young PC emerged from a side room and approached them. 'They're finished now, guv,' he said to Butler. 'You can go in and talk to him.'

29

Danny Street was sitting on the side of the bed, looking decidedly sorry for himself. His right arm was heavily bandaged. He glanced up as they came in and scowled. 'Ah, for fuck's sake. What do you want?'

Valerie smiled at him. 'That's not much of a welcome, Danny.'

'I've just been shot. You think I'm fit to talk to you lot?'

Butler sat down beside him. 'It's a minor injury. You'll live. Which is more than might be said for your pal, Squires.'

Danny narrowed his eyes. 'Squires? Is that his name? He ain't my pal. I hardly know the geezer.'

'You just happened to be standing next to him when someone decided to try and take you out.'

'What makes you think it was me they were after?'

'Just a wild guess,' Butler said.

Danny shook his head. 'Nah, I don't reckon so. I'm not the one who ended up with two bullets in me back.'

Valerie leaned against the wall and folded her arms. 'So, do you want to tell us what happened, Danny?'

'Nothin' to tell, love,' Danny said. 'One minute I'm standing there, then I hear the noise, three bangs ... one, two, three ... next thing, he's on the ground and I've got blood pouring out me arm.'

Valerie didn't respond to the 'love'. She knew he was only trying to wind her up. 'Perhaps we could go back a bit. What was Jeremy Squires doing there in the first place?'

Danny's lips slid into a contemptuous grin. 'Jesus, I think even you can manage to work that one out.'

'Are you saying he was a regular?'

'No idea,' Danny said. 'I ain't seen him there before, but that don't mean nothin'. I don't spend much time at Belles these days. Might be a regular, might not.'

Butler shifted on the bed. 'So take us through what happened.'

'Starting at the beginning,' Valerie said. 'From when you first noticed him.'

Danny glanced from one to the other. 'Is he going to make it, this Squires guy? How bad is he?'

'Why?' Butler asked. 'You worried about what he might say?'

'Why should I be worried? I've got nothin' to hide. I'm the innocent victim here.'

'Well, that's a first,' Butler said.

Danny scowled at him. 'You want my help or not?'

'Just get on with it, will you?'

Danny waited a while as if his feelings were hurt and he needed some time to recover. 'Okay,' he said. 'This is how it went. Sol comes over to my table at around eight o'clock with this grey-haired geezer I've never seen before. Bloke wants to talk to me, apparently. So I tell him to take a pew, and Sol clears off. Anyway, turns out he's parked his motor in the Staff Only spaces on the forecourt and wants to make sure it'll still be there when he leaves – not towed or clamped, right?'

Valerie heaved out a sigh, not even attempting to hide her scepticism. 'Oh, come on, Danny. You really expect us to believe that?'

'It's the truth, I'm telling you. This guy's in love with his motor, a brand-new Discovery it is. Can't bear the thought of anything happening to it.'

'So why didn't he just ask Solomon Vale if he could park it there?' Butler asked.

'Why talk to the monkey when you can talk to the organ grinder? Anyway, you can tell he's the kind of bloke who likes to go straight to the top. And, seeing as he's been so respect-ful, asking for permission and the like, I tell him it's okay so long as he doesn't make a habit of it.'

'Right,' Butler said. 'And then?'

'And then I tell him to take a pew. Why not?'

'Very sociable of you.'

'Yeah, well, that's the way I am, Mr Butler. Plus, he looked to me like the kind of geezer who had a few bob – nice clothes, nice watch – so I figured it was worth it. I mean, he may as well spend his cash in Belles as anywhere else, right?'

'You're all heart.'

'And then what?' Valerie asked.

Danny gave a shrug, a gesture he instantly regretted. The movement of his shoulders must have sent a pain down his arm because he visibly winced and hissed out a breath. 'What do you mean?'

'Did you talk to him, did he talk to any of the girls?'

'Yeah, we had a chat.'

'About?'

Danny pondered on this for a moment. 'Cars,' he said eventually. 'Yeah, we talked about cars for a while. And then after about ten minutes or so he looks at his watch and acts kind of surprised at what the time is. He gets up and says he has to go.'

'Bit odd, isn't it?' Valerie asked. 'Ten minutes? He hardly had time to appreciate the atmosphere.'

'You know what I reckon?'

'Enlighten us.'

'I reckon he got cold feet. He was looking round all the time, checking out the other customers. I've come across his type before – they've got the hots and fancy an eyeful, but don't want to be spotted by someone they know. Worried about it getting back to the missus or the boss or whoever pulls their strings.'

Valerie studied him with care. Although Danny Street was a well-practised and proficient liar, he didn't seem as cocky as he normally was. Some of that might have been down to the fact that someone had just tried to take him out, but she suspected something else. 'That must have been a disappointment. There you were, thinking he was going to spend a bundle, and he just ups and leaves.'

'It happens. Anyway, I was gasping for a fag so I decide to walk out with him, take a look at that fancy motor he'd been banging on about. And that's when it happened.' Danny made a shooting gesture with two fingers of his left hand. 'We'd only been there thirty seconds and bang!'

'Let's go back a bit,' Butler said. 'So you're coming out of the club. Was anyone else around?'

'Only Sol on the door.'

'Okay, so you're walking away from the door and towards the street. What do you see?'

'We were talking. I didn't really notice. Bit of traffic, people going by. But it's always busy round there.'

'So you didn't hear anything before the shots, didn't notice anyone hanging around the gates?'

Danny gave a snort. 'What, some geezer with a shooter in his hand? Yeah, sure.'

'If it was a man,' Val said.

'What you saying? That some bloody tart shot me?'

Valerie could see the indignation in his face. Being shot by a man was one thing, by a woman was quite another. 'I've no idea, but I'm keeping an open mind.'

'Yeah,' said Danny resentfully. 'Maybe it was some tart trying to kill the geezer. The bitch certainly couldn't shoot straight. Maybe it was his wife.'

'How do you know he was married?' Valerie asked.

Danny smirked. 'Had the ball and chain on his finger, didn't he? Anyway, you can always tell. Half the men who come to Belles are hitched.'

'So you didn't see anything?' Butler asked.

'Not a thing. One minute we were looking at the motor, the next . . . '

'Okay, we get the picture. And after the shots, you didn't hear anything else? Someone running away, the sound of a car accelerating?'

'No. Shit, I'd just been shot. How much listening do you

think I was doing? I was on my fuckin' knees, mate, bleeding to death for all I knew.'

Valerie looked at his bandaged arm and rolled her eyes. 'It was only a flesh wound.'

Danny glared back at her. 'So, are we done here? Much as I love talking to you, I'd prefer to piss off home and get stuck into a bottle of Scotch.'

Butler rose to his feet. 'You know the score,' he said. 'We'll need to talk to you again.'

'Yeah, yeah. Don't leave the country, huh?'

'You've got it.'

'Oh, Mr Butler?' Danny said.

'Yes?'

'Try not to be too disappointed. You know, about me still being alive and all.'

Butler grinned. 'We already had the champagne on ice.'

Valerie turned to Butler as soon as the door was closed and they were back in the corridor. 'He's lying.'

'Course he's lying. The guy can't help himself. Question is, which part is he lying about?'

'Most of it, if past experience is anything to go by.'

Butler scratched his forehead. 'Trouble is, you start making a list of people who might have a grudge against him and you come up with half the population of London.'

'Maybe Squires can shed some light.'

'If he makes it.'

Butler glanced up and down the corridor. 'It's going to be a while before he's out of surgery. You fancy taking a look at the scene of the crime?'

30

Ava lay sprawled on the sofa, watching TV and enjoying the peace and quiet of the flat. Tash and Hannah had gone up West for a meal and wouldn't be back until late. She picked up the bar of chocolate, snapped off a row and popped a chunk in her mouth. It was a sad indictment of her social life that she had nowhere to go and no one to see on a Saturday night. Sad and single. She glanced at the chocolate. And if she carried on this way – sad, *fat* and single.

She flicked through a few channels, searching for something decent to watch. Well, she might be on her own, but at least she was free from Hannah's clutches. It had not been a comfortable experience being cross-examined by her earlier. Hannah was like a Rottweiler; once she got her teeth into you, she wouldn't let go. And Ava didn't like lying. Not that she had lied, exactly, but she hadn't told the truth either.

Ava turned on her side and yawned. Back to work on Monday. Were things okay with her and Chris Street? She thought so. They'd cleared the air if nothing else. Perhaps now life could get back to normal, or as normal as it ever could be when you were working for a villain.

She was wondering if she could be bothered to go to the kitchen and make a fresh cup of coffee when she heard the sound of the key in the lock. It was only twenty to ten and way too early for the two of them to be back – unless they'd had a row. Quickly, she sat up, ready to shoot off to the bathroom, claiming she'd been about to take a shower if the atmosphere was frosty. She'd had enough of Hannah for one day.

There were, however, more than two voices coming from the hall. Seconds later, Tash appeared with her arm around a weeping Lydia.

'You won't believe what's happened,' Tash said. 'Have you heard?'

Ava rose to her feet. 'What? What is it?'

Tash gently led Lydia to the sofa and sat her down. She fussed around for a moment, plumping cushions and squeezing her on the arm, before looking up again. 'Jeremy Squires has been shot. He's in the hospital now. They're operating on him.'

Lydia made a small choking sound, burying her face in the ragged piece of tissue she was holding.

Ava didn't know who he was. 'Jeremy . . . ?'

'Amanda's husband,' Tash said. 'You remember, Amanda? She was at Beast on Thursday when we went to the show.'

'Oh, right.' Ava recalled her now, an elegant blonde woman Tash had rushed off to speak to.

'Twice,' mumbled Lydia. 'He was shot twice.'

'Twice,' Tash repeated. 'Lydia called me. She was really upset, so we called round at her place to pick her up. We didn't think she should be alone.'

Ava wasn't so sure about the 'We'. Hannah had followed them in wearing the kind of pained expression that suggested that she knew she should be feeling sympathetic but couldn't quite summon up the energy. Instead, she had her gaze firmly fixed on Tash's arm draped around Lydia's shoulder.

'Of course not,' Ava said. 'God, I'm really sorry. Is he a good friend of yours, Lydia?'

Lydia shifted the tissue from her mouth and began twisting it around her fingers instead.

'He used to . . . he used to come into the shop a lot. And Amanda. He's really nice. They both are. I don't understand why . . . how could . . .' But then she rapidly dissolved into tears again.

'It's all right, it's all right,' Tash murmured.

'Why don't I make a cup of tea?' Ava said. 'Something hot and sweet for the shock, yeah?'

'I'll give you a hand,' Hannah said.

Hannah shut the kitchen door behind them and raised her eyes to the ceiling. 'God, I don't mean to sound insensitive, but that girl's such a drama queen. I mean, she hardly knows the guy, not really.'

Ava switched on the kettle and got some mugs out of the cupboard. She wondered if Lydia was closer to Squires than anyone realised. Could they have been having an affair? It wasn't impossible, and it might account for the evasiveness that Hannah had been banging on about earlier. 'It's still a shock, even if it's someone you don't know that well.'

Hannah, ignoring the comment, carried on. 'So there we are, right in the middle of our meal when she rings up, blubbing down the phone, and next thing Tash has promised to go straight round. I mean, why did she even call Tash? Why didn't she call you?'

'Er ...' Ava found herself caught on the hop again, and had to improvise. 'Oh, she probably tried. My phone's in the bedroom. It's been re-charging.' Ava sent a mental prayer up to the gods that her mobile, which was sitting in her bag on the kitchen table, wouldn't suddenly start ringing. 'I don't think she has the landline number.'

Hannah sat down, clearly peeved at the interruption to her evening. And then, as if not wanting to leave Tash alone with Lydia, she quickly stood up again. 'I suppose I'd better go and offer some support.'

She was almost at the door when Ava asked, 'Where did it happen? The shooting, I mean. Was it in Kellston?'

'No, not Kellston. It was at the club that your boss owns. Belles, is it?'

Ava gave a start. 'What?'

'Yes, right outside. In the car park. I mean, what was the guy even doing at that place? He must be a complete sleazeball. Oh, and one of the Streets was shot as well.'

Ava felt the blood drain from her face. Her voice, when it finally emerged, sounded thin and croaky. 'What? Which one? Who was it?'

Hannah gave a shrug. 'I've no idea.'

Ava shot across the kitchen and into the living room. Her heart was in her mouth. 'Lydia, Hannah's just told me that one of the Streets was shot. Do you know who it was?'

Lydia raised her eyes, red-rimmed and still full of tears. 'Erm . . . the younger brother, I think. Danny, is it?'

'Are you sure?'

Lydia snuffled and gave a small nod. 'I think so. That's what Morton said. He was the one who called me.'

'Okay, thanks.' Ava retreated into the kitchen and slumped down at the table. She felt guilty at the relief that was flowing over her. *It wasn't Chris.* Thank God for that. He might be a pain in the arse, but she wouldn't want to see him hurt.

'Was it him?' asked Hannah, sounding indifferent as to whether it was or not.

'No.'

'Well, that's something. At least you're not unemployed again. Do you need a hand with those teas or can you manage?'

'I can manage.'

'Okay,' Hannah sighed. 'I suppose I'd better go and help out.'

As soon as she'd left the room, Ava stood up and closed the door again. She grabbed her phone out of her bag and called Chris Street.

'Hi,' she said as soon as he answered. 'It's me. I've just heard. Is Danny all right?'

'News travels fast. Yeah, he's fine. Not too bad. It was only a flesh wound. They discharged him a while back.' He paused and then added, 'He's here at home, milking it for all it's worth, expecting the rest of us to wait on him hand and foot.'

'At least it's not too serious. What about the other guy?'

'Still in hospital.'

'Do you have any idea what happened?'

Chris barked out a laugh. 'Yeah, some geezer took a shot at Danny and missed . . . twice.'

'Not much of a marksman, then.'

'You're not wrong there.'

There was a brief silence before Ava said, 'Were you there? Were you at Belles when it . . . when he was shot?'

'Why? Were you worried that it might have been me who copped the bullet instead?'

'No. Why should I have been?' And then concerned that this sounded unnecessarily defensive, she quickly added, 'Although I have been on the lookout for a cheap Mercedes. You have to grab your chances when you can.'

'Love you too, babe,' he said.

'Okay, well if you need me for anything, I'll be around tomorrow. Just give me a call.'

'Thanks, but I reckon we're okay. See you Monday, yeah?'

Ava said goodbye and hung up. She sat for a moment, staring down at the phone and then dropped it back in her bag. She got up, made the teas, put them on a tray and took it through to the living room.

By now Lydia had calmed down a bit. She was still white-faced, still obviously shaken, but she had stopped crying. She wrapped her hands around the mug and mumbled, 'Thanks. I'm really sorry about this. I didn't . . . I didn't know what else to do . . .'

'You did the right thing,' Tash said. 'You should be with friends at a time like this. And you're staying here with us tonight. I'm not having you going back to an empty flat.'

'Oh, I couldn't.'

'Of course you can. We insist. Tell her she has to stay, Hannah.'

'Yes, it's probably for the best,' said Hannah through gritted teeth.

'You don't mind do you, Ava?' Tash asked.

'No, not at all. You're more than welcome.'

'Thank you,' said Lydia, raising her wide blue eyes to them all. 'You're all being so ... so nice ... and so kind ... and I know I'm behaving like a child. I can't help it, I just ...' She bent her head again, her fair hair falling around her face.

'Hey,' said Tash, putting an arm round her shoulder. 'Come on. I'm sure he'll be okay. He's in the hospital. They'll take good care of him.'

'But what if he ...'

'Don't think like that. You have to stay positive.'

While Tash was trying to reassure Lydia, Hannah stretched out her legs and took a sip of tea. She looked at Ava over the rim of the mug. 'You'd better be careful,' she said. 'It could be Chris Street next.'

31

Chris Street had already come to the same conclusion as the police. Whoever had fired the gun outside Belles must have been aiming for Danny. It was the only rational explanation. He took the glass of Courvoisier and placed it on the small table beside his brother.

'So, have you drawn up a shortlist yet?'

'No need, bro. Like I said, they didn't come looking for me.'

Chris sat down, leaned back, crossed his legs and stared at him. It was impossible to tell whether Danny was in some kind of psychological denial or if he was just taking the piss; there was so much junk swimming around in his bloodstream that he wouldn't know reality if it slapped him in the face. 'You reckon?'

'Who'd want to kill a great guy like me?' Danny sniggered. 'It wouldn't be natural.'

Terry was standing at the window, looking out at the

snow. 'You know who. I fuckin' warned you. Why didn't you listen?'

Danny snorted. 'You think Delaney did this?'

'Who else? You should have stayed away from his mad bitch of a daughter.'

'Shit, Delaney didn't do it.' Danny drank some of the brandy and grinned. 'If he'd wanted me dead, I'd be dead. You think that goon he employs would have accidentally pumped two bullets into somebody else?'

'There wasn't much light,' Chris said.

'There was enough. It wasn't him. Christ, if Delaney's going to waste every man who shags his daughter, he'll be taking out contracts for the rest of his life.'

'Where is she, anyway? Shouldn't she be here playing doctors and nurses?'

'Where's Ava?' Danny retorted. 'She ain't here either.'

'I've not just been shot.'

'Yeah, well, if you had been, you sure as hell wouldn't want some tart fussing round.'

Terry kept his back to them, his shoulders hunched. 'She's big trouble. You know she is.'

Danny rolled his eyes. 'This isn't about her. How many times? Jesus! Whoever did this, they were amateurs. And it wasn't me they were after, it was him.'

'But why?' Chris asked. 'Who the hell is this guy, Squires?'

'How should I know? He's just some punter. We got talking and when he left, I went outside with him. Wanted a fag, didn't I? See, that's what I mean. No one could have *known* I'd be out there. It was him they were waiting for.'

Chris wasn't so sure. And he reckoned Danny was hiding

something. God, Danny was *always* hiding something. 'What did Old Bill say?'

'Nothin' worth repeating. It was Butler and that blonde cow from Cowan Road.'

'Middleton,' Chris said. 'She must have thought all her Christmases had come at once.'

'Apart from the fact I'm still breathing.'

'Yeah, apart from that.' Chris paused and then said, 'Course it could have been Wilder. He's mad enough to try and take you out.'

Danny curled his lip. 'What, that fuckin' pansy? He wouldn't have the nerve.'

Chris could have mentioned that the 'fuckin' pansy' was currently screwing Jenna, but decided not to share that particular humiliation. It would be common knowledge soon enough.

'Wilder,' repeated Terry as if the name had only just penetrated his brain.

'What do you reckon?' asked Chris. 'I'd sure as hell put him in the frame.'

Terry glanced over his shoulder. 'That's Lizzie's boy,' he said. 'Why would he want to do something like that?'

'Why does Wilder do anything? Why does he send dead rats through the post?'

Terry pulled on his ear for a moment, his forehead puckered in a frown. 'You should talk to Lizzie. She'll sort him out.'

There was a short uncomfortable silence before Danny barked out a laugh. 'What the fuck are you going on about? Lizzie's six foot under. What do want me to do – dig her up?'

'Leave it,' said Chris, throwing his brother a warning glance.

Terry's frown grew deeper, his expression one of incomprehension. He blinked a couple of times and then turned his back on them again.

Chris looked past his father to the garden that lay beyond, the long oblong of white with its snow-covered trees and bushes. Trojan patrolled the perimeter, his nose close to the ground, searching for the scent of any poor creature, human or animal, that he could hunt down and tear limb from limb.

'You okay, Dad?' he asked.

Terry didn't answer.

Chris had the sense of a thread being pulled, of a slow but distinct unravelling. Everything was coming apart. Everything was changing, and not for the better.

32

DI Valerie Middleton was back at her desk at the crack of dawn on Sunday morning. With the overtime sheets pushed to one side, she was sifting instead through the witness statements taken after the shooting at Belles. They made for pretty thin reading. Solomon Vale, who had probably been best placed to view the incident, could add little to what Danny Street had already told them. She thought back to the interview that had been conducted in the opulent if somewhat tacky surroundings of the club office.

'So, talk us through what you saw, what you heard,' Butler said. 'Let's start with the arrival of the victim, Jeremy Squires.'

Solomon, who seemed way too big for the chair he was sitting on, leaned forward with his hands splayed across his huge thighs. 'Squires? That his name?' He waited a few seconds, looking from Butler to Valerie, before continuing. 'It was about eight, I reckon. He pulled into the car park, the far part by the exit, and then came over to the door.'

'Had you ever seen him before?'

'Don't reckon so, but there's lots of people come and go. Can't remember all of them.'

'But he's not a regular?'

Solomon smiled, showing a row of straight white teeth. 'Don't reckon so,' he said again. 'But then all you honkies look the same to me.'

Valerie gave him a thin smile in return. 'What did you say to him?'

'Huh?'

'The car park's only for staff, isn't it? Did you tell him that he couldn't park there?'

'I didn't tell him nothin',' Solomon said. 'Didn't get the chance. He comes up to me and says that he wants to speak to the boss. I ask him what it's about, but don't get no joy. He's insistent. Yeah, that's the word, *insistent*. Only wants to talk to the guy at the top. Now, normally, I'd want a bit more information before I go bothering the boss, but this guy looks kind of official, like a lawyer or something, so I figure he might be expected and just take him on through.'

Butler placed his elbows on the table and steepled his fingers. 'When he asked for the boss, did he use a name? I mean, did he specifically ask for Danny Street?'

'Nah,' Solomon said. 'The boss. That's all he said. But Danny was the only one here, so that's who I took him to see.'

'How did Squires seem?' Valerie asked.

'Seem?'

'Was he impatient, anxious, calm?'

Solomon thought about this for a moment and then gave

219

a shrug of his mighty shoulders. 'He seemed like the sort who was used to getting what he wanted.'

'So you take him through to the club. What happens then?'

'I take him over to Danny's table. The guy says something to him – I don't hear what, it's noisy in there with the music – and then the guy sits down. I figure everything's okay and so I head back to the door.'

'Did you get the impression that they knew each other?'

Solomon raised his hands, palms upward. 'Didn't get no impression, man. Couldn't say one way or the other. It's Saturday night and it's getting busy. I got other things on my mind.'

Butler and Valerie waited, but he had nothing more to add.

'And then what happened?' Butler prompted.

'And then I don't see him again until he and Danny come out.'

'Which is how long?'

'Couldn't say for sure. Fifteen minutes, maybe.'

'Quarter of an hour,' Butler said. 'Doesn't say much for the quality of the entertainment.'

'Or maybe it was *so* good, he just couldn't take the excitement.'

'Even you don't believe that.'

Solomon grinned. 'Anyway, Danny stops to light a fag and the other guy walks on over to his car. Danny goes over to join him and next thing I hear is the noise. Three shots in a row, quick, one after the other. I run over there and the two of them are on the ground by the car. Danny's bleeding from the arm, but he's okay. The grey-haired guy's not looking so good though. He's got two holes in his back and he's not moving.'

'Did you look around?' Valerie asked. 'You must have wondered if the gunman was still there.'

'Must have done. Probably. Only natural, ain't it?' Solomon frowned while he tried to think back. 'I didn't notice nothin', though.' His lips slid into a half smile. 'I mean, there were people on the street, cars going by, but no one standing by the gates with a gun in their hand.'

Valerie inclined her head. 'How did you know the shots came from there?'

'Where else could they have come from? The guy had his back to the gate. He was shot in the back. Therefore . . . '

'Could have come from one of the buildings,' Butler suggested.

'That would have meant a rifle. Didn't sound like rifle shots to me.'

Valerie gave a nod. 'Okay. So what next?'

'Next, I check out the guy on the ground. He's still got a pulse but nothin' to write home about. So I call an ambulance, pronto.'

'And Danny?'

'What about him?'

'What's he doing?'

Solomon sat back and folded his arms across his chest. 'What do you think he's doing? Dancing the light fandango? The guy's just been shot, man. He's trying his best not to bleed to death.'

'It was only a flesh wound,' Valerie said.

'He don't know that. All he knows is that it hurts like shit and that's a mighty lot of blood pumping out of his arm.'

Butler gave a nod. 'Did he say anything to you while you were waiting for the ambulance to come?'

'I dunno. Some, I guess. He was in shock. I wasn't exactly thinking straight myself. I think he asked about the geezer, whether I thought he would make it or not.'

'Where was Danny in relation to Squires?'

Solomon frowned again as if suspecting some trickery to the question. 'What?'

'Squires was lying face down on the ground, right?' Butler said. 'So where exactly was Danny? By his feet, by his hips, by his chest?'

'Erm . . . close by. Pretty near. He was sitting down. By his chest, I guess.'

'Did he touch him, try and move him?'

'If he did, I didn't see it. But then I wasn't looking all the time. There was a crowd starting to gather so I got up and tried to shift them back. No one needs an audience, right, not when they've just been shot.'

Valerie was brought back to the present by the sight of DCI Butler strolling across the incident room. He was wearing a heavy overcoat dusted with snow and a green-and-blue-check scarf. The blinds were open and she gave him a wave.

'Morning,' he said as he came through the door. 'How did I guess I'd find you here at this ungodly hour?'

'Oh, you know me. I can't resist a good attempted murder. It is still *attempted*, isn't it? Any news from the hospital?'

Butler pulled out a chair and sat down. 'It's touch and go.

He's still in intensive care. I've got a couple of PCs with him just in case he was the intended victim. They'll let me know if he comes round. The bullets have gone off to Ballistics, but until we find the gun ...'

'Do we know anything about it yet?'

'Only that it's an automatic or semi-automatic. The boys found the shell casings on the ground. Oh, yes, and the third bullet lodged in the wall so, looking at the trajectory, it's pretty clear that whoever fired the gun was standing by the gates.'

'Must have been one cool customer,' Valerie said. 'Anyone could have seen them.'

'Cool or crazy. Take your pick.'

Valerie pondered on this for a while before belatedly remembering her manners. 'Would you like a drink? Tea, coffee?'

'Is it any better than that dishwater at the hospital?'

'Marginally.'

'Go on, then. I'll have a tea. One sugar, please.'

Valerie went through to the drinks machine in the incident room and came back a couple of minutes later with two plastic cups. She put them on the desk and sat down again. 'I was just reading through Solomon Vale's statement,' she said. 'There was something I wanted to ask you.'

'Ask away,' Butler said. He picked up the cup, took a sip and gave a nod. 'I've tasted worse.'

'Why did you ask whether Danny Street had moved Squires?'

'Ah,' Butler said. 'Good question. There's something of a mystery there. You see, there was a lot of blood down the side of Squires's jacket, some on the front left side of his shirt and even some in his left-hand jacket pocket. It didn't come from the bullet wounds. The jacket's still with Forensics, but I'm willing to bet that the blood is Danny's.'

'You think Danny moved him before the ambulance came?'

'He must have done. Question is, why? What was so important that even though he'd been shot himself, and must have been in considerable pain, he still felt the need to go rummaging through Squires's pocket?'

'His wallet?' Valerie suggested.

'Yeah, that was the first thing that sprang into my mind too, but his wallet wasn't there. It was in the back pocket of his trousers. And that, surely, would be the next place you'd look. Except he didn't. There wasn't a drop of blood, not one.'

'Maybe he didn't have time.'

'But that would normally be the first place you'd search. No, I reckon he was after something else.'

'Any ideas?'

Butler stirred his tea with the skinny plastic spoon. 'Not a clue.'

'I still think Danny was the intended target. You know he's been seeing Vic Delaney's daughter, Silver?'

Butler glanced up at her. 'No, I didn't. You think Delaney might have been showing his disapproval?'

'Would you like it if your daughter was dating Danny Street?'

'No,' Butler said. 'But then I wouldn't be that happy if my son was dating Silver Delaney either.'

'You've got a point.'

'Hardly a marriage made in heaven. Not sure if I buy Delaney for this, though. He'd be more likely to rough Danny up, try and warn him off, rather than actually put a bullet in him.'

'Who knows? Daddies and their daughters.'

Butler drank some more of his tea, his face tight and pensive. 'The other thing is, how would anyone be sure that Danny was even going to go outside last night? I mean, later, yeah, when the club closed, but not at that time.'

'He's a smoker,' Valerie said. 'Perhaps he makes a habit of nipping out for a fag.'

'But then he'd probably stay near the entrance, wouldn't he? And that would make him a pretty hard target for someone standing at the gate – it must be what, twenty, twenty-five yards? Well, unless they were a pro, but a pro doesn't accidentally pump two bullets into the wrong victim. Plus, if Danny's telling the truth, he doesn't spend much time at Belles, so why would anyone expect to find him there?'

'Because he was followed?'

'And then the tail stands around in the freezing cold hoping that Danny might show his face before closing time? No, it doesn't add up.'

'But who'd want to shoot Squires?' Valerie glanced down at the open file. 'Did you get a chance to talk to the wife?'

'Amanda. Yeah, briefly. She can't make any sense of it either. They were due at a dinner party in Whitechapel at seven-thirty, an important one too, by all accounts. Another local councillor called Barnes and his missus. Squires was hoping to bend the guy's ear about some planning application. And then, just as they were about to leave, Squires claims he's got an emergency at work and has to go into the office for half an hour. He calls a cab for her and says he'll join her later.'

'And then off he trots to Belles.'

'Exactly,' Butler said. 'So unless he was overtaken by an uncontrollable urge to view a glistening pair of naked breasts, my guess would be that he had pressing business with Danny Street.'

'Glistening?' she asked, arching her brows.

Butler grinned. 'So I've heard.'

'So you reckon Solomon Vale was lying when he said Squires didn't ask for Danny by name?'

'Through his teeth,' Butler said. 'But then what do you expect? He works for the Streets. He and Danny had a good ten minutes to cobble a story together before the ambulance or the cops got there.'

'I don't suppose Mrs Squires knows if her husband made a habit of visiting clubs of ill-repute.'

'Says he wasn't the type, but who can tell? The wife's often the last to know.'

Valerie sighed. 'I can't believe there weren't any witnesses. Shoreditch is always packed on a Saturday night. You'd think someone passing by would have noticed a gun-toting loiterer.'

'Except by the time people realised they were gunshots, the perp had already cleared off. And whoever it was, they didn't run. They didn't draw any unnecessary attention to themselves.'

Valerie was aware that they'd only got a handful of witness

statements from people who'd been on the main road. 'So what happened to the crowd Solomon was talking about?'

'Most of them disappeared as soon as the boys in blue arrived. Usual thing of not wanting to get involved, or not wanting their Saturday night to be put on hold by having to hang around and make a statement. We've put out a request for witnesses on the news, but I'm not holding my breath.'

'Probably wise.'

'Anyway, there is one other thing I meant to mention. When I was at the hospital one of the nurses said . . . ' Butler's mobile started ringing and he reached into his pocket. 'Sorry, hang on a sec.' He pressed a button and put the phone to his ear. 'Butler.'

Valerie watched as he listened to the caller. She saw his expression change, his face growing grave.

'Okay, thanks for letting me know. I'll see you back at the station.' Butler ended the call, tapped the mobile against his chin and looked over at Valerie.

'Bad news I take it?'

'Squires died ten minutes ago.'

'Damn.'

Butler rose to his feet and put on his overcoat. 'Well, it's not *attempted* murder any more. I suppose I'd better talk to the wife again.'

Valerie didn't envy him that particular job. 'Before you go, what were you saying, about the nurse?'

'Oh, yes. It's probably nothing, but when Squires was first brought in, he was drifting in and out of consciousness. She claims he kept saying the name Ava. Could have been

Amanda, of course – he wouldn't have been speaking that clearly – or maybe it's a pet name for her.'

'Ava?' repeated Valerie sharply.

'Name mean something to you?'

'Yes,' she said. 'It does. You might want to sit down again for a minute.'

33

When Ava got out of bed and wandered into the living room, it was to find the sofa empty and the blankets neatly folded. She went through to the kitchen where Tash was sitting at the table, gazing into space.

'Has Lydia gone?'

'Ages ago. I was up at seven and she wasn't here then. She left a note.' Tash picked up the scrap of paper and handed it to her. 'Do you think she's all right? I'm worried about her.'

Ava read the note which said simply *Thanks for everything. So sorry to have been a nuisance. I'll call you later. Love Lydia x.* 'I'm sure she's okay. It's just the shock of it all.' She put the note down and went to put the kettle on. 'I mean, you don't expect it, do you, someone you know getting shot like that.'

'Maybe I should go round. I've tried calling her, but she isn't picking up. It just keeps going to voicemail. She's only down the road. It wouldn't take me five minutes.'

'She might be asleep,' Ava said. 'I don't suppose she got much kip last night. Why don't you give it an hour or two, see if she calls you back?'

As if she didn't know what to do with herself, Tash folded her arms and unfolded them again, sat back and then forward. Her hands began a restless dance on the table. 'She was so upset. I've never seen her like that before.'

'You haven't known her that long.'

Anger flashed into Tash's eyes. 'God, now you're sounding just like Hannah,' she snapped. 'I suppose *you* think she was overreacting too.'

'Did I say that?'

Tash glared at her for a moment, her eyes bright with reproach, her cheeks flushed pink. But then as rapidly as her rage had sprung up, it shrivelled away again. She rubbed at her eyes and shook her head. 'Sorry, I didn't mean that. I shouldn't have ... I'm just ... It's just that Lydia's all on her own. She hasn't got anyone to look out for her.'

'It's okay,' Ava said. 'It doesn't matter. I understand.' And she understood, she thought, a lot more than Tash probably realised. What might have started off as 'a bit of fun' had turned into something more serious. Tash's feelings were written all over her face. Her love for Lydia might be unrequited, but that didn't make it any less genuine. 'Let's have some coffee and then I'll walk round with you if you want.'

'Would you?'

'Course I will. Where's Hannah? Is she still in bed?'

'No, she's gone home. She's got one of her moods on. You know what she's like. If I pay anyone else even the slightest bit of attention, she gets the hump.'

Ava made two mugs of instant coffee and put them down on the table. 'Well, Hannah's never been what you'd call the easy-going sort.'

Tash almost managed a smile. 'You can say that again.'

'Actually there was something I meant to ask you about Lydia.' Ava sat down and paused for a moment while she tried to think of the right way to phrase it.

'What is it?'

Ava noticed that Tash's voice had an eagerness to it, the eagerness that comes from needing to talk about the person you're in love with. She had a question to ask, but didn't want to get Hannah into trouble. Things were fraught enough between the couple without her adding fuel to the fire. 'Erm ... I was just wondering how Lydia knew Guy Wilder. I mean, she's not lived here long, has she? It doesn't really matter. I'm just being curious.'

'Guy? Oh, that was down to Maggie.'

'Maggie?'

'Yeah, Lydia was in the Fox one night and she was talking about how her mum came from Kellston and asking if there was anyone in the area who might have known her. Maggie suggested Guy. He grew up here and he knows lots of people.'

'Is her mum not ...'

Tash gave a little shake of her head. 'No, she died about nine months ago. An overdose.'

Ava pulled a face. 'Oh, that's terrible. Was it ... was it deliberate or didn't she mean to do it?'

'Lydia doesn't know. There wasn't a note or anything. She says her mum had serious problems: drink, drugs, bad relationships and the rest. They were always moving around from

231

place to place, never settling anywhere. They were living in Glasgow when she died.' Tash sipped on her coffee and gazed over the rim of the mug. 'She reckons the only time her mum was happy was when she was growing up in Kellston. At least, that's what she told her. I think that's why Lydia came down here.'

Ava was surprised by how much Tash appeared to know. Lydia clearly wasn't quite as evasive as Hannah thought. Or at least not with everyone. 'And her dad? Is he not on the scene?'

'No, she doesn't know who he is. She doesn't have a name or anything.'

'She's been through a lot, then. It's not surprising that she's gone to pieces over this shooting.'

'You see?' Tash said. 'You understand, so why can't Hannah?'

Ava suspected that Hannah already understood more than she wanted to. It was never easy knowing that the person you loved was interested in someone else. 'So was Guy Wilder useful? Could he tell Lydia anything?' she asked, trying to get the conversation back on track.

'Yeah, a bit. Guy's younger than her mum, but he knows a lot of local history.'

'Is that another way of saying local gossip?'

Tash smiled. 'Maybe. But whatever you think, Guy's been good to her. He even helped her find the flat on Barley Road.'

'I don't think anything. I barely know the man.' Although that wasn't strictly true. She knew that he had sent a dead rat to Terry Street and that he was sleeping with Chris's ex-wife. But then she also knew that someone had murdered his mother and that he believed Terry Street had arranged it. The whole situation was a mess, a simmering volcano waiting to explode.

Suddenly the doorbell rang and Tash leapt up, relief spreading over her face. 'That must be her. I'll get it.'

Ava put the kettle on again, getting ready to offer more tea and sympathy, but when Tash came back upstairs it wasn't Lydia that she had in tow but a couple of plainclothes female officers. 'It's the police, Ava. They want to talk to you.'

Ava felt her heart jump into her mouth. It had to be bad news. 'What's happened? Is it Mum? Is it Dad?'

'No, nothing like that,' said the tall blonde woman. 'My name's DI Valerie Middleton and this is DS Laura Higgs.' She flashed her identification badge. 'We'd like to talk to you about a shooting that took place last night at a club called Belles.'

'What?' asked Ava. 'I don't understand.'

The other cop, the shorter, brown-haired one, threw a glance towards Tash. 'Is it all right to talk to you here or would you rather come down the station?'

'Here,' Ava said, her heart beating too quickly in her chest. 'We can do it here. But I don't get it. What's this got to do with me?'

'Do you want me to stay?' Tash asked.

Ava shook her head. 'No, it's okay. It's fine.' She looked at the cops and gestured towards the kitchen table. 'You'd better sit down.'

34

Ava sat on one side of the table and the two officers sat on the other. She looked at the women, more bewildered now than afraid. 'I really don't see how I can help you.'

DS Higgs stared sternly back at her. 'Perhaps you could let us be the judge of that.' There was hostility in her voice, an edge of nastiness, as if Ava had already been judged and found wanting.

DI Middleton's manner was less aggressive. 'But you have heard about the shooting?'

'Yes.'

'So perhaps you could tell us about Jeremy Squires.'

Ava frowned. 'Tell you? Tell you what? I don't even know the man.'

Higgs made a huffing sound in the back of her throat. 'You don't *know* him?'

'That's what I said. I've never met Jeremy Squires. I don't even know what he looks like.' Ava paused and then quickly added, 'Why should I? Who said I did?'

DI Middleton didn't answer her directly. 'You work for Chris Street, don't you?'

'Yes, I'm his driver.' Ava couldn't figure out where they were going with all this, but anxiety was starting to stir in her stomach.

'*Just* his driver?' Higgs asked.

Ava was about to say yes again when she suddenly recalled her conversation with Chris in Connolly's. She was, as least as far as Danny Street was concerned, his girlfriend too. Had Danny mentioned that to the police? But why should he? Aware that the officers were waiting for a response, she didn't have time to think it through properly. She made a fast decision that if she denied the relationship it might make her look suspicious, as if she had something to hide. 'Is that any of your business? I don't see what it has to do with the shooting.'

Higgs gave a smug smile. 'So more than just his driver, then?'

'We're friends,' Ava said, deliberately fudging the issue. 'We go way back. I've known him since I was a kid.'

'And have you had contact with Chris Street since the shooting?'

'Of course I have. His brother was shot too, remember? I wanted to make sure he was okay.'

'So you called him rather than him calling you?' Middleton asked.

'Yes.'

The detective inspector left a short pause before asking, 'How did you hear about it? The shooting, I mean?'

'How?'

'It's a simple enough question,' Higgs snapped.

Ava stared back at her. She was under interrogation, but couldn't figure out why. 'When my flatmate came home. She told me.'

'What time was that?'

'I don't know. About a quarter to ten. I'm not sure exactly. You'd have to ask her.'

'And how did she know about it?'

'From a friend.'

'And this friend's name?'

Ava hesitated. The last thing Lydia needed, especially in her current state, was the police knocking on her door, but she couldn't see any way of avoiding a straight answer. 'She's called Lydia, Lydia Hall.'

Higgs leaned forward with a gleam in her eye. 'And how did Lydia know?'

Ava had been around enough cops in her early years to be wary of their intentions. Her father's inability to keep his mouth shut had got him banged up on more occasions than she cared to remember. Although she wasn't guilty of anything – her conscience was clear – she was still reluctant to say too much. 'Look, what's all this about? I don't understand why you're asking these questions. I don't know anything about the shooting, other than it happened last night and it happened at Belles.'

DI Middleton gave her a patient if not entirely friendly smile. 'We're just trying to establish a few facts.'

'And what kind of facts would those be?'

'Perhaps if you could explain the connection between this Lydia Hall and Jeremy Squires?'

'Nothing close,' Ava said. 'She works in a gallery on the

high street. Beast? The taxidermy place? Jeremy Squires and his wife are collectors; they go in there a lot. I think her boss rang her when he heard about the shooting.'

Higgs inclined her head. 'And why should he do that?'

Ava gave a sigh. 'Why do you think? I presume he didn't want her to hear it from someone else or on the news or the radio.'

'But Squires and his wife are just customers,' Higgs said.

Ava gave a shrug. 'So what? It's still a shock when someone you know gets shot.'

Higgs reached into her handbag and took out a notepad and pen. She flicked through the pages before glancing up at Ava again. 'Could we have the address of this Lydia Hall.'

'Barley Road, but I don't know the number.' Ava gestured towards the living room. 'You'll have to ask Tash.'

DI Middleton painted on her smile again. 'So, Ava, let's get back to Jeremy Squires. You're sticking by your claim that the two of you have never met?'

There was something about the way she said 'claim' that set Ava's teeth on edge. 'No, never.'

'This is just routine, nothing to worry about, but would you mind telling us what you were doing last night, between the hours of . . . say seven and ten?'

'Me?' exclaimed Ava, her heart missing a beat. Suddenly her mouth had gone dry. 'What . . . why . . . what do you want to know that for?'

DI Middleton kept on smiling. 'As I said, just routine. There's not a problem, is there?'

'Yes,' said Ava, fighting to keep her voice steady. 'If you're accusing me of a crime, then yes, there's one mighty big problem. What do you think – that I ... that I had something to do with it?'

'No one's accusing you of anything.'

'Really? Only it's starting to sound that way.'

'If you've got nothing to hide,' said Higgs sharply, 'then you won't mind answering the question.'

Ava glared at her. 'I was here. I was in all night.'

'And there's someone who can verify that?'

'No, there isn't anyone who can verify that,' said Ava angrily. 'I could have quite easily nipped out, driven down to Belles and shot a man I don't know just for the hell of it!'

Higgs looked smug, as if Ava's response had revealed something useful. 'There's no need to get upset.'

'There's every need,' Ava retorted. She gave herself a mental prompt to try and stay calm. Losing her cool wasn't going to get her anywhere. 'Look, I was in all night, okay? I made dinner, watched some TV and read a few magazines. And before you ask me what I watched, it wasn't anything in particular. I was just channel hopping.' She paused and then added. 'Oh, I did watch the National Lottery, but sadly my numbers didn't come up.'

'And during that time,' Higgs asked, 'did you call anyone or did anyone call you?'

'No. The only call I made was to Chris Street at about half ten.'

Higgs scribbled in her notebook and Ava peered across the table trying to read it. But the notebook was upside down and the writing, a series of squiggles, seemed to be in a kind of shorthand.

DI Middleton shifted forward a little, a frown settling

between her eyes. 'We have a bit of a mystery,' she said. 'Perhaps you can help us out.'

'Me?'

'Yes, you see Mr Squires was conscious for a while when he was first taken into hospital. He was heard to repeat a name several times. Do you know what that name was?'

Ava shook her head. 'How should I know?'

Middleton left one of those short pregnant pauses. 'Well, the peculiar thing is that the name he kept saying was Ava.'

The words hit Ava like a fist in her stomach. She felt the blood drain from her face. 'What? I don't understand . . . He can't have meant me. How could he? He can't have. It must be someone else. I'm not the only person in the world called Ava.'

Middleton lifted her shoulders a fraction. 'But you see the problem we have? I mean, look at it from our point of view. Last night two men were shot and one of them was Danny Street. You drive for his brother, Chris. Jeremy Squires keeps repeating the name Ava. Perhaps there's another Ava that we haven't come across yet. What do you think the chances are?'

'But this is crazy!' Ava exclaimed. 'It's mad, completely mad! I swear to you, I don't know this guy.' She looked wildly around the kitchen as if somewhere, in one of its corners, there might be the evidence she needed to prove her innocence. 'I don't, I honestly don't!'

DS Higgs watched her with a kind of dull weariness as if she'd seen this act a thousand times before and hadn't believed it the first time.

But then, out of the blue, Ava suddenly found a straw to grasp at. 'You can ask him when he comes round again. I'll even come to the hospital. He'll tell you! He'll tell you this had nothing to do with me.'

Higgs glanced quickly at her boss, eager to be the one to reply. Middleton gave her a curt nod. 'I'm afraid that won't be possible. Mr Squires died from his injuries this morning.'

'He's dead?' said Ava, barely able to squeeze out the words. She felt her throat constrict as fear and alarm swept through her body. If he was dead then he couldn't clear her name and if he couldn't clear her name then . . .

'Yes,' Higgs said. 'Mr Squires won't be telling us anything.'

DI Middleton stared at Ava gravely. 'So, if there's anything *you'd* like to tell us, anything you might have forgotten to mention, now might be the time to do it.'

Ava shook her head. 'I've told you everything. I've told you the truth.'

'Well,' said Middleton as she rose to her feet, 'we'll want to talk to you again. Not planning on going anywhere, are you?'

'No.'

'Good. We'll be in touch.'

Ava remained seated at the table as the two officers left. She dropped her head into her hands and covered her face. She felt cold and panicky, like an animal trapped in a snare. This couldn't be happening to her, it couldn't. In a matter of minutes her life had slipped from the normal, from the everyday, into a weird surreal nightmare.

Ava heard the coppers talking to Tash and then the heavy click of the front door closing.

Seconds later, Tash came hurrying into the kitchen. 'What is it? What's going on? Why did they want to know where Lydia lives?'

'Squires is dead,' Ava said. 'He died this morning.'

Tash raised a hand to her mouth. 'Oh God!'

'You'd better call Lydia and warn her that the police will be paying a visit. Leave a message if she doesn't answer.'

'But why did they want to talk to you?'

'I'll tell you in a minute,' Ava said. 'You'd better call Lydia first.' As Tash went into the living room, Ava snatched up her phone and rang Chris Street's number. It went straight to voicemail. 'Damn it,' she murmured. Then, as heard the beep, she said, 'It's me. It's Ava. Call me back as soon as you get this. It's urgent.' As soon as she'd hung up, she quickly dialled again. This time the phone was answered on the second ring. 'Dad? Thank God you're there. I need to talk to you. Can I come round?'

35

As Silver carelessly manoeuvred the black Mazda MX-5 around the bend, she clipped the edge of the pavement, sending a judder through the car. Danny swore softly under his breath. 'For fuck's sake! You know how much this motor cost? Concentrate, can't you? At least try and keep the damn thing on the road.'

Silver tossed her head and glared at him. 'You drive, then. Oh, no, I forgot – you can't. You've only got one good arm. I'm doing you a bloody favour here. At least try and show some gratitude.'

'A favour? You're in this as deep as I am. If I hadn't got hold of those photos, you'd be looking forward to making new friends down Holloway by now.'

Silver looked at him again and shrugged. 'I still don't see why we need to do this. Why don't you just give him a bell?'

'Because this needs the personal touch. Squires is brown

bread, ain't he? Singing with the angels. Morton's going to be shitting himself, wondering if his little sideline is about to be exposed. What if he panics and starts shooting his mouth off to the filth?'

'Do you think he might?'

'You can never tell with people like that. It ain't worth the risk.'

'So what are you going to do?'

Danny grinned. 'What I'm going to do, hon, is make sure that he's more afraid of me than he is of the law.'

'With one arm?'

'Yeah, with one arm. Why, do you reckon I can't? There's more than one way to scare the shit out of tossers like him.' Danny glanced over his shoulder at the cars behind. 'Go round the block a couple of times. I want to make sure we ain't got a tail.'

'We haven't,' she said.

'And how the fuck would you know? The only time you use the rear-view is when you're admiring your pretty little face.'

Silver flicked back her long fair hair, glanced in the mirror and smiled. 'Only pretty? Squires said I was beautiful.'

'Yeah, well, Squires was trying to get into your knickers.'

'Or maybe he had more taste than you.'

'Taste?' Danny snorted. 'The guy collected dead animals. How fuckin' tasteful is that?'

Silver indicated left and swung the car round again. 'You see? There's no one behind us. I was right. Come on, tell me I was right.'

Danny lit a cigarette, a procedure that took twice as long as it normally would because of his injured right arm. 'Just 'cause the guy ain't up our backsides, don't mean he ain't there. Slow down a bit. I want to make sure.'

Silver took her foot off the gas and cruised through the back streets at a steady twenty. 'What did the cops say at the hospital?'

'They figure the bullets were meant for me.'

'Maybe they were. Who'd want to kill Squires?'

'How should I know? He could have been up to all sorts. Just 'cause he's Mr Respectable don't mean he's whiter than white.'

'You think the cops will want to talk to me?'

'Why should they? It ain't nothin' to do with you.'

Silver pursed her lips, annoyed at being dismissed so casually. 'It is too. Who's to say I wasn't there? The old man's got plenty of guns. I could have gone down Belles and tried to blow your bloody brains out.'

Danny drew on his fag and laughed. 'Yeah, be just like you to kill the wrong fuckin' bloke.'

'Maybe I won't miss next time.'

'Maybe I'll get in there first.'

Silver shook her head. 'You couldn't kill me, babe. You know you couldn't.'

'Nah,' he said. 'You're right. Who would drive me around if you were six foot under?'

'Maybe Ava would oblige – if you asked her nicely.'

'Did Squires ask you nicely?'

'You should know,' Silver said. 'You've got it all on film.'

Danny opened the window and threw the fag end out. 'Not any more, hon. I've got rid of it. And all the photos too.'

Solomon Vale had brought the envelopes round last night after the filth had finally let the staff go. The black man had handed them over without a word, got back in his car and pissed off home. Danny had made a bonfire at three o'clock in the morning, destroying all the evidence.

'Shame about that,' Silver said.

'It's not safe to hang on to anything, not with the filth on the prowl.'

'We can get some more,' she said. 'Once they've lost interest, we can start again.'

Although the blackmail gig had been a lucrative one, Danny suspected that it had probably run its course. 'I dunno. We'll see.'

Silver pulled up round the corner from Beast and killed the engine. She took off her seat belt and went to open the door.

'What are you doing?'

'We're going to see Morton, aren't we?'

Danny shook his head. 'Nah, not *we*, babe. Best I do this on my own.'

Silver narrowed her eyes, her mouth becoming sulky. 'What?'

He leaned across, took hold of her chin with his left hand and pulled her head around. He kissed her roughly, his tongue probing her mouth as his hand roamed down over her breasts and her stomach before coming to rest between her legs. He waited until he felt her respond before moving his lips away from hers and whispering in her ear. 'We don't want him getting distracted, hon. One look at you and he won't be listening to a word I say.'

Silver, although partly mollified, wasn't giving up yet. 'But it's not fair,' she said, like a disappointed child. 'You can't just leave me here on my own.'

'I'll be five minutes,' he said. 'Ten at the most. This is important, babe. I need him to be concentrating, not staring at your tits.'

Silver glanced down, admiring the generous curve of her own breasts, before looking up at him again. 'Ten minutes,' she said. 'And if you're not back by then I'm going to take this fuckin' car and dump it on the Mansfield.'

'You do that,' he said, 'and you'll end up in the same bloody morgue as Squires.'

'You've been warned.'

'So have you.' Danny got out of the car, closed the door and bent down to grin at her. She gave him the finger. He gave her the finger back. As he walked off down the road, he took a quick look at his watch. Twenty past ten. He made a mental note of it. Silver was nuts enough to actually carry out the threat.

The front display window of Beast was covered by a metal grille. The gallery was closed on Sundays, but Danny was sure that Morton Carlisle would be here. He was always here. And if he wasn't in the main part of the shop, he'd be in the basement ripping the guts out of some dead animal. He rang the bell, two short rings. While he waited he stamped his feet in the snow and looked up and down the street, his eyes quickly scanning everyone who passed by. Had the filth got a tail on him already? He didn't think so, but you could never be too careful.

Thirty seconds passed and then a minute. Danny put his left hand to the side of his face and peered in between the metal slats covering the reinforced glass door. He rang the bell again, this time keeping his finger on it. 'Come on, you fucker,' he hissed. If one thing was for certain it was that he wasn't leaving until he'd done what he'd come to do.

Eventually, there was movement from inside. Morton appeared from the rear of the gallery and looked towards the door. He saw Danny and stopped dead in his tracks. For a moment, Danny thought he was going to do a runner, retreat back into his office, but finally he made up his mind, carried on forward, unlocked the door and opened it.

'What the hell are you doing here?' Morton hissed through the metal grille. 'Are you mad?'

'Let me in. We need to talk. Do you want to do it here or shall we go somewhere more private?'

Morton hesitated again, but only for a second. With shaking hands he fiddled around with the locks until he was eventually able to lift up the grille. As soon as Danny had stepped inside, he quickly slammed it shut again.

'Good choice,' Danny said.

Morton stared at him. 'He's dead, you know.'

'Of course I fuckin' know. Why do you think I'm here?'

Morton's hands began a frantic dance, rising up to his chin, falling down to his hips. His eyes were wide and full of panic. 'What if they find out? What if the police realise he was being blackmailed and—'

'And what?' Danny said. 'They can't prove nothin', not if we all stay calm and keep our mouths shut.' He gave Morton's shoulder a shove. 'Come on, shift it! Get away from the door.'

The two of them went through to the office at the back where Morton slumped down at his desk and put his head in his hands. 'You shouldn't have come here,' he said. 'It's asking for trouble.'

Danny stayed on his feet, looming over him. 'Not as much trouble as we'll be in if you lose your nerve, mate. You're not going to do that, are you, Morton? I'd be really disappointed if you did.'

Morton Carlisle looked up at him, his forehead shiny with sweat. 'The man's dead,' he said hoarsely. 'If the police find out about the pictures, about ... they'll think *we* did it, they'll think we killed him.'

'Yeah,' Danny said. 'So let's make sure they don't find out, huh? I mean, so far as they're concerned, you're just a business associate, nothing else. There's no reason to suspect you of anything unless you give 'em reason to. So we keep calm, yeah? Keep a lid on it.'

Morton Carlisle had gone a sickly colour. His face had a greenish hue as if he was about to throw up. 'I didn't sign up to this. I don't know. A man's been murdered, shot dead in cold blood. It's not ... I can't ...'

Danny suspected that the time for reasoning was over. He sat on the corner of the desk, pulled the flick knife from his pocket and leaned forward, placing the blade against Morton's throat. 'This ain't a discussion, mate. I don't give a fuck what you think.' He pushed the tip of the blade into the soft flesh, pressing it hard enough to pierce the skin. A thin stream of blood trickled out.

'Please,' Morton begged, his body going rigid. His eyes stared pleadingly into Danny's. 'No, please.'

There was something about his pathetic desperation that made Danny want to plunge the knife in deeper. He could cut straight down into the throat or, if he moved the blade sideways, he could slice neatly through the carotid artery. Either way, it would all be over in a matter of seconds. Even with his left hand, he was more than capable of performing the act. And he was tempted, sorely tempted. It would mean one less loose end to worry about.

'Please,' Morton croaked. 'I won't . . . I won't say anything. I swear.'

Danny gazed down at him, revelling in the power he held. One simple move and he could shut Morton's mouth forever. But was it worth the risk? Probably not. The filth would be crawling all over the place and God knows what they'd find. Well, he knew one thing they'd find and that was a lot of unexplained cash. That's if Morton kept it here. But where else would he keep it? It wasn't safe to put blackmail money into a bank account.

'Please,' Morton begged again.

Slowly Danny lowered the knife, returned the blade to the sheath and shoved it back in his pocket. 'It's your lucky day, Morton.' He rose to his feet and gave a slow shake of his head. 'Just don't make me sorry I didn't finish the job huh?' At the door, he stopped and turned around. 'Oh and a word to the wise. You may want to change your shirt. There's a little blood on the collar.'

36

Ava couldn't keep still. She'd been at her father's for over an hour, jumping up every so often and going over to the window to look out across the Mansfield Estate. Any minute she expected to see a couple of squad cars drive through the main gates and pull up outside Haslow House. It wasn't that long since she'd been stressing about her father being arrested and now she had her own freedom to worry about too.

'Sit down,' Jimmy Gold said. 'You're making me nervous.'

Ava scanned the horizon one more time before returning to the kitchen table. 'Sorry. I can't help it. I just keep thinking . . .' She sat down, put her hands around the mug and tried to get warm. Even though the central heating was on, she felt cold and shivery, as if a sliver of ice was lodged in her bloodstream.

'Well don't. Nothing's going to happen. They were only fishing, love. All they've got is a name. How's that going to stand up in a court of law?'

Ava jerked up her head. 'You think they might arrest me?'

'No, that's not what I'm saying. Of course not. How many women are there in London called Ava?'

'A few, probably, but how many of them are connected to the Streets? That's how they're going to think. That's how *I'd* think if I was them. I'd figure it was too much of a coincidence.'

'Yeah, well, a coincidence is all it is. Stop getting ahead of yourself. Come tomorrow, they'll be digging around in his business, in his past, in his family life. Something's bound to come to light.'

'And if it doesn't?'

'There's still nothing to connect you to the shooting.'

Ava chewed on her nails. She remembered the eyes of the brown-haired cop, hard and suspicious and cynical. *That* woman had her well and truly in the frame. 'Since when has that stopped the cops from fixing someone up?'

'I think even they'd need a bit more than a whispered name from a dying man.'

'But what if there is more?' said Ava, her imagination starting to run riot again. 'What if they find something else?'

'There isn't anything to find, love.'

'Well there *shouldn't* be,' she said. 'But what if ... God, I don't know. I've just got a really bad feeling about all this. Do you think I should see a solicitor?'

Jimmy Gold pulled a face. 'Why waste your money on a brief when you don't need one? Give it a day or two and see what happens next.'

She knew that he thought she was overreacting, and maybe he was right. She didn't want to make it look like she had something to hide. Although a visit from the law hadn't been unusual in the days of her childhood, it was the first time in her life that *she* had been the focus of their interest. Her nerves were jangling and she couldn't think straight. She picked up the mug, sipped at the lukewarm coffee and put the mug down again. 'Do nothing, then? Just sit around and wait.'

'What else can you do?'

Ava glanced at her phone that had remained silent since she'd arrived. 'Why hasn't he called me back? I left a message ages ago.'

'Who's that, love?'

'Chris Street. I called him after the cops had been round.'

'Maybe he's had a visit too. Old Bill's going to want to talk to Danny again. Bound to. He's their number one witness.'

Ava was starting to wish that she'd never taken the driving job. Ever since she'd started, there had been trouble, first with Guy Wilder and now the shooting. She had thought that she could cope with working for a villain, but now she wasn't so sure. She remembered the gun that she had slipped into her bag – but that couldn't have anything to do with the death of Squires. No, there were hundreds, maybe thousands of guns swirling around in the underworld of London.

'What is it?'

Ava wrinkled her nose. 'Nothing.'

'Why don't you talk to the girl you were telling me about, this Lydia Hall? She knew Squires, didn't she? Maybe she can shed some light on why he said the name Ava.'

'I would do if she was in any fit state. But I'm not sure that she knew him that well. Or maybe she did. I've no idea, to be honest.'

'Could be worth a go.'

'I think the cops are going to see her. Probably so they can try and dig the dirt on yours truly.'

'Not that you're getting paranoid or anything.'

'I've a right to be paranoid,' she said, forcing a semblance of a smile. 'Everybody's out to get me.'

Suddenly Ava's mobile went off, its ring sounding unnaturally loud in the quiet of the kitchen. She snatched it up, hoping that it was Chris Street. But it wasn't his name showing on the screen. 'Ah, it's only Tash,' she said as she lifted the phone to her ear. 'Hi there, you okay?'

Tash, however, was obviously far from okay. Ava couldn't make out what she was saying. It was just a hurried series of mumbles interspersed with sobs. 'Tash? Tash? Slow down. I can't hear you properly. What's going on? What's happened?' There was a long pause and then Hannah came on the line.

'You'd better get back,' she said. 'There's been some bad news.'

Ava's fingers tightened around the phone. 'What is it?'

Hannah hesitated as if unwilling to speak the words out loud. But then she took a deep breath and said, 'It's Lydia. She's dead. She's taken an overdose.'

37

DI Valerie Middleton gazed at the empty double bed with its rumpled sheet. They had removed the body of the girl half an hour ago, but her imprint still remained. How old had she been? Twenty-five, twenty-six perhaps. A pretty, fair-haired girl with nothing to live for. A quarter-full bottle of whisky sat on the bedside table alongside an empty bottle of anti-depressants.

Suicides always filled Valerie with an almost overwhelming sense of sadness. It was the loneliness of it that got to her most, those final moments that had been spent in a solitary determination to end it all. There was no note, no final scribbled words of explanation. What could be so bad, so unendurable that Lydia Hall had felt unable to go on? It had to be connected to the murder of Squires.

DS Higgs came back into the bedroom and glanced at the bed. 'What do you reckon, guv? A guilty conscience or a broken heart?'

Valerie knew that she had to turn off her emotions and put on her professional head if she wanted to think clearly. 'No sign of the gun, I take it?'

'No, but she could have dumped it straight after, dropped it in a bin or somewhere. The boys have finished searching the flat. It isn't here. In fact, there isn't much here at all, not even a computer. We've bagged her phone, but that's about the sum of it.'

Valerie wasn't surprised that the search had been completed so quickly. Lydia Hall had possessed very little. The flat was sparsely furnished with only the bare essentials. The girl had made no attempt to prettify it, to put up pictures or add any feminine touches. There were no furry scatter cushions, no family photos, no ornaments or plants. It hadn't been so much a home as a roof over her head.

'Okay, I'll sort out the bedroom. Tell the boys they can go.'

As Higgs left the room, Valerie walked over to the window. It was only by chance that they had found the body at all. With Butler back at the scene of the crime and no real leads other than the mutterings of a dying man, she had decided that they might as well follow up on Ava Gold's story and see how much Lydia knew about the shooting.

The flat was a small one-bedroom conversion on the ground floor of a three-storey Victorian house on Barley Road. The building, situated at the far end of the road, was in the less desirable part without the nice view over the green. Higgs had rung the bell a couple of times, but there had been no response. Valerie wasn't sure what had made her try the handle – nobody kept their homes unlocked in Kellston even if they were in – but the door had offered no resistance and had swung smoothly open.

Valerie frowned. Had she known even as she stepped inside? There had been no smell – it was too early for that – but there had been something about the silence, a kind of still brooding quality that hung in the air like a pall. She had called out the girl's name. 'Lydia? Lydia, it's the police.'

They had gone into the chilly living room. Nothing. The bedroom was off to the right. She had hesitated before she'd turned the brass-coloured doorknob, a sense of unease washing over her. The curtains were closed, but a lamp was on beside the bed. And in the soft light she had seen the girl with her fair hair spread over the pillow like a fan. Not asleep. She was definitely not asleep.

Valerie had gone through the motions, feeling for a pulse even though she knew it was useless. The body was already cool. They had been too late, way too late to even have had a chance of saving her. The pathologist had estimated the time of death in the early hours of the morning, maybe one or two o'clock. They had no idea as yet how many pills she had taken, but mixed with the whisky they would have acted quickly.

Turning away from the window, she walked back over to the bed and with a gloved hand picked up the empty bottle and read the small print on the label. Amitriptyline. The prescription had been made out for a Karen Hall, not Lydia Hall. Sister? Mother? Or maybe just another name she had used. Valerie bagged the container, along with the bottle of whisky and the glass.

Higgs appeared again, her voice cool and brisk. 'Ready, guv?'

'Why do you think she left the front door open?' Valerie asked. 'What was the reason for that?'

'Maybe she wanted someone to find her before it was too late.'

'But no one was going to drop round at that time of night.'

'Unless she made a call, told someone what she was planning on doing.' Higgs paused and then added, 'Or in case she changed her mind and called an ambulance. People do. And you wouldn't want them wasting valuable time while they tried to get in.'

Valerie was aware that they would never know for certain. What had gone on in Lydia Hall's mind would always remain a mystery. Someone, of course, would have come round eventually: her boss, a friend, even the police if she was reported as missing. Had she wanted to make it easy for them? Had she preferred her body to be discovered as soon as possible? Perhaps the truth was more mundane – that she had simply forgotten to lock the door behind her.

'What are you thinking?' Higgs asked. 'You got doubts about the suicide?'

'No, not really. There's no sign of a struggle. I mean, it's not impossible that she was murdered, but I don't think so.'

'So what next?'

Valerie gave a sigh. 'We try and track down the family, if there is any, and break the bad news. Has Tash Reed gone home?'

'Yeah, Annie ran her back. Said she'd stay with her until her friend got there.'

It had been unfortunate that Tash Reed had turned up when she had, shortly after they'd discovered the body. Finding the front door ajar, the girl had walked straight into the flat. Valerie remembered her expression as the two of them had come face to face in the living room, the eyes growing wide, the slow dawning of horror. Death was never easy to deal with, but when you stumbled on it unexpectedly . . .

Valerie straightened her shoulders and glanced over at Higgs. 'Time for another visit to Market Square, I think.'

38

Ava, who had run most of the way back from the Mansfield, slipping and sliding on the ice, was now perched on the edge of one of the armchairs trying to get her breath back. It still hadn't sunk in properly. *Lydia was dead. Lydia had committed suicide.* These were facts and yet she didn't seem able to process them properly. She felt numb rather than emotional. It was as if the shock had paralysed the part of her brain that dealt with such terrible things.

Her gaze jumped between her flatmate and the two cops. Tash's eyes were red with crying. Hannah was doing her best to comfort her, but it was an impossible task. Tash had started by blaming herself for not going round to Barley Road earlier in the morning and then, when she discovered that this would have made no difference, blamed herself instead for not staying up with Lydia last night.

'I didn't even hear her leave,' Tash said. 'She was going to sleep on the sofa, but she must have slipped out as soon as we went to bed.'

'And what time was that?' DS Higgs asked.

Tash opened her mouth, but only a thin mewling sound emerged.

'About a quarter to twelve,' said Hannah, taking over. 'Yes, I'm pretty sure. Twelve at the latest.'

DI Middleton leaned forward, laying a hand lightly on Tash's arm. 'We understand that this is a difficult time, an awful time, and we're really sorry to be asking all these questions, but it's the only way we're going to find out what happened.'

'You know what happened, don't you?' said Hannah sharply. 'She went home and then she—'

Tash visibly flinched, stopping her girlfriend in her tracks. Then she swallowed hard and stared at DI Middleton. 'Why?' she asked, in a small trembling voice. 'Why did she do it?'

'Perhaps if we could go over the events of the evening,' said Middleton softly. 'Lydia phoned you, yes? While you were out having a meal?'

'She was hysterical,' Hannah said.

'Upset,' Tash insisted, shifting a couple of inches away and glaring at her. 'She wasn't hysterical. Why are you saying that?'

'She was more than just upset, Tash. You know she was. When we picked her up from the flat, she couldn't stop crying.'

'Well what do you expect when she'd just found out that ... that someone she knew had been shot?'

Hannah glanced at the cops and gave a shrug. 'It just seemed ... I don't know. I mean this was before the man had even died.'

'You thought it was an overreaction?' DS Higgs suggested. 'Disproportionate?'

Hannah gave another shrug. She wasn't going to deny it, but she wasn't going to risk Tash's wrath by agreeing out loud either.

'Lydia was sensitive,' Tash said. 'Fragile. Things, they ... they affected her differently to other people.'

'And what time did you get the call?' Middleton asked.

'Nine-ish,' Hannah said. 'Yes, it was definitely about nine.'

Higgs scribbled in her notebook.

'What about her family?' Middleton asked. 'Do you know where they are, how we might contact them?'

Tash, if she had heard the question, showed no indication of it. She covered her mouth with her fist and stared down at the floor.

'I don't know about any family,' Hannah said. 'To be honest, she was more Ava's friend than ours.'

The two cops both stared at Ava. Finding herself the sudden focus of their attention, she shifted uncomfortably in her seat. Oh God, why had Hannah had to say that? She'd barely known Lydia. In fact, she'd only met her on three occasions: at Beast, on Friday when they'd gone to the Fox and last night when the poor girl had been falling apart. But she could hardly admit to that, not in Hannah's presence at least. Tash had enough problems without her adding to them.

'Sorry?' Ava said, playing for time and pretending that her mind had been elsewhere. 'What was that?'

'Lydia's family,' said Higgs, her eyes boring into Ava. 'She must have mentioned them to you.'

'Oh, erm . . .' Ava quickly thought back to the conversation she'd had with Tash that morning in the kitchen, trying to remember exactly what she'd said about Lydia and her past. 'She didn't talk about her family much. I know her mum died about nine months ago. I think that she was still . . . still trying to come to terms with it.'

'And her father?' Higgs asked.

Ava shook her head. 'No, she never knew her father. She never mentioned any brothers or sisters either. She only moved here in July so I haven't really known her that long.'

'Do you know where she lived before?'

'Glasgow,' Ava said. 'But I got the impression that she and her mother moved around a lot.'

'Do you know what her mother was called, her Christian name?'

'Sorry, I've got no idea.'

Higgs kept her eyes fixed firmly on Ava. If the sergeant's stare was designed to intimidate, it worked. Ava had that icy, anxious feeling again. Although she had nothing to hide – other than the irrelevant matter of Tash's infatuation with Lydia – she felt like the guilty party. *Stay calm. Keep your head. Don't let them see that you're rattled.* Like her dad had said, they were only fishing, but she knew they were after something big.

'And what about boyfriends?' Higgs asked. Her gaze left Ava for a second and flicked over towards Tash and Hannah. 'Or . . . er . . . partners? Was she seeing anyone?'

Ava gave a thin smile. 'Are you trying to ask if she was a lesbian?'

'Was she?'

'No, I don't think so. And if she did have a boyfriend, she never mentioned him to me.'

DI Middleton crossed her long slender legs and smoothed out her skirt. 'And did she ever mention Jeremy Squires to you? I mean, before last night.'

'No, not that I remember.'

'So he wasn't a particularly close friend or, if he was, she didn't want people to know about it.'

Tash's head jerked up suddenly. 'What are you . . . what do you mean?'

But everyone knew what the inspector meant.

'You suspect there might have been something going on between them,' said Hannah, articulating a collective thought. 'You think they might have been having an affair.'

Middleton gave a cool shake of her head. 'All we're doing at the moment is trying to establish her state of mind, to make some sense of why she'd choose to take her own life a few hours after Jeremy Squires and Danny Street were shot.'

Ava frowned. 'But she didn't even know that Squires was dead when she . . . when she did it.' She sat back and folded her arms. 'No, that doesn't add up. If she was in love with him, then surely she'd want to stick around, make sure he was okay.'

'Unless . . . ' Hannah said.

There was a short pregnant silence while the 'unless' settled over the room. Ava instantly knew what was being implied: people killed for love or because they had been rejected. Was it possible that Lydia had followed Squires to Belles and shot him in the back? It seemed unlikely, but not impossible. It was true that Lydia had been grief-stricken, but had that been a sign of a guilty conscience or simply the response of a girl who was already in a highly emotional state after losing her mother?

Suddenly, Tash realised what her girlfriend was suggesting. 'No, no way! That's ridiculous! How could you even . . .' Tash glared at Hannah, her eyes brimming with anger and tears. Then she looked over at Valerie Middleton. 'She wouldn't. She *couldn't*. Lydia was a gentle person. She was kind. She wouldn't harm a fly.'

'But you've got to admit, it was hardly a normal reaction,' Hannah said.

Tash turned on her again. 'And what would you know about *normal*!'

Ava winced. If Hannah had any sense she'd shut her mouth and keep it shut before she completely alienated Tash and blew their relationship right out of the water. But of course, Hannah couldn't let it go.

'I'm only saying. I've a right to say what I think, haven't I?'

'Not when you're thinking those sorts of things.'

'And since when did you become an expert on Lydia Hall? You hardly knew the girl.'

'I knew her a damn sight better than you did!'

DS Higgs glanced slyly from one to the other, her lips slightly parted like a hungry predator sensing a good feed coming. Ava had disliked her the first time they'd met and her opinion hadn't altered. She was always wary of cops – she'd seen too many of them as a kid – but this one made her more uncomfortable than most. There was something cold, almost reptilian about the woman. Before the exchange between Tash and Hannah got out of hand, and things were said that couldn't be unsaid, Ava quickly tried to defuse the situation. 'Come on. We're all upset. Let's not . . . Lydia wouldn't have wanted this.'

'*Some* of us are upset,' Tash said, glancing pointedly at Hannah.

Hannah glared back at her. 'Meaning?'

It must have been crystal clear to everyone, especially Hannah, that Tash's feelings for Lydia ran deep. Normally, Ava wouldn't have volunteered any information to the police – it went against the grain – but now she saw it as the only way to stop Tash from blurting out something she might later regret.

'Guy Wilder might be able to help. He was friendly with Lydia.'

DS Higgs's gaze slithered back to her. 'Guy Wilder?'

'Yes, you know, from the wine bar on the high street. He might be able to tell you more about the family. When she first moved here, she was trying to find people who might have known her mum and someone pointed her in Guy's direction.'

'And did he know her mother?' Higgs asked.

'No, I don't think so. He's too young. But like I said, they became friends. She might have mentioned something to him, something useful.' Wilder, she was sure, wouldn't appreciate her tip-off to the cops, but hopefully he'd never find out it was her.

'How friendly?' Higgs said.

'Pardon me?'

Higgs scowled, suspecting that Ava knew exactly what she meant. 'Did they go out together? Where they ever in a relationship?'

'Oh, no, I don't think so. Well, if they were, she never said.'

Ava could see DI Middleton's brain ticking over at this new piece of information. She felt slightly bad about landing him in it, but they would probably have found out eventually. All she was doing was speeding up the process. Anyway, a man who sent a dead rat through the post didn't deserve too much consideration.

The inspector raised her chin a little, her interest piqued. She was about to say something when a phone started ringing. It took Ava a few seconds to realise it was hers. 'Sorry,' she said as she reached around the chair to her coat pocket, pulled the mobile out and checked the screen. It was Chris Street. Typical of him to ring back when the cops were here.

Ava stood up and looked over at DI Middleton. 'Sorry,' she said again. 'I won't be long, but I have to take this.' She went into the kitchen, closed the door behind her, pressed the button and lifted the phone to her ear. 'Finally,' she said, skipping the niceties. 'Where have you been? I've been trying to call since this morning.'

'Nice to talk to you too. What's the problem?'

'The problem is . . .' And Ava embarked on a fast somewhat garbled account of everything that had happened since she'd talked to him last. She kept her voice low, sure that DS Higgs was straining her ears to try and hear what was being said. Every now and again he'd say, 'Slow down, slow down,' but eventually she got to the end. There was a long pause after she'd finished as though he was still trying to digest it all.

'So what are you saying? That this girl Lydia killed Squires?'

'No. I don't know. Maybe. No one seems to know anything for sure.' Her fingers gripped the phone more tightly and there was a slight tremor to her voice that she couldn't control. 'But the police have latched on to Squires repeating the name Ava at the hospital. They think I had something to do with the shooting.'

'He can't have been talking about you.'

'Try telling that to the cops. I mean, put yourself in their shoes: I work for you, Danny was with Squires at Belles, and Squires kept saying my name after he was shot. They're hardly going to write it off as coincidence. And I was in on my own last night so I don't even have an alibi.'

'Shit,' he said. 'That does look bad.'

'You see?'

'You can't even get a date on a Saturday night?'

Ava scowled down the phone. 'Oh, I'm glad you think it's so damn funny.'

'Hey, I'm only trying to lighten the mood. You need to stop stressing. If Old Bill had you in the frame you'd be down the nick by now. They're just going through the motions. Look, do you want me to come over?'

Ava hesitated, but then made up her mind. 'No, I don't think that's a good idea. Not with the law here. And I don't have a clue how long they'll be. Just have a word with Danny and see if he can shed any light on it, will you? Maybe Squires mentioned another Ava to him or . . . Jesus, I don't know. Just try and find out anything you can. I'll see you tomorrow, yeah? I'll pick you up at the usual time.'

They said their goodbyes and Ava hung up. The events of the past twenty-four hours were starting to catch up with her. Things had been happening at such a pace that she hadn't really had time to absorb them, but now she found herself thinking of Lydia and the stark cold truth of her death. Could she have done more, done anything, to stop her from killing herself? The horror of it all was slowly sinking in.

Ava had to gird herself before going back into the living room. When she did, she was relieved to see that the two officers were on their feet and preparing to leave. Tash was still sitting on the sofa, her face pale and drawn. Hannah was preparing to show the officers out. But just as she thought the ordeal was over – at least for now – DI Middleton turned, fixed her in her sights and said, 'Just one last thing.'

'Yes?'

'I was wondering why Lydia didn't call you last night. Why did she call Tash instead?'

Ava drew in a breath. It was the second occasion that she had faced the question. The first time, when Hannah had asked, she had come up with a glib response about her mobile being on recharge, but that wouldn't do for the cops. When they checked Lydia's phone, if they hadn't already done so, they'd see that she hadn't even tried to ring her. Instantly Ava saw how bad this could look. They might come to the conclusion that she hadn't been called because she was involved in some way, because she already knew about the shooting, because . . . But Ava didn't have time to run through all the dire possibilities. The inspector was still waiting for a reply.

'Erm, I'm not really sure.' Ava, starting to panic, rapidly searched for a plausible answer. 'But, well, it might have been because when I saw Lydia on Friday, I mentioned that I was going to Norfolk this weekend to see my mum. Perhaps she thought there was no point in ringing me if I was that far away.'

'But you didn't go,' Middleton said.

Ava met the gaze of the inspector and fought against the urge to look away. 'No, I changed my mind.'

'Any particular reason?'

'The weather,' replied Ava, surprised by how easily the lie rose to her lips. 'I didn't want to drive through the snow.' From the corner of her eye she was aware of Hannah staring at her and she sent up a silent prayer that once, just for once, the woman would keep her big mouth shut.

39

Noah, who was ostensibly making preparations to open the bar, was actually eavesdropping on the conversation that was taking place on the leather sofas directly in front of the counter. The two police officers had arrived five minutes ago. Initially, he thought they'd come about the shooting at Belles. It was common knowledge, especially among the local constabulary, that there was no love lost between Guy and the Street family.

Although the news of Lydia Hall's suicide had come as a shock – sudden death was always shocking – it had not entirely surprised him. Lydia had always seemed a brittle, fragile kind of girl, highly-strung and prone to extreme emotions. He had not known her long, only a few months, but long enough to be aware that her mental state was not an entirely balanced one. He was pretty sure that she had provided the dead rat that Guy had sent to Terry Street.

DI Middleton was the cop doing most of the talking. She

was a tall, attractive blonde in her mid-thirties, dressed in a tailored, navy blue suit that flattered her curves. 'So, you think her mother's name was Karen Hall?'

'Yes,' Guy said. 'Karen, I'm pretty sure it was Karen. Lydia thought I might know someone who had known her mother. Of course *my* mother probably did, but as you're aware . . .'

Noah watched as Middleton gave a nod. Lizzie Street had been murdered several years back and wouldn't be telling anyone anything. 'But the name wasn't familiar to you?'

'It didn't ring any bells, but it was a long time ago. I think she said that her mother left the area when she was about sixteen. I doubt if I was even born then.'

'What do you think Lydia hoped to achieve?'

'Achieve?' Guy echoed. 'I don't know if she wanted to *achieve* anything. I think she was just . . . just searching for somewhere she could call home. I got the impression that she'd had a rather unstable background, that she'd moved around a lot, never settled anywhere. Perhaps she was just looking for some roots.'

'Do you know if she had other family?'

'She didn't mention anyone.'

'Did she have a boyfriend?'

'I've no idea.'

'But you were friends. Didn't the subject ever crop up?'

Guy sat forward, resting his hands on his knees. Since hearing the news, two short, deep lines had engraved themselves into the space between his eyes. 'Well, I'd say we were friendly rather than friends.'

'I'm not sure I understand the distinction.'

Guy made a loose gesture towards their surroundings. 'I

run a bar, Inspector, which means I get to meet a lot of people. And talk to a lot of people. I did have a few chats with Lydia, but to be honest it wasn't anything more than that. When she first came here she didn't know anyone. I suppose I felt sorry for her. She came across as ... I don't know ... a bit of a lost soul.'

'So not close, then?'

'No, not close, but I liked her. And I'm sorry, really sorry, to hear about what's happened.'

There was a short respectful silence before the other cop, the harder-faced, younger woman said, 'Did Lydia ever mention the name Jeremy Squires to you?'

'Squires? Wasn't he the man who got shot last night?'

'Yes.'

'No, never. Did they know each other?'

'Apparently so.'

Guy pulled a face. 'Really? But you can't think ... I mean, she didn't ... there's no connection between the two events, is there?'

'That's what we're trying to find out. Did *you* know Mr Squires?'

'Only by sight. He came here occasionally, not very often.'

'But of course you do know Danny Street.'

Guy gave a thin smile before raising both his hands, palms out. 'Not guilty,' he said. 'I was here all night until closing. There are plenty of witnesses if you'd like to check.'

DI Middleton joined the conversation again. 'No one's accusing you of anything, Mr Wilder.'

'I'm pleased to hear it.'

'We're just trying to shed some light on why Lydia Hall should take her own life.'

'Well, I wish I could help, but apart from the obvious . . .'

'The obvious?'

Guy gave a shake of his head, followed by a long sigh. 'That she was unhappy. That she couldn't see an end to that unhappiness. Isn't that why most people commit suicide?' He looked at his watch and then back at the two women. 'I wish I could help you more, but if you don't have any further questions, I really should be getting on. We're due to open shortly.'

While Guy showed the officers out, Noah picked a lemon out of the bowl and started slicing it up. He waited until the door had closed before raising his eyes again. 'Why did you lie to them?'

Guy sauntered over to the bar. 'About what?'

'You know what. About Lydia's past, about her mother, about everything you told her.'

'Oh that,' he said dismissively. 'Why should I help the police? Let them do their own investigating.'

40

By Monday morning the snow had turned to a sleety rain, making the pavements of Kellston even more perilous than the day before. As DI Valerie Middleton walked down from Cowan Road police station, her boots slipping and sliding on the icy surface, she knew that if she wasn't careful she'd end up on her backside. With her left hand holding on to her umbrella she pulled her right hand out of her pocket to give her better balance. Already she was regretting that she hadn't brought the car. The cold, nipping at her nose and ears, made her shiver. The breath escaped from her mouth in small steamy clouds.

It was a relief when she finally reached Connolly's and was able to push open the door and step into the welcome warmth of the café. The breakfast shift was in full swing and most of the tables were occupied. The room smelled of fried bacon, coffee and damp coats. Jeff Butler was sitting right at the back, his head bent in concentration as he tucked into a

Full English. She ordered a cappuccino from the counter, waited for it to be frothed and poured, and then went over to join him.

'Morning,' she said, pulling out the chair opposite to his. 'Fuelling up?'

'Valerie,' he said. 'Good to see you.' He gestured with his fork towards the plate. 'Comfort eating. The wife's gone to Oslo on a business trip so I'm having to fend for myself.'

'Ah, fending. Is that what you call it? Well, I'm sure she'll be overjoyed to come home and find you three stone heavier.'

Butler laughed while he cut into a slice of bacon. 'So what's bubbling with the Squires case? You want to go first or shall I?'

Valerie glanced towards his plate and smiled. 'You eat and I'll talk. That way your food won't go cold.' She took a sip of coffee while she gathered her thoughts. Although they'd liaised over the phone, they hadn't had a chance of a proper catch-up. Five minutes later, having run through a detailed account of the previous day, she was done.

'So that's pretty much it,' she said, summing up. 'The one linking factor between all these events appears to be Ava Gold. Squires reportedly said the name Ava while he was dying in hospital, she's involved with Chris Street, Danny Street was with Squires when he was shot, and she was friends with Lydia Hall.'

'But she still denies that she even knew Squires.'

'Yes.'

Butler mopped up some egg with a piece of fried bread. 'And where's the motive? A woman spurned? Lydia has an affair with Squires, gets dumped, shoots him in the back, calls

275

her friends, cries for a few hours and then, full of remorse, kills herself. Where did she get the gun?'

'Maybe Ava got it for her. I'm sure the Streets have a whole artillery stashed away somewhere. And that could explain why Lydia didn't call her on Saturday night. Plus the fact that she'd accidentally shot Danny too.'

Butler put his knife and fork down and sighed. 'Jesus, it would help if we were actually sure who the intended target was. I thought you were more inclined towards Danny Street.'

'I was until Lydia Hall decided to end it all.'

'But if Lydia did shoot Squires, then why was he saying the name Ava?'

'Perhaps Lydia and Ava were in it together.'

Butler wiped with mouth with his napkin. 'Except Squires couldn't have seen who shot him. He had his back to the gate.'

'I know. But I still think she's involved in one way or another. We just have to find out how.'

'Well, maybe something useful will turn up today. I've got a couple of officers going into Squires's office this morning and we'll be doing a trawl through his bank accounts to see if there's anything interesting there.'

'What about Danny Street? You went to see him again, didn't you?'

'Oh, he's sticking to his story,' said Butler. 'It's a pile of bollocks of course, and he knows that we know it, but unless we can prove the real reason for the meeting we're pretty much buggered.'

'What does he say about the blood on the jacket? It is his, I take it?'

'Yes, a perfect match. Says he tried to help Squires, that it must have been transferred then.'

'Be the first time Danny Street ever tried to help anyone.' Valerie picked up a spoon and poked at the froth on her cappuccino. 'And the wife? Have you managed to talk to her again?'

'She's still in shock, but claims her husband didn't have any enemies that she knew of. The name Ava didn't mean anything to her either, although I get the feeling – and it is just a feeling – that our Mr Squires may not have been the entirely faithful sort.'

'A hunch?'

'Yeah, she wasn't exactly forthcoming when it came to their personal life. I don't know, I could be wrong, but we'll ask around, see if any of his friends or business associates are willing to dish the dirt.'

'She knew Lydia Hall, though, didn't she?'

'Yes, although only through Beast. She met her quite a few times at the shop, but they never socialised as such.'

Valerie's eyebrows shifted up a notch. 'Well, *she* might not have. Doesn't mean that Squires wasn't seeing Lydia on the quiet.'

Butler pushed his plate to one side. He drank some tea and glanced around the café before his gaze came to rest on Valerie again. 'Maybe we're making this too complicated. What if Squires wasn't the target? There's a list of people as long as my arm who'd be more than happy to see the back of Danny Street.'

'And Lydia Hall?'

'The shooting of Squires could have been the straw that

broke the camel's back. She's unhappy, possibly even clinically depressed. Maybe she was involved with Squires or maybe she just liked the guy, and the shock of it all simply sent her over the edge.'

Valerie thought about this for a moment but then shook her head. 'Sorry, I don't buy it.'

'No, I didn't think you would.' Butler grinned at her. 'Not sure if I do either, to be honest. Just thought I'd throw it in the pot for the hell of it.' He paused and then said, 'So what about this call, the one she got from her boss about the shooting? Maybe he can tell us something.'

'We're still trying to get hold of Morton Carlisle. I've been ringing his mobile – his number was on Lydia's phone – but he's not answering.'

'So how about we walk down the road and ask him in person?'

Valerie's hands tightened around the cup she was holding. 'What, go to the gallery?'

Butler laughed. 'What's the matter, Val? Do stuffed animals give you the creeps?'

'No, that *place* gives me the creeps.'

He looked puzzled for a second, but then his expression abruptly changed to one of mortification. 'Ah, God, I'm so sorry. I forgot all about ... Christ, I should have thought.'

Valerie, who spent more time than she should trying *not* to think about it, offered up a faint semblance of a smile. 'Well, I'm glad you didn't. I don't want to be remembered forever as the cop that almost got killed by the Whisperer.'

Butler gave an understanding nod. 'Hey, look, why don't I go on my own? I can nip down the road, have a word and then come back. You stay here and get yourself another coffee.'

Valerie was tempted to take him up on the offer – she had no desire to step inside that building again – but knew that would be giving in to her fear. 'Aren't you supposed to face your demons?'

'Can I let you in on a secret? It's not obligatory.'

Valerie lifted her left hand from the cup and ran her fingers through her hair. 'No, I can't spend the rest of my life avoiding the place.'

'Are you sure?'

'Come on,' she said, rising to her feet. 'Let's get over there before I lose my nerve and bottle it.'

Outside, she walked as quickly as she dared on the slippery pavement. Now that she'd made the decision, she was eager to get it over and done with. They crossed the road and started heading north towards the former undertaker's. Butler made small talk, but she was only listening with half an ear. Her heart had started to pound in her chest. It was almost three years but she could still remember every second of her ordeal, every wave of panic, every desperate plea she had uttered, every scorching rush of pain as the burning cigarette was pushed into the soft flesh of her shoulder. Gerald Grand's voice whispered in her ear: *Of the woman came the beginning of sin, and through her we all die.*

Valerie swallowed hard, trying to force down the fear. It was over, done with. Grand was in jail and would most certainly die there. She was the lucky one, the one who had got away. She had to hold on to that. If she continued to let the events of that day haunt her, then he would still have control,

279

would still be pulling her strings from behind prison bars. She couldn't, *wouldn't*, allow that to happen.

They came to the gallery and stopped outside. Butler reached for the door, but then hesitated and withdrew his hand. He looked at her. 'Are you sure? You don't have to do this.'

'Just do it,' she said, trying to keep her voice light. 'If I feel a fit of hysteria coming over me, I'll let you know.'

Butler smiled. 'Somehow I don't associate you with fits of hysteria.'

'Let's hope it stays that way.'

Butler pushed open the door and they stepped inside. The inside of the gallery was filled with a vast array of animals in glass cases and domes. Such was the surreal nature of the place that Valerie was temporarily distracted from her own fears and anxieties. She had read about taxidermy being back in fashion, but had not been prepared for the sheer quantity of creatures on show. Her gaze flicked quickly over rabbits, voles, weasels, mice, rats, fish and snakes – and they were just the exhibits closest to her. A large brown bear, its expression less than friendly, was standing guard by the wall.

'Nature in all its abundance,' Butler murmured. 'Skinned and stuffed in Kellston.'

'Not tempted to an impulse purchase, then?'

'I'll pass.'

A tall, stooped man with a shock of white hair and a salesman's smile approached from the rear of the room. 'Good morning, good morning,' he said, rubbing his hands together. 'Welcome to Beast. Not so nice out there today.'

'Morton Carlisle?' Butler asked.

'That's right.'

'I'm DCI Jeff Butler and this is DI Valerie Middleton.' He held out his ID.

Carlisle gave it a cursory glance. 'Ah,' he said, his face instantly dropping. 'Is this about poor Mr Squires?'

'And Lydia Hall,' Valerie said.

'Lydia?' he said, frowning. 'I'm afraid she hasn't come in today. It's not like her, not like her at all, but I think she may be too upset about ... Well, it's not always easy to cope with these things. I've tried calling her but ...'

'You haven't heard?'

'Heard?' he said. 'Heard what?'

Valerie prepared herself to break the news. 'Is there somewhere we can go? An office, perhaps?'

Carlisle's mouth opened, his lips parting as if to demand an answer to his original question. But then he thought better of it. 'This way,' he said, turning and walking back in the direction he had come from.

The inside of the building was so altered that Valerie had no immediate reminders of her experiences there. It was only as they passed the open door to the basement that she received an unwelcome jolt. A smell, something like formaldehyde – perhaps it was formaldehyde – floated up the stairs and caught in the back of her throat. She shuddered, her eyes instinctively closing for a second.

'Are you all right?' asked Butler softly.

'Fine,' she said, smartly bringing down the shutters on the part of her mind that held the details of the past. 'I'm fine.'

Morton Carlisle took them into a small office off to the right where they all sat down and the bad news was imparted.

Valerie watched him carefully as she told him about Lydia's suicide. The shock on his face seemed genuine, although his skin was so bloodless it was impossible to tell if he actually paled or not. Butler asked if he wanted a glass of water.

Carlisle shook his head. 'She's dead? I can't believe it. She's dead?'

It was another few minutes before Valerie felt able to ask the questions that she had to ask. 'We need to track down her family, if she has any left. Did she mention any relatives to you?'

'Relatives? No, no I don't think so.' Carlisle's hands shifted around the desk as if he didn't know what to do with them. 'I got the impression that she was alone.'

'And as a person, what was Lydia like?'

'Like?'

'You know – quiet, bubbly, reliable, happy, sad . . . '

Carlisle pondered on this for a moment. 'Reliable, yes, certainly. That's why I was so surprised when she didn't turn up this morning. And hard-working too. I wouldn't say she was an especially extrovert person, but then I wouldn't call her shy either. I suppose she was rather . . . self-possessed.' His right hand reached for a piece of paper, moved it a quarter of an inch and then moved it back again. 'And polite. She was always good with the customers.'

Butler leaned forward. 'Jeremy Squires was a customer.'

Carlisle made a slight movement of his head, almost a nod but not quite. 'Yes, indeed.'

'Did Lydia know him well?'

'Well?' Carlisle repeated.

'Did they seem friendly towards each other?'

'Like I said, Lydia is ... *was* always good with the customers. She had a nice manner. Jeremy and Amanda made regular visits to the gallery. They're keen collectors. They've got an excellent eye.'

And an excellent bank balance, Valerie thought, judging by the price tags she'd noticed on her way through the rooms. 'So she would have seen quite a lot of them. Did Jeremy ever come in on his own?'

Carlisle hesitated again, concerned perhaps about the direction the interview was taking.

'Occasionally, but I don't see what that has to do with—'

'We're just trying to get some background,' Butler said. 'Nothing to worry about.'

Valerie continued with her questions. 'And would they have been alone together, or are you always here?'

Carlisle went back to fiddling with the sheet of paper. He gave it a long hard stare and then raised his eyes to the inspector. 'I'm not quite sure what you're getting at.'

'I'm just trying to establish the nature of their relationship.'

'There *wasn't* any relationship,' said Carlisle firmly. 'Well, nothing beyond the normal parameters of business.'

'Are you certain of that?'

'He's a married man, for heaven's sake.' Carlisle cleared his throat. 'He and Amanda are ...were ... No, there was nothing like that going on. I'd have noticed. I'd have known about it.'

Valerie wasn't so sure. Couples who were having illicit affairs would take extra care in the company of others. 'Okay,' she said. 'But now, can I take you back to Saturday night. How exactly did you hear about the shooting of Jeremy Squires?'

Carlisle seemed to relax a little, as if now on safer ground. 'Eddie Barnes called me. I've known him for years. He was having a dinner party and the Squires had been invited, but only Amanda turned up. Jeremy was supposed to be joining them later but . . . well, you know what happened next. The police found Amanda's number on his phone and called to let her know. Once she was on her way to the hospital, Eddie gave me a ring.'

'And then you rang Lydia,' Valerie said.

'That's right.'

'Why?' asked Butler.

'Pardon me?'

Butler leaned his elbows on the desk. 'Why exactly did you call her? If Jeremy was just a customer, why the urgency in letting Lydia know?'

A frown settled on Carlisle's forehead. 'There wasn't any urgency except . . . I don't know. I suppose I didn't want her to see it on the TV.' His hands resumed their restless dance, his fingers intertwining, parting, coming together again. 'I called a few people, not just Lydia.'

Valerie suspected that Carlisle was the kind of man who revelled in passing on bad news. He had probably called everyone he knew to relay the information and gossip about how a respectable businessman like Squires had been shot outside a sleazy lap-dancing club in Shoreditch. 'Do you know where she was when you called her?'

Carlisle shook his head. 'She didn't say. I didn't think to ask.'

'Could you hear any noise in the background – traffic, music, the TV, that kind of thing?'

'No, I don't think so. Nothing that I recall.'

'And how did she react when you told her?'

Carlisle lifted a hand to his face and rubbed at his chin. 'She was ... upset ... shocked ... she didn't say much.'

'So she sounded surprised?'

'Of course she was surprised. I mean, you read about this kind of thing, see it on the news, but you don't expect ...'

'No,' Valerie said.

'But I had no idea that she'd take it so badly. Is that why she ...? But surely not. Was there a note? Did she say why?'

'I'm afraid not. How long had Lydia been working here?'

'Since the summer. July. Yes, it was the beginning of July, I believe.' Carlisle moved his hands down into his lap and then back on to the table again. 'It really is too terrible. A young girl like that. Dreadful. What a waste.'

Valerie wasn't sure what made her ask the next question. Simple curiosity, perhaps, as to how Lydia Hall had ended up here. 'How did she get the job? Was it through an advert, an agency?'

Carlisle frowned again. 'What does that matter?'

'It probably doesn't, but if you could just humour me.'

'Well, as it happens it was Guy Wilder. He asked me to consider her. He knew I was looking for a new assistant and thought she might be suitable.'

Valerie glanced quickly at Butler, but of course he hadn't been there at the interview with Wilder. 'Oh,' she said, feigning ignorance. 'So Lydia was friendly with Mr Wilder?'

'Yes. I believe so. She used to go to the bar quite often.'

Valerie gave a nod. 'Okay. Thank you.'

With her questions finished as regards Lydia Hall, Butler continued with his own line of enquiry.

'How well did you know Jeremy Squires?'

'Oh, I've known him for years. He's a collector, a business acquaintance. Sometimes our paths crossed at various social events.'

'And what kind of a man was he?'

Carlisle gave a light shrug of his shoulders. 'Decent, honest, trustworthy. A family man. He was a councillor too, you know. Yes, he was well liked and respected in the local community.'

'Mr Perfect, then?'

Carlisle's mouth turned down at the corners. 'Well, I doubt if many of us qualify for that particular status. All I'm saying is that *I've* never heard a bad word said about him.'

'And when was the last time you saw Mr Squires?'

'Now, let me see . . . it must have been last Thursday. Yes, that was the day we had the exhibition. He came in the afternoon with his wife.'

'And who did he talk to?'

Carlisle raised his hands in an exasperated fashion. 'I really have no idea, Chief Inspector. The gallery was crowded. I don't follow my clients around to see who they're conversing with.'

'Was Danny Street here by any chance?'

The question, coming out of the blue, clearly flustered Carlisle. 'No. What? Why should he be?'

'But you do know him?'

'Yes. No. I mean, I know *of* him. I know who he is. But we're not . . . I'm not personally acquainted with him.'

Butler left a short silence during which Carlisle didn't meet his gaze. 'Okay, well, I think that's about it.' He looked at Valerie. 'You all done?'

'Only one last thing. Does the name Ava mean anything to you, Mr Carlisle?'

'Ava? Do you mean Ava Gold?'

Valerie stared across the desk. 'You know her?'

'Hardly. I've met her once . . . no, twice. A dark-haired girl, yes? But I always remember names. It's something that I pride myself on. She was here last Thursday as it happens. She came to the exhibition.'

Valerie's eyes flashed with interest. 'Did she indeed. Do you know if she came with anyone?'

'I'm afraid not. As I mentioned earlier, it was a busy day. When I spoke to her – and that was only briefly – she was on her own.'

Valerie pushed back her chair and stood up. 'Thank you for talking to us. We appreciate it, especially at this difficult time.'

Carlisle looked relieved as he escorted them back to the front door. 'A tragic business. I'm only sorry I couldn't be of more help.'

As soon as they were on the street, Valerie turned to Butler and said, 'Well, there's a turn-up for the books. Ava and Squires in the same place at the same time last week. So much for the two of them never having met.'

41

Ava dashed from the Kia to the Mercedes, shook the rain from her hair, turned on the heat and then sat and waited for Chris Street to come out of the house. It was a miserable morning, cold and wet and grey. The rain was bucketing down, hammering on the roof of the car and streaming down the windscreen. She had a strangely claustrophobic feeling, as if her darkest thoughts were closing in on her.

She drummed her fingers on the wheel, impatient to be off. Where was he? The longer she had to wait, the more time she had to dwell on things. Lydia's face rose into her mind and she tried to push it away. With suicide, there was always a legacy of guilt. It was impossible to still those persistent voices, those nagging doubts about whether you could have done more.

All the same, she preferred to be here rather than at home. The atmosphere at the flat was fraught, with Tash and Hannah barely talking to each other. The relationship was on its knees, slowly disintegrating, and it was only a matter of time before it all fell apart. And that, of course, wasn't the only thing she had to worry about. A man she didn't know had called out her name as he lay dying. *Ava, Ava*. What the hell was she supposed to do about that?

Suddenly, above the sound of the rain, she heard the front door slam and seconds later Chris was climbing into the car.

'Morning,' he said. 'Still at liberty, then? I thought you might be running errands for some fat dyke in Holloway by now.'

She gave him a cool look. 'Ha, ha. I'm glad you find it all so amusing.'

'Still got Old Bill on your back?'

'Yes. They're convinced, unsurprisingly, that I must have something to do with Squires. Did you manage to find out anything from Danny?'

Chris pulled his seat belt across, shaking his head at the same time. 'Sorry, he disappeared before I got the chance to have a proper talk. But he said he'd meet us in the Fox at lunchtime. You can ask him all you want then.'

'Oh, okay,' she said, not entirely looking forward to the rendezvous. Danny Street freaked her out and she didn't relish the prospect of having to be closer than a few feet from him or to ask him anything face to face. She'd been hoping that Chris would ask the difficult questions for her. 'So where to? Where do you want to go?'

'Shoreditch.'

'Belles? Isn't it closed? I thought the cops would still be crawling all over the place.'

'They are. I want to go to Maple Street. You know where that is?'

Ava breathed out a sigh as she drove the Merc through the gates and on to Walpole Close. 'Why do you always ask me if I know where places are? I've been driving round London for years.'

'Are we a touch irritable this morning?'

'Yeah, well, you'd be irritable if . . . '

Chris Street glanced at her, raised his hand and rubbed at his chin. 'Oh, shit, sorry. I should have thought. Was that girl – Lydia is it? – was she . . . was she a good friend of yours?'

'No,' she said. 'I hardly knew her, but that's half the problem.'

'You've lost me.'

And then, before she knew it, Ava was telling him all about Tash's infatuation and how she'd had to cover when Hannah started asking questions. 'So you see, the cops now think that I was the one who was close to Lydia and even if Tash tells them the truth, they're not going to believe her. They're just going to think that she's covering because we're mates.'

'My, those lesbians have mighty complicated love lives.'

Ava snorted. 'Well, I don't think you need to be lesbian to have complications in that department. If I remember rightly it wasn't that long since you were rushing round to Wilder's with—'

'Yeah, yeah, no need to remind me. I get it. We all make mistakes, huh?'

She gazed through the rain-soaked windscreen as the wipers flipped back and forth. 'Anyway, none of that explains why Jeremy Squires was calling out my name.'

'The guy had just been shot. He was probably delirious.'

'But why Ava, for God's sake? Why, of all the names in the world, did he have to pick on mine?' She tapped the wheel in frustration. 'You're sure Danny didn't say anything after the shooting? I mean, he was there with Squires. He must know something.'

'He says they were chatting about cars.' Chris gave her a sideways glance. 'What do you reckon, then? Was Lydia the one? Did she do it?'

'I've no idea. There's nothing to suggest that she was actually involved with Squires, but then there's nothing to say she wasn't either. And she was upset, *really* upset, on Saturday night. But . . . I don't know . . . It's all a damn mess.'

'Maybe Lydia mentioned your name to him and it just kind of stuck in his head.'

'So much so that he's calling it out on his deathbed?'

'Well . . .'

'Exactly. It doesn't make a blind bit of sense.'

By the time they reached the border of Shoreditch, Ava hadn't gleaned any more information than she'd had on waking up that morning. She felt frustrated and anxious, scared that her life was about to spiral out of control. Although she kept telling herself that the police couldn't prove anything – there was nothing to prove – the tightness in her chest remained.

She manoeuvred the Mercedes carefully through the line of traffic until they arrived at Maple Street. When they reached a wide office block covered in scaffolding and tarpaulins, Chris told her to pull in beside it. He sat and stared at the building for a minute or two.

'Not much work going on,' he said eventually.

'It's not really the weather for it.'

'But not inside either. Look, it's all locked up.'

Ava peered through the rain. 'What is this place?'

'It's supposed to be Borovski's new casino. But I heard a rumour that he's pulled out, that he's decided to open up in Whitechapel instead. Seems like that rumour could be true.'

'And that matters because?'

'Because we've got a deal with him. Or at least, we thought we had. And now he's pissing off somewhere else.'

'And hasn't told you.'

'Not a word. He was trying for that place in Whitechapel for ages, but couldn't get the planning permission. That's why he decided to come here.'

'Must have twisted someone's arm. Maybe he's got a friend on the council.'

'Bunged them a fortune, more like.' Chris raked his fingers through his hair. 'Shit, this is all I need.' He opened the door to the car. 'There must be someone about. I'm going to have a butcher's.'

As soon as Chris had left, Ava got out her mobile and called her father. His voice, when he answered, sounded strained and hoarse.

'Are you okay, Dad?'

'It's just a bit of flu, love. Nothing to worry about. I'll be right as rain in a couple of days. How are you? No more trouble from the law, I hope.'

'Nothing serious,' she said, not wanting to burden him with her concerns when he was ill. 'Are you sure you're all right? You sound terrible.'

'Yeah, I'm fine.'

'And no problems with, you know, what we were talking about ...' She didn't want to mention the robbery. Ava doubted if the police had a tap on his landline phone, but you could never be sure. If they suspected her of murder, they could probably do anything they liked. And what about her own phone? She knew that it was possible to place a tap inside it, but were there other ways of listening in?

'No, love. No problems at all.'

'Good,' she said, relieved that she had one less thing to worry about. At least for the moment. 'Why don't I call by after I've finished work? I can bring some food over, save you cooking for yourself.'

'You don't need to do that.'

'I want to,' she said. 'I'll see you later.'

Chris came hurrying back through the rain just as she was hanging up. 'Any joy?' she asked as he got into the car, but one look at his face told her everything she needed to know. 'Bad news, I take it.'

'It's that all right. I found a security guy who said work stopped a week ago. And he doesn't reckon it's going to start again anytime soon. Place is up for sale again.'

'Ah,' she said. 'Well, I hope you haven't sent your Russian friend the falcon yet. Maybe Carlisle will give you a refund.'

'I'll shove that fuckin' falcon up Borovski's arse! Jesus, I bet this is down to Wilder.'

'You can't be sure of that.'

'No, but I can take a bloody good guess.'

Fearing that he might be about to do something rash, she said, 'Just promise me that you're not going to go over there and start waving that gun about.'

'I couldn't if I wanted to.'

'Huh?'

Chris, as if he'd said more than he intended to, quickly looked away from her.

'What do you mean?' she asked.

Slowly, he turned his face to meet her gaze again. He hesitated, but then decided to come clean. 'It's missing. I don't know where it is.'

'What? How can it be missing?'

He gave a shrug. 'It was in the pocket of my other overcoat. I meant to take it out, put it somewhere safe, but then I forgot all about it. And then this morning . . . I was going to lock it in the safe, but . . . '

'Jesus, how long has it been missing for?'

'How the hell would I know? One day, three days? I haven't seen it since Friday. Danny says he hasn't taken it. The old man says the same. Course either of them could be lying. And Dad can't remember what he was doing yesterday, never mind a few days ago.'

'So who else has been to the house?'

'Only Silver. Oh, and the cleaning woman, Mrs Phillips, but somehow I can't see her as an avid arms collector.'

Ava thought about the gun that had been used to kill Squires. Could it have been the same one? Perhaps Silver had taken it, but she'd hardly try and shoot her own boyfriend. Unless Danny had persuaded her to kill Squires, his perfect alibi being that he was standing right beside the guy when he was shot. 'Silver, then. Have you asked her?'

'She denies it, but she's mad enough. Come to that, she's nuts enough to take a shot at Danny. Those two are . . . ' He pulled a face. 'They're both crazy. They're as mad as each other and off their heads most of the time.'

'So what are you going to do?'

'What can I do? It might turn up again. It might not. I'll just have to wait and see.'

Ava gazed up towards the dark, cloud-filled sky. This wasn't good news, not good at all. Could it really be a coincidence that the gun had disappeared at the same time as the fatal shooting of Squires? Somehow she doubted it.

42

The Fox was busy, doing a brisk lunchtime trade. While they stood at the bar, waiting to be served, Ava scanned the pub for Danny. There was no sign of him. A small part of her hoped that he wouldn't show, but the bigger part wanted desperately to find out what he knew about Squires.

Eventually Maggie McConnell came over and said, 'Hello, dear. Sorry to keep you waiting. How's Tash bearing up?'

'Not so good. It'll take a bit of time, I guess.'

'It's such a shame. Give her my love. That poor Lydia; it doesn't bear thinking about.'

Chris ordered the drinks, a pint for himself and a Coke for Ava. As Maggie was taking the money she asked him, 'And how's your father now?'

'He's fine,' said Chris sharply. 'Why shouldn't he be?'

Maggie raised her eyebrows and retreated to the till.

'She was only asking,' Ava said. 'No need to bite her head off.'

'Looking for gossip, more like.'

They found a free table against the wall and sat down. 'Didn't you mention that you were thinking of trying to buy this place? You won't have a hope if you get on the wrong side of Maggie.'

'I haven't a hope anyway. The old man's not interested.'

'Couldn't you raise the money yourself?'

'I might have had a fighting chance if the Borovski deal had gone through, but that's dead in the water now.' He took a mouthful of his pint and glowered down at the table. 'Bloody Wilder's seen to that.'

'You don't know that for sure. You can't know that it was him.'

'So why do you think he was schmoozing the Russian at that Beast place?'

'I didn't say he was schmoozing, just that they were ... talking to each other.'

'Friendly, you said. *More* than friendly. No, Wilder's behind this. You can bet your life on it. Somehow he's managed to persuade Borovski to change his plans and open the casino in Whitechapel instead. God, Wilder's going to pay for this. I'm going to make damn sure he does.'

Before Chris could begin to dwell on Guy Wilder's ruination of his life, Danny turned up with Silver in tow. She was wearing white trousers, white boots and a white fur jacket. On a snowy day, Ava thought, she'd be in danger of disappearing entirely from view. While Danny went to the bar, Silver slid into the bench and stared across the table.

'So, you're Ava.'

'That's me.'

Silver inclined her head as if to study her better. Her blue eyes blatantly roamed across her face and down the upper part of her body. Finally, she turned to Chris and nodded. 'She's pretty.'

'I'm sure she's pleased you think so,' he said drily.

Ava looked from one to the other. 'I am here, you know.'

'I'm just looking out for him, hon,' Silver said. She gave a weird little giggle. 'Poor Chris hasn't had much joy on the girlfriend front recently.'

Ava suddenly remembered that she and Chris were supposed to be a couple. With everything that had happened recently, the pretence felt somewhat farcical. However, as she didn't want to embarrass him, she had no choice but to play along. 'I guess he's the fussy type. Some men are like that.'

Chris shifted uncomfortably beside her. She guessed that he felt as awkward as she did about the whole situation.

Danny came back with a couple of shorts on a tray. He kept his right arm down by his side and carried the tray in his left hand. He sat down beside Silver and gave Ava a nod. 'I hear the filth have been giving you grief.'

'You could say that. They're trying to figure out why Jeremy Squires kept saying my name. I don't suppose you have any idea, do you?'

'Me?' Danny said. 'Not a clue. Sorry, love. I only met the man for five minutes, walked out to the car park with him and next thing I know some bastard's put a bullet in my arm.'

'So he didn't mention my name to you?'

'Nah, he didn't. Did you know the bloke, then?'

'No,' Ava said. 'I didn't. That's what makes it all so weird.'

'I wouldn't worry about it,' said Danny dismissively. 'Cops can't arrest you for being called Ava. Least they couldn't last time I looked. They'll soon get sick of hassling you, sweetheart, move on to some other poor sod.'

Ava was quickly beginning to realise that the meeting was a waste of time. Danny, if he knew anything, wasn't going to spill the beans. She was still in the dark and that was the way it was going to stay.

Silver looked at Chris again. 'We heard about Jenna,' she said slyly. 'Is it true about her and Wilder?'

'Why should I care? She's my ex not my missus. I don't give a fuck what she does.'

'Wilder, though,' said Silver, deliberately goading him. 'Why him? Is she trying to piss you off or what?' She smiled, showing a row of small white pearly teeth. 'The bitch deserves a slap. You want me to give her a slap for you, babe?'

'I think I can fight my own battles, thanks all the same.'

'Well, if you change your mind . . .'

'I won't.'

Silver, disappointed, turned her attention to Ava. 'So where are you from, then?'

From here, originally. From Kellston.'

'She's Ted Gold's daughter,' Danny said. 'I told you that.'

'*Jimmy* Gold,' Ava said. 'Ted's my uncle.'

Danny frowned. 'Jimmy? I don't remember him. Did he work down the car lot?'

'Sometimes.' Ava wasn't surprised that he didn't remember her dad. Ted was a loud flamboyant character and her father, a quieter sort, had always been in his shadow.

'So where do you live?' Silver asked.

'Here in Kellston.'

'Whereabouts?'

'Market Square.'

'Really? What number?'

Ava was reluctant to tell her – she didn't see why she wanted to know – but couldn't think, off the cuff, of a good enough reason as to why she shouldn't. 'Forty-six,' she said eventually.

'Forty-six,' Silver repeated carefully as though she was mentally filing the information away. 'So why don't you ever come round to Walpole Close if you live so near?'

'I do come round. I'm there every morning.'

Silver flashed her teeth again. 'You know what I mean. How come you never stay over? Or are you two not . . . '

Ava was rapidly coming to the conclusion that Silver had no boundaries when it came to social interaction. The girl was either devoid of any social graces or just deliberately provocative. Ava glanced at Chris, smiling thinly. 'Why don't you tell her, hon. Why don't you explain why I never stay over?'

'Because it's none of her business,' Chris said. 'Silver should learn to keep her nose out of things that don't concern her.'

But Ava could see that his attempt to deflect was only going to inflame her curiosity rather than satisfy it. Before Silver embarked on a closer interrogation, she quickly piped up, 'Actually, it's because of the dog. He doesn't like being left on his own. And he doesn't get on with other dogs so . . . '

'Oh, what kind of a dog is he?' Silver asked.

'A Staffie,' Chris said, obviously feeling that he now needed to contribute something to the ongoing lie. 'He's a Staffie

300

called George. Now can we move on or would you like to know what brand of dog food he eats and where he likes to shit?'

Silver giggled. 'You're so funny. Ain't he funny, Danny?'

'Yeah, bleedin' hilarious,' Danny said. 'I need another drink. I'll get a round in, yeah?' He stood up and looked down at Chris. 'Give us a hand, eh. I can't carry all the glasses with this arm.'

As soon as the two of them had left, Silver leaned forward and said conspiratorially, 'So what's the real story with you and this Squires bloke? It's okay, you can tell me. I won't tell another soul.'

Ava stared at her. 'What?'

'Why was he saying your name, hon? There must have been something going on. Were you and him . . . you know?'

'There was nothing going on, nothing at all. I've never met the bloke before in my life.'

Silver tapped the side of her nose with a finger. 'Oh, okay, I get you. Hush, hush, yeah? Don't worry, I'll keep shtum.'

'There's nothing to keep shtum about. I've never—' But Ava quickly shut up again. She suspected that the more she protested her innocence, the guiltier she would seem and so decided to change the subject. 'How long have you and Danny been together?'

'Not long.' Silver swept back her long fair hair and laughed. 'You know what my dad says about him? He says he should be fed to the pigs. He says it's a shame that bullet didn't go six inches to the left. He says the world would be a better place if Danny Street was dead and buried and the worms were feeding on his corpse.'

Ava's eyes widened. 'Your dad seems to have a lot to say on the matter.'

'Yeah, he's a complete bastard.'

Ava couldn't work out if Silver was deliberately trying to shock her or if she had no filter at all on what came out of her mouth. She glanced towards the bar, hoping that Chris would come back soon.

Silver placed her hand over Ava's. Her fingers were cool, but her eyes were bright and glittering. 'You know what I think, hon? I think you and me are going to be the very best of friends.'

Ava felt her heart sink. With all the shock, horror and heartache of the last few days the very last thing she needed was a friend like Silver.

43

DI Valeric Middleton ran through the CCTV coverage for the tenth time, peering intently at the screen. She watched as the two men, Squires and Danny Street, came out of Belles. Danny stopped to light a cigarette. Squires kept on walking until he was out of view. The film was too grainy to read the expression on his face. He was walking quickly, though, as if he was in a hurry. There was about thirty seconds of Solomon Vale standing alone by the entrance – no one else going in or coming out – before Vale sprinted over towards the part of the car park that wasn't covered by the cameras.

She went back to the start and ran it again, this time freezing the action as soon as Street and Squires appeared at the door. She moved her face closer to the computer and then sat back and fiddled with the zoom button until she'd homed in on the lower part of the jacket Squires was wearing.

Just as she was printing out a copy of the image, there was a knock on the office door.

'Come in.'

Jeff Butler appeared, holding aloft a brown paper bag. 'Lunchtime update,' he said. 'I hope you haven't eaten already.'

Valerie glanced towards the clock on the wall. It was one fifteen. 'God, is it that time already?'

'It certainly is, and I've got some news.'

'Good, I hope.'

'It's certainly interesting.' Butler sat down, put the bag on her desk and took out two large takeaway cups. 'I got a coffee for you, tea for me, and a couple of sandwiches. What do you prefer, ham or cheese and tomato?'

'Thanks. I'll have the cheese.'

Butler delved into the bag again and passed her the sandwich. He peeled the wrapper off his own, took a hearty bite and started chewing.

'Hey, don't keep me in suspense,' Valerie said. 'I don't care if you talk with your mouth full.'

Butler grinned and swallowed. 'But my poor old mum, God rest her soul, would turn in her grave. "Manners maketh man" was one of her favourite sayings, along with "Get your feet off the furniture; you're not living in a bleedin' doss house."' He laughed and then looked thoughtful for a second. 'But I digress. Sorry. What I came to tell you is that we've got information from the bank about Squires's personal bank account, and guess what?'

'Oh, please don't make me guess. I'm no good at guessing.'

'Okay, then. This is how it goes. At two forty-two on Saturday afternoon, Jeremy Squires went to his local branch and pulled out ten thousand big ones in cash.'

Valerie gave a low whistle. 'Now that is interesting. I take it the wife can't shed any light on why he did that?'

'Not a clue. And as the money wasn't found on him, I'd say our Mr Squires gave it to someone else.'

'Like Danny Street, for example.'

'It is the first name that springs to mind.'

Valerie tore a corner off her sandwich. 'And why would he do that?'

'Only two reasons you'd hand over an amount like that in cash – either a dodgy deal or blackmail.'

'And if you were a betting man?'

'Blackmail,' Butler said. 'If it was a deal, what was the hurry? Why would he have to rush over to Belles, missing the start of a dinner party that had probably been on his calendar for weeks? No, this was something that happened quickly, that took him by surprise. We checked his phone and he got a call around midday from a number we can't trace. It was from a pay-as-you-go, but it's been disconnected.'

'So, if we're presuming blackmail, we're probably talking a woman.'

'*Cherchez la femme*,' Butler said.

'Well, we haven't got far to look. The lady's name was clearly on his mind when he took two bullets in his back.'

'Ava Gold?'

'The very same.' Valerie ate some of her sandwich and took a sip of coffee. 'All the connections are there. She works for the Streets and probably not just as a driver. They pick a victim, set him up, take a few compromising snaps and Bob's your uncle – a handy and virtually risk-free stream of income in these difficult financial times.'

'Ah, the old honeytrap scenario. Simple but effective.'

'Especially when the man has a reputation to maintain.'

'And a wife to keep happy.'

Valerie reached across to the corner of her desk, removed the sheet of paper from the printer and put it in front of him. 'Look at this,' she said. 'Squires has got his hand in his pocket, but I'm sure there's something else there too. You can't see it clearly, but . . . '

Butler peered down at the printout. 'Yes, you could be right. We'll get the techie boys to take a look, see if they can clean up the image.'

'If it was a set of photos, it would account for why Danny Street was so desperate to get them back. But what happened to them next? Do you think he had them at the hospital?'

Butler shook his head. 'No, he wouldn't have taken the risk, not after a shooting. And they weren't found at the scene.'

'Which leaves Solomon Vale. He probably gave him the cash too.'

'And the chances of Vale admitting to any of that?'

'Zero,' Valerie said.

Butler chewed on his sandwich for a while. 'If we're right about this and it was a blackmail scam, then where does Lydia Hall fit in?'

'I'm not sure yet, but she was friends with Ava.' Valerie frowned while she thought about it some more. 'Maybe the two of them were in it together. Lydia could have provided the names of possible victims – she'd know who flashed the cash at Beast – and then Ava set them up. Danny Street puts the screws on and collects the money. Squires gets shot on the night of the pay-off, Lydia feels guilty about her part in it all and kills herself.'

Butler smiled. 'It's a theory.'

'Got a better one? And it would explain why Lydia didn't call Ava after she heard the news.'

'Although she did go to Market Square.'

'Yes, but she thought Ava had gone away for the weekend. She didn't expect to see her there.'

Butler sat back, putting his hands behind his head. 'But if you're right, then who the hell shot Squires? Who's got the motive? His blackmailers aren't going to want him dead. It's the very last thing they want. The police start sniffing around, poking into bank accounts and the whole gig goes up in smoke.'

'Maybe we should pull in Ava Gold, have another word.'

'No, let's hold fire for now. We'll do a bit more digging first, see what else we can find out.'

'What did Danny Street say when you asked him about Ava?'

Butler lowered his arms, folding them across his chest instead. 'Said he didn't know anyone called Ava. When I reminded him of the Ava Gold who's been driving his brother around he claimed to have forgotten all about her. Said she'd slipped his mind, that the two of them hadn't been going out for long.'

Valerie gave him a thin smile. 'So they are an item, then.'

'Looks that way.'

There was a knock on the door and DS Higgs put her head round. 'Excuse me, guv.' She flapped some sheets of paper in the air. 'We've just had news from Glasgow. You're going to want to see this.'

44

Valerie took the three sheets from Higgs's hand. 'What have we got?'

'Death certificate for a Karen Hall. Turns out she was Lydia's mother. She died from an overdose in February this year. In Glasgow, like we thought. We've been able to trace her birth certificate and Lydia's too.'

Valerie's face changed as she glanced through the copies of the documents. She sucked in a breath and released it as quickly. 'Well, that's a turn-up for the books.'

'Thought you'd say that, guv.'

Butler sat forward, his eyes filled with anticipation. 'I hate to break up the party, ladies, but would either of you two care to share?'

'Sorry,' said Valerie, passing over the sheets of paper. 'Here, why don't you take a look for yourself.'

Butler barked out a laugh as he read. 'God, I didn't see that coming.'

'A blast from the past,' Valerie said.

'It's that all right. Jesus, I didn't think I'd be seeing that name again in a hurry.' He read from one of the documents. 'Karen Hall, née Quinn. Yeah, she was one of Tommy's daughters.'

Valerie glanced up at DS Higgs. 'You'd better sit down.'

Higgs pulled up a chair next to DCI Butler. 'You weren't around when the Quinns were operating, were you, guv?'

'Do you mind?' he said. 'It must be forty years since Joe Quinn was murdered. I'm not that bleeding old.'

'Sorry, guv.'

'Mind, when I joined up there were still plenty of cops around who *did* remember him. They were a powerful family, the Quinns. Not quite in the Kray league, but close enough. They ran Kellston before Terry Street took over. Joe was a right nasty bastard by all accounts.'

Valerie, who had only a sketchy history of the family, said, 'Wasn't he murdered by his sons?'

Butler gave a nod. 'One of them. The other, Tommy – that was Lydia's grandfather – got done for attempting to dispose of the body. His missus took off as soon as the verdict came in, cleared off to Spain and took the kids with her.'

'Karen obviously came back at some point.'

'No father on the birth certificate for Lydia,' Butler said, glancing down. 'Could be useful to know who that was.'

Valerie looked at Higgs. 'Do we have a marriage certificate for Karen?'

'Still trying to track it down. That's if she ever did get married; she could just have changed her name.'

Valerie took two large swigs of coffee. She was in need of a caffeine boost, something to stimulate her brain as they tried to put the pieces together. 'So what are we all thinking? Did

Lydia come to Kellston simply because her mother had grown up here or did she have a more sinister reason?'

Higgs was the first to offer up an opinion. 'Wasn't there a rumour that Joe Quinn's sons might have been innocent? That Terry Street was the one who murdered Joe, rather than his sons.'

'Yeah,' Butler said. 'But that's all it was – a rumour.'

Valerie looked across the desk. 'Lydia might have thought otherwise. We don't know what she was told as she was growing up. What if she came back to try and find out what really happened? Ava Gold said that Lydia was searching for people who knew about the past, about her mother.'

Higgs gave a snort. 'That's if you can believe anything Ava Gold says.'

Jeff Butler flicked through the documents again, even though he'd already absorbed all the information. It was a way of occupying his hands while his mind went to work. Eventually he put the papers back on the desk and said, 'So basically we could still be looking at Lydia as our gunman – or gun*woman* – and we're back to the intended victim being Danny Street rather than Squires.'

Valerie gave a nod. 'If Lydia was looking for some kind of revenge, maybe she thought that killing Terry's son was better than killing Terry himself. An eye for an eye, that kind of thing. Terry murdered her mother's grandfather, Joe Quinn, and had his two sons locked up for something they hadn't done. One of those sons was her mother's father, Tommy. Maybe she saw it as a kind of justice.'

'Except there's no evidence that Terry did kill Joe,' Butler said.

'Yes, but we're talking about what Lydia *thinks*, what she *believes*. What did her mother tell her? We just don't know. What we do know is that Karen Quinn had a troubled exist-ence and maybe she blamed Terry Street for that. It could have been enough to bring Lydia back to Kellston, to try and right the wrong that ruined her mother's life.' Valerie stopped, took a breath and gave Butler a wry smile. 'Yes, it's just another theory. But if she shot Squires by mistake, it might have been enough to push her over the edge.'

'What about the gun?' he said. 'We were wondering if Ava Gold might have got it for her, but she's hardly likely to have handed over a weapon that was going to be used to kill her boyfriend's brother.'

'Unless she didn't know who Lydia really was.'

Higgs flapped a hand impatiently. 'I don't see how she couldn't have known. They were friends, weren't they? That Ava Gold's in this up to her neck.'

Butler gazed at the ceiling for a moment, tracing a crack that was running in a zigzag from one side to the other. 'Someone must have known who she really was.'

'Guy Wilder,' Valerie suggested. 'If she went to talk to him about her mother, then she must have told him what her mother's maiden name was.'

'So why didn't he say anything?' Higgs asked. 'We were at the bar yesterday and he didn't even mention it.'

Butler laughed. 'Say anything? *His* mother was one of the biggest villains in the East End. He might run a legitimate business, but he's still his mother's son.'

Valerie reached for her coat. 'I think it's time we had another word with Mr Wilder.'

45

Mondays were never that busy at the bar and now, with the last of the lunchtime trade starting to drift away, Noah found himself at a loose end. Standing behind the bar, he gazed with irritation at the debris on the counter. Jenna had gone off to talk to some girls in the corner, leaving her jacket, bag, scarf, gloves, phone and newspaper all in a heap on the counter. He didn't see it as his job to protect her belongings. Why should he? It would serve her right if some light-fingered customer helped himself on the way out.

Guy was sitting on one of the leather sofas with the grey-haired bloke, Borovski. Noah wasn't happy about that either. Guy had gone out of his way to try and make sure that the Russian didn't open his casino on the borders of Kellston. Although he wasn't privy to all the ins and outs, he did know that Guy had spent the last month schmoozing Jeremy Squires and his councillor pals. Had money changed hands? He suspected so.

There had only been one reason why Guy had got himself involved in the business of the casino, and that was to spite the Streets. No casino meant no protection money and that wouldn't please Terry and his sons. Still, that was the whole point of it. Guy would do just about anything to piss off the Streets. One day, and it was a day that was rapidly approaching, he'd go too far.

Noah gave a weary shake of his head, picked up Jenna's copy of the *Evening Standard* and leafed through the pages. It wasn't long before he came across a report of the shooting at Belles. There was a photograph of Squires and beside it one of Danny Street. He scanned through the article, but it didn't tell him any more than he already knew.

Guy stood up and walked Borovski to the door. The two men shook hands and then the Russian crossed the road to where his chauffeur was waiting in the smart black Bentley. Guy came over and leaned on the bar.

Noah tapped the newspaper. 'Belles,' he said.

'They found out who did it yet?'

'Not when this went to print.'

'Does it mention Lydia?'

'No, nothing.'

'Lydia?' Jenna said coming up behind Guy. She glanced down at the newspaper to see what Noah was reading. 'Was that the Lydia that was here on Saturday?'

Noah gave Guy a sharp look. 'Lydia was here?'

'After the bar closed,' Jenna said. 'After you left. It was about half twelve. She turned up out of the blue wanting to talk to you. She was upset about something. Guy got her a coffee while I went upstairs.'

'Me? Why would she—'

Guy cut in quickly. 'I figured the last thing you needed was a drunken Lydia turning up on your doorstep after a long night in the bar, so I made her a coffee in the hope she'd sober up and I'd be able to persuade her to go home.'

'You didn't tell me,' said Noah tightly, frowning at Guy. It was a big fat lie – at least the part about Lydia wanting to see him – but he wasn't going to say anything in front of Jenna.

Guy gave a shrug. 'Didn't I? It must have slipped my mind.'

'So what's this Lydia got to do with that?' Jenna asked, staring at the paper again. 'What's she got to do with what happened at Belles?'

'Nothing,' Guy said.

'So why did you just ask if she was mentioned?'

'Oh, only because she knew Squires vaguely. That's what she was upset about when she came here. She'd met him a few times in the shop she works in. To be honest, she's a bit of a drama queen. She barely knew him, but that's Lydia for you, always getting emotional over one thing or another.'

Noah could feel his heart beginning to race. He closed the paper, folded it over and put it back on top of Jenna's jacket. He gave her a quick glance, wondering if she'd swallowed the story. She wasn't the sharpest knife in the drawer, but she wasn't entirely stupid either. However, he suspected that any concerns she might have revolved more around sexual jealousy than anything else. She wasn't really interested in the shooting, only in whether Guy could be trusted or not.

Noah checked the clock on the wall. 'I'm going to close up.' He looked pointedly at Guy and said as casually as he could

314

manage, 'And I need a word about those, er . . . promotions we were discussing. Do you think you'll have time before this evening?'

'Sure,' said Guy blithely. 'We're just going upstairs to grab a coffee. Half an hour and then I'm all yours.'

Jenna leaned across the bar, laid a hand on her jacket, fluttered her eyelashes and said, 'Noah, sweetheart, you don't mind if I leave my things down here, do you? It'll save me carting it all up to the flat.'

'Sure,' Noah said. 'No problem.'

'Thanks, babe. You're an angel.'

Noah got rid of the last of the customers and locked the door. He leaned against it for a moment waiting for his heart rate to slow. It had taken every last inch of willpower to stop himself from dragging Guy into the back and demanding some answers straight away. But he couldn't do that. He couldn't do anything that might make Jenna suspicious.

He spent most of the next half-hour pacing distractedly round the bar. Lydia Hall had been here on Saturday night. Lydia had been here and then she had gone home and killed herself. Jesus! And Guy hadn't said a word. Not a single goddamn word. He wondered, not for the first time, whether she might actually have done the shooting. The cops hadn't come straight out and said it, but why else would they be so interested in her death and how well she knew Squires?

When he heard the footsteps on the stairs, he made himself scarce, waiting in the back until Guy had seen Jenna out. Did that woman ever do any work? She owned a lingerie shop in Chigwell – courtesy of her divorce settlement – but didn't spend much time there. He waited, full of impatience, while

315

she chattered on and on. Jesus, was she never going to leave? It was only after long lingering kisses had been exchanged and goodbyes been murmured that the front door finally opened and closed.

Noah, unable to contain himself any longer, stormed back into the bar. 'Why the hell didn't you tell me?'

Guy gazed calmly back at him. 'Because I knew you'd react like this.'

'And what's that supposed to mean?'

'That you'd get in a panic, that you'd go off on one.'

Noah shook his head in frustration. 'For God's sake, you were the last person to see Lydia alive. She came here before she went home and . . . What did she say? Why did she come here?'

'You know what she was like. She'd heard about the shooting, got in a state and—'

'Heard about it or *did* it?'

Guy gave a shrug. 'Well, you could never tell with Lydia. What was real and what was fantasy? She always lived in a world of her own. Anyway, she was in a state. I made her coffee, calmed her down and offered to walk her home. And that was it – the last time I saw her.'

'But what did she say?'

'It was kind of garbled. To be honest, she wasn't making much sense. She'd had a few drinks. She wasn't . . . wasn't thinking straight. She was rambling.'

Noah began pacing again, up and down, up and down. 'I mean, how would someone like Lydia even get hold of a gun?' He stopped suddenly and stared at Guy. His heart missed a beat. 'Oh, please God, tell me you didn't.'

Guy pulled a face. 'How was I to know what she was planning? That's if she even did it. A couple of weeks ago, she told me that she didn't feel safe living alone, that someone had tried to break in to her flat. She said she was going to buy a gun to protect herself. What was I supposed to do?'

'Supposed to do? Christ almighty! Not hand her a bloody gun for starters. Are you completely bloody mad?'

'Yeah?' Guy said. 'And if I hadn't, what would she have done then? Gone out and tried to buy one on the street. And probably got herself arrested or mixed up with God knows what sort of lowlifes and ended up in a ditch somewhere. And yeah, maybe it was a mistake, but I thought she just wanted the gun to make her feel better, to feel safe.'

Noah's hands clenched with anxiety. 'What if the police find out?'

'And how are they going to do that?'

'Well, even if they don't, they still might think that you put her up to it. As soon as they find out who she is – and they will find out – they'll be knocking on the door again wanting to know why you lied to them.'

'That's my problem. You think I can't deal with the cops?'

Noah was infuriated by his nonchalance, by his apparent indifference to the trouble that was brewing. Couldn't he see how bad it was going to look? 'You should never have filled her head with all that stuff, all those rumours about the past. She was impressionable. You know she was.'

'They weren't rumours. You think my mother didn't know the truth? She knew it inside out. She knew *everything* about Terry Street. I wasn't going to lie to the girl. She wanted answers and I gave them to her.'

'You wanted to cause trouble for the Streets.'

Guy gave a shrug. 'So what? Terry Street had my mother murdered. What's a little trouble compared to that?'

'You don't know that for sure.'

'I know how Terry's mind works. Sitting in that prison cell for all those years, hearing stories about her, watching as she grew more and more powerful. He couldn't stand it. He was the boss and he needed everyone to know it.'

Noah was quiet for a moment. 'Maybe Lydia did shoot Danny Street. Maybe she meant to kill him and accidentally killed Squires instead.'

'She might have,' Guy said. 'She might not. But either way, so far as the cops are concerned, it's nothing to do with me or you. There's no reason why they should ever find out that Lydia was here on Saturday.'

'How can you say that? What about Jenna? She saw her. She knows she was here.'

'So what?'

Noah sat down, briefly covered his face with his hands and then looked up at Guy again. 'What happens when she finds out that Lydia's dead?'

'If she finds out.'

'It's going to be splashed all over the papers when . . . *if* the police find a link with the shooting. And anyway, she's over here often enough. What if she hears someone talking about her suicide?'

'Then I'll sit down and have a chat with her. I'll tell her that Lydia was drunk, that she wasn't making any sense, that I had no idea she was going to go home and top herself. I'll explain how I don't want the cops crawling all over my life and making it a misery. God, the woman was married to Chris Street. I'm sure she knows how to keep her mouth shut.'

But Noah wasn't so sure. Jenna and Guy hadn't been together long. Just how loyal would she be when push came to shove? Then again, Guy Wilder could be very persuasive when he put his mind to it. He was still pondering on this when another more urgent thought leapt into his head. 'What about the gun? Did they find it at her flat? What if it's still got your prints on? Did you wipe it – did you wipe it before you gave it to her?'

'You don't need to worry about the gun.'

'What do you mean, I don't need to ...' Noah's eyes widened in alarm. He jumped to his feet. 'Shit, tell me she didn't bring it with her. She did, didn't she? But you've got rid of it, right? Jesus, Guy, tell me you've dumped the fucking thing!'

'I will – once everything calms down.'

'No, not later. Now. You've got to get rid of it *now*! What if the cops search upstairs?'

'Why should they?'

As his heart thumped ever harder in his chest, Noah could feel himself starting to sweat. He wiped his forehead with the back of his hand. 'What's the matter with you? It could be the bloody murder weapon for all you know. Let me take it. I'll ... I'll ...'

'You'll what? Chuck it in the river, put it in a bin, bury it in Epping Forest? And what if someone finds it? No, it's safer here. I feel better knowing exactly where it is.'

'You're mad. You can't take that risk.'

319

Guy smiled, his eyes bright with amusement. 'Chill out, you'll give yourself a coronary. Stop worrying. Everything's under control.' He patted Noah on the shoulder and walked behind the bar. 'Do you fancy a drink? I know I could do with one.'

'You know what I want, Guy? I want the bloody truth for once. Do you think there's any way you could manage that?'

Guy inclined his head and stared at him. 'The truth,' he repeated. 'Are you sure?'

'Yes, of course I'm damn well sure.'

'Well then, you'd better sit down and I'll bring that drink over. I think you're going to need it.'

46

Ava got into the Mercedes, shut the door, leaned back and gave a long sigh of relief. 'Thanks for that,' she said. 'You could have warned me.'

Chris slid his seat belt across his chest. 'I told you what my brother's like. He never says more than he wants to – and most of what he does say is complete and utter bollocks.'

'It's not him I'm talking about.' She glanced out of the window towards the Fox. 'Has that girl got a screw loose or is it just me?'

'Oh, Silver. Yeah, she's crazy, mad as a box of frogs.'

'You know what she said while you two were at the bar? After informing me that the two of us were going to be great friends, she asked what you were like in bed. Well, she didn't quite put it quite like that, but I'll spare your blushes.'

Chris laughed. 'I hope you gave me a glowing report.'

'I told her it was none of her damn business.' She leaned

forward again and started the engine, keen to get away from the pub. 'I mean, what kind of person asks a question like that five minutes after you've been introduced?'

'I thought you women talked about that stuff.'

'Yeah, right. It's always top of the agenda whenever we meet for the first time. We tend to skip the usual formalities, like where you come from or what you like to do, and get straight down to the nitty-gritty. *Hey, what's your boyfriend like in the sack?*

'You mean that's not true?' he said. 'God, I'm disappointed. I always imagined—'

'No, no, no!' she interrupted, raising a hand. 'Kindly keep the dark corners of your imagination to yourself. I don't want to hear it. I've already got an imaginary boyfriend and an imaginary dog. That's as much as I can handle in one day.' She swung the Mercedes out of the car park and headed for the high street. 'And George? What's all that about? How could you call my dog George?'

'What's wrong with George?'

She gave him a sideways glance. 'So do you think we got away with it? Do they believe we're a couple?'

'Well, you could have been a little more affectionate, but they'll probably just put that down to your uptight nature.'

'I'm not uptight.'

'Says the girl who refuses to talk about her boyfriend's prowess in the bedroom.'

'Prowess?' she repeated, raising her eyebrows. 'Is that what you call it?'

He grinned at her. 'You don't know what you're missing.'

She rolled her eyes. 'Spare me. And just out of interest,

how long exactly are you planning on keeping this beautiful relationship going?'

'Why, are you bored of me already?'

'Promise me one thing. When the time comes, I can dump you, right? A girl's got her pride to consider.'

Chris took his phone out of his pocket, checked his messages and gave a grunt. 'You'd think she could at least send a text.'

'Who's that?'

'Jenna,' he said. 'I've been trying to get hold of her since Friday. She won't answer my calls, doesn't reply to my texts. I mean, for God's sake, all I want to do is talk to her. Five minutes – you'd think she could spare me that.'

'Perhaps she doesn't want to talk.'

'Why do you say that?'

Ava shot him a quick glance. 'Probably because she knows what you're going to say and doesn't want to hear it. She must have been told that you turned up at Wilder's and that you weren't in an altogether good frame of mind. I imagine she's waiting for you to calm down a bit before she makes contact.'

'I'm perfectly calm,' he said through gritted teeth. 'I just want to know what the hell she's playing at.'

'Which, roughly translated, means you don't care what she does so long as she doesn't do it with Wilder, huh?'

Chris's grey eyes darkened. 'There are thousands of men out there, hundreds of thousands. Why did she have to pick him?'

Ava, trying to lighten the mood a little, said, 'Good thing I'm not the jealous sort or I might not take too kindly to you banging on about your ex.' She saw his expression and grimaced. 'Oh right, sorry, not a subject for humour. I'll shut up, shall I?'

Chris didn't reply. He turned his face away, gazed out of the window for a while and then went back to staring at his phone as if by the very force of his will he could make it spring into life.

Ava felt suddenly uneasy about it all. If Jenna kept on ignoring him, he might snap and do something stupid. What if he decided to go back to the bar or go to her home and have it out with her? If he wasn't careful, he'd end up getting arrested for harassment – or worse. She opened her mouth but then smartly closed it again. She wasn't his keeper and it wasn't her place to lecture him on what he should or shouldn't do.

Ava tried to push her concerns aside, to concentrate on the road ahead. Anyway, she had problems of her own to deal with. The way things were going, she'd probably be the one to get arrested. The meet with Danny had been disappointing. She'd tried not to raise her expectations, but a part of her had still hoped for a glimmer of enlightenment as regards Jeremy Squires and the uttering of her name. And what had she learned? A big fat nothing.

She swung a right at the northern end of the high street and skirted around the Mansfield Estate until she came to Lincoln Road. She travelled another twenty yards and then pulled the car on to the forecourt of the Lincoln Pool Room and switched off the engine.

Chris unfastened his seat belt. 'You may as well come in,' he said. 'I need to look through the books. I'll be half an hour or so. Do you play pool?'

'No.'

'Well, you can grab a drink or a cup of coffee. Save you sitting out here on your own.'

Ava, although she'd never been inside the Lincoln, had heard plenty about it. It was another of the businesses owned by the Streets, a place where the local boys hustled, did their dodgy deals, drank too much lager and then beat the shit out of each other on a Saturday night. She hesitated, but decided that, on balance, it was probably safer being inside than sitting alone outside in a spanking new Mercedes.

She got out of the car and walked with Chris towards the entrance. The wide low-slung building was painted white and adorned with a generous smattering of graffiti. Two of the windows had cracks running down them and another was boarded up. The bins were overflowing and sodden heaps of litter – empty crisp packets, tin cans and fag ends – had gathered in the pools of rainwater.

Inside, the clicking of the pool balls merged with the rhythmic complaints of a rapper sounding off about his 'bitch'. The place was surprisingly busy for a Monday afternoon and about three-quarters of the tables were in use. The furniture, designed for utility rather than comfort, consisted of a line of hard bench seats set back against the wall. Chris headed towards the bar running along the left side of the hall.

The man behind the counter was wearing jeans and a checked shirt with the sleeves rolled up. He was in his sixties, but still solid-looking. He had a creased leathery face and a nose that had been broken more than once.

'Lenny,' Chris said. 'How are you doing?'

'Not so bad, ta. How's that brother of yours? I heard you had a spot of bother at Belles.'

'Makes a change from here, eh? Yeah, he's fine. You know Danny, he always bounces back.' Chris turned to Ava. 'This is Big Lenny,' he said. 'He's run this joint for the last twenty years. Lenny, this is Ava, a friend of mine.'

Ava noticed how he didn't introduce her as his driver. She smiled at Lenny. 'Hi.'

Lenny gave her one of those curt nods that certain types of East End men seemed so fond of – a spare acknowledgment of her existence and nothing more – and immediately turned his attention back to Chris. 'You want to come through to the back?'

'Sure.' Chris glanced at Ava. 'You want something to drink?'

'Thanks. I'll have a Coke.'

'A Coke for the lady, please, Lenny.'

Lenny obliged with a half pint of something flat and brown. He put the rather grubby glass down on the counter without even looking at her.

'Thanks,' she said.

Lenny walked off to the end of the bar and flipped open the counter.

'You'll be okay on your own?' Chris asked.

'I'll see you later.'

After he'd gone, Ava sat down on a bar stool and gazed across the pool hall. The clientele was predominantly young and male, although there were a few girls playing too. She watched the two boys closest to her as they strutted round the table lining up their shots, but her mind was only half on the game. The other half was already drifting back to the messy killing of Jeremy Squires. Somehow, she had managed to get herself embroiled in the death of a man she hadn't even known. How had that happened? One minute she'd been living an ordinary, predictable existence, the next she was being interviewed by a pair of cops who clearly had her in the frame for murder.

Ava gave a shudder as she reached for the glass. She took a tentative sip of the cola-type liquid – it definitely wasn't Coke – and almost spat it out again. It was warm and flat and decidedly nasty.

'Yeah, tastes like gnat's piss, doesn't it?'

She turned to see Solomon Vale standing next to her. She glanced from him to the glass and then back up at him again. 'All things considered, I think that might be a slur on the virtues of gnat's piss.'

Solomon grinned, pulled up a stool and sat down next to her. 'So how's the driving going?'

'The car's outside. You want to check it for dents?'

'Is someone feeling a touch defensive?'

'Sorry,' she said. 'It's not been the best couple of days. I've had the cops on my back about the shooting at Belles.'

'You and me both,' he said.

'Yes, but they don't think you're involved.'

Solomon looked her up and down and smirked. 'You? Why would they think that?'

Ava stared back at him. 'There's no need to act so surprised. Why not me? Don't you think I'm capable? You shouldn't be fooled by appearances. For all you know, I could be a fully trained assassin.'

Solomon took a swig from his bottle of water, thought about it and then placed the bottle on the counter. 'In my experience, small as it is, fully trained assassins don't tend to hang about once they've done the job. They get their well-paid asses out of the picture as fast as they possibly can.'

'You reckon?'

'I reckon.'

Ava gave a shrug. 'So maybe they just think I'm the sort of woman who goes around shooting men on a Saturday night. Either way, they're sure I had something to do with it. Believe me, I know when a copper's serious or not. I've been there, seen the hunger in their eyes.'

Solomon gave her another incredulous look. 'You?'

'No, well, okay, not me exactly, but my dad's been banged up more times than I've had hot dinners. I know coppers. I know what they're like.'

'But I still don't get it, babe. Why should they be giving you hassle?'

Ava explained to him about Squires calling out her name, making her a primary suspect so far as Old Bill were concerned. 'So you see, I'm right in the middle of it all without having a clue how I managed to get there.' Sensing that a thin thread of hysteria was starting to creep into her voice, she quickly moved on. 'But enough about me. Are you working here at the moment?'

'If you can call it that.' Solomon's eyes raked the room with something like contempt. 'I'm stuck here until Belles opens again. That could be days, weeks even.'

'The prospect of which doesn't fill you with joy and happiness.'

'No,' he said. 'The prospect sure as hell doesn't.'

Ava nudged her glass away, not intending to drink any more of the vile substance it contained. 'Well, don't expect me to feel sorry for you. I just spent the last hour in the Fox with Silver Delaney.' As soon as she said it, she wondered if she shouldn't have. She barely knew Solomon and anything she said could easily find its way back to Danny. 'I mean, I'm sure she's very nice once you get to know her properly, but—'

'That girl's about as nice as a cobra with a headache.'

Ava smiled with relief. 'Oh, right. So it's not just me then.'

'No, babe, it's not just you.'

Suddenly, above the noise of the music, the chatter and the clicking pool balls, there was the sound of a disturbance coming from the entrance. A frazzled-looking guy rushed into the pool room and waved his arms at Solomon. 'Hey, Sol, come and give me a hand, will you? It's all kicking off out here.'

With an obvious show of reluctance, Solomon rose to his feet. 'Just what I need,' he murmured. As he was walking away from her, he looked back over his shoulder and said, 'You want to stay away from Silver. She won't do you any favours. She's trouble, that one.'

'Thanks. I sort of gathered that.'

For a second he looked as though he was about to say something else, but then he gave a small shake of his head and strode off towards another kind of trouble.

47

DI Valerie Middleton stared hard at Guy Wilder. Most law-abiding people would show some concern at having been caught out lying to the police, but he was cool as a cucumber. He sat back on the leather sofa with his legs crossed, his whole body posture as relaxed as it could be. He didn't betray even a hint of anxiety. She was wondering now whether they ought to have taken him down the station and conducted the interview there. He was in his comfort zone here in the bar and nothing seemed to faze him.

'So,' she continued, 'are you saying that you didn't know that Lydia Hall's mother was actually Karen Quinn?'

Guy frowned, pausing before he replied. 'To be honest, she might have mentioned it, but Lydia talked about all sorts of things. I wasn't always listening properly.' He flashed a charming smile at Valerie. 'It's the curse of the barman, having customers tell you their life story, all their childhood miseries, their marital problems. After a while, you tend to switch off.'

'But that name would have meant something to you.'

'Would it?'

'The Quinns were a big family in these parts, powerful, important. Terry Street used to work for them and then took over after Joe was murdered.'

'It's all a long time ago, though, isn't it? Ancient history.'

'But you must have heard the rumours about Terry's rise to power. That he was the one who killed Joe and not his son. Did you tell Lydia about that? She would have been interested, wouldn't she?'

'She might have been, but no, I didn't tell her anything. I've found it's never wise to repeat rumour and gossip. Mind, if that was what she was after, I'm sure she wouldn't have had too much difficulty in tracking it down. Kellston's full of people who wouldn't think twice about filling her head with all sorts of rubbish.'

DCI Butler, who'd been quiet until this point, leaned forward and put his hands on his knees. 'But none of that *rubbish* came from you?'

'No, none of it came from me.'

'Still, you can see how Lydia might have taken against Terry Street, might have wanted to hurt him or his family. Her mother, Karen, lost her grandfather and her father. Joe Quinn was murdered, Tommy Quinn was banged up. Lydia could easily have blamed Terry for all her mother's problems and for her eventual overdose. Did you know Lydia's mother committed suicide too?'

'Yes,' Guy said. 'She did tell me that. She also told me that her mother was a drug addict and an alcoholic.'

'So you did listen sometimes,' Butler said.

Guy flashed his smile again. 'If you hear something repeated enough times, you tend to remember it.'

Valerie, who was more than aware of the bad blood between Guy Wilder and the Streets, was sure that he was hiding something. She couldn't believe that he hadn't talked to Lydia about the Quinns. He wouldn't have been able to resist it. But was he actually involved in what she did next or was he simply trying to distance himself? When it came to murder, people often got defensive. She glanced around the bar, all clean and tidy and ready for opening in the evening. There was no sign of Noah Clark today. She looked back at Guy. 'Did Lydia own a gun?'

Guy laughed. 'A gun? Where on earth would Lydia get a gun from?'

'Not too difficult round here,' Butler said.

'You can't seriously think that she shot that Squires bloke. Not little Lydia. She didn't have it in her.'

'How would you know? You've already told the inspector that you weren't especially close. Why couldn't she have done it? What was to stop her?'

Guy's shoulders rose and fell in a casual shrug. 'Nothing, I suppose. She just never struck me as the type who'd do anything so . . . so violent. And *why* would she? What did Squires ever do to her?'

Butler looked down, ran his fingertips along the glass top of the table, and then slowly looked up again. 'Maybe it wasn't Squires she was aiming for. Maybe it was Danny Street.'

'Danny?'

'Why not? She might have seen it as payback for all the damage Terry Street inflicted, or allegedly inflicted on her

332

family. When she found out she'd got it wrong, that she'd shot the wrong man by mistake, she took her own life. Or perhaps she always planned to do that anyway.'

'You don't think that's a little . . . far-fetched?'

Valerie kept her eyes fixed on him as she asked the next question. 'When was the last time you saw Lydia?'

Guy's face remained expressionless. 'Oh, it must have been last week sometime. Let me see . . . Wednesday or Thursday? No, hang on, it was definitely Thursday. There was an exhibition at Beast and Noah and I went along to provide the cocktails.'

'And did you speak to her?'

'In passing. We said hello, not much else. It was too busy. They had a good turnout. She was showing people around, dealing with the buyers. We were doling out the booze.'

'And how did she seem?'

'Fine, but like I said, I barely spoke to her.'

'And when the show was over?'

'We packed up and left. That was it.'

Valerie glanced at Butler. She knew that Wilder had reached the limit on what he was prepared to tell them. He had his story and he was sticking to it. They couldn't prove that he was lying, any more than he could prove that he was telling the truth. The law, however, was on his side. Without any evidence, there was nothing they could accuse him of.

'Okay,' said Butler, rising to his feet. 'That's it for now. Thanks for your time. If you remember anything else, perhaps you'll let us know.'

Valerie stood up too. 'One last thing. Do you know a woman called Ava Gold?'

Guy shook his head. 'No, I've never heard of her.'

'She was a friend of Lydia's – in her late twenties, dark hair, dark eyes, a pretty girl, Italian-looking. She was at the show on Thursday.'

'Was she? Sorry, it doesn't ring any bells.'

'Maybe Noah would remember her. Is he here today?'

Guy glanced at his watch. 'In an hour or so. I'll ask him if you like.'

'Thank you.'

Valerie and Jeff Butler left the bar and stepped outside on to the pavement. A freezing wind swept along the high street, the icy air stinging their faces. Butler turned up the collar of his coat. 'Out in the cold,' he said. 'The story of our lives.'

'He knows more than he's saying.'

Butler gave a weary sigh. 'They always know more than they're saying. That's the trouble with this damn job.'

48

Tuesday morning dawned grey and cold with a thin mist hanging over the rooftops. Ava stood by the kitchen window and gazed down on the empty market square. She'd got up early, unable to sleep, and for the past hour the hands of the clock had moved around the face at a snail's pace. It was only twenty past seven and she wasn't due to pick up Chris until ten o'clock.

Before going to work, she planned to head over to the Mansfield Estate to see her dad and drop off some provisions. He was down with the flu, full of aches and pains and in a sorry state. She had visited him yesterday, early in the evening, and taken over soup and rolls, aspirin, whisky, honey and lemon. She didn't like him being on his own when he was ill, but he'd insisted he could cope, refusing her offer to stay over and take care of him.

Tash wandered into the kitchen in her dressing gown and slumped down at the table. She had a dazed, red-eyed look and Ava suspected that she hadn't had much sleep either.

'There's a brew in the pot. Shall I pour you one?'

'Thanks,' Tash said. 'You been up for long?'

'A while. Is Hannah still in bed?'

'No, she left last night. I told her to. Not much point in her being here really. She doesn't understand.'

Ava poured out the tea and placed the mug in front of her. 'Maybe she understands too much.'

Tash looked up, frowning. 'What do you mean?'

'Your feelings for Lydia. I think she must have guessed by now how you felt about her. And Hannah isn't good at dealing with things like that.'

'It's not as though anything was going on. Lydia was never interested in me, not in that way.'

'But you were interested in her.'

Tash lowered her head and drank some tea, her long brown hair falling round her face like a curtain. 'None of it matters any more.' She was quiet for a moment and then she glanced up again. 'Have the police been back in touch?'

Ava felt her stomach lurch. 'No, not since Sunday.' She stared down into the square, fearing that a couple of cops might roll up at any second and haul her off to the nick. 'I don't imagine I've seen the last of them, though.'

'It's all my fault. God, I'm sorry. I should never have pretended that Lydia was your friend rather than mine. If it hadn't been for that—'

'That's not why they're so interested in me. Honestly, Tash, it isn't. Don't beat yourself up about it. It's the whole name thing – Jeremy Squires saying "Ava" at the hospital – that's what's got their antennae buzzing. They can't figure it out and I can't either.' She moved away from the window and sat down. 'Did you ever meet him? Did you ever meet Squires?'

Tash shook her head. 'No, and Lydia never mentioned him. I'm sure she didn't.'

'I met up with Danny Street yesterday. He claims he hasn't got a clue.'

'You don't believe him?'

'Put it this way, if he does know anything, he sure as hell isn't willing to tell me.'

'Can't Chris have a word?'

'He's already tried. It's a waste of time.' The more Ava dwelled on it, the more fearful she became. She jumped up again and went over to the window. She felt sick inside, like a condemned man waiting for the hangman to arrive. Too anxious to hang around in the flat, she decided to get out. 'I think I'll go over to my dad's. He's an early riser; he should be up by now.'

'Is he feeling any better?'

'I hope so. He looked like death warmed up yesterday.' As soon as she said it, Ava winced. 'Oh, sorry, I didn't think. Me and my big mouth. Sorry, I shouldn't have ... '

'Will you stop apologising. I'm not so delicate that you can't mention the word in my presence. Give him my love, yeah? I hope he gets well soon.'

'What are you going to do?' Ava didn't like to think of her alone in the flat while she was out all day. 'Are you sure you'll be okay?'

'I'll be fine.' Tash managed a feeble smile. 'Go on, clear off. I'll see you later.'

Ava gave her shoulder a squeeze as she passed by on her way to the living room. 'Bye then. You take care.' She picked up her bag and her phone, went into the hall and took her coat off the peg. She hesitated for a moment, glancing back towards the kitchen, but then opened the front door and closed it behind her.

She pulled on her coat as she hurried down the stairs, eager now to put some distance between her and the flat. She couldn't help worrying about the cops turning up. Being innocent didn't always mean that you wouldn't be punished. Miscarriages of justice happened; she'd read about them in the paper, seen them on the news.

Outside, the air was so cold that it made her flinch. She shivered as she put her head down and dashed across the square. Yesterday's rain had turned the snow to ice and her feet slipped as she made her way to the high street. Here, the traffic was already building up with the early morning commuters trying to beat the rush.

As she waited at the Pelican, she glanced to her right and saw a commotion down by the green. There were several police cars with flashing lights, an ambulance and a small crowd of onlookers. She was too far away to see what was happening and wasn't going to take a detour to satisfy her curiosity. Anyway, she had no desire at the moment to be any closer to the law than she had to be.

When the lights changed, she quickly crossed the road and started walking north. She went past Connolly's, the door opening as she passed to release a brief rush of warm air and a snatch of music from the radio. There was a Co-op on the corner and she went inside to stock up on the essentials for her dad. She put milk, bread, tea, butter, sugar, loo roll, tissues and a newspaper into her basket, and then added soup and a few ready meals that he could just pop in the microwave.

With a carrier bag hanging off each arm, she left the store, took a right turn off the high street and traipsed along Mansfield Road until she came to the entrance to the estate. At this time of day she didn't feel so nervous about being alone in the concrete jungle. Hopefully, all the muggers, junkies and other unsavoury characters would still be tucked up in bed.

She took the main path up to Haslow House, pushed open the door and stepped into the cold malodorous foyer. Wrinkling her nose at the smell, she wondered if she should risk taking the lift. She didn't fancy lugging two heavy carrier bags up three flights of steps. On the other hand, she didn't much fancy being trapped in a stinking broken-down lift either. Erring on the side of caution, she decided to take the stairs.

By the time she reached her father's flat, Ava was out of breath. She trudged along the landing until she reached number thirty-one where she put the bags down and rang the bell. It was a minute or so before he answered the door and his face fell as soon as he saw her.

'Ava, love, what are you doing here?'

'Oh, thanks, lovely to see you too. What kind of a welcome is that?' She picked up the bags again and held them aloft. 'I brought you some shopping. So are you going to invite me in or what?'

He stood aside and waved her in. 'Yeah, yeah, of course. Sorry, love. Ta. You just took me by surprise. I didn't expect to see you today.'

'What kind of a daughter leaves her old man to fend for himself when he's sick?' She went through to the kitchen and put the bags on the table. 'How are you feeling by the way, any better?' It was only at that moment, as she studied him properly, that she realised how ill he actually looked. His face was pale, almost ashen, and there was a faint sheen of sweat on his forehead. And then she noticed that he was wearing his overcoat. 'God, you weren't thinking of going out, were you? You shouldn't. It's freezing out there.'

'I was just ... er ... going to nip out for a paper.'

She took the *Daily Mirror* out of one of the bags and handed it to him. 'Here, never say I don't anticipate your every need.'

He didn't, however, look as pleased as he might have done. 'Oh, right.'

'Why don't you take off your coat and get that kettle going while I put this stuff away?' She watched him out of the corner of her eye as she opened the fridge and started to unpack. Something was bugging him and it wasn't just a dose of flu. He was acting in a shifty kind of way and kept glancing at his watch. 'What's the matter? Do you need to be somewhere?'

'No, no,' he said too quickly, turning his back to mess about with cups and spoons and sugar. 'Where would I need to be?'

'Well, nowhere I hope, not in your state.' She closed the fridge door, went to stand beside him and folded her arms across her chest. 'What's going on, Dad?'

'Nothing, nothing's going on.'

'So why are you acting all antsy?'

'I'm not.'

'Yes, you are.'

The kettle boiled and he carelessly slopped water over the teabags. 'You're imagining it. Pass me the milk, will you?'

Ava went back to the fridge and took out the plastic bottle. He finished making the tea, but as he carried the two mugs to the table, she noticed how his hands were shaking. She stared at him with worry in her eyes.

'I suppose you'll need to get off to work soon,' he said as he sat down.

'Sounds like you want to get rid of me.'

'Course not, love, it's always great to see you, but I wouldn't want you getting in trouble with that boss of yours.'

As Ava didn't intend to spend the rest of the day stressing over what he might or might not be up to, she decided to call his bluff. 'You know what? I think I'll give Chris a call and tell him I can't make it today. I don't think you should be on your own at the moment.'

Her father's eyes widened with alarm. 'You can't do that!'

'Why not?'

'I mean you *shouldn't* do that. You've only just started the job. How's it going to look if you start taking time off already? I'm okay, I'm fine. There's no need to put yourself out. It's a touch of flu, that's all. I'll be right as rain in a few days.'

'Okay,' Ava said. 'Let me put it another way. I'm not leaving this flat until you tell me what the hell you're up to. I know you, Dad, and I know when you're hiding something.'

Lifting his hands, he seemed on the point of proclaiming his innocence, but then he slowly dropped them back to the table. He shook his head. 'Best you don't know, love. I don't want to get you involved.'

'Oh, Christ,' she said. 'Tell me it isn't another job?'

'Nah, it's not. I promise. I swear to you.'

'What then? What's so important that you feel obliged to leave the comfort of a nice warm flat when you're sick as a dog?'

He drank some of his tea, sighed and peered at her over the rim of the mug. 'There's a problem.'

'So share it with me.'

'It's to do with Finian's.'

'I thought that went off without a hitch.'

He nodded. 'It did, sweet as a nut, but the gear still hasn't been shifted. It's been in a lock-up over Dalston way. And last night two of the lads who were in on the job got nabbed on another robbery. Ryan reckons there's a chance that they might grass us up or at least tell the law where the gear's been stashed.'

'Is that Ryan Moore?' she asked, frowning. Moore was one of Ted Gold's old pals, a slippery customer who, like her uncle, was more than adept at wriggling out of tricky situations and leaving some poor sucker to take the fall.

'Yeah, that's him.'

'I wouldn't trust that guy as far as I could throw him.'

'Ah, Ryan's okay. He's sound enough.'

And that, she thought, was her dad all over. How many times had Moore screwed him over in the past? Yet her father had, it seemed, a singular inability to learn from experience. 'So what does he want you to do now? You said you were just the driver, that you wouldn't have to do anything else.'

'Yeah, but that was before the two lads got nicked. We need to get rid of the gear, pronto. Ryan and Lee have already emptied the lock-up into the van. All I have to do is deliver it to Chingford.'

'You?' she said, her voice full of indignation. 'That was never the deal. Why should you have to do it? Why can't one of them drive the van?'

'Fair's fair, love. They took a big risk going to Dalston. For all they knew, the cops could have been lying in wait for them. They did their bit and now I need to do mine.'

'You don't *need* to do anything,' she insisted. 'And anyway, you're not fit to leave the flat, never mind drive a bloody van.'

'It won't take me long,' he said, glancing at his watch again. 'I can be there and back in an hour or so. All I have to do is deliver the goods and that's it. It's straightforward. No risk.' He rose to his feet, but almost immediately lost his balance, swayed a little and slumped back down again.

Ava stared at him. 'Look at the state of you. You can barely stand. This is crazy. You'll have to call Ryan, tell him you can't do it. Tell him you're sick, for God's sake.'

'I can't, love. I said I'd do it and I will.'

She could see that for her father it was a matter of pride, of reputation. If he backed out now, he'd lose face and he couldn't bear that. The trouble was that he'd probably collapse on the job and end up crashing the van. From there it would be a small step from hospital to a prison cell. Suddenly, she realised that there was only one way out. *She* would have to do it.

'Where's the van? Where do you need to pick it up from?'

'It's parked in Tierney Street,' he said. 'And it's legit, love, not nicked or nothing so there's no reason why I should be stopped. But I have to get it back by twelve. That's the arrangement. Any later and the guy who's made the loan will report it as stolen.'

'And you've got a name for the man you're delivering to?'

'Course I have. It's Lenny Crew. He's got a warehouse near the old dog track.'

'Okay,' she said, stretching out her hand. 'Give me the keys.'

'What?'

'I'll do it. I'll take the van over to Chingford.'

Her father shook his head. 'No way, Ava. No! I'm not letting you do that.'

'I don't see that you have a choice. Take a look in the mirror, Dad. You're like the walking dead. You're never going to make it over there. You'll be lucky to make it down the stairs.'

'I'll be fine. You think I'm going to let you risk your whole future by driving around with a load of dodgy gear?'

'You just said there wasn't any risk.'

'Hardly any risk, but that's not the point. You never know what's going to happen. Some idiot jumps a red light or runs into the back of you and it's game over. This is my problem, love, not yours. I'll be the one to sort it out.'

'Except there's every chance that you'll be the one running the light or doing the crashing, and then what? How do you think Ryan Moore's going to react when he finds out all his hard work's gone for a burton? He'll be none too happy when you wrap that van round a lamppost either.'

'I'm not going to do that.'

'No,' she said, 'you're not. Because you're not going to drive the damn thing. Be sensible, Dad, just for once in your life. Let me do this. If you don't and something happens to you, I'll never forgive myself. And Jesus, you know what else? I really can't cope with any more prison visiting.'

He gazed across the table at her, his eyes full of sadness and regret. He knew she was right, but was still unwilling to make that final decision.

'Please,' she begged. 'Please let me do this.'

Finally he gave in. 'Okay,' he said, 'but I'm coming with you. I'm not letting you do this on your own.'

Ava shook her head. 'No, no way. I don't want that. You'll only make it harder for me. I don't want to have to worry about you getting sick on the way there. If we have to stop or pull in somewhere, we'll only draw attention to ourselves.'

'If anything happens, your mother will never talk to me again.'

'She never talks to you anyway. Come on, please, give me the keys. The longer we argue about it, the less time we have.'

His overcoat was hanging over the back of the chair. Eventually, reluctantly, he turned around, dug into the pocket and pulled out the keys to the van. Even then he didn't pass them over immediately. 'This isn't right, love. I can't—'

'You can,' she said, reaching out to grab them before he changed his mind. Once they were safely in her hand, she stood up and got ready to go. 'Now, tell me exactly where this warehouse is.'

Three minutes later, Ava was jogging down the stone steps of Haslow House. Nerves fluttered in her stomach as she rounded the stairwell and headed for the ground floor. What was she doing? It was crazy. Well, yes, it might be crazy, but it was still a damn sight less crazy than allowing her father to do it.

Once she was down in the foyer, she paused for a moment to gather her thoughts. She had to stay calm, stay focused. All she was doing was driving a van to Chingford. *Don't think about what's in the back of it. Don't think about stolen goods. Don't think about getting caught.* She swallowed hard before she pushed open the door and hurried through the estate towards Tierney Street.

The white Luton van was parked exactly where her father had said it would be, halfway down the street and alongside the launderette. Her fingers tightened around the keys as she approached, her eyes darting from side to side in case anyone was watching. What if the cops were here and lying in wait? She glanced over her shoulder, afraid that she might be being followed. She considered walking on past the van and going round the block just to make sure, but then decided it would only be a waste of time. Even if the police were here they'd be keeping out of sight.

Standing beside the van, Ava took one last look round before finally unlocking it. Then she took a deep breath, jumped inside and slammed the door. For the next few seconds, she sat there, hunched over the wheel, waiting for the worst to happen. She was so tense she could feel a thin ache running along her shoulder blades and down the length of her spine.

Eventually, when it sank in that the coast was apparently clear, she put the key in the ignition and started the engine. Almost immediately her phone began to ring. She jumped.

Damn! Who was that? Snatching the phone out of her bag, she looked at the screen. It was Chris. She thought about ignoring it – it was another two hours before she was due to pick him up – but then decided that she'd better speak to him. If the traffic was bad she might not get back in time for ten o'clock.

'Hello,' she said.

'Ava? It's Chris.' His voice sounded harsh and urgent. 'Where are you? Are you at home?'

'No, I'm, er . . . I've just been to see my dad.'

'Something's happened. Have you heard?'

'What? What is it?'

There was a harsh intake of breath from the other end of the line. 'It's Jenna. She's dead. She's been murdered.'

49

It took Ava a moment to process the information. Jenna dead, murdered? As the horror slowly seeped into her brain, a shiver ran through her. 'What?' she said again.

'I didn't do it. I swear to you, I didn't. And I can't go home. I can't get the Merc. Danny says the cops are there. They're waiting for me. The bastards will try and pin this on me. I know they will.'

Ava shook her head, trying to work through the shock of it all. She remembered the police cars gathered at the green, the flashing lights, the growing crowd of onlookers. 'But if you run, they'll be sure you're guilty.'

'They're already sure. They've got me right in the frame. I need to get out of Kellston. I need to get out of here fast.'

She knew what he was asking and her heart sank. She didn't answer straight away. Once she'd committed herself there would be no going back.

'Ava, I swear I didn't do it. I give you my word.'

'I know. I believe you,' she said, although she was still too shocked to know what she truly believed.

'I need to get away before I get collared. Anywhere. It doesn't matter. Just somewhere I can lie low for a while.'

'Where are you?'

'The old railway arches,' he said. 'Near Albert Street.'

Ava knew the place, abandoned and derelict, the haunt of some of the local toms. Her fingers tightened around the phone. What choice did she have? She couldn't say no. She couldn't turn her back when he'd asked for help. Before long, there'd be cops crawling all over Kellston; it would only be a matter of time before they flushed him out. 'Wait there,' she said. 'I'll be five minutes.'

Rather than taking the more direct route along the high street – a route that would have involved passing the green – she wound around the back streets instead. This proved more problematical than she'd anticipated. The van was a longer, wider vehicle than she was used to and several times she came uncomfortably close to scraping the cars parked on either side of the narrow streets.

Although she wanted to get there in a hurry, she couldn't afford to put her foot down. *Concentrate,* she ordered herself. *Don't think about anything but getting this damn van from A to B.* But her mind refused to listen. What was she doing? Inevitably, her thoughts reeled back to Friday, to Chris's rage when he'd found out about Jenna and Guy Wilder. Even yesterday, he'd still been trying to get hold of her, pestering her with calls and texts. What if he'd snapped, lost his temper and . . . But no, she couldn't believe that he'd actually killed her. Chris Street was capable of many things, but surely not that.

By the time she reached the arches it was almost half past eight. She cruised slowly along the empty street keeping her eyes peeled. The crumbling redbrick construction had once been occupied by barbers, cobblers, bakers and mechanics, but all those enterprises had long since ceased to exist. Now it was used only by the dispossessed, the homeless seeking shelter for the night, the junkies or the prostitutes needing somewhere dark and lonely to conduct their private business.

When she reached the end of the street, she pulled up, leaving the engine running. She waited, drumming her fingers on the wheel. Where was he? She peered through the misty air at the gaping, sinister holes of the arches. Sometimes the council came along and boarded them up, but within a few hours the boards would all be torn down again.

After a minute, when he still hadn't appeared, she got out her phone and called him. 'I'm here,' she whispered, even though there was no one to hear her. 'I'm in the white van. Where are you?'

A few seconds later Chris emerged from one of the arches. He had the appearance of a fugitive, his head bent, his shoulders hunched. As he hurried towards the van, she lifted a hand and bit down on her knuckles. What was she doing? Shortly, she would not just be in possession of a pile of stolen gear, but also of a man on the run – a man who was suspected of murder. How much worse could it get? Before she had too much time to think it through, he'd already jumped into the cab beside her.

'I thought you'd be in the Kia,' he said.

She looked at him. His body was tense, his face tight and grim. 'You okay?'

'I will be – as soon as we get clear of here.'

Ava pulled away from the kerb, trying to decide on the best route to take. She couldn't go anywhere near the high street. It was too risky with all the police around. She would have to loop around and head for Chingford that way. 'So what happened? Do you know?'

Chris shifted in the seat, shifting forward and then shifting back, his dark eyes scanning the road. 'All I know is that she's dead. She was found on the green this morning. I had a meet with someone, early, down at the Hope. A bit of business, nothing important. I was on my way there when Danny rang, said Jenna had been murdered and the cops were at the house. I didn't have the car so I legged it over to the arches. It was somewhere to lie low until I figured out what to do next.'

'But why should the cops think it was you? I mean, I get that she's your ex and the rest but—'

'It's more complicated than that.'

Ava felt her stomach tighten. She stared out at the slow-moving traffic on Roman Road, willing it to move faster, for the lights to stay on green. She suspected she might regret her next question, but it leapt from her mouth before she could silence it. 'How? How is it complicated?'

He drew in a breath, averted his face for a moment and then glanced back. 'I got a text from her last night at about ten to eleven, saying she had to speak to me urgently, to meet her by the green. I tried to call her, but her phone was turned off.'

'And you went?'

'Yeah, I went. I hung around but she was a no-show. I tried her phone again, but it was still going straight to voicemail. I waited half an hour or so and then went home. I thought she was just fucking me about. I had no idea that . . .' He rubbed hard at his face. 'She must have been there, though. She must have already been . . .'

'Didn't you think it was odd, her calling so late?'

'Not really. That was how Jenna was. She liked to snap her fingers and have people come running.'

'But not many women would choose to meet at the green at that time of night. Bit of a dark and lonely place for a rendezvous with an unhappy ex.'

Chris's eyes flashed as if she was accusing him of something, but then he blinked and shook his head and gave a shrug. 'I presumed she meant *by* the green, not actually on it. It's not dark there. There's plenty of light from the streetlamps. And anyway, I thought she'd probably parked her car there. I presumed she was in Kellston seeing Wilder, and it's not always easy to find a space near the bar. I thought she'd wait in the car.' His right hand clenched and unclenched on his thigh. The corners of his mouth turned down. 'Jesus, I don't know what I thought. Maybe I wasn't even thinking. I just wanted to see her, to find out what the hell was going on.'

Ava realised now why the cops would have him firmly in the frame. They'd find the text on Jenna's phone and know that she had gone to meet Chris at the green. It wouldn't take a genius to put together a credible case against him. How long before they heard about his angry visit to Wilder's on Friday?

There were plenty of witnesses to it. And then there were all the texts he must have sent to her over the past few days. He would come across as a man running out of patience, a vengeful, jealous man who couldn't cope with the fact that his ex had moved on. Not to mention that the moving on was being done with his old enemy, Guy Wilder.

Chris took out his phone and started to scroll through the menu. 'I'm going to ring Danny, see what's going on.'

'No,' she said sharply, a memory jumping into her head of a thriller she'd recently seen on TV. 'You should turn that off. Can't the cops track you through your phone?'

'Shit,' he murmured, jabbing at the button.

'I think you have to take the battery out, maybe the sim card too. But whatever you do, don't use it again, not while . . . not until this is all sorted out.' She took her own mobile out of her pocket and threw it into his lap. 'Here, you'd better do mine too.'

While Chris sorted out the phones, Ava stared hard at the road ahead. By now they had reached the roundabout on Lea Bridge Road and she tried to concentrate as they merged on to the North Circular. Here the traffic was manic, a rushing, roaring crush of vehicles. She hunched over the wheel, watching the cars in front and behind, desperately trying to anticipate if any of them were about to do something stupid. She couldn't afford to get caught up in an accident.

'I have to go to Chingford,' she said. 'My dad was supposed to be delivering some stuff, but he's too sick. I'm going to a warehouse near the old dog track. It's probably best if the guys there don't see you. You might get recognised. What do you want me to do? I could drop you off somewhere and pick you up later.'

'What's in the van?' he asked.

'You don't want to know. You've got enough to worry about. Let's just say it's not strictly legit and the sooner I get rid of it, the happier I'll be.'

He gave a dry laugh. 'You must be thinking the same of me.'

Ava glanced at him. 'If I thought you were a murderer, I wouldn't be sitting next to you. The thing is, I have to get this van back to Kellston by twelve. Have you thought about where you want to go? So long as it's not too far, I'll take you.'

'Chingford's good,' he said. 'I've got an old mate there. He'll sort me out, get me somewhere safe to stay for a few days.'

'Are you sure?'

'Yeah, you can drop me off by the cemetery.' He paused and then said, 'You know the filth will be waiting for you when you get back? They're bound to be. What are you going to say to them?'

Ava felt a faint sense of panic well in her throat. 'I haven't figured that out yet. I'll think of something. One good thing is that the Kia's been parked in Violet Road since yesterday. They don't know about the van so they can't prove that I was the one to take you anywhere.'

'They'll still give you a hard time.'

'They can't prove anything,' she said again, although she couldn't quite disguise the tremor in her voice. Another grilling from the police was the last thing she needed. She saw the signs for Chingford and flipped on the indicator as she headed for the slip road. They were not far off now. Another five minutes and they'd be there.

They were quiet for a while, both lost in their own thoughts. By the time Chris spoke again, they were on Old Church Road approaching Chingford Mount cemetery. There was nowhere she could safely pull in and so she turned right and passed through the gates on to the main drive.

'This is fine,' he said after she'd gone about fifty yards. 'I can walk through from here.'

She stopped the van and looked around. It was still early and the only other people in sight were a man shifting dirt with a forklift and a couple of kids on bikes. A squirrel crossed the road in front of them, paused, gazed at them with curiosity and then scurried up a tree. 'How will I get in touch with you?'

'You don't. It's better that way.'

'Is it?'

He turned his head and smiled. 'Thanks, Ava. I won't forget this.'

She forced a weak, trembling smile in return. What if the cops caught up with him and threw him in jail? These could be his last few hours as a free man. 'Oh, don't worry. I'll make damn sure you don't.'

'Bye, then.'

As he went to get out of the van, Ava reached for his arm. 'Take care of yourself, huh?'

She wasn't quite sure what happened next. He turned back towards her, his fingers closing around her hand. There was an intake of breath. His? Hers? She couldn't be sure. Their eyes locked and neither of them looked away. For a few seconds they were as still as the grey stone angels in the graveyard. She couldn't say who broke the spell, which one of them made the first move, but suddenly his face was close to hers. His lips brushed gently against her lips, his mouth slowly covering her mouth. Every sensible neuron in her brain told her to pull away, to stop, to not be such a bloody fool, but her body told her something entirely different.

50

Back at Cowan Road station, Valerie Middleton went straight to the Ladies' and washed her hands with the kind of manic thoroughness that would have shamed a sufferer of OCD. No matter how many murders she dealt with, she always had the same feeling of being unclean, of being in some way polluted by the act.

The victim had been found behind the bushes by a woman walking her dog at around seven thirty this morning. She'd been shot through the heart. There was no sign of a struggle and no sign of sexual assault, although they wouldn't know for sure until after the autopsy had been done. The pathologist had put the death roughly between the hours of nine and twelve last night.

It hadn't taken long to put a name to the victim. Even before the contents of her bag had been examined, one of the first officers at the scene had identified her as Jenna Dean, the ex-wife of Chris Street. Though the body had now been

357

removed, the green remained taped off while the SOCOs combed the ground. Valerie also had a team going door-to-door, questioning all the local residents. One of them, surely, must have heard that shot.

She shook her wet hands and stared at her reflection in the mirror. Her face looked tired, as if the burden of the investigation had already started to weigh her down. She'd never been one to jump to premature conclusions, but this murder had all the hallmarks of a domestic. The text in the send box of Jenna's mobile phone had told them pretty much all they needed to know: last night Jenna Dean had arranged to meet with Chris Street and now she was dead.

While Valerie carefully dried her hands, she continued to think about the killing. Street, unsurprisingly, had disappeared. If he'd left directly after the murder, he could be miles away by now. But he hadn't taken the Mercedes, so how had he got away? He could have taken a cab – they'd have to check that out – or borrowed a car or got someone else to drive him. His girlfriend, Ava Gold, was a distinct possibility. She was also missing, although her flatmate swore that she'd been in all night. But what would Tash Reed know? She hadn't been aware that Lydia Hall had left on Saturday night so how could she be sure that Ava hadn't slipped out too?

Valerie returned to the mirror and made some final unnecessary adjustments to her hair. Then she pushed back her shoulders, took a deep breath and prepared herself for battle. During her first few years in the job she'd worked for a senior officer who had always referred to murder as a kind of war with the police on one side and the perpetrator on the other. It was their job, and their duty, to hunt down the enemy and take him prisoner. Although it was a particularly masculine perspective, she had never quite been able to shake the analogy from her head.

Upstairs, the incident room was buzzing. There was the bustle of officers coming and going, the exchange of information, the clicking of fingers on keyboards, the constant ringing of the telephones. Valerie went to the desk where DS Laura Higgs was working and peered over her shoulder at the sheet of paper she was studying.

'Is that Jenna Dean's phone log?'

Higgs gave a nod. 'Yes, guv. There are over twenty texts from Chris Street since Friday. He wasn't a happy bunny. Did you know she was seeing Guy Wilder?'

'Wilder? You're kidding. God, he wouldn't have been too pleased about that.'

'You can say that again. He was giving her a shedload of grief, although there's no sign of her having replied until last night. Looks like she'd had enough of being hassled and decided to meet him face-to-face.'

Valerie could imagine how Chris Street would feel about his ex taking up with Wilder. The two men detested each other and never bothered to hide it. 'What about Street's mobile?'

'We're still waiting for the phone company to get back to us. You know what they're like. It could take a while.'

'Guv?' DC Preston called from the other side of the room. 'Got a call for you. DCI Butler.'

Valerie gave him a nod and then said to Higgs, 'Get someone over to Wilder's place and bring him in. Let's see if he can shed any light on what happened last night.' She walked quickly to Preston's desk and picked up the phone. 'Jeff, hi, sorry. I was just about to call you.'

'I heard there was another shooting. Is it true? Is the victim Chris Street's ex-wife?'

'Yes, Jenna Dean.'

Butler gave a low whistle. 'Being connected to the Streets doesn't sound like good news at the moment. Got any obvious motives yet?'

'How does a complicated love life sound for starters? It appears she was dating Guy Wilder.'

'Jesus,' Butler said. 'I bet that went down like a lead balloon. Your man Street wouldn't have liked that one little bit. So you've got the ex-husband and the current boyfriend. Which one's your money on? Or are you going for a rank outsider?'

Valerie was used to the apparently callous way some officers responded to an unnatural death. It was a protective barrier, a way of distancing themselves. Everyone had their own coping mechanisms. 'Well, Chris Street appears to have done a runner. He's not at home and we've searched Belles, the Lincoln and all his other usual haunts. His phone's turned off too.'

'Narrows the odds. Anything on the weapon that was used?'

'Not yet. Are you thinking it might be the same gun used in the Belles shooting?'

'It's not beyond the realms of possibility. There does seem to be a suspicious amount of fatal activity revolving around the Streets at the moment.'

'I'll keep you up to date,' she said. 'Nothing new your end, I suppose?'

'You suppose right. Look, I'll try and drop by this evening. I know you'll be up to your ears, but if you have a minute, maybe we can grab a drink, exchange notes.'

'Sounds good,' she said. 'See you later, then.'

Valerie walked back across the room, sat down opposite DS Higgs and started going through the scene-of-crime photographs. Jenna Dean was lying on her side, her eyes still open, her long blonde hair soaked by the rain. The victim was wearing a short, dark red dress and knee-high boots. Her lipstick matched the colour of her dress. The single bullet wound in her chest matched the colour of her lipstick. An expensive Cartier watch was still on her wrist, as were a couple of fancy-looking rings. This was no mugging, then, but they already knew that.

'Why do you think she got out of the car?' Valerie asked.

Higgs glanced up. 'Guv?'

The distinctive bright pink Cherokee Jeep had been parked by the green and thoroughly examined by Forensics. 'It was raining, wasn't it? And no woman wants to stand about in the rain and the cold if she doesn't have to. Why didn't she wait in the car for Chris Street and have the conversation where it was warm and dry? We know he didn't get in because his prints aren't on the passenger door.'

'Maybe she didn't want to be that close to him. Maybe she waited until she saw him arrive and then got out. She was probably intending to keep it short and simple – *Leave me alone* – before going on to the bar to see Wilder. But then Street got mad and—'

'And what? Dragged her on to the green? Wouldn't she have struggled, shouted for help?'

'He wouldn't need to do any dragging if he was pointing a gun at her.'

Valerie pulled a face. 'Bit risky when you're standing on the high street. Anyone could have seen him.'

'Except it was raining. And no one takes much notice of anything when it's pouring down.'

'I suppose.' Valerie frowned as she continued to flick through the pictures. Near the bottom of the pile was a photo of Jenna's striped umbrella, which had blown across the green and got entangled in some bushes. The spokes were bent and twisted, the fabric spattered with mud. She gazed at it for a while, the image imbued with a kind of poignancy. In her mind, it seemed to sum up all the waste and futility of a life taken prematurely.

Fifteen minutes later, news came from the officers who'd been despatched to Wilder's: Guy Wilder was down in reception and demanding to see his solicitor. Valerie raised her eyes to the ceiling, knowing that would mean yet another delay. But there was nothing she could do about it. Being Jenna Dean's current boyfriend, Wilder was bound to feel under pressure, under suspicion even. And no one these days, especially in a murder case, would set foot in an interview room without legal protection.

While she waited, she turned her attention back to Ava Gold. The girl still hadn't returned to the flat in Market Square. DCs Joanne Lister and David Franks had been to the Mansfield Estate to see her father, but Jimmy Gold hadn't been cooperative.

DC Lister, a pale-faced officer with a mop of red hair, stood in front of Valerie's desk and shook her head in frustration. 'He said he'd seen her briefly this morning, but doesn't know where she is now. He claims that he thought she was going on to work and insists that she couldn't have known anything about the murder or Chris Street disappearing. He says she wouldn't get involved in anything like that. But then, he's her dad. He is going to say that, isn't he? He was lying, guv, I know he was.'

'I'm sure you're right.'

'Do you think we should pull him in?'

'No,' Valerie said. 'Let's leave him be for the moment. When ... *if* Ava comes back, she might head for his flat rather than her own. She might reckon it's a safer bet. Let's not give her any reason to think otherwise. We'll get a car down to the Mansfield in case she shows up.'

DC David Franks, a tall solid guy who loomed over Lister, asked, 'Is she likely to come back, guv? I mean, if she's just helped Chris Street do a runner, isn't she going to stay with him?'

'Well, we don't know anything for sure yet. Why don't the two of you head over to Market Square and keep an eye on the flat?'

51

Ava, although trying not to think about the kiss as she drove towards the old dog track, was actually thinking of nothing else. It hadn't meant anything. Of course it hadn't. It was just one of those mad, impulsive actions fuelled by adrenalin, fear and anxiety. When you were afraid, you reached out for someone ... anyone who might bring you some temporary comfort. And it wasn't as if she had *those* sorts of feelings for him. She liked him well enough, but she wasn't falling in love. No, she absolutely, definitely wasn't falling in love.

'Watch the road,' she murmured to herself. 'Don't get distracted. Don't mess up now.' The traffic was heavy and there were roundabouts to negotiate. All it would take was a second's loss of concentration and she would plough straight into the backside of the car in front.

But despite the good advice to herself, she still couldn't contain her worries about him. The police would check out all his known friends. Were they aware of the mate in

Chingford? Could the guy even be trusted? Rewards were often offered for suspected murderers and greed could easily overrule old loyalties. And she should have reminded Chris not to pull any money out from a cashpoint; that would be another way the police could track him down, or at least get a vague idea of his whereabouts.

Ava drummed her fingers on the wheel as she waited at a red light. She had to stop stressing about him. He wasn't stupid and hopefully he wouldn't do anything stupid. And he was innocent, wasn't he? She instinctively felt that he was, but what if her instinct was skewed, if she'd got it all wrong?

The niggling doubt gnawed away at her. She tried to push it aside, but the voice couldn't be silenced completely. Chris had been angry at Jenna, more than angry. He'd felt betrayed and humiliated. He'd also had a gun, although he claimed it had gone missing. Was he telling the truth? All it took was a red mist to descend, a momentary loss of self-control and there was no going back.

She blinked twice, trying to wash away the doubt. It was too late now to change her mind. All she could do was stand by her convictions and pray that she hadn't been taken for a fool. Up ahead she could see the old dog track – and now there was something else to worry about. What if the cops had got Lenny Crew under surveillance? Perhaps he was a known fence. Perhaps one of the guys who'd been arrested had tipped the wink to the cops about where the gear was going be offloaded.

She was a hundred yards past the track before she spotted the warehouse, a wide grey metal structure with the name *Crew & Lambert* emblazoned across the front. She had a sudden impulse to just drive on past, to not take the chance, but then thought of her dad and knew that she couldn't do it. After uttering a quick prayer – *Please God, don't let me get nicked* – she indicated left, went into the slip road, turned on to the forecourt of the warehouse and pulled in by the main entrance.

Seconds later, a tubby middle-aged man with thinning brown hair and suspicious eyes emerged from behind the double doors. He came alongside the van, put his hands on his generous hips and stared at her.

Ava wound down the window. 'Hi. Are you Lenny Crew?'

'Yeah,' he said.

'Got a delivery for you.'

'A delivery?' he said, a deep frown settling on his forehead. 'I ain't expecting no delivery.'

Ava stared back at him. She didn't know how these things worked. What was she supposed to say now? She could hardly blurt it out – *Hey, remember that dodgy load of electricals you arranged to buy? Well, here they are!* – and without being sure of what was acceptable and what wasn't, she felt reluctant to name names either. As she was pondering on what to do next, Ryan Moore suddenly appeared at the doors. He hurried over and grinned at her.

'Ava, love. What are you doing here?'

'Dad's sick,' she said, laying it on thick. 'He's bad. He's had to go to hospital, but he didn't want to let you down so . . . '

Lenny Crew glanced at Ryan. 'What's going on here?'

'Don't worry,' Ryan said, giving him a slap on the back. 'This is Jimmy's daughter, Ava. She's sound. She's fine.' He looked back at her. 'No problems, then?'

'Sweet as a nut,' she said, recalling her father's words about the original job. 'But I'm in a hurry. I need to get to the hospital. Where do you want the van?'

Lenny Crew jerked his thumb, his eyes still less than friendly. 'Round the back,' he said. He was, she imagined, the type of man who believed that women were only good for two things – domestic chores and shagging – and had no place at all in the masculine world of crime.

Ava drove the van round to the back of the warehouse where there were a number of storage depots. One of them had its doors rolled open and she waited there. After a short while, Lenny and Ryan appeared in her rear-view mirror. Their heads were close together and Lenny still looked peeved by the unexpected change in the arrangements. She had never expected to be pleased to see Ryan Moore, but on this occasion it was a godsend. If he hadn't been here, she was pretty sure that Lenny, fearing a set-up, would have sent her on her way.

'You want to reverse in?' Ryan said, walking up to her and gesturing towards the open depot.

'Sure.'

Ava carefully manoeuvred the vehicle until she could slide it easily into the open space. Then she switched off the engine, jumped out of the cab and gave the keys to Ryan. He opened the rear of the van and messed about with the tailgate. She stared at the gear piled high in the back. Jesus, it was like an Aladdin's cave! There must have been hundreds of boxes and until they were unloaded she wouldn't be able to get away. Aware that she needed to get the van back by twelve, she rolled up her sleeves and nodded at the two men. 'Right, let's get this lot shifted.'

Ryan kept up a steady stream of chatter while they moved the stolen goods, but Lenny barely said a word. Spurred on by fear – what if the cops suddenly showed up? – she threw herself wholeheartedly into the job, and with the three of them working flat out, they managed to finish in under fifteen minutes. By the time all the boxes had been transferred, her face was flushed from the exertion and she could feel a trickle of sweat running down her spine.

Ryan closed up the back of the van and passed the keys back to Ava. 'Drive carefully, then.'

'I always do.'

'And sorry about your dad, love. Give him my best.'

She could have done with a breather, but her desire to get away outweighed any physical needs. Quickly, she clambered into the cab, closed the door and smiled at Ryan through the open window. 'I will, ta. See you around.'

'Ain't you forgetting something?'

Ava stared back at him. 'Sorry?'

Ryan grinned, took a large wad of notes out of his pocket and offered them up to her. 'Don't want to leave without your dosh.'

She gazed at the notes, knowing that she couldn't turn up in Kellston with an unexplained pile of cash. Not when the police would be waiting for her. They'd think Chris had paid her to help him get away. 'Oh, er . . . why don't you sort it out with Dad? I'll get him to give you a bell when he's feeling better.'

'You sure?'

'Yeah, yeah, no worries. That'll be fine. Bye, then.' She looked at Lenny. 'Bye.'

Lenny gave her a brusque nod, turned around and walked off towards the warehouse. She thought his manners left a lot to be desired, but she wasn't about to kick up a fuss. Who cared what he thought of her? He was just a dinosaur male with a pea-sized brain. Glad that she was finally making her escape, she gave Ryan a cheery wave, started the engine and set off for the road.

The drive back seemed to take forever. The sense of relief she felt at having finally freed herself of the stolen goods was tempered by her ongoing anxiety about Chris. There would also be the inevitable repercussions of her going missing. She had to think of a story, no matter how thin, to tell the cops when they picked her up.

The traffic was especially bad as she hit the outskirts of Kellston and it took her twenty minutes to reach Tierney Road. The spot where the van had originally been parked was now occupied and she had to go round the block three times before she finally found a space in Cherry Street.

Once the van was successfully in place, she leaned back and briefly closed her eyes. *Thank God.* It was done. It was over. But she didn't have time to hang about. Now she had to face the rest of it. Quickly, she sorted out her mobile, putting the battery and the sim card back in. She knew the police could track her whereabouts through the phone, but could they also listen in to conversations? She didn't dare take the risk.

Five minutes later, having bought herself a phone card, she was standing in a booth at the railway station. It was possible that the cops had put a tap on her dad's line, but she was hoping that they wouldn't have been able to organise it this quickly. Anyway, she didn't have a choice about calling him.

She'd have to take the chance and hope for the best. She punched in the number and listened to it ring. It was answered almost immediately.

'Hello?'

'Dad?'

He answered with the sound of panic in his voice. 'Ava? Where have you been? What's going on? I've been trying to call you.'

She put one hand over her left ear, trying to block out the noise of the station announcements. 'I'm fine. Everything's okay. Sorry, my phone's playing up. Have the cops been round about Jenna?'

'They're looking for you. I didn't tell them nothing. I said I'd seen you today, but only for ten minutes. Is it true? Did Chris Street really—'

'No,' she said. 'I don't think so, but God knows what's going on. All I heard was that she'd been killed.' She thought it best to keep quiet about the rest – what her father didn't know, he couldn't inadvertently let slip. 'Look, the van's on Cherry Street. I've left the keys over the rear wheel, driver's side. You'd better get the owner to pick it up quickly. Oh, and I told our mutual friend that you'd had to go to hospital, just in case he asks.'

'Hospital?'

'Just tell him it was suspected pneumonia, something like that. I'll explain when I see you.'

'Ava—'

'Dad, I've got to go. Don't worry. I'll speak to you later.' She hung up before he had the chance to say anything else. Leaving the station, she looked warily to the left and right.

She needed to get back on the high street, but didn't dare go past the green. It would still be crawling with cops and one of them might recognise her.

Instead, she took the long way round, walking through the back streets until she was able to swing back on to the main road further up. Here, she dived into the first clothes store she came to, made a fast perusal of the racks, chose three cheap T-shirts and paid for them at the counter. When questioned, she was going to tell the police that she'd spent the morning shopping. It was hardly a rock-solid alibi, but it was better than nothing.

Ava walked back towards Market Square, her heart starting to thump in her chest. She came to Connolly's and thought about going inside for a coffee. It was tempting. Anything that involved putting off the fateful moment was tempting. But she knew it had to be faced. It wasn't going to go away and the longer she left it, the harder it would be.

She was at the end of Market Street when she saw the two cops, a man and a woman, sitting in an unmarked car near the flat. They were illegally parked on a double yellow line. Even though she'd been expecting it, her impulse was to turn and run. She had to dig deep into the meagre remains of her courage to keep on walking towards them.

52

DI Valerie Middleton looked across the table at Guy Wilder and his solicitor. The latter was a slick piece of work, dressed in a suit that had probably cost more than she earned in a month. His name was Hugo Pinner and his attitude was one of supercilious impatience. He frequently sighed and glanced at his watch as if to remind her that his client's time was important and shouldn't be wasted. He was, she thought, a man with an over-inflated sense of his own importance.

Guy Wilder, however, was harder to fathom. Although clearly shaken by Jenna Dean's death, he did not appear to be in any way devastated. Considering his girlfriend had just been murdered, he was remarkably calm.

'So,' she continued, 'when exactly did your relationship with Jenna Dean begin?'

Wilder's hands rested comfortably on the table. 'Recently. Very recently, in fact. Only a couple of weeks ago. I've actually known her longer than that, but only in passing, to say hello to, that kind of thing.'

'And you knew she was Chris Street's ex-wife?'

'Of course.'

'And that didn't bother you?'

Wilder lifted his shoulders in a casual shrug. 'Why should it?'

'You didn't think Chris Street might find it . . . provocative?'

'What exactly are you trying to imply, Inspector?' Pinner cut in. 'I don't see how—'

But Wilder waved his objection away with a flap of his hand. 'It's okay, Hugo. I don't mind answering the question.' He focused his gaze back on Valerie and gave a slight smile. 'You can't always help who you're attracted to. And if I was to automatically eliminate any woman who'd had a past relationship, there wouldn't be many left to date.'

Valerie stared back at him. She found the response disingenuous – he must have known how Street would react – and decided to pursue the matter. 'But Chris Street wasn't happy about it? Would that be a fair assessment?'

'I have no idea what goes on in Chris Street's head. But yes, I believe he did express some displeasure. He turned up at the bar Friday lunchtime, shouting the odds, looking for me. I wasn't there, but my business partner Noah Clark was. There were plenty of other witnesses too. He was acting in a . . . how shall I put it? . . . a somewhat threatening manner.'

'And what did you do about it?'

'Do?' he repeated, raising his eyebrows.

'Did you call the police and report him?'

'No.'

'Why not?'

Wilder sat back and crossed his legs. 'Well, to be honest I presumed it was just bluster. He's the type of man who doesn't like to lose face. He was obviously bothered by my seeing Jenna – even though they're no longer together, and haven't been for a long time – and decided to kick up a stink about it. I never thought for a second that she might be in any danger. He was directing his anger at me rather than her.'

Valerie suspected that Guy Wilder had taken pleasure in winding up his old adversary. It was hard to tell whether he'd had any genuine feelings for Jenna or whether she had simply been a means to an end. 'Did you view the relationship as serious, as one that was going somewhere?'

Wilder produced that slight smile again. 'Who's to know what's going to become serious or not? It was early days. We were simply enjoying each other's company. I liked her. She was good fun.'

Good fun, Valerie thought, wasn't exactly a ringing endorsement of the relationship. It suggested something light and superficial. The roots of murder tended to be fixed in strong, powerful emotions and there was little evidence of those in Wilder – at least not in regards to Jenna Dean. She could not, however, entirely rule him out as a suspect. Chris Street might be top of the list, but it was wise to keep an open mind. She gave DS Laura Higgs a quick sideways glance, letting her know that she was free to continue with her own set of questions.

'Perhaps we could move on to last night,' Higgs said. 'Had you arranged to meet Jenna?'

'No,' he replied. 'No firm arrangement. She was busy, seeing friends, but said she might drop by later. I did try and call her – it must have been about a quarter to eleven – but her phone was off.'

'So you didn't see or hear from her yesterday?'

'Yes, we talked earlier in the day. About one o'clock, I think it was. That was the last time we … that was the last time I heard from her.'

'You weren't worried when she didn't turn up?'

'No, not at all. I presumed she was still up West with her friends.'

DS Higgs shuffled the files on the table, opened the top one and looked at the contents. She left a short pause before glancing up again. 'How did Jenna feel about the situation with Chris?'

'How do you mean?'

'Was she worried, annoyed, indifferent?'

Guy Wilder's gaze roamed briefly around the room before coming back to rest on Higgs again. 'I'd say she was more irritated than anything else. He'd been bombarding her with calls and texts all weekend. She was trying to ignore him, but he clearly wasn't getting the message.'

'And did she mention the idea of meeting up with him?'

'No, but if she'd chosen to do so, it would have been entirely up to her. I wouldn't have tried to influence her decision one way or another.'

'Even though he'd been making threats? Weren't you worried for her, afraid for her safety?'

'In retrospect, I clearly should have been. I believed, wrongly as it transpired, that it was me he had the problem with.'

'Although you knew that she was being *bombarded* – wasn't

that the word you used? – with calls and text messages from him.'

Pinner tried to interject again, but Wilder made the same stop gesture with his hand. 'Jenna showed me the texts. There was nothing specifically threatening about them. They were more *tedious* than anything else. Still, I'm sure you already know that. You do have her phone, don't you? You must have read them.'

It was true, Valerie thought, that there was nothing in the messages to suggest that Jenna was in any imminent danger. They mostly consisted of requests that she call him back immediately. Their sheer volume, however, should have set alarm bells ringing. 'Why do you think she asked him to meet her last night?'

'Did she?' Wilder looked surprised by this piece of information. 'I didn't know that.'

'She sent him a text telling him to meet her at the green.'

Wilder shook his head. 'She must have . . . I don't know . . . Maybe she'd decided it was the only way to put a stop to all the harassment. Obviously, she wouldn't want to meet him in the bar – not when I was there – and I shouldn't think she'd want to go to his house either. When she came to see me, she often parked by the green. I suppose she must have been intending to come over after she'd finished talking to him.'

'You don't think it's odd?' Valerie asked. 'I mean, that she didn't call you, tell you that she was on her way?'

Wilder's clear blue eyes gazed directly into hers. 'Perhaps she wanted to surprise me.' He inclined his head and gave a sigh. 'Why are we even doing this? You know who killed her. We both know.'

'Is my client a suspect?' Pinner asked. 'Only if he is, then—'

Valerie smiled thinly back at him. 'Mr Wilder is simply helping us with our enquiries.'

'Well, I think my client has been more than generous with his time. So if you don't intend to charge him with anything, may I suggest we bring this interview to a close?'

53

The rain was bucketing down, hitting the pavement at speed and streaming down into the gutters. Michael Raynard stood for fifteen minutes, sheltering in a doorway. He waited until he was sure that the shop had no customers before quickly crossing the high street and going into Beast. He opened the door – there was a light dinging sound – closed it carefully behind him and shook the rain from his hair. He flipped the sign over from OPEN to CLOSED and drew the bolt across.

Morton Carlisle, alerted by the bell, wandered out from the office at the back. His salesman's smile wavered. 'I'm sorry. What are you doing?'

'Closing up for the day,' Raynard said.

Carlisle stared at him. 'I don't . . . Why? Why are you . . . ?'

'I've come for a private viewing. I don't want us to be disturbed.'

'We don't do private viewings, not without an appointment.'

'I don't need an appointment.'

A nervous tic danced at the corner of Carlisle's mouth. 'I don't ... What ... What's going on?'

Raynard ran a hand along the top of one of the glass cabinets. 'Please don't be difficult, Morton. I'm not in the mood. Let's just keep this simple, huh?'

'What is it you want? Money? Is that it?' Carlisle's hands moved restlessly from his sides, to his chest, to the back of his neck. 'We don't ... we don't keep cash on the premises.'

'You can't pay for what I want. No, that's not it at all.' Raynard gave a small impatient shake of his head. 'I'm here to talk about Silver Delaney.'

'What? Who?'

'You don't recall her? How odd. I've always thought of her as a rather memorable sort of girl.'

Carlisle swallowed hard, his Adam's apple jumping in his throat. 'I don't know who you're talking about. I'd like you to leave, please, or I'm ... I'm going to call the police.'

'The police? Are you sure about that?' From the long inner pockets of his dark grey overcoat, Raynard pulled out a baseball bat. He slapped it twice into the palm of his hand, producing a dry thudding sound. He gazed down at the cabinet. 'The trouble with broken glass is that it makes such a mess, don't you find?' He glanced up again, his eyes hard and cold. 'You end up picking up the pieces for weeks.'

'No!' Carlisle pleaded. 'Please! Don't ... don't ...'

But it was already too late. The bat descended on the cabinet with enough force to shatter the glass into a thousand pieces. The noise ripped through the room, making Carlisle jump with fright. His eyes widened at the same time as his mouth fell open. The mounted red fox tumbled to the floor and Raynard stamped on its neck with the heel of his boot. 'I've never been keen on foxes. Vermin, that's all they are.' Slowly, he looked up. 'Shall we start again, Morton?'

Carlisle was now backing away, both hands raised in a defensive gesture. 'W-what do you want? Tell me what you want, but please don't . . .'

Raynard advanced towards him, glancing to his left and right as if trying to decide which cabinet to choose next.

'Please!' Carlisle begged again. 'Stop this. Anything . . . tell me . . . only please . . .' His hands shifted up to his face, clenching into fists and squeezing against his cheeks. 'Do you have any idea what these exhibits are worth?'

Raynard gave a low mirthless laugh. 'Silver Delaney,' he said again. 'You do know her, don't you? She came to see you here not so long ago. She came with Danny Street.'

'Oh, h-her,' Carlisle stammered. 'Yes, the girl, the fair-haired girl. Is that her name? I didn't know. I swear I didn't.'

Raynard continued to pat the bat softly into the palm of his hand. 'Mr Delaney has concerns about his daughter. Like any decent father, he worries about the company she keeps.'

'What's that got to do with me?'

'I want to know what she was doing here.'

A thin film of sweat had erupted on Carlisle's forehead. 'Nothing. I mean, she just came with him. He was . . . he wanted to buy something . . . from the gallery.'

'At night?'

Carlisle swallowed hard again, his eyes fixed on the bat. 'He . . . he called me, said he needed an item urgently. For a client. A business partner. He had to have it for the following day. A falcon, that's what he bought. Yes, yes, a gyrfalcon, I remember it now. It was a very fine example of . . . ' He ran his tongue along his dry lips. 'I hardly spoke to her, I swear. She was just here, with him. Nothing else.'

Raynard inclined his head. 'Why don't I believe you, Morton?'

'I'm telling the truth. I swear. That was . . . '

The bat flew more widely this time, its aim random and more destructive. The noise was loud, a shattering, splintering explosion of sound. Three cabinets, two domes and a smaller case containing a single hummingbird, all dissolved into shards.

'No! Please . . . '

'Final chance,' Raynard hissed. 'And then this room becomes a fuckin' glass factory.'

As the bat rose up into the air again, Carlisle stretched out his arms. 'No, no, stop it! I'll tell you. I'll tell you everything.' A thin pathetic whine leaked out of his mouth. 'It wasn't me. I didn't want to do it. They made me.'

'Keep talking.'

'They . . . he . . . he wanted names, customers, men, well-off men who spent a lot of money here.'

Raynard gave a bleak, tight-lipped smile. 'And why exactly would he want those?'

Carlisle's tongue flicked out again, quickly dampening his lips. His eyes looked frantically around the room, towards the door and then back at Raynard. But still he didn't speak.

'You're running out of time here, mate. No one's coming to help. There's only you and me. Please don't try my patience. You've got five seconds. Five, four, three—'

'All right, all right. I'll tell you. Just don't ...' Carlisle wrapped his arms protectively around his chest and stared down at the floor. 'It was a ... a blackmail scam. He wanted the names so he could set them up, make some money.'

'Set them up?'

'You know?' Carlisle's eyes, full of fear, flicked up again. The pale, parchment skin of his face was pulled taut over his cheekbones and ridged with pink. 'With a woman.'

'With Silver Delaney?'

'I don't know. I swear. He never told me. All I did was provide him with the names.'

Raynard gave a sneer. 'And take the money. You did take the money, Morton, didn't you?'

'Some. Not much. I didn't want to do it. He threatened me, said I had to. I was scared of him. He's crazy, violent. He wouldn't take no for an answer. I didn't have a choice.'

'Oh, there's always a choice, Morton. You could have gone to the law, got some protection. Most people would do that, don't you think?'

'I was scared of him,' Carlisle repeated. 'You don't know what he's like.'

Raynard scratched his head with his left hand, while he slapped the bat gently against his thigh with his right. 'How many men are we talking about here? Are there pictures? Videos?'

'Only a few ... men, I mean. Four or five. Street didn't show any pictures to me.' Hurriedly, he added. 'I wouldn't have wanted to see them.'

'Sure you wouldn't,' Raynard sneered. 'A nice respectable guy like you.' He released a long audible breath. 'Mr Delaney

382

isn't going to be happy. No, he isn't going to be happy at all. His little girl mixed up in something like this.'

'It was nothing to do with me. I didn't think—'

'Save it,' Raynard said. 'I don't give a toss what you thought.'

Carlisle's voice was tight and strained. 'What are you . . . what are going to do now?'

'Not up to me, is it? But Mr Delaney doesn't like people taking advantage of his daughter. No, he takes a very dim view of things like that.'

'It's Danny Street who's behind all this, not me. He's the one you should be talking to.'

'I'm sure I'll get around to it.'

'It wasn't my fault. I didn't . . . '

'Yeah, I get it. Nothing's your fault, huh? I'll be sure to pass the message on.' Raynard looked around the room, wrinkling his nose. 'Bit of a mess, this place. You should get it cleaned up, Morton. It doesn't give a good impression to the customers.' He turned on his heel and began to walk away.

Carlisle stared silently after him. He was holding his breath in case the man started wielding his bat again. There was the crunch of boots on broken glass. The man glanced out through the door, making sure the coast was clear before he slid back the bolt. Then, without a backward glance, he stepped out on to the street and strode away.

Carlisle took a few seconds to recover his composure before hurrying over to the door to lock it again. He leaned against it for a moment, feeling the cold sweat sliding down his back. What now? What should he do now? His guts turned somersaults, bile rising into his throat. It might be over for the time being, but it was only an adjournment. Judgement hadn't yet been passed and when it was . . .

Quickly, with shaking legs, he pushed himself forward and half-ran, half-staggered to the office. He snatched up the phone and dialled the number. It was answered not by Danny Street, but by Silver Delaney.

'Hey, Morton,' she said in her drawl. 'How are you doing, hon?'

'I need to speak to Danny. Is he there?'

'Nah, he's not here.'

'Where is he? Do you know where he is? I have to speak to him. It's urgent, for God's sake.'

'What's going on, hon? What's happening?'

'What's happening? You want to know what's happening?' There was a distinctly hysterical edge to his tone. 'What's happening is that I've just had a visit from a friend of your father's. Tell Danny to get round here straight away. Straight away, do you hear me? Otherwise I'm going to the police.'

54

Ava was feeling the kind of exhaustion that comes from having to lie consistently. Her body felt heavy as lead. She was trying to stay focused, to keep her story simple and to not embellish it with any unnecessary detail. The same questions were being asked over and over again. It was now three o'clock in the afternoon and her head was beginning to spin.

In front of her were DI Valerie Middleton and DS Laura Higgs. Sitting to her left was a duty solicitor called Vanessa West. The woman, in her mid-twenties, although competent was not especially reassuring. Ava suspected her of being intimidated by the two senior police officers.

'Let's go over last night again,' Higgs said. Her gaze, hard and nasty, bored into Ava.

Ava glanced at her solicitor. 'Do I have to keep on doing this?'

Before Ms West had the opportunity to reply, DI Middleton

said, 'If you wouldn't mind. Just one more time, so we're all perfectly clear on the details.'

Ava wondered if the two officers were playing good cop, bad cop. If that was the case then Higgs definitely qualified as the latter. Ever since their first meeting on Sunday, the sergeant had been quite blatantly antagonistic, as if she had taken an instant dislike to her and was now intent on proving her guilty of anything.

'If you wouldn't mind,' DI Middleton said again.

Ava, seeing that her solicitor wasn't going to intervene, wearily embarked on her story again. 'Okay. I was in all night, watching TV. My flatmate Tash was there with her girlfriend, Hannah. We had a pizza for dinner – mozzarella and tomato – then the two of them went down to the Fox. That was about eight o'clock. I stayed in. They got back about eleven twenty. I was just going to bed. I said goodnight and that was it.'

'And you didn't make or receive any phone calls during this time?'

'No. You've got my mobile. You can check. And you can check the landline too.'

Higgs directed another fierce glare at her. 'Although Chris Street could have come round to the flat while Tash and Hannah were out.'

'He could have, but he didn't.'

'And you're absolutely sure about that?'

'Absolutely sure.'

Higgs continued to press on with her theories. 'If Chris Street arrived at the flat before your flatmate and her friend returned from the pub, he could have hidden in your bedroom until the girls were asleep and then the two of you could have left together.'

'He didn't. We didn't. And look, why would he come to me anyway? He's got family, a father, a brother. He'd trust them more than he would trust me.'

'But you're his girlfriend,' Higgs said.

And there was another can of worms that Ava didn't want to open. No one was going to believe her if she said that they had just been pretending. It would sound ridiculous. 'So what? You really think I'd be the first person he'd turn to?'

For all the dark, nightmarish qualities of the interview, Ava was aware of one shining ray of light. Now she knew that Jenna had been murdered last night, she was certain of Chris's innocence. If he had killed her, then why would he have hung around to the morning before trying to make his escape? Even if he'd been worried about the Merc being stopped, he could easily have borrowed Danny's car or his father's to get away. He could have pulled money out of his account, driven to the airport and been 500 miles away by now.

'And what about this morning?' DI Middleton said.

Ava sighed before diligently repeating the reply she'd already given so many times before. 'I went over to the Mansfield to see my dad at about eight o'clock. He's ill. He's got the flu. I bought some shopping for him on the way there.'

Higgs leaned forward, her eyes flashing again. 'So you were on the high street. Are you saying you didn't notice any activity around the green?'

'I saw some police cars and an ambulance.'

'And you didn't wonder what was going on?'

Ava released another thin sigh. 'Yes, I wondered, but this is Kellston. It's not that unusual to see a few cops around. Anyway, I was more concerned about my dad. I went to the Mansfield, stayed with him for about ten, fifteen minutes and then started walking back towards the flat.'

'And that's when you got the phone call from Chris Street?'

'Yes. He told me he didn't need me today and that he'd see me tomorrow.'

'And that's all.'

'That's all.'

'And how did he sound?'

Ava raised her hands. 'Ordinary, normal. I don't know. I was on the street. There was a lot of noise, cars going by and the rest.'

'You didn't think it was odd, him cancelling like that?'

'No, not at all. Some days he doesn't need me.'

Higgs continued to glare at her. 'So then you decided to go clothes shopping?'

'Why not?'

'Except none of the clothes stores were open at that time. It can't have been more than, what, half eight by then?'

'Window shopping,' Ava said. 'I couldn't be bothered to go back home. I thought I'd have a look in the windows first and see if there was anything I fancied.'

'So you're claiming that you spent all morning looking at clothes?'

'Yes,' Ava said. 'Although I didn't buy much, a few T-shirts and that was it.'

'It appears your phone was disconnected for a couple of hours. We were trying to contact you, but couldn't get through.'

'Was it?' said Ava, feigning surprise. 'I didn't know that. It was working fine last time I used it.'

The interview continued in this vein for a further twenty minutes. Although Ava couldn't prove what she'd been doing, it couldn't be disproved either. So long as no one had seen her driving the van, she was safe. In truth, they were more interested in what had happened last night, and for that she had an alibi in Tash. Well, an alibi of sorts. There was, of course, no reason why she couldn't have crept out of the flat in the middle of the night.

Eventually, after DI Middleton had once again explained the likely repercussions of helping a murderer to evade justice, she was told she could go. Relief flowed over her. Although she knew that she wasn't out of the woods yet, at least she had got a temporary reprieve.

Ava pulled on her coat in the foyer of the station and made her way out of the doors. It was raining, but she didn't care. She put up her umbrella and gulped in the cold winter air, glad to be out of the small stuffy room and away from the glare of her interrogators. *Thank God.*

She had got as far as the corner of Cowan Road when she heard quick footsteps behind.

Turning, she saw DS Higgs hurrying towards her. For one terrible second, she thought a vital piece of evidence had come to light and she was about to be arrested. Her chest tightened and her pulse began to race. 'What is it? What do you want?'

'You don't mind if I have a quick word, do you?'

'Actually, I do,' Ava snapped back. 'You've had plenty of time to talk to me, over two hours in fact. And shouldn't my solicitor be present?'

'Oh, I don't think your solicitor would want to hear this,' said Higgs slyly. 'It's about your dad and it's a little on the delicate side.'

Ava stared at her through the grey gloom of the afternoon. She could hear the rain, a steady patter, falling against the canopy of the umbrella. 'What about Dad?'

'He's done a bit of time inside, hasn't he?'

Ava gave a shrug. 'What of it?'

'Be a shame to see him banged up again. I mean, he's getting on a bit now. It gets harder as you get older, all those long empty days stretching in front of you. Not to mention all those young bulls wanting to prove themselves. You'd be surprised how many inmates get attacked, killed even in prison.'

'What are you trying to say?'

'I'm saying that we know about the robbery at Finian's. We know your father was the driver.'

Ava felt the shock like a blow to the stomach. For a second she was speechless, her thoughts racing, her heart pounding in her chest. 'That's not true. You're trying to fix him up. You're trying to get at me through him.'

'Good try, Ava. The whole innocent act may fool some people, but it doesn't wash with me.'

'So why haven't you arrested him, then?'

DS Higgs smirked at her. 'We will – unless you're prepared to tell us where Chris Street is. Give us his location and we may be prepared to overlook the matter. Have a think about it, love. You've got twenty-four hours.'

'I can't tell you what I don't know.'

'Twenty-four hours. It's time to decide where your loyalties lie.'

55

Ava was still in turmoil, her head spinning, her stomach churning, as she climbed the stairs to the flat in Market Square. Higgs had issued her with an ultimatum and she didn't think the sergeant was bluffing. They knew about her dad. They knew about the robbery. Oh Christ, what was she going to do? She was stuck between a rock and a hard place. On the one hand, she couldn't condemn her father to what might be a lengthy prison sentence, on the other she felt unable to betray Chris Street.

She took out her key and put it in the lock. The truth was that she didn't even know exactly where Chris was. He could easily have moved on from Chingford by now. But still she baulked at the idea of giving the cops even that small clue. And how much evidence did they really have against her dad? Maybe not enough to convict him. She had twenty-four hours to figure out what to do. The clock was ticking and she couldn't even think straight.

As soon as she opened the door, Tash rushed out of the living room. 'You're home!' She gave Ava a hug and then, still holding on to her arms, leaned back a little and studied her more closely. 'Are you okay? I've been so worried about you. I thought they might have … What did the police say? They've been here too. They wanted to know all about last night. Have they found him yet? Have they found Chris Street?'

'Hey,' said Ava, forcing a smile as she tried to mask her fear and confusion. 'One question at a time. And first I need to take a long hot shower. I've been stuck down that place for hours.'

Tash finally let go of her. 'But they haven't charged you with anything?'

'Not yet,' said Ava, shrugging out of her coat and hanging it on the peg by the door. 'But I'm sure that won't stop them from trying. Look, I'll just grab that shower and then I'll tell you all about it.'

'I'll make you a coffee.'

'Haven't we got anything stronger than that? I need a proper drink, the stronger the better.'

'There's some of Hannah's Johnnie Walker left. We can finish that off.'

'Sounds like a plan.' Ava watched as Tash went off towards the kitchen and then she made her way wearily to the bathroom. Inside, she took off her watch, placing it on the window ledge, and then she stripped off her clothes, leaving them where they fell on the floor. She turned on the tap and stepped under the powerful jets, standing motionless as the hot water flowed over and around her.

It must have been two minutes, maybe three, before her muscles finally started to relax. She raised her face and closed her eyes. The day, which had started off with a simple visit to her father, had somehow turned into a nightmare: stolen goods, a murdered woman, a man on the run for murder, a two-hour interrogation, lies, deceit and evasion.

DS Higgs loomed into her thoughts and she instinctively flinched. What the sergeant had done wasn't legal, but she could hardly report her. Not when her dad was guilty as accused. Should she ring him, tell him about the threat? But what would that achieve? There was nothing he could do about it, other than sit and worry about when the cops might turn up. He wasn't the type to try and make a run for it.

She squeezed a pool of shower gel into the palm of her hand and lathered every inch of her body. She felt dirty, and not just from the dust and grime of the city. There was a more subtle pollution that came from sitting in a police interview room and telling lies for two hours. She washed her hair and scrubbed her fingernails, trying to purge herself of all the horror of the day.

Eventually, when she was as clean as she would ever be, she turned off the shower. She stepped out on to the cool lino, wrapped a towel around her, brushed her teeth, put on her watch, picked up her discarded clothes and then padded to the bedroom. The light was fading fast. She glanced down at the square, at the people passing through, before pulling the curtains across and switching on the lamp.

Ten minutes later, dressed in jeans and a white long-sleeved T-shirt, she sat curled up on the sofa. The story she was telling Tash was a highly edited version of the day's events, almost identical to the one she had told the cops. She didn't like lying to her, but what else could she do? Sometimes the truth was a burden that shouldn't be shared.

'The police went to see Hannah too,' Tash said. 'They turned up at her office.'

'I bet she was well pleased about that.'

'About as pleased as she'll be when she finds out that we've polished off her whisky.'

'And very nice it is too,' said Ava, taking another sip from her glass. She hadn't eaten since breakfast and the malt was going straight to her head. The sensation was a pleasant one, softening the sharp scary edges of her fears and anxieties. She knew that it was only a temporary reprieve – tomorrow her problems would still be there – but even a short escape was welcome. There was only so much anyone could take in a day.

'Do you think he did it?' Tash asked. 'Do you think Chris Street murdered her?'

'No. Why should he? He wasn't overjoyed about Jenna seeing Guy Wilder, but he wasn't going to kill her for it.'

Tash didn't look convinced. 'So why's he disappeared?'

'Because he knows he'll be top of the list when it comes to suspects.' Ava gave a light shrug. 'Well, I presume that's the reason. From what I can gather, he was supposed to meet up with her last night. It puts him in the frame, but that doesn't mean he did it.'

'It doesn't mean he didn't either.'

'I suppose not. It just ... it doesn't seem to add up. It doesn't feel right.'

Tash peered at her over the rim of her glass. 'Sometimes

feelings can get in the way of the truth. It's easy to see people the way you want to see them.'

'Do you think Lydia killed Jeremy Squires?'

Tash hesitated, mulling it over before she answered. 'I didn't want to, not at the beginning. I couldn't believe she was capable. I thought I knew her, but I didn't, not really. I only saw what she wanted me to see.'

'You think I'm kidding myself about Chris?'

'I'm not saying that. But you never really know what goes on in someone else's head. He and Jenna had history. He might have only meant to threaten her, to scare her, and then . . .'

Ava wanted to protest his innocence, but instantly dismissed the idea. Tash might grow suspicious and start to realise that she knew more than she was saying. 'Maybe you're right.'

Tash glanced at her watch, leaned down and picked up her mobile from the coffee table. 'I've just got to make a quick call. I was supposed to be taking some samples over to that new hat shop in Covent Garden, but I can change it, go another day.'

'No, don't do that. You should go. You've got to go.'

'I don't want to leave you here on your own, not when—'

'I'll be fine, Tash. Honestly I will. Please go. I'll feel really bad if you don't.'

Tash frowned at her. 'I don't know.'

'You *have* to. Hey, there's been enough bad stuff happening recently without you throwing away this opportunity as well. It won't look good if you cancel at the last minute. They might not even agree to see you again.'

'Do you think?'

'Just go, will you? Oh, and brush your teeth before you leave. You don't want to turn up stinking of whisky.'

The flat seemed unnaturally quiet after Tash had left. It was twenty past four and dark outside. Ava thought about making something to eat, but couldn't summon the energy to get off the sofa. She poured herself another glass of whisky and gazed into the amber liquid. Drowning her sorrows in booze probably wasn't the greatest idea, but she didn't have a better one at the moment.

Although she tried to control them, her thoughts inevitably drifted back to Chris. That kiss. That soft shivery *meaningless* kiss. Why had she allowed it to happen? It complicated things. Confused things. It confused *her*. She sighed into the silence of the room. There were some men it was better to stay away from. Alec Harmer was one of them and she'd learned that lesson the hard way. She wasn't about to make the same mistake again.

Ava lay back, closed her eyes and felt the tiredness wash over her. She hungered for release, for a chance to forget everything for a while. She turned on her side, yawned and curled up her legs. Two minutes later, she was asleep.

56

DI Valerie Middleton leafed through the results of the autopsy on Jenna Dean. There was nothing unexpected there. The woman, thirty-one years of age, had been in good health at the time of her demise. Time of death: between ten and eleven last night. Cause of death: a single gunshot to the chest. No evidence of any sexual assault or of any kind of a struggle. The bullet had been removed from the body and sent to ballistics.

Forensics hadn't come up with anything useful either. With all the heavy rain overnight, parts of the green had turned into a quagmire. Mud could often be a good medium for the retention of footprints, but not on this occasion. The piece of ground where the body was found had been churned up first by the dog that had sniffed her out and then by its owner.

She looked across the desk at DS Laura Higgs. Although she had her own office, she preferred to be present in the incident room when a major inquiry was on the go. 'Anything more on Chris Street yet?' They had put out an appeal on the lunchtime news, requesting information on his whereabouts. There had been plenty of 'sightings', ranging from Portsmouth to Glasgow, from airports to ferry terminals, but nothing solid and nothing that could be verified.

'I don't reckon he's gone that far. He'll be hiding out some-where, waiting for the dust to settle. We need to find a way to flush him out.'

'Such as?'

'I'm still working on that. If he left in a hurry, he might not have much money on him. He'll need to find a way to get hold of some. Maybe he'll get in touch with his father or Danny or Ava Gold.'

'I don't know,' Valerie said. 'Men like him usually keep a stash at home, a few grand just in case of emergencies.'

'A few grand doesn't go far – not when you're on the run. He wouldn't dare stay in a hotel – too much chance of getting recognised – so someone's probably hiding him. And that kind of protection, unless it's your nearest and dearest, tends to cost a bomb.'

The door to the incident room opened and Jeff Butler came hurrying towards them. 'Have you heard?'

'What is it?' Valerie asked.

'I just got a call from my mate in ballistics. It was the same gun. The same gun was used to kill Jeremy Squires and Jenna Dean.'

Although the news was a breakthrough, Valerie was irritated by the fact that he had heard before she had. An old boys' club was in operation in the force, a club from which she felt permanently excluded. 'Really?' she said, trying to keep the tightness from her voice. 'Now that's interesting.'

'Isn't it just?' If he noticed her annoyance, he didn't show it. 'Exactly the same striation pattern on the bullets. No doubt about it.'

'Why don't you grab a chair, Jeff?'

Butler looked around, took a chair from an empty desk and sat down beside her. 'I don't get it, though. Chris Street kills Jenna Dean. Yeah, that's straightforward enough. But shooting Danny Street, shooting his own brother. Why would he do that?'

Valerie raised her eyebrows. 'Oh, I don't know. I'd probably want to shoot him if he was *my* brother. But, putting that personal prejudice aside, perhaps it was just a mistake. It was dark in the car park and he wouldn't have had much time.'

'But why kill Squires anyway? We already know that he'd pulled the money out of the bank.'

'So maybe he changed his mind, got to Belles and decided that he wasn't going to pay up after all. Threatened to go to the police and blow the whole blackmail scam out of the water. Danny couldn't risk that, so he put in a call to his brother and kept Squires talking until Chris had a chance to get to the club.'

Butler nodded. 'And then Danny took the money before the ambulance arrived, passed it on to Solomon Vale and hey presto, problem solved.'

'It has a certain kind of logic to it.'

'It does,' Butler agreed.

'Although we can't be sure that the same person did both the shootings. If that gun belonged to the Streets, it could just as easily have been Terry that finished off Squires.'

'That guy doesn't know what day of the week it is,' said Higgs, glancing up at the other two. 'When I interviewed him, he kept getting confused, thinking that it was his wife who'd just been killed. He kept saying: "Is Lizzie dead? Has someone killed Lizzie?" He couldn't get it into his head that it was Chris's ex I was talking about.'

Butler gave a nod. 'Yeah, I've heard some rumours. Terry's been doing a few odd things lately.'

'For real, you think?' Valerie asked. 'Or is it just his way of avoiding difficult questions?'

'Well, you never know with Terry, do you?' Butler leaned back and frowned. 'And where does this leave us with Lydia Hall? It looks like she didn't kill Squires after all.'

'Unless . . .' Valerie said.

'Unless?'

'Well, I suppose it's not impossible that she dropped the gun at the scene. Solomon Vale could have picked it up, taken it into the club and then given it to Chris Street.'

'Which blows the Chris Street shooting Jeremy Squires scenario out of the window.'

'It does. But it would explain how the same gun was used for both of the killings.' Valerie gave a sigh. 'Although we still haven't got a motive for Lydia killing Squires.'

Butler stood up and gave Valerie a nod. 'I'll leave you to mull that one over. I'd better get off. I've got someone to see. You still on for that drink, later?'

'Should be. Unless Chris Street pops up in the meantime.'

'We live in hope.'

After he'd gone, DS Higgs looked over at Valerie. 'DCI Butler seems to be spending a lot of time here.'

Valerie frowned at her. 'He's investigating a murder, a murder involving the Streets. Why shouldn't he be here?'

'Oh, no reason. I was just wondering if he prefers the company at Cowan Road to all those big burly guys down at Shoreditch.'

Valerie gave her an icy stare. 'Meaning what exactly?'

'Not meaning anything, guv. He's a nice guy. You could do worse.'

'What? It's not like that. There's nothing ...' Valerie stopped abruptly, realising that she didn't need to explain herself to the likes of Higgs. But then, fearing that she might be the subject of office gossip, she couldn't resist adding, 'It's a purely professional relationship. He's married, for God's sake.'

'*Was* married. His wife cleared off to Oslo over six months ago. Dumped him for some Norwegian banker. Although banker probably wasn't the word the DCI used.'

It was news to Valerie, but she tried not to show her surprise. 'Well, it's none of our business, is it? His private life is his own. So shall we just get on with the job in hand?'

Higgs gave her a smug smile, before lowering her gaze to the heap of papers in front of her. 'Yes, guv.'

A few minutes later, DC Preston came over to the desk, loitering for a moment until Valerie raised her head.

'Yes?'

'I've just finished interviewing two of the customers who were drinking in Wilder's last night.' He looked quickly at his notes. 'Jane Wainwright and Tessa Marsden. They were sitting near the door and claim that Guy Wilder left the bar at about ten thirty and didn't come back until about ten, fifteen minutes later.'

'They're sure?'

'Absolutely sure. They say they remembered because he got back just before closing. And he was wet, guv, like he'd been out in the rain.'

'You think they're reliable witnesses?'

'Seem to be, guv. Neither of them has got any kind of record; I ran a check.'

'Okay,' Valerie said. 'Why don't you organise a car, get down to Wilder's and pull him in again.'

As Preston walked off, Higgs stared across the desk at Valerie. 'You don't really think he had anything to do with it? Chris Street killed Jenna Dean. He must have done. We should check out those girls properly. Who's to say that Danny Street or his old man hasn't paid them to put Wilder in the frame?'

'We will check them out if Guy Wilder denies it, but let's hear what he has to say for himself first.'

57

DS Higgs turned up her collar against the rain and hurried along to the end of Cowan Road where Franny Keats was waiting for her in his clapped-out Cortina. She climbed into the passenger seat and closed the door, wrinkling her nose at the smell of the interior. It stank of dope, fag smoke, lager and sweat.

'You ever think about cleaning this heap of crap?' she asked, shifting away the debris at her feet.

'What'd I want to do that for?'

'I dunno. So you don't catch the plague?'

Franny Keats lit a fag and glared at her. He was one of her regular snitches, a junkie off the Mansfield who supplemented his benefits with regular payments from informing on the lowlifes of Kellston. 'What do you want?' he asked. 'Or did you just come here to have a pop?'

'Got a job for you – that's if you think you're up to it.'

'What sort of job?'

'The sort that involves drinking lager all night in the local pubs and bars. Should be right up your street.'

Franny took a draw on his fag, releasing the smoke in a long thin stream. He narrowed his eyes. 'What's the catch?'

'No catch. I just want you to spread some news around. I want you to tell every local villain you come across that Chris Street is in the clear over Jenna Dean. I want you to tell them that you've heard Guy Wilder's been charged with her murder.'

Franny thought about this for a while. 'That true?'

'What difference does it make if it's true or not?' She pulled fifty quid out of her pocket and handed it over to him. 'Here. This should be enough to keep you going. And don't fuck me about, Franny, 'cause I'll be checking up on you. If that rumour isn't going strong in a couple of hours, I'll hunt you down and make you pay.'

'No need to be like that,' he said sulkily, folding the notes and slipping them into his pocket. 'When have I ever let you down?'

'Don't get me started. Just do it, okay? And make it sound convincing.'

Franny stroked the wheel with the palms of his hands. 'Fifty quid don't go far,' he said. 'Not in some of the joints round here. What if I run out of cash? Can't stand there with an empty glass, can I?'

Higgs hissed out a breath. 'Jesus, I'm not the bloody Bank of England.'

'Ah, come on,' he wheedled. 'Just another score. That'll see me right.'

Although she'd been expecting the request, she pretended that she hadn't. 'A score? You're taking the piss!'

Franny's hungry eyes gazed back at her. 'Ten, then. And I'll make sure the word gets around real good.'

With a feigned show of reluctance, she pulled another tenner from her bag. 'You'd better. And you need to get your arse in gear right now.'

'I'm on it,' he said, grinning.

Laura Higgs got out of the car, glad to be escaping the stench. She wasn't under any illusions that Chris Street was suddenly going to come out of hiding when he heard the news, but it might be enough to make him drop his guard. He might take a chance that he wouldn't normally take. Yeah, one mistake, one tiny slip, and they'd have the murdering bastard.

58

Fifteen minutes after she'd fallen asleep, Ava was abruptly woken by the sound of her phone. Her eyes blinked open and for a moment, confused, she wasn't sure where she was. The phone kept on ringing. Quickly she got to her feet, stumbled across the room, found her bag, rummaged in it and snatched up the mobile. 'Yes?'

'It's Solomon,' a deep voice said. 'Sol. I just wanted to make sure you're okay.'

'Oh, Sol. Hi. Yes. A bit tired, that's all. Sorry, it's been a long day.' She gave her head a shake, trying to free it from the bleary daze of sleep. 'They had me down Cowan Road for two hours.'

'They didn't charge you with nothing?'

'No.'

'I had the third degree too. Fuckin' bastards turned my flat over. I mean, how much searching does it take to figure out that a man over six foot tall *ain't* hiding in the wardrobe?'

'They make a mess?'

'Hard to tell. It's not too tidy at the best of times.' He laughed. 'But that ain't the point. It's the principle, right?'

'Yeah, it's the principle.'

'So are you sure you're okay?'

'Getting there,' she said.

'Good.'

Ava wanted to ask him about Chris – she was sure that the two of them must have been in touch or how else would Sol have got her number? – but was afraid of saying too much over the phone. The law could be listening in and it wasn't worth taking the risk. Just as she was trying to think of a subtle, roundabout way of addressing the subject, the doorbell went. She jumped, thinking it might be the police again. 'Sorry,' she said, 'there's someone at the door.'

'Who is it?'

'I don't know. Hang on a sec.' She walked over to the window, pulled back the curtain and looked down into the square. She saw the top of a fair head and then a familiar face gazing up. 'Oh no,' she murmured into the phone. 'It's Silver Delaney.'

'Silver? What the hell's she doing there?'

'God knows, but she's seen me so I'll have to go down. I'll get rid of her and call you back, okay? Just give me five minutes.'

Ava hung up. The last thing she needed was company – especially Silver's company – but there was no way round it. If only she hadn't looked out of the window . . . but it was too late for that. There was no way of avoiding her and so she went downstairs and opened the door.

Silver's face was pinched and tight. She leapt forward, grabbing hold of Ava's arm. 'You've got to come, you've got to come right now! It's about Chris. Danny needs to talk to you.'

'Danny?'

'Yes, you've got to come,' said Silver, pulling at her sleeve. 'It's urgent.'

'Okay, okay, I'll just get my coat.'

'You don't need your coat. He's only round the corner.'

'I need my keys, though. Hold on, I won't be a minute.' Ava rushed back upstairs, grabbed her coat and keys and ran back down the stairs again. 'What's going on?'

'Danny's got news. He'll explain. He'll tell you everything. But we've got to be quick.'

Ava put on her coat as she accompanied Silver across the square, keeping her eyes peeled for the police. Would they be watching out for her, keeping her under surveillance in case she made contact with Chris? But she wasn't making contact with him so she didn't need to worry. There was no law against talking to his brother.

'I knew you'd come,' said Silver, slipping her arm through Ava's. 'I told him you would. I always know these things. I said *Ava's the type of girl who never lets anyone down.*'

The combination of the winter cold, the rain and her sudden exit from the warm flat, made Ava shiver. Or maybe it wasn't just that. Silver seemed hyper, charged-up. Had she taken something? Coke or crack was the first thing that sprang to mind. The girl's red spike-heeled shoes tapped rhythmically against the pavement, a noise that for some reason set Ava's teeth on edge.

They went up Market Street and turned left on to the high

street. Silver began to walk even faster now, pulling Ava along beside her. 'We're almost there. Not far to go.'

Ava glanced over her shoulder, but couldn't spot anyone following them.

'Don't worry,' Silver said. 'There's no one there. I checked. I made sure. I looked all around the square.'

They came to a stop outside Beast. There was a CLOSED sign on the door, but Silver took out a set of keys, chose one and put it in the lock.

'What are we doing here?' asked Ava as the door swung open. She didn't understand why Danny would be at the taxidermist's. And why was the shop closed? It wasn't even five o'clock yet. She hung back, alarm bells going off in her head. This didn't feel right. It didn't feel right at all.

Silver grabbed hold of her elbow and dragged her roughly over the threshold. 'Come on. Quickly! We can't keep him waiting.'

Before she knew it, Ava was standing inside the shop. It was dark inside, but there was a thin light coming from the back. Silver slammed shut the door and pulled the bolt across. As her eyes gradually grew accustomed to the gloom, Ava realised that the place had been trashed; cabinets had been broken and there was glass all over the floor. Near her feet lay the wretched remains of a red fox, its head almost severed from its neck.

'What the—' But as she turned to look at Silver, the words stuck in her throat. The girl was pointing a small black gun directly at her chest.

59

Silver's face had taken on an odd expression. Her eyes were gleaming, her lips strangely twisted. A small gob of spittle nestled in the left-hand corner of her mouth. 'Get moving,' she ordered, gesturing with the gun.

'What are you doing?' Ava whispered.

'The basement,' Silver hissed back. 'Go down the stairs. Over there, through that door where the light's coming from.'

'I don't understand. Why are you—'

'Shut up!' Silver snapped. 'Start walking. Do what I tell you, Ava. Don't make me mad.'

Shocked and bewildered, Ava headed for the rear of the shop. She heard the thin crunch of the glass beneath her feet and from behind her the sound of Silver's soft panting breath. She carried on walking until she came to the top of a flight of grey stone steps. By now her heart was thumping, dread knocking in her chest.

'Down the stairs,' Silver urged.

But Ava hesitated, panic surging through her body. She looked down into the basement as if she was staring into the jaws of hell. If she went down, would she ever come back up again?

Silver shoved the barrel of the gun into her spine. 'I can shoot you right here, right now. Is that what you want, Ava? Is that what you really want?'

With leaden legs, Ava slowly began the descent. Silver closed the door behind them. She listened out for any sound that might warn her that someone else was present. Was Danny Street waiting for her? And if he was, then why? All she had done was help his brother escape. Why should she be punished for that?

She clung on to the wooden rail as she put one foot in front of another. Above her a single bare bulb hung from the slanting ceiling. Jesus Christ, if only she'd never looked out of that window. If only she hadn't answered the door. If only . . . But those regrets weren't going to help her now. She had just made what might turn out to be the biggest mistake of her life.

When she reached the bottom of the steps, Ava stopped. Ahead of her, at the end of a short corridor was a large well-lit room. The door was open. The smell of formaldehyde hung on the air. She felt the fear rising into her throat and tried to swallow it down.

'Go on,' ordered Silver, prodding her again with the gun. 'Why have you stopped? You mustn't stop. You have to carry on.'

Ava knew she had no choice. Holding her breath she

advanced, the brightness of the fluorescent light making her squint. As her vision cleared, the first thing she noticed was a long workman's table in the centre of the room. Its wooden surface was covered with sharp metal tools, wire, clay, animal skulls, skin and bones. Then, as she shifted her gaze a fraction, her stomach gave a lurch. There *was* someone else in the room, only it wasn't Danny Street.

Morton Carlisle sat propped up against the wall, his head lolling forward, his legs stretched out in front of him. There was a bullet wound close to his collar bone and the left side of his shirt was covered in blood. His chest was still rising and falling, quick shallow breaths as if his lungs were straining to work. A thin wheezing sound came from his mouth.

Ava automatically moved towards him. 'God, what have you done?'

Silver started waving the gun around again. 'Leave him! Leave him alone! Don't touch him!'

Ava stopped in her tracks, glancing quickly over her shoulder. 'You have to get an ambulance,' she said. 'Do you want him to bleed to death?'

That small weird smile appeared on Silver's face again. 'Yes,' she said. 'That's exactly what I want.'

Ava's heart skipped a beat. She looked towards Carlisle and then back at Silver. 'Why? Why would you want that?'

'That's my business,' said Silver sulkily. She pushed out her upper lip, pouting at Ava. 'Sit down over there.' She pointed towards the right where there was an old stained porcelain sink set into a steel counter, but then shook her head. 'No, not there. Sit down by him. I want to be able to see you both. But don't touch him, right? You mustn't touch him.'

Ava moved forward, skirted around the corner of the table and kept on walking until she reached the limp bleeding figure of Carlisle. She turned and slid slowly down the wall. She wrapped her arms around her shaking knees and stared up at Silver. 'What now?'

Silver seemed to relax a little now that she had both of them safely in her sights. She didn't answer the question, though. Instead she said, 'Did you know that this used to be a funeral parlour?'

The last thing Ava needed was to be reminded of death, but she knew that the only way of avoiding it was to try and find a way to engage with her captor. She had to play for time. She had to keep her talking until she figured out a plan. 'Yes, I remember it from when I was a kid. Tobias Grand & Sons.'

'Do you know what they used to do in here?'

'No.'

'This was where they embalmed the bodies. Danny told me. Danny watched it done once. He watched a dead girl's insides being sucked out through a tube. Is that gross or what?'

'Where is Danny?' Ava asked.

Silver leaned against the table and scowled at her. 'He's not here. Why would he be here? This has nothing to do with him.'

'Okay,' said Ava, trying to keep her voice calm while her thoughts ran riot. 'I was just wondering. It doesn't matter.' Her eyes fixed on the gun. Was it the gun that Chris had lost? It had to be. It looked the same, but she was hardly an expert. 'Is that your gun?'

'It's mine now,' Silver said. 'Finders, keepers. And it's loaded.' She looked at Carlisle and gave her little-girl giggle. 'But you already know that. And the thing is, when it goes off, nobody can hear a thing. It's the walls, you see, nobody can hear through these walls.'

Ava gazed up at Silver, seeing for the first time the spatters of blood down the front of her white coat. She hadn't noticed it before. The light had been too dim. She must have been standing close to Carlisle when ... but she didn't want to dwell on that. 'Have you used it before?'

'Before?' Silver repeated, a tiny frown settling on her forehead. Then suddenly her brow cleared. 'Oh, I get it. You mean Jenna Dean, don't you? Now if anyone deserved to die, that bitch did.'

'Did you kill her?' Ava tried not to make the question sound like an accusation.

'Might have done,' Silver said. 'Then again, I might not. What do you think?'

'I don't know.' Ava wasn't sure if she wanted to know either. She wondered how long it would be before anyone noticed she was missing. A few hours, maybe even longer. Tash would probably presume that she'd gone to see her dad. She wouldn't start to worry until later tonight. And then, even if it was reported, who would think to look for her in Beast? 'Why have you brought me here?'

'You know why.'

Ava shook her head. 'I thought we were friends. Didn't you say that, in the Fox? Didn't you say that we were going to be the best of friends?'

'That was before.'

'Before what?'

'Before Daddy found out about . . .' Two stripes of pink appeared on Silver's cheekbones. She glared down at Carlisle. 'That bastard told Raynard everything.'

'I don't know who Raynard is.'

Silver gave a sigh of exasperation as if Ava's ignorance knew no bounds. 'Works for my dad, don't he? He came here. He came here asking questions and that stupid bastard spilled his guts.'

Ava realised now what had happened upstairs. Raynard's powers of persuasion had clearly gone beyond the verbal. She gave Carlisle a quick sidelong glance, unsure as to whether he was even conscious or not. How long could he survive for? Fifteen minutes, twenty? How long before all the blood leaked out of his body? 'He shouldn't have done that,' she said, trying to ingratiate herself. 'People should know when to keep their big mouths shut.'

'That's what I told him. But he wouldn't listen. Kept saying that he was going to call the filth.' Silver gave a high-pitched laugh, a sound that had a faintly hysterical edge to it. 'The filth, for fuck's sake!'

'So you had to stop him. Of course you did.'

'Yes,' Silver said. 'That's what I had to do.'

While they were talking Ava was looking surreptitiously around the room. So far as she could tell the only way of escape was back up the steps. Had Silver locked the door? She didn't know. She'd heard it close, but wasn't sure if a key had been turned or not. Anyway, she'd never even make it that far. Now that she was sitting on the floor, she was at a distinct disadvantage. In the time it would take her to get up, to make a lunge at Silver, the crazy girl would have pulled the trigger. She cursed the fact that she hadn't made a move upstairs where the light was bad and she might have stood a better chance.

'I still don't see why we can't be friends,' Ava said. 'I'd never grass to the police. They had me down the station for two hours this afternoon and I never said a word.'

'Ava Gold,' Silver murmured. 'Silver and Gold, silver and gold – do you get it?'

'Sure,' Ava said, smiling back at her. 'Doesn't that make us a team, you and me?'

'We could have been friends, but it's too late now.'

'It's never too late,' Ava insisted.

Silver gave a shrug. She didn't look convinced. Her fingers tightened around the gun.

'Why did . . . why did Morton want to talk to the police?' asked Ava tentatively.

Silver's eyes glittered, her face growing angry. 'It was all his fault,' she spat, glaring at Carlisle. 'It was, it really was. He *wanted* her to do it. He wanted Ava to do all those dirty things with those men. He wanted her to fuck them. That's not right, is it?'

'No,' Ava said.

'And now Daddy's mad and he doesn't love his little girl any more. So Morton has to be punished. And Ava has to be punished too. She has to be made to pay for all the trouble she's caused. Do you see?'

What Ava saw was that she wasn't going to get out of this damn place alive if she didn't do something soon.

60

It was almost fifteen minutes now since Valerie had got the call from DC Lister, informing her that Danny Street's girlfriend had turned up at Market Square and taken Ava Gold to Beast. There was no doubt in the inspector's mind as to what was going on: Chris Street was holed up in the taxidermy shop and the clan was gathering to help with his escape.

She sat in the car, her eyes firmly fixed on the door. She had made the decision not to go in. Chris Street was a dangerous fugitive. He was wanted for murder and if he could kill his ex-wife he wouldn't think twice about shooting a copper. There were three unmarked cars and a van parked in the street as well as officers posted discreetly at the rear of the building. All of the officers at the scene were armed.

'It could be hours before he comes out,' Higgs said.

'So we'll wait.'

'Guy Wilder's brief was just arriving as we left. He'll do his nut.'

'Let him.'

Higgs gave a self-satisfied kind of smile as if she was pleased by the prospect of having Hugo Pinner standing around twiddling his thumbs – or maybe she was feeling smug about something else entirely. Valerie suspected that her sergeant didn't always play by the rules, that she was the type of officer who liked to cut corners, believing that the end always justified the means.

'What do you reckon, guv? Is Morton Carlisle an accomplice or a hostage?'

'Hard to say, but I don't reckon he's as squeaky clean as he likes to make out.' Valerie had taken an instant dislike to Carlisle, but she still wasn't sure whether that was down to the man himself or the business he ran. There was something creepy about all those dead, stuffed animals, something that made her flesh crawl.

'I wonder why Street chose here,' Higgs said.

'Because it's the last place we'd think of looking. He probably got a kick out of hiding right under our noses.'

Valerie was pretty sure that he'd be down in the basement, the most secure part of the building and the most difficult to penetrate. If they broke in through the front or the back, he'd hear them coming – there was bound to be someone listening out – and officers could be targeted, picked off one by one, as they passed through the door. Another option was to seal off the area and let Street know that they were there, but that might create a hostage situation that could go on for days. So, for the moment, she had decided to sit it out. There was a different kind of risk in waiting for him to come to them – that a member of the public might get hurt – but hopefully it would all be over in seconds. They would have the element of surprise on their side.

'Guv,' said Higgs, shifting forward. 'Look who it is.'

Valerie smiled as she saw Solomon Vale striding down the high street, walking quickly in their direction. 'Well, fancy that,' she said. 'Another staunch member of the firm coming to help out in his boss's time of need.'

Solomon Vale went up to Beast, tried the door, which was locked, and rattled the handle. He peered in through the glass. He rang the bell, stood back. Then he stepped forward again and hammered on the door.

'Jesus Christ!' Higgs said. 'What the hell is he doing?'

Valerie frowned. Vale couldn't be drawing more attention to the place if he tried. What was he playing at? It didn't make sense. Unless ... She suddenly wondered if they'd been sussed, if this was some sort of distraction technique while Street tried to get out round the back. Snatching up the radio, she warned the officers at the rear of the building to be alert. But then, after peering briefly through the door again, Vale appeared to give up. He gave the handle one last rattle and started walking away from the shop.

Valerie didn't know what was going on, but she had to make a fast decision. 'Let's take him,' she said. She got on the radio again, put out the order and sat back and waited.

Thirty seconds later, Solomon Vale had been swiftly and discreetly removed from the high street and installed in the back of an unmarked car. He hadn't put up a struggle.

Although he was a big man, he knew when he was outnumbered. He also knew when to pick his fights.

Valerie climbed into the car beside him. 'Solomon,' she said. 'How nice to see you again.'

Vale lounged in the corner of the seat, his arms folded across his chest. 'No need to go to all this trouble, Inspector. You want a date, all you got to do is ask.'

She smiled thinly back at him. 'You want to tell me what you're doing here?'

'Now how about that for a coincidence? I was just going to ask the very same question. Here I am, walking down the street, minding my own business and next thing . . .'

'Why were you trying to get into Beast?'

'Same reason anyone wants to go there. I was looking to buy me a nice stuffed parrot to cheer up the living quarters.'

'Nothing to do with Chris Street, then?'

To give him his due, Vale made a pretty good job of looking surprised. 'Chris? I don't know what you're talking about.'

'Don't mess me about, Solomon. I'm really not in the mood.'

Vale glanced towards the shop and then, as if a light had suddenly dawned, he gave a light mocking laugh. 'What, you think Chris is in there?'

'Isn't that why you're here?'

'I've already told you why I'm here.'

'And we both know that that's a load of bullshit.'

Vale placed a hand over his heart. 'Aw, now you're hurting my feelings, Inspector, and just when I thought we might have a future together.'

Valerie gave a snort. 'Well, sorry to disappoint. And sorry to inform you that for the foreseeable future at least, you're going to be sitting down Cowan Road police station. If Chris Street is in there, we don't want you tipping him off.'

She made to get out of the car, but then, unexpectedly, Vale said, 'Hang on a moment. Is Ava Gold in there?'

'Any reason why she should be?'

Vale hesitated. It went against the grain for him to tell the law anything, but there was clearly something on his mind. He glanced towards the two officers in the front seat. 'I want a word,' he said. 'On our own, just you and me.'

'That's not possible,' DS Higgs said from the passenger seat.

But Valerie waved her objection aside. She wanted to hear what Vale had to say and wasn't concerned about being alone in the car with him. She'd known him long enough to be sure that he wasn't any kind of danger to her. 'Five minutes,' she said. 'And if you're messing me about, Solomon, I'll charge you with wasting police time.'

Higgs shot her a look 'Are you sure, guv, only—'

'I'm sure,' said Valerie firmly.

Higgs reluctantly followed DC Preston out of the car. As soon as the door had closed, Valerie turned to Vale. 'So what's on your mind?'

'Ava Gold,' he said. 'She is in there, ain't she? She's in there with Silver Delaney.'

'What makes you think that?'

He leaned forward, splaying his hands on his thighs. 'Look,' he said, glancing at her. 'I'm gonna tell you something and it's God's honest truth. Chris Street *ain't* in there. I know that for a fact. Don't ask me how I know 'cause I ain't gonna tell you. Just take it from me, huh?'

'So you just want me to walk away? What do you think, that I was born yesterday?'

'I don't want you to walk nowhere,' he said. 'What I want is for you to go in there and get Ava Gold out.'

'What?'

'This is serious. I ain't messing. That Silver – she's cracked. She ain't right in the head. You hang around here for as long as you like, but I reckon only one of those girls is gonna come out again.'

Valerie felt a wave of apprehension flow over her. 'Get talking, Solomon. What the hell's going on?'

He shifted in his seat, clearly torn between his discomfort in talking to a cop and the consequences if he didn't. 'Okay, this is how it is. 'Bout an hour ago, I was down the Lincoln. Silver and Danny Street are in there too. He goes for a slash and his phone starts ringing. She answers it, starts talking to someone called Morton. She ain't happy; I can see that from the look on her face. She's as nice as pie to him over the phone though. Then, soon as they've finished chatting, she grabs her coat and hotfoots it out of the joint without another word.'

Valerie shook her head, still unsure as to where this was going. 'And?'

'Well, I don't think nothin' of it at the time – why should I? – but then half an hour later I give Ava a call, just to see how she's doing and all. We're talking when Silver turns up at her place, out of the blue, ringing the bell, and Ava says she has to go down and answer it 'cause she's looked out the window and Silver's seen that she's there. "I'll call you back in five minutes," is what she says. So I wait for ten minutes and she still ain't called back so I try her phone but it just rings and rings. I keep on trying, but she doesn't answer. So I figure something's wrong and I head down here.'

'But why Beast? Why here?'

'I tried Ava's flat first, but there's no one there. And well, there ain't too many Mortons in Kellston so I figured it had to be this one that Silver had been talking to.'

Valerie gave a small exasperated sigh. 'But I still don't see why you think Ava's in any kind of danger.'

'Call it a hunch,' he said. 'But not the kind of hunch that you want to be ignoring. Silver's involved in bad stuff. I can't say more than that. I know she's Danny's girlfriend, but it comes down to loyalty, don't it? Me and Chris go way back. He and Ava . . . well, he wouldn't want to see her get hurt.'

Valerie had to make a tough decision about what to do next. She didn't think Solomon was lying. What if he was right about only one of the girls coming out again? She opened the car door, stepped out and leaned down. 'Stay here,' she said.

Solomon gave a nod. 'You know,' he said, 'I bet you could get that shop door opened real quiet if you put your mind to it.'

She walked down the street, her thoughts in tumult. Should she go in? Shouldn't she? Both options could have their consequences. Quickly, she got into another car where Higgs was waiting for her.

'Guess what, guv? A call's just come through from the station. Noah Clark wants to talk to you urgently.'

But Valerie had other things on her mind. 'What does he want? Whatever it is, it's going to have to wait.'

Higgs left a short dramatic pause before delivering her news. 'Well, what he wants, apparently, is to confess to the murder of Jenna Dean.'

61

Silver Delaney was getting jumpy and agitated. She paced alongside the table, muttering to herself and shifting the gun from one hand to the other as if she was tired of holding it but didn't dare put it down. Ava's fear was starting to escalate. Whatever the girl had taken was beginning to wear off and soon she'd need another fix. Except she couldn't get what she needed here. If she wanted more gear, she'd have to leave Beast. And if she was going to leave the building, she had some unfinished business to deal with first.

'Why don't we go to my flat?' Ava suggested. 'I've got some stuff. We could have a smoke.'

Silver stared at her, her eyes full of suspicion. 'Ava's not allowed to leave.'

'Don't you fancy a smoke? I could certainly do with one. And then we could ... we could have a chat about things.'

Silver began playing with the tools on the table, using her free hand to pick up the sharp-bladed scalpels and put them down again. 'You have to take the fur off first,' she said, glancing up. 'Or the skin. You have to peel it away so you can chuck away the shit inside – the guts and everything. You want to keep the skeleton, though. You need to keep the bones.'

'Right.'

'Morton told me all about it, you see. He liked to talk about it. Not when Danny was around, of course, but other times ... when it was just the two of us.' She picked out a small bleached skull and held it up for Ava to see. 'What do you think this is?'

'I don't know. A rat, maybe? Something like that.'

'A rat,' Silver murmured. 'Someone sent a rat to Terry.' She gave a giggle. 'Trojan tried to eat it. He ran round and round the office and ripped its stupid little head off.'

'Did he?'

'Chris doesn't like rats. Did you know that?'

'No,' Ava said.

'He's scared of them. They give him goosebumps. They make the hairs on the back of his neck stand on end.' Silver gave her a sly look. 'What are you afraid of, Ava?'

Ava gazed back at her, trying to think of an answer that didn't involve a crazed female wielding a gun. 'Spiders,' she said eventually. 'I don't like the way they scuttle.'

Silver's mouth slid open, revealing her small white teeth. 'Imagine someone putting a big black spider on your face when you're fast asleep.'

Ava gave an involuntary shudder. 'I'd rather not.'

Silver stood up straight again. She looked first at the gun and then at her two hostages. 'This is getting boring now. Where's Danny? Do you know where Danny is?'

Ava, sensing a gap in Silver's sense of reality, grasped the opportunity with both hands. 'He's at Market Square. He's at the flat.'

'What's he doing there?'

'He's waiting for you . . . for *us*. We should get going. He'll get the hump if we keep him hanging around.'

'Who cares? I don't give a fuck.'

Ava felt a stab of dismay, but she wasn't giving up just yet. 'Course you don't. Why should you? But he's got the stuff, hasn't he? He's got the gear.' She was taking a calculated risk – Silver might decide to shoot her there and then – but with few other options she reckoned it was a gamble worth taking.

Silver considered this for a moment, her desire for a fix glistening in her eyes. 'What about him?' she asked, glaring at Carlisle.

'What about him?' said Ava, making her voice sound suitably callous. 'Leave him here. Lock the door. No one's going to find him until it's too late.'

'You think?'

'Yeah, or you can come back later if you want. We can both come back.'

There was a long silence in the room. Ava could feel her heart beating in her chest, a heavy thump that grew stronger by the second. She thought she felt Carlisle move beside her, but didn't dare look at him. Slowly, very slowly, she rose to her feet. 'You ready, then?'

Silver frowned, her hand tightening around the gun again. 'You're not supposed to leave,' she said. 'Daddy won't like it.'

'Then I'll come back. I'll come back after we've been to see Danny. Your dad won't even know that I've been gone.'

427

Silver put her thumb in her mouth and stared at her.

'I promise,' Ava said. 'I won't tell him if you don't.'

Eventually, Silver gave a nod.

Ava walked slowly up the steps, overly aware of the girl's presence behind her. She knew that at any second her life could end. All it would take was one slight squeeze of that trigger. Her legs were trembling, a cold knot forming in her stomach. She found herself thinking about her mum and dad, about how they would cope if she died in this place. A lump lodged in her throat. She thought about everything she'd been through today, how many lines she'd crossed and how much she'd got away with. Everybody's luck ran out eventually.

Five steps to go. Four, three, two, one. When she reached the top, Ava breathed a sigh of relief. The worst part was over. She was sure it was. She reckoned she was strong enough to overpower Silver, to wrench the gun from her, but she wasn't about to do anything rash. She had to keep cool, stay calm and choose exactly the right moment.

Ava kept on walking towards the door. The broken glass crunched beneath her feet. *Be patient. Be smart.* She reached up and slid back the bolt. Then she turned to look at Silver. 'You'd better put the gun away. Someone might see it.'

'It's dark,' Silver said. 'No one's going to notice.'

Ava decided not to argue with her. She'd come this far, she didn't want to blow it now. At some point Silver would drop her guard and when she did, that would be the time to pounce. 'Okay,' she said. 'Whatever you think.' As she opened the door and stepped out on to the street, she felt a second even greater wave of relief. Greedily, she gulped in the cold evening air. A steady rain was falling and she raised her face to the sky, grateful to be free again.

Silver closed the door behind them. Perhaps she sensed that something was wrong because she instantly flinched, a thin hissing sound escaping from her lips.

Suddenly, Ava found herself blinded by a strong white light. It seemed to fall all around her, wrapping her in its glare, pinning her to the spot. Immediately, she raised her hands to her eyes.

'Don't move! This is the police. Stay where you are!'

Ava froze, but Silver didn't. Perhaps Silver's response was automatic, instinctive, but her hand jerked up and the gun came with it. There was one loud bang and the next thing Ava knew she was spinning backwards, a blinding pain running through her body. She was vaguely aware of a volley of different-sounding shots, of a cry, a series of shouts, of her own sense of falling before she crashed against the glass of the door. She wondered if she was dying, if this was it, the end, the grand finale. And then all her thoughts splintered . . . and then there was nothing.

62

DI Valerie Middleton sat in the hospital corridor, her heart as heavy as stone. There had been no choice – she knew there hadn't – but shooting dead a nineteen-year-old girl wasn't any copper's idea of a job well done. If there had been another way, she would have taken it, but it had come down to whether Ava Gold would live or die.

Oblivious to the activity around her, she sank into a morass of self-examination and self-doubt. Had she been too quick to judge, to jump to the wrong conclusions? Now that she knew the truth, it was all too easy to see the mistakes that had been made. She had wanted to believe that Chris Street was guilty of murder and that belief had coloured the whole investigation.

Valerie sighed as she leaned back against the wall and closed her eyes. It was ten o'clock and the day wasn't over yet. The long interview with Noah Clark had exhausted her and left a bad taste in her mouth. Everything she'd thought had been true had been turned on its head. She'd got most of it wrong and was still trying to come to terms with it.

Morton Carlisle, once he'd come out of surgery and recovered enough to talk, had been keen to give his version of events. They had at least got it right about the blackmail scam. Danny Street and Silver Delaney had targeted half a dozen men, including Squires, names passed on to them by Carlisle. He was pleading coercion, that he'd been forced into doing it, but it would be up to a jury to decide whether he was telling the truth or not.

And then there was Danny Street. They'd picked him up a couple of hours ago. He was pleading ignorance, of course, claiming that he knew nothing. Would they be able to gather enough evidence to convict him? It would depend, she thought, on whether any other blackmail victims would come forward.

Sensing a movement, Valerie blinked open her eyes. Jeff Butler was standing in front of her. He thrust a takeaway cup of coffee into her hand and sat down. 'You okay?'

'I've been better.'

'It was a tough call, but you did the right thing.'

'Did I?'

Butler placed a hand gently on her arm and nodded. 'Of course you did. If you hadn't ordered them to shoot, Ava Gold would be lying in the morgue right now.'

'But it's not just about this evening, is it? It's about everything else, all the other stuff that led up to it.'

'You played it by the book, Val. This whole investigation has been ... Jesus, you know what's it's been like. Two murders, one gun, a whole bloody spider's web of lies and contradictions. Even Einstein couldn't have figured this one out.'

Valerie opened the lid on the coffee and took a sip. 'Noah Clark,' she murmured.

Butler huffed out a breath. 'You want to explain it to me? I've got a grasp on the basics, but the detail's still eluding me.'

'He killed her. He killed Jenna Dean.'

'But why?'

Valerie gazed up at the ceiling before she slowly lowered her gaze again. 'The things we do for love.'

'What? He was in love with Jenna Dean?'

'No, not Jenna,' she said, slowly shaking her head. 'Guy.'

Butler's eyebrows shot up. 'So he was ... they were ...'

'Apparently so.'

'Oh.'

'But that's not why he murdered her. I mean, it wasn't jealousy that made him do it. He knew that Guy was only sleeping with her to goad Chris Street. No, what scared him was the thought that Guy had gone too far this time and that Street wasn't going to settle for idle threats.'

'And the only way to protect Guy Wilder was to kill Jenna?'

'Yes, if he could frame Street at the same time.' Valerie thought back to the interview room, to Noah Clark's dark eyes full of pain. 'I don't think he planned it. He saw an opportunity and took his chance. Guy didn't know whether Jenna was coming to the bar on Monday night or not, but Noah saw her drive past about ten twenty-five – that pink Jeep of hers was pretty distinctive – and knew that she'd be parking in her usual place up by the green.'

'So he followed her there.'

Valerie, taking another large sip of coffee, was grateful for the caffeine rush. It gave her a lift, relieving some of her fatigue. 'He ran upstairs, got the gun and some gloves, and then went out the back door. By the time he got to the green, she was just getting out of the car. She must have spent a few minutes checking her make-up, that sort of thing. He told her that Guy had had an accident at a friend's house in Barley Road, a fall, and that he was on his way to see him. Barley Road runs parallel to the high street, along the far side of the green, so the quickest way to get there was to walk straight across.'

'And she believed him – about the accident, I mean?'

'Sure. Why wouldn't she? He was Guy's friend. He was good old reliable Noah.'

Butler raked his fingers through his hair and sighed. 'So the two of them hurry across the green, Noah grabs her, pushes her into some bushes and shoots her. Then he sends the text from her phone to Chris Street, telling him to come over and meet her, thereby putting him at the right place at more or less the right time.'

'That's pretty much the gist of it.'

'A bit risky, wasn't it? Anyone could have heard that gun go off.'

'Except you don't think it's a gun, do you? It's not the first thing that springs to mind. You presume it's a car backfiring, something like that.'

'And the gun?'

'He says it belonged to Lydia Hall, that she turned up in a state late on Saturday night, looking for Guy and saying that

433

she'd shot Jeremy Squires. Noah says he took the gun off her, that he was worried she might hurt someone else or herself. He also claims that Guy was asleep, that he didn't know anything about it. Personally, I don't believe him, but that's his story and he's sticking to it.'

'So Lydia did kill Squires.'

'Yes, but she didn't mean to. According to Noah, she was obsessed with what Terry Street had done to her family. And I'm reading between the lines here, but I get the impression that Guy had been egging her on. He wanted her to hate the Streets as much as he did.' Valerie paused for a moment, glancing along the long hospital corridor. 'Anyway, she went to Belles and when she reached the gates she saw Danny Street coming out of the main entrance with a smaller grey-haired man who she mistakenly thought was Terry. The light wasn't good and she only got a fleeting glance.'

'But she decided to shoot him anyway.'

'She decided it had to be him because he was with Danny.'

'Jesus,' Butler said.

'Exactly.'

They were both quiet for a moment. The night-time sounds of the hospital flowed over and around them, the click of footsteps on lino, the rattle of a trolley, the gentle snoring of one of the patients from a ward nearby.

Jeff Butler was the first to speak again. 'So, Noah Clark – why the big confession? It wasn't as if we were banging on the door.'

'We pulled Guy Wilder in for questioning again this afternoon. A couple of customers had claimed that on Monday night he'd left the bar before closing and was missing for about ten minutes. I think he probably realised that Noah wasn't there and went outside to look for him. But anyway, before he could be interviewed, the whole Beast thing happened and Wilder was left kicking his heels at Cowan Road. Of course, Noah started to worry – he didn't know what was going on – and then someone came into the bar and told him that Guy had been charged with the murder of Jenna Dean.'

'And he believed them?'

'He couldn't see why else Guy would have been gone so long. Of course a simple phone call would have told him all he needed to know, but he'd had a few drinks and wasn't really thinking straight. He panicked, reckoned Guy was going down for murder and came rushing to the rescue.'

'The things we do for love,' said Butler, echoing her earlier sentiment.

Valerie glanced at him. 'You don't have to stay, you know. I'm fine. I'm going to talk to Ava Gold and then I'm heading off.'

'I'm not doing anything else. Might as well keep you company.' Butler gave a shrug. 'I was working on a murder inquiry, but it appears to have been solved.'

'Haven't you got a home to go to?'

'At the moment? No, not much of one.'

Valerie remembered what Higgs had told her about Jeff Butler and his wife. 'I know what it feels like,' she said softly. 'When I split up from Harry, I couldn't stand all the gossip. It drove me crazy.'

Butler gave a wry smile. 'Ah, so you've heard.'

'The rumour mill continues to turn. Try not to let it get to you. At the time I felt like the whole station was talking about me. It passes, though. People forget, things move on.'

'And in the meantime?'

'In the meantime, you just have to grin and bear it.' Valerie put her empty cup down on the seat beside her. 'But if you're still up for that drink, I wouldn't say no. I need one after the day I've had.'

63

Ava lay still on the bed while the doctor and nurse fussed around her, examining the gunshot wound in her hip and the cut to her head that she'd got when she'd fallen against the door at Beast. With her eyes, she followed the doctor's fingers as he checked her line of vision. She'd been lucky. She knew she had. If Silver had raised the gun just a little bit higher, she could have been lying in an entirely different place.

Outside the door, DI Valerie Middleton was waiting to talk to her. Silver Delaney was dead and there were questions to be answered. She thought about Silver and shivered. What had happened to that girl to turn her into the monster she'd become? Ava didn't want to think about it.

Tash had been in earlier and told her about Noah Clark's confession. That was good. It meant Chris was in the clear. No more running, no more hiding. Ava had talked to her dad on the phone. He'd wanted to visit too, but she'd ordered him to stay at home and keep his germs to himself.

She'd be out in a day or two and then everything would get back to normal. Except, would it? The threat that DS Higgs had made still lay heavily on her mind. Would they arrest him for the robbery at Finian's? She hoped and prayed that they wouldn't.

After ten minutes, the medical staff pronounced her likely to live and left her alone in the room. She waited for the inspector to appear, dreading the moment, but knowing that it couldn't be avoided. The experience would have to be relived, the horror revisited. But then, then it would be over and she might finally get some sleep.

As she mentally prepared herself for the forthcoming interview, it suddenly occurred to her that Chris had told her that the gun he'd taken into Wilder's wasn't loaded. Had he been lying or had Silver put the bullets in herself? She stirred slightly, felt the pain in her hip and winced. Men like Chris lied about all sorts of things. It didn't do to trust them, to put much faith in what came out of their mouths.

Several more minutes passed before she heard a small commotion in the corridor. There was the sound of footsteps, of voices slightly raised. DI Middleton said, 'I'm sorry, but you can't go in there—'

'Ten minutes,' a male voice said. 'It's the least you can do after falsely accusing me of murder.'

Ava recognised that voice, and a few seconds later she recognised the face too. Chris Street strode into the room and grinned at her. He was wearing his long dark overcoat and his hair was damp from the rain. 'Up for visitors?' he said. He held out a brown paper bag. 'I come bearing gifts. Or grapes, as it happens. Do you like grapes?'

'You're back.'

'I am indeed.' He put the bag on the table and perched on the edge of the bed. 'How are you feeling?'

'Like I've been shot.'

He frowned. 'I suppose this means you won't be at work tomorrow.'

'Due to circumstances beyond my control.'

'That's the trouble these days. You can't get the staff. If they're not reversing your Merc into a wall, they're out there getting themselves shot.'

A smile flickered at the corners of her mouth. 'Sorry to inconvenience you. Perhaps you could ask your brother to choose his girlfriends more wisely in the future.'

'I can ask, but I can't promise anything.'

Ava suddenly became serious again. 'Look, I need to know something before the cops come in.' Quickly, she told him about DS Higgs and the threat to arrest her father if she didn't come clean as to Chris's whereabouts. 'Do you think they will? Do you think they'll charge him?'

'No,' he said firmly. 'I don't. If the delightful DS Higgs does have any evidence, she'll be burying it right now. She's not going to want you telling the world what she threatened to do. It won't look good for her if you make a complaint.'

'Are you sure you're right?'

'I'm always right.'

Ava relaxed a little. She moved her head on the pillow and gazed up at him. She felt a faint tingling that she put down to the drugs she'd been given. 'So are you okay?'

'Right as rain.' His face suddenly grew solemn. 'I owe you one.'

'That's what friends do,' she said. 'Watch out for one another.'

He gave her a long lingering look, his gaze travelling over her face and searching out her eyes. 'Is that what we are – friends?'

Ava felt a light blush rise to her cheeks. She didn't answer him directly; she still needed time to sort out how she felt. 'But you're right, you do owe me. Sixty quid, as it happens. You still haven't coughed up for that ticket the cops gave me.'

Have you read them all?

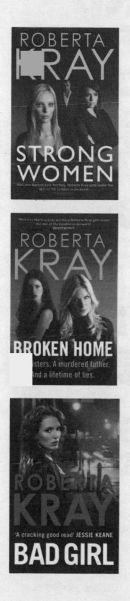

STRONG WOMEN

THE VILLAIN'S DAUGHTER

BROKEN HOME

NOTHING BUT TROUBLE
Some people are just born bad

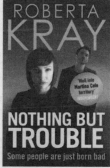

BAD GIRL

STREETWISE

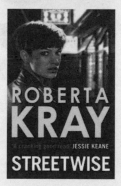